THE TEXAN SCOUTS
A Story Of
The Alamo And Goliad

by

Joseph A. Altsheler

THE TEXAN SCOUTS
A Story Of The Alamo And Goliad

by Joseph A. Altsheler

Copyright © 2023

ISBN: 978-93-57488-00-6

Published by

DOUBLE 9 BOOKS

2/13-B, Ansari Road
Daryaganj, New Delhi – 110002
info@double9books.com
www.double9books.com
Tel. 011-40042856

ABOUT THE AUTHOR

Joseph A. Altsheler was born on April 29, 1862, in Three Springs, Hart County, Kentucky, to Joseph and Louise Altsheler. He was a newspaper reporter, editor, and author of popular juvenile historical fiction. He wrote fifty novels and at least fifty-three short stories. Seven of his novels were in sequence.He worked as an editor at the Louisville Courier-Journal in 1885. In 1892, he started to work for New York World and then as the editor of the World's tri-weekly magazine. He wrote children's stories due to a lack of suitable stories.On May 30, 1880, Altsheler married Sarah Boles and had a son named Sidney. In 1914, during World War I Altsheler and his family were in Germany and they were forced to remain there.Altsheler died at the age of 57, on June 5, 1919, in New York. His wife, Sarah Boles died after 30 years. Their bodies are buried at the Cave Hill Cemetery in Louisville, Kentucky. Although each of the thirty-two novels constitutes an independent story, Altsheler suggested reading in sequence for each series (that is, he numbered the volumes). You can read the remaining eighteen novels in any order.

CONTENTS

CHAPTER I.
IN THE STORM

The horseman rode slowly toward the west, stopping once or twice to examine the wide circle of the horizon with eyes that were trained to note every aspect of the wilderness. On his right the plains melted away in gentle swell after swell, until they met the horizon. Their brown surface was broken only by the spiked and thorny cactus and stray bits of chaparral.

On his left was the wide bed of a river which flowed through the sand, breaking here and there into several streams, and then reuniting, only to scatter its volume a hundred yards further into three or four channels. A bird of prey flew on strong wing over the water, dipped and then rose again, but there was no other sign of life. Beyond, the country southward rolled away, gray and bare, sterile and desolate.

The horseman looked most often into the south. His glances into the north were few and brief, but his eyes dwelled long on the lonely land that lay beyond the yellow current. His was an attractive face. He was young, only a boy, but the brow was broad and high, and the eyes, grave and steady, were those of one who thought much. He was clad completely in buckskin, and his hat was wide of brim. A rifle held in one hand lay across the pommel of his saddle and there were weapons in his belt. Two light, but warm, blankets, folded closely, were tied behind him. The tanned face and the lithe, strong figure showed a wonderful degree of health and strength.

Several hours passed and the horseman rode on steadily though slowly. His main direction was toward the west, and always he kept the river two or three hundred yards on his left. He never failed to search the plains on either side, but chiefly in the south, with the eager, intent gaze that missed nothing. But the lonesome gray land, cut by the coiling yellow river, still rolled before him, and its desolation and chill struck to his heart. It was the depth of the Texan winter, and, at times, icy gusts, born in far mountains, swept across the plains.

The rider presently turned his horse toward the river and stopped on a low bluff overlooking it. His face showed a tinge of disappointment, as if his eyes failed to find objects for which they sought. Again he gazed long and patiently into the south, but without reward.

He resumed his ride parallel with the river, but soon stopped a second time, and held up an open hand, like one who tests the wind. The air was growing perceptibly colder. The strong gusts were now fusing into a steady wind. The day, which had not been bright at any time, was turning darker. The sun was gone and in the far north banks of mists and vapor were gathering. A dreary moaning came over the plain.

Ned Fulton, tried and brave though he was, beheld the omens with alarm. He knew what they portended, and in all that vast wilderness he was alone. Not a human being to share the danger with him! Not a hand to help!

He looked for chaparral, something that might serve as a sort of shelter, but he had left the last clump of it behind, and now he turned and rode directly north, hoping that he might find some deep depression between the swells where he and his horse, in a fashion, could hide.

Meanwhile the Norther came down with astonishing speed. The temperature fell like a plummet. The moan of the wind rose to a shriek, and cold clouds of dust were swept against Ned and his horse. Then snow mingled with the dust and both beat upon them. Ned felt his horse shivering under him, and he shivered, too, despite his will. It had turned so dark that he could no longer tell where he was going, and he used the wide brim of his hat to protect himself from the sand.

Soon it was black as night, and the snow was driving in a hurricane. The wind, unchecked by forest or hill, screamed with a sound almost human. Ned dismounted and walked in the lee of his horse. The animal turned his head and nuzzled his master, as if he could give him warmth.

Ned hoped that the storm would blow itself out in an hour or two, but his hope was vain. The darkness did not abate. The wind rose instead of falling, and the snow thickened. It lay on the plain several inches deep, and the walking grew harder. At last the two, the boy and the horse, stopped. Ned knew that they had come into some kind of a depression, and the full force of the hurricane passed partly over their heads.

It was yet very dark, and the driving snow scarcely permitted him to open his eyes, but by feeling about a little he found that one side of the dip was covered with a growth of dwarf bushes. He led the horse into the lower edge of these, where some protection was secured, and, crouching once more in the lee of the animal, he unfolded the two blankets, which he wrapped closely about himself to the eyes.

Ned, for the first time since the Norther rushed down upon him, felt secure. He would not freeze to death, he would escape the fate that sometimes overtook lone hunters or travelers upon those vast plains. Warmth from the blankets began gradually to replace the chill in his bones, and the horse and the bushes together protected his face from the driven snow which had been cutting like hail. He even had, in some degree, the sense of comfort which one feels when safe inside four walls with a storm raging past the windows. The horse whinnied once and rubbed his nose against Ned's hand. He, too, had ceased to shiver.

All that afternoon the Norther blew with undiminished violence. After a while the fall of snow thinned somewhat, but the wind did not decrease. Ned was devoutly thankful for the dip and the bushes that grew within it. Nor was he less thankful for the companionship of his horse. It was a good horse, a brave horse, a great bay mustang, built powerfully and with sinews and muscles of steel. He had secured him just after taking part in the capture of San Antonio with his comrades, Obed White and the Ring Tailed Panther, and already the tie between horse and rider had become strong and enduring. Ned stroked him again, and the horse, twisting his neck around, thrust his nose under his arm.

"Good old boy! Good fellow!" said Ned, pinching his ear. "We were lucky, you and I, to find this place."

The horse neighed ever so gently, and rubbed his nose up and down. After a while the darkness began to increase. Ned knew that it was not a new development of the storm, but the coming of night, and he grew anxious again. He and his horse, however secure at the present moment, could not stay always in that dip among the bushes. Yet he did not dare to leave it. Above on the plain they would receive the full sweep of the wind, which was still bitterly cold.

He was worn by the continued buffetings of blast and snow, but he did not dare to lie down, even in the blankets, lest he never wake again, and while he considered he saw darker shadows in the darkness above him. He gazed, all attention, and counted ten shadows, following one another, a dusky file. He knew by the set of their figures, short and stocky, that they were Mexicans, and his heart beat heavily. These were the first Mexicans that any one had seen on Texan soil since the departure of Cos and his army on parole from captured San Antonio. So the Mexicans had come back, and no doubt they would return in great force!

Ned crouched lower, and he was very glad that the nose of the horse was still under his arm. He would not have a chance to whinny to his kind that bore the Mexicans. But the horse made no attempt to move, and Ned watched them pass on and out of sight. He had not heard the sound of footsteps or voices above the wind, and after they were gone it seemed to him that he had seen a line of phantoms.

But he was sure that his own mortal eyes had beheld that for which he was looking. He and his comrades had been watching the Rio Grande to see whether the Mexicans had crossed, and now he at least knew it.

He waited patiently three or four hours longer, until the wind died and the fall of snow ceased, when he mounted his horse and rode out of the dip. The wind suddenly sprang up again in about fifteen minutes, but now it blew from the south and was warm. The darkness thinned away as the moon and stars came out in a perfect sky of southern blue. The temperature rose many degrees in an hour and Ned knew that the snow would melt fast. All danger of freezing was past, but he was as hungry as a bear and tired to death.

He unwrapped the blankets from his body, folded them again in a small package which he made fast to his saddle, and once more stroked the nose of his horse.

"Good Old Jack," he murmured—he had called him Old Jack after Andrew Jackson, then a mighty hero of the south and west, "you passed through the ordeal and never moved, like the silent gentleman that you are."

Old Jack whinnied ever so softly, and rubbed his nose against the boy's coat sleeve. Ned mounted him and rode out of the dip, pausing at the top of the swell for a long look in every direction. The night was now peaceful and there was no noise, save for the warm wind that blew out of the south with a gentle sighing sound almost like the note of music. Trickles of water from the snow, already melting, ran down the crests. Lighter and lighter grew the sky. The moon seemed to Ned to be poised directly overhead, and close by. New stars were springing out as the last clouds floated away.

Ned sought shelter, warmth and a place in which to sleep, and to secure these three he felt that he must seek timber. The scouts whom he had seen were probably the only Mexicans north of the Rio Grande, and, as he believed, there was not one chance in a thousand of meeting such enemies again. If he should be so lucky as to find shelter he would sleep there without fear.

He rode almost due north for more than two hours, seeing patches of chaparral on both right and left. But, grown fastidious now and not thinking them sufficient for his purpose, he continued his northern course. Old Jack's feet made a deep sighing sound as they sank in the snow, and now there was water everywhere as that soft but conquering south wind blew steadily over the plain.

When he saw a growth of timber rising high and dark upon a swell he believed that he had found his place, and he urged his horse to renewed speed. The trees proved to be pecans, aspens and oaks growing so densely that he was compelled to dismount and lead Old Jack before they could force an entrance. Inside he found a clear space, somewhat like the openings of the north, in shape an irregular circle, but not more than fifteen feet across. Great spreading boughs of oaks had protected it so well that but little snow had fallen there, and that little had melted. Already the ground in the circle was drying.

Ned uttered an exclamation of relief and gratitude. This would be his camp, and to one used to living in the wilderness it furnished good shelter. At one edge of the opening was an outcropping of flat rock now quite dry, and there he would spread his bed. He unsaddled and unbridled his horse, merely tethering him with a lariat, and spread the horse blanket upon the flat rock. He would lie upon this and cover himself with his own blankets, using the saddle as a pillow.

But the security of the covert tempted the boy, who was now as hungry as a bear just come from winter quarters. He felt weak and relaxed after his long hours in the snow and storm, and he resolved to have warm food and drink.

There was much fallen wood among the trees, and with his strong hunting knife he whittled off the bark and thin dry shavings until he had a fine heap. Working long with flint and steel, he managed to set fire to the shavings, and then he fed the flames with larger pieces of wood until he had a great bed of glowing coals. A cautious wilderness rover, learning always from his tried friends, Ned never rode the plains without his traveling equipment, and now he drew from his pack a small tin coffee pot and tiny cup of the same material. Then with quick and skillful hands he made coffee over the coals and warmed strips of deer and buffalo meat.

He ate and drank hungrily, while the horse nibbled the grass that grew within the covert. Glorious warmth came again and the worn feeling departed. Life, youthful, fresh and abounding, swelled in every vein.

He now put out all the coals carefully, throwing wet leaves upon them, in order that not a single spark might shine through the trees to be seen by an enemy upon the plain. He relied upon the horse to give warning of a possible approach by man, and to keep away wolves.

Then he made his bed upon the rock, doing everything as he had arranged it in his mind an hour before, and, wrapped in his blankets, fell into the soundest of sleeps. The south wind still blew steadily, playing a low musical song among the trees. The beads of water on the twigs and the few leaves that remained dried fast. The grass dried, too, and beyond the covert the snow, so quick to come, was equally quick to go.

The horse ceased to nibble the grass, looked at the sleeping boy, touched his blankets lightly with his nose, and walked to the other side of the opening, where he lay down and went to his own horse heaven of sleep.

It was not many hours until day and Old Jack was a light sleeper. When he opened his eyes again he saw a clear and beautiful winter day of the far south. The only clouds in the sky were little drifting bits of fine white wool, and the warm wind still blew. Old Jack, who was in reality Young Jack, as his years were not yet four, did not think so much of the covert now, as he had already eaten away all the grass within the little opening but his sense of duty was strong. He saw that his human master and comrade still slept, apparently with no intention of awakening at any very early date, and he set himself to gleaning stray blades of grass that might have escaped his notice the night before.

Ned awoke a little after the noon hour, and sprang to his feet in dismay. The sun was almost directly over his head, showing him how late it was. He looked at his horse as if to reproach his good comrade for not waking him sooner, but Old Jack's large mild eyes gave him such a gaze of benignant unconcern that the boy was ashamed of himself.

"It certainly was not your fault," he said to his horse, "and, after all, it probably doesn't matter. We've had a long sound sleep and rest, and I've no doubt that both of us will profit by it. Nothing seems to be left in here for you to eat, but I'll take a little breakfast myself."

He did not relight the fire, but contented himself with cold food. Then resaddling, he left the grove and rode northward again until he came to a hill, or, rather, a swell, that was higher than the rest. Here he stopped his horse and took a glance at the sun, which was shining with uncommon brilliancy. Then he produced a small mirror from the pocket of his hunting shirt and held it in such a position that it made a focus of the sun's rays, throwing them in a perfect blazing lance of light.

He turned the flaming lance around the horizon, until it completed the circle and then he started around with it again. Meantime he was keeping a close watch upon every high point. A hill rose in the north, and he looked at it longest, but nothing came from it. There was another, but lower, hill in the west, and before he had completed the second round with his glass a light flashed from it. It was a brilliant light, almost like a sheaf of white incandescent rays. He lowered his own mirror and the light played directly upon his hill. When it ceased he sent back answering rays, to which, when he stopped, a rejoinder came in like fashion. Then he put the little mirror back in the safe pocket of his hunting shirt and rode with perfect confidence toward that western hill.

The crest that Ned sought was several miles away, although it looked much nearer in the thin clear air of the plains, but he rode now at increased speed, because there was much to draw him on. Old Jack seemed to share in his lightness of spirit, raising his head once and neighing, as if he were sending forth a welcome.

The boy soon saw two figures upon the hill, the shapes of horse and man, outlined in black against the sun, which was now declining in the west. They were motionless and they were exaggerated into gigantic stature against the red background. Ned knew them, although the distance was far too great to disclose any feature. But signal had spoken truly to signal, and that was enough. Old Jack made a fresh burst of speed and presently neighed once more. An answering neigh came back from the hill.

Ned rode up the slope and greeted Obed White and the Ring Tailed Panther with outstretched hands.

"And it's you, my boy," said Obed, his eyes glistening. "Until we saw your signal we were afraid that you might have frozen to death in the Norther, but it's a long lane that has no happy ending, and here we are, all three of us, alive, and as well as ever."

"That's so," said the Panther, "but even when the storm was at its worst I didn't give up, Ned. Somehow, when things are at the blackest I'm always hopin'. I don't take any credit fur it. I was just born with that kind of a streak in me."

Ned regarded him with admiration. The Ring Tailed Panther was certainly a gorgeous object. He rode a great black horse with a flowing mane. He was clad completely in a suit of buckskin which was probably without a match on the border. It and his moccasins were adorned with thick rows of beads of many colors, that glittered and flashed as the sunlight played upon them. Heavy silver spurs were fastened to his heels, and his hat of broad brim and high cone in the Mexican fashion was heavy with silver braid. His saddle also was of the high, peaked style, studded with silver. The Panther noticed Ned's smile of appraisement and smiled back.

"Ain't it fine?" he said. "I guess this is about the beautifullest outfit to be found in either Texas or Mexico. I bought it all in honor of our victory just after we took San Antonio, and it soothes my eyes and makes my heart strong every time I look at it."

"And it helps out the prairies," said Obed White, his eyes twinkling. "Now that winter has made 'em brown, they need a dash of color and the Panther gives it to 'em. Fine feathers don't keep a man from being a man for a' that. What did you do in the storm, Ned?"

"I found shelter in a thick grove, managed to light a fire, and slept there in my blankets."

"We did about the same."

"But I saw something before I reached my shelter."

"What was that?" exclaimed the two, noting the significance in Ned's tone.

"While I was waiting in a dip I saw ten Mexican horsemen ride by. They were heavily armed, and I've no doubt they were scouts belonging to some strong force."

"And so they are back on this side of the Rio Grande," said Obed White thoughtfully. "I'm not surprised. Our Texans have rejoiced too early. The full storm has not burst yet."

The Panther began to bristle. A giant in size, he seemed to grow larger, and his gorgeous hunting suit strained at the seams.

"Let 'em come on," he said menacingly. "Let Santa Anna himself lead 'em. We Texans can take care of 'em all."

But Obed White shook his head sadly.

"We could if we were united," he said, "but our leaders have taken to squabbling. You're a Cheerful Talker, Panther, and you deserve both your names, but to tell you the honest truth I'm afraid of the Mexican advance."

"I think the Mexicans probably belonged to Urrea's band," said Ned.

"Very likely," said Obed. "He's about the most energetic of their partisan leaders, and it may be that we'll run against him pretty soon."

They had heard in their scouting along the Rio Grande that young Francisco Urrea, after the discovery that he was a spy and his withdrawal from San Antonio with the captured army of Cos, had organized a strong force of horsemen and was foremost among those who were urging a new Mexican advance into Texas.

"It's pretty far west for the Mexicans," said the Panther. "We're on the edge of the Indian country here."

But Obed considered it all the more likely that Urrea, if he meditated a raid, would come from the west, since his approach at that point would be suspected the least. The three held a brief discussion and soon came to an agreement. They would continue their own ride west and look for Urrea. Having decided so, they went into the task heart and soul, despite its dangers.

The three rode side by side and three pairs of skilled eyes examined the plain. The snow was left only in sheltered places or among the trees. But the further they went the scarcer became the trees, and before night they disappeared entirely.

"We are comin' upon the buffalo range," said the Panther. "A hundred miles further west we'd be likely to strike big herds. When we're through fightin' the Mexicans I'm goin' out there again. It's the life fur me."

The night came, dark and cold, but fortunately without wind. They camped in a dip and did not light any fire, lying as Ned had done the night before on their horse blankets and wrapping themselves in their own. The three horses seemed to be contented with one another and made no noise.

They deemed it wise now to keep a watch, as they might be near Urrea's band or Lipans might pass, and the Panther, who said he was not sleepy at all, became sentinel. Ned, although he had not risen until noon, was sleepy again from the long ride, and his eyes closed soon. The last object that he saw was the Panther standing on the crest of the swell just beyond them, rifle on shoulder, watching the moonlit plains. Obed White was asleep already.

The Panther walked back and forth a few times and then looked down at his comrades in the dip. His trained eyes saw their chests rising and falling, and he knew that they were far away in the land of Nowhere. Then he extended his walk back and forth a little further, scanning carefully the dusky plain.

A light wind sprang up after a while, and it brought a low but heavy and measured tread to his ears. The Panther's first impulse was to awaken his friends, because this might be the band of Urrea, but he hesitated a moment, and then lay down with his ear to the earth. When he rose his uneasiness had departed and he resumed his walk back and forth. He had heard that tread before many times and, now that it was coming nearer, he could not mistake it, but, as the measured beat indicated that it would pass to one side, it bore no threat for his comrades or himself.

The Panther did not stop his walk as from a distance of a few hundred yards he watched the great buffalo herd go by. The sound was so steady and regular that Ned and Obed were not awakened nor were the horses disturbed. The buffaloes showed a great black mass across the plain, extending for fully a mile, and they were moving north at an even gait. The Panther watched until the last had passed, and he judged that there were fully a hundred thousand animals in the herd. He saw also the big timber wolves hanging on the rear and flanks, ready to cut out stray calves or those weak from old age. So busy were the wolves seeking a chance that they did not notice the gigantic figure of the man, rifle on shoulder, who stood on the crest of the swell looking at them as they passed.

The Panther's eyes followed the black line of the herd until it disappeared under the northern rim of darkness. He was wondering why the buffaloes were traveling so steadily after daylight and he came to the conclusion that the impelling motive was not a search for new pastures. He listened a long time until the last rumble of the hundred thousand died away in a faint echo, and then he awakened his comrades.

"I'm thinkin'," he said, "that the presence of Urrea's band made the buffaloes move. Now I'm not a Ring Tailed Panther an' a Cheerful Talker for nothin', an' we want to hunt that band. Like as not they've been doin' some mischief, which we may be able partly to undo. I'm in favor of ridin' south, back on the herd track an' lookin' for 'em."

"So am I," said Obed White. "My watch says it's one o'clock in the morning, and my watch is always right, because I made it myself. We've had a pretty good rest, enough to go on, and what we find may be worth finding. A needle in a haystack may be well hid, but you'll find it if you look long enough."

They rode almost due south in the great path made by the buffalo herd, not stopping for a full two hours when a halt was made at a signal from the Panther. They were in a wide plain, where buffalo grass yet grew despite the winter, and the Panther said with authority that the herd had been grazing here before it was started on its night journey into the north.

"An' if we ride about this place long enough," he said, "we'll find the reason why the buffaloes left it."

He turned his horse in a circuit of the plain and Ned and Obed followed the matchless tracker, who was able, even in the moonlight, to note any disturbance of the soil. Presently he uttered a little cry and pointed ahead. Both saw the skeleton of a buffalo which evidently had been killed not long and stripped of its meat. A little further on they saw another and then two more.

"That tells it," said the Panther succinctly. "These buffaloes were killed for food an' most likely by Mexicans. It was the shots that set the herd to runnin'. The men who killed 'em are not far away, an' I'm not a Ring Tailed Panther an' a Cheerful Talker if they don't belong to Urrea's band."

"Isn't that a light?" said Ned, pointing to the west, "or is it a firefly or something of the kind?"

A glowing spark was just visible over the plain, but as it neither moved nor went out the three concluded that it was made by a distant fire.

"I think it's in chaparral or among trees," said Obed, "or we would see it more plainly. It's a poor camp fire that hides its light under a bushel."

"I think you're right an' it must be chaparral," said the Panther. "But we'll ride toward it an' soon answer our own questions."

The light was more than a mile away and, as they advanced slowly, they saw it grow in size and intensity. It was surely a campfire, but no sound that they could yet hear came from it. They did not expect to hear any. If it was indeed Urrea and his men they would probably be sleeping soundly, not expecting any foe to be near. The Panther now dismounted, and the other two did likewise.

"No need to show too high above the plain," he said, "an' if we have to run it won't take a second to jump back on our horses."

Ned did not take the bridle of his horse as the others did. He knew that Old Jack would follow as faithful as any dog to his master, and he was right. As they advanced slowly the velvet nose more than once pressed trustfully against his elbow.

They saw now that an extensive growth of chaparral rose before them, from the center of which the light seemed to be shining. The Panther lay down on the prairie, put his ear to the ground, and listened a long time.

"I think I hear the feet of horses movin' now an' then," he said, "an' if so, one of us had better stay behin' with ours. A horse of theirs might neigh an' a horse of ours might answer. Yon can't tell. Obed, I guess it'll be for you to stay. You've got a most soothin' disposition with animals."

"All right," said Obed philosophically, "I'd rather go on, but, if it's better for me to stay, I'll stay. They also serve who stand and hold the reins. If you find you've got to leave in a hurry I'll be here waiting."

He gathered up the reins of the three horses and remained quietly on the plain, while Ned and the Panther went forward, making straight for the light.

When they came to the edge of the chaparral they knelt among the bushes and listened. Now both distinctly heard the occasional movement of horses, and they saw the dusky outlines of several figures before the fire, which was about three hundred yards away.

"They are bound to be Mexicans," whispered the Panther, "'cause there are no Texans in this part of the country, an' you an' me, Ned, must find out just who they are."

"You lead the way, Panther," said Ned. "I'll follow wherever you go."

"Then be mighty careful. Look out for the thorns an' don't knock your rifle against any bush."

The Panther lay almost flat. His huge figure seemed to blend with the earth, and he crept forward among the thorny bushes with amazing skill. He was like some large animal, trained for countless generations to slip through thickets. Ned, just behind him, could hear only the faintest noise, and the bushes moved so little that one, not knowing, might have credited it to the wind.

The boy had the advantage of following in the path made by the man's larger figure, and he, too, was successful in making no sound. But he could hear the stamp of horses' feet clearly now, and both to left and right he caught glimpses of them tethered in the thickets. His comrade stopped at last. They were not more than a hundred yards from the fire now, and the space in front of them was mostly open. The Panther, crouching among the bushes, raised his finger slowly and pointed toward the fire.

Ned, who had moved to one side, followed the pointing finger and saw Urrea. He was the dominant figure in a group of six or seven gathered about the flames. He was no longer in any disguise, but wore an officer's gorgeous uniform of white and silver. A splendid cocked hat was on his head, and a small gold hilted rapier swung by his side.

It may have been partly the effect of the night and the red flame, but the face of Urrea had upon Ned an effect much like that of Santa Anna. It was dark and handsome, but full of evil. And evil Ned knew Urrea to be. No man with righteous blood in his veins would play the spy and traitor as he had done.

"I could shoot him from here," whispered the Panther, who evidently was influenced in a similar way, "then reach our horses an' get away. It might be a good deed, an' it might save our lives, Ned, but I'm not able to force myself to do it."

"Nor I," said Ned. "I can't shoot an enemy from ambush."

Urrea and the other men at the fire, all of whom were in the dress of officers, were in a deep talk. Ned inferred that the subject must be of much importance, since they sat awake, discussing it between midnight and morning.

"Look beyond the fire at the figures leanin' against the trees," whispered the Panther.

Ned looked and hot anger rose in his veins.

CHAPTER II.
THE CAPTIVES

Ned had not noticed at first, but, since his eyes were growing used to the dim light, and since the Panther had pointed the way, he saw a dozen men, arms bound tightly behind them, leaning against the trees. They were prisoners and he knew instinctively that they were Texans. His blood, hot at first, now chilled in his veins. They had been captured by Urrea in a raid, and as Santa Anna had decreed that all Texans were rebels who should be executed when taken, they would surely die, unless rescue came.

"What shall we do?" he whispered.

"Nothing now," replied the Panther, in the same soft tone, "but if you an' Obed are with me we'll follow this crowd, an' maybe we can get the Texans away from 'em. It's likely that Urrea will cross the Rio Grande an' go down into Mexico to meet Cos or Santa Anna. Are you game enough to go, Ned? I'm a Ring Tailed Panther an' a roarin' grizzly bear, but I don't like to follow all by myself."

"I'm with you," said Ned, "if I have to go all the way back to the City of Mexico, an' I know that I can speak for Obed, too."

"I jest asked as a matter of form," said the Panther. "I knowed before askin' that you an' Obed would stick to me."

There was a sudden gust of wind at that moment and the light of the fire sprang higher. The flames threw a glow across the faces of the prisoners. Most of them were asleep, but Ned saw them very distinctly now. One was a boy but little older than himself, his face pale and worn. Near him was an old man, with a face very uncommon on the border. His features were those of a scholar and ascetic. His cheeks were thin, and thick white hair crowned a broad white brow. Ned felt instinctively that he was a man of importance.

Both the boy and the man slept the sleep of utter exhaustion.

Urrea rose presently and looked at his prisoners. The moonlight was shining on his face, and it seemed to Ned to be that of some master demon. The boy was far from denying many good qualities to the Mexicans, but the countenance of Urrea certainly did not express any of them that night. It showed only savage exultation as he looked at the bound men, and Ned knew that this was a formidable enemy of the Texans, one who would bring infinite resources of cunning and enterprise to crush them.

Urrea said a few words to his officers and then withdrew into a small tent which Ned had not noticed hitherto. The officers lay down in their blankets, but a dozen sentinels watched about the open space. Ned and the Panther crept slowly back toward the plain.

"What is our best plan, Panther?" whispered the hoy.

"We can't do anything yet but haul off, watch an' then follow. The chaparral runs along for a mile or two an' we can hide in the north end of it until they march south an' are out of sight. Then we'll hang on."

They found Obed standing exactly where they had left him, the reins of the three horses in his hands.

"Back at last," he said. "All things come to him who waits long enough, if he doesn't die first. Did you see anything besides a lot of Mexican vaqueros, fuddled with liquor and sound asleep?"

"We did not see any vaqueros," replied the Panther, "but we saw Urrea an' his band, an' they had among them a dozen good Texans bound fast, men who will be shot if we three don't stand in the way. You have to follow with us, Obed, because Ned has already promised for you."

The Maine man looked at them and smiled.

"A terribly good mind reader, that boy, Ned," he said. "He knew exactly what I wanted. There's a lot of things in the world that I'd like to do, but the one that I want to do most just now is to follow Urrea and that crowd of his and take away those Texans. You two couldn't keep me from going."

The Panther smiled back.

"You are shorely the right stuff, Obed White," he said. "We're only three in this bunch, but two of 'em besides me are ring-tailed panthers. Now we'll just draw off, before it's day, an' hide in the chaparral up there."

They rode a mile to the north and remained among dense bushes until daylight. At dawn they saw a column of smoke rise from Urrea's camp.

"They are cookin' breakfast now," said the Panther. "It's my guess that in an hour they'll be ridin' south with their prisoners."

The column of smoke sank after a while, and a couple of hours later the three left the chaparral. From one of the summits they dimly saw a mass of horsemen riding toward Mexico.

"There's our men," said the Panther, "an' now we'll follow all day at this good, safe distance. At night we can draw up closer if we want to do it."

The Mexicans maintained a steady pace, and the three pursuers followed at a distance of perhaps two miles. Now and then the swells completely shut Urrea's band from sight, but Ned, Obed and the Panther followed the broad trail without the slightest difficulty.

"They'll reach the river before noon," said the Panther. "There ain't any doubt now that they're bound for Mexico. It's jest as well for what we want to do, 'cause they're likely to be less watchful there than they are in Texas."

The band of Urrea, as nearly as they could judge, numbered about fifty, all mounted and armed well. The Mexicans were fine horsemen, and with good training and leadership they were dangerous foes. The three knew them well, and they kept so far behind that they were not likely to be observed.

It was only a half hour past noon when Urrea's men reached the Rio Grande, and without stopping made the crossing. They avoided the quicksands with experienced eyes, and swam their horses through the deep water, the prisoners always kept in the center of the troop. Ned, Obed and the Panther watched them until they passed out of sight. Then they, too, rode forward, although slowly, toward the stream.

"We can't lose 'em," said the Panther, "so I think we'd better stay out of sight now that they're on real Mexican soil. Maybe our chance will come to-night, an' ag'in maybe it won't."

"Patience will have its perfect rescue, if we only do the right things," said Obed.

"An' if we think hard enough an' long enough we're bound to do 'em, or I'm a Ring Tailed Panther an' a Cheerful Talker fur nothin'," said the Panther.

Waiting until they were certain that the Mexicans were five or six miles ahead, the three forded the Rio Grande, and stood once more on Mexican soil. It gave Ned a curious thrill. He had passed through so much in Mexico that he had not believed he would ever again enter that country. The land on the Mexican side was about the same as that on the Texan, but it seemed different to him. He beheld again that aspect of infinite age, of the long weariness of time, and of physical decay.

They rode more briskly through the afternoon and at darkness saw the camp fires of Urrea glimmering ahead of them. But the night was not favorable to their plans. The sky was the usual cloudless blue of the Mexican plateau, the moon was at the full and all the stars were out. What they wanted was bad weather, hoping meanwhile the execution of the prisoners would not be begun until the Mexicans reached higher authority than Urrea, perhaps Santa Anna himself.

They made their own camp a full two miles from Urrea's, and Obed and the Panther divided the watch.

Urrea started early the next morning, and so did the pursuing three. The dawn was gray, and the breeze was chill. As they rode on, the wind rose and its edge became so sharp that there was a prospect of another Norther. The Panther unrolled from his pack the most gorgeous serape that Ned had ever seen. It was of the finest material, colored a deep scarlet and it had a gold fringe.

"Fine feathers are seen afar," said Obed.

"That's so," said the Panther, "but we're not coming near enough to the Mexicans for them to catch a glimpse of this, an' such bein' the case I'm goin' to put it between me an' the cold. I'm proud of it, an' when I wrap it aroun' me I feel bigger an' stronger. Its red color helps me. I think I draw strength from red, just as I do from a fine, tender buffalo steak."

He spoke with much earnestness, and the other two did not contradict him. Meanwhile he gracefully folded the great serape about his shoulders, letting it fall to the saddle. No Mexican could have worn it more rakishly.

"That's my shield and protector," he said. "Now blow wind, blow snow, I'll keep warm."

It blew wind, but it did not blow snow. The day remained cold, but the air undoubtedly had a touch of damp.

"It may rain, and I'm sure the night will be dark," said Obed. "We may have our chance. Fortune favors those who help themselves."

The country became more broken, and the patches of scrub forest increased in number. Often the three rode quite near to Urrea's men and observed them closely. The Mexicans were moving slowly, and, as the Americans had foreseen, discipline was relaxed greatly.

Near night drops of rain began to fall in their faces, and the sun set among clouds. The three rejoiced. A night, dark and wet, had come sooner than they had hoped. Obed and Ned also took out serapes, and wrapped them around their shoulders. They served now not only to protect their bodies, but to keep their firearms dry as well. Then they tethered their horses among thorn bushes about a mile from Urrea's camp, and advanced on foot.

They saw the camp fire glimmering feebly through the night, and they advanced boldly. It was so dark now that a human figure fifty feet away blended with the dusk, and the ground, softened by the rain, gave back no sound of footsteps. Nevertheless they saw on their right a field which showed a few signs of cultivation, and they surmised that Urrea had made his camp at the lone hut of some peon.

They reckoned right. They came to clumps of trees, and in an opening inclosed by them was a low adobe hut, from the open door of which a light shone. They knew that Urrea and his officers had taken refuge there from the rain and cold and, under the boughs of the trees or beside the fire, they saw the rest of the band sheltering themselves as best they could. The prisoners, their hands bound, were in a group in the open, where the slow, cold rain fell steadily upon them. Ned's heart swelled with rage at the sight.

Order and discipline seemed to be lacking. Men came and went as they pleased. Fully twenty of them were making a shelter of canvas and thatch beside the hut. Others began to build the fire higher in order to fend off the wet and cold. Ned did not see that the chance of a rescue was improved, but the Panther felt a sudden glow when his eyes alighted upon something dark at the edge of the woods. A tiny shed stood there and his keen eyes marked what was beneath it.

"What do you think we'd better do, Panther?" asked Obed.

"No roarin' jest now. We mustn't raise our voices above whispers, but we'll go back in the brush and wait. In an hour or two all these Mexicans will be asleep. Like as not the sentinels, if they post any, will be asleep first."

They withdrew deeper into the thickets, where they remained close together. They saw the fire die in the Mexican camp. After a while all sounds there ceased, and again they crept near. The Panther was a genuine prophet, known and recognized by his comrades. Urrea's men, having finished their shelters, were now asleep, including all the sentinels except two. There was some excuse for them. They were in their own country, far from any Texan force of importance, and the night could scarcely have been worse. It was very dark, and the cold rain fell with a steadiness and insistence that sought and finally found every opening in one's clothing. Even the stalking three drew their serapes closer, and shivered a little.

The two sentinels who did not sleep were together on the south side of the glade. Evidently they wished the company of each other. They were now some distance from the dark little shed toward which the Panther was leading his comrades, and their whole energies were absorbed in an attempt to light two cigarritos, which would soothe and strengthen them as they kept their rainy and useless watch.

The three completed the segment of the circle and reached the little shed which had become such an object of importance to the Panther.

"Don't you see?" said the Panther, his grim joy showing in his tone.

They saw, and they shared his satisfaction. The Mexicans had stacked their rifles and muskets under the shed, where they would be protected from the rain.

"It's queer what foolish things men do in war," said Obed. "Whom the gods would destroy they first deprive of the sense of danger. They do not dream that Richard, meaning the Panther, is in the chaparral."

"If we approach this shed from the rear the sentinels, even if they look, will not be able to see us," said the Panther. "By the great horn spoon, what an opportunity! I can hardly keep from roarin' an' ravin' about it. Now, boys, we'll take away their guns, swift an' quiet."

A few trips apiece and all the rifles and muskets with their ammunition were carried deep into the chaparral, where Obed, gladly sacrificing his own comfort, covered them against the rain with his serape. Not a sign had come meanwhile from the two sentinels on the far side of the camp. Ned once or twice saw the lighted ends of their cigarritos glowing like sparks in the darkness, but the outlines of the men's figures were very dusky.

"An' now for the riskiest part of our job, the one that counts the most," said the Panther, "the one that will make everything else a failure if it falls through. We've got to secure the prisoners."

The captives were lying under the boughs of some trees about twenty yards from the spot where the fire had been built. The pitiless rain had beaten upon them, but as far as Ned could judge they had gone to sleep, doubtless through sheer exhaustion. The Panther's plan of action was swift and comprehensive.

"Boys," he said, "I'm the best shot of us three. I don't say it in any spirit of boastin', 'cause I've pulled trigger about every day for thirty years, an' more'n once a hundred times in one day. Now you two give me your rifles and I'll set here in the edge of the bushes, then you go ahead as silent as you can an' cut the prisoners loose. If there's an alarm I'll open fire with the three rifles and cover the escape."

Handing the rifles to the Panther, the two slipped forward. It was a grateful task to Ned. Again his heart swelled with wrath as he saw the dark figures of the bound men lying on the ground in the rain. He remembered the one who was youthful of face like himself and he sought him. As he approached he made out a figure lying in a strained position, and he was sure that it was the captive lad. A yard or two more and he knew absolutely. He touched the boy on the shoulder, whispered in his ear that it was a friend, and, with one sweep of his knife, released his arms.

"Crawl to the chaparral there," said Ned, in swift sharp tones, pointing the way. "Another friend is waiting at that point."

The boy, without a word, began to creep forward in a stiff and awkward fashion. Ned turned to the next prisoner. It was the elderly man whom he had seen from the chaparral, and he was wide awake, staring intently at Ned.

"Is it rescue?" he whispered. "Is it possible?"

"It is rescue. It is possible," replied Ned, in a similar whisper. "Turn a little to one side and I will cut the cords that bind you."

The man turned, but when Ned freed him he whispered:

"You will have to help me. I cannot yet walk alone. Urrea has already given me a taste of what I was to expect."

Ned shuddered. There was a terrible significance in the prisoner's tone. He assisted him to rise partly, but the man staggered. It was evident that he could not walk. He must help this man, but the others were waiting to be released also. Then the good thought came.

"Wait a moment," he said, and he cut the bonds of another man.

"Now you help your friend there," he said.

He saw the two going away together, and he turned to the others. He and Obed worked fast, and within five minutes the last man was released. But as they crept back toward the chaparral the slack sentinels caught sight of the dusky figures retreating. Two musket shots were fired and there were rapid shouts in Mexican jargon. Ned and Obed rose to their feet and, keeping the escaped prisoners before them, ran for the thickets.

A terrific reply to the Mexican alarm came from the forest. A volley of rifle and pistol shots was fired among the soldiers as they sprang to their feet and a tremendous voice roared:

"At 'em, boys! At 'em! Charge 'em! Now is your time! Rip an' t'ar an' roar an' chaw! Don't let a single one escape! Sweep the scum off the face of the earth!"

The Ring Tailed Panther had a mighty voice, issuing from a mighty throat. Never had he used it in greater volume or to better purpose than on that night. The forest fairly thundered with the echoes of the battle cry, and as the dazed Mexicans rushed for their guns only to find them gone, they thought that the whole Texan army was upon them. In another instant a new terror struck at their hearts. Their horses and mules, driven in a frightful stampede, suddenly rushed into the glade and they were now busy keeping themselves from being trampled to death.

Truly the Panther had spent well the few minutes allotted to him. He fired new shots, some into the frightened herd. His tremendous voice never ceased for an instant to encourage his charging troops, and to roar out threats against the enemy. Urrea, to his credit, made an attempt to organize his men, to stop the panic, and to see the nature of the enemy, but he was borne away in the frantic mob of men and horses which was now rushing for the open plain.

Ned and Obed led the fugitives to the place where the rifles and muskets were stacked. Here they rapidly distributed the weapons and then broke across the tree trunks all they could not use or carry. Another minute and they reached their horses, where the Panther, panting from his huge exertions, joined them. Ned helped the lame man upon one of the horses, the weakest two who remained, including the boy, were put upon the others, and led by the Panther they started northward, leaving the chaparral.

It was a singular march, but for a long time nothing was said. The sound of the Mexican stampede could yet be heard, moving to the south, but they, rescuers and rescued, walked in silence save for the sound of their feet in the mud of the wind-swept plain. Ned looked curiously at the faces of those whom they had saved, but the night had not lightened, and he could discern nothing. They went thus a full quarter of an hour. The noise of the stampede sank away in the south, and then the Panther laughed.

It was a deep, hearty, unctuous laugh that came from the very depths of the man's chest. It was a laugh with no trace of merely superficial joy. He who uttered it laughed because his heart and soul were in it. It was a laugh of mirth, relief and triumph, all carried to the highest degree. It was a long laugh, rising and falling, but when it ceased and the Panther had drawn a deep breath he opened his mouth again and spoke the words that were in his mind.

"I shorely did some rippin' an' roarin' then," he said. "It was the best chance I ever had, an' I guess I used it. How things did work for us! Them sleepy sentinels, an' then the stampede of the animals, carryin' Urrea an' the rest right away with it."

"Fortune certainly worked for us," said Ned.

"And we can find no words in which to describe to you our gratitude," said the crippled man on the horse. "We were informed very clearly by Urrea that we were rebels and, under the decree of Santa Anna, would be executed. Even our young friend here, this boy, William Allen, would not have been spared."

"We ain't all the way out of the woods yet," said the Panther, not wishing to have their hopes rise too high and then fall. "Of course Urrea an' his men have some arms left. They wouldn't stack 'em all under the shed, an' they can get more from other Mexicans in these parts. When they learn from their trailers how few we are they'll follow."

The rescued were silent, save one, evidently a veteran frontiersman, who said:

"Let 'em come. I was took by surprise, not thinkin' any Mexicans was north of the Rio Grande. But now that I've got a rifle on one shoulder an' a musket on the other I think I could thrash an acre-lot full of 'em."

"That's the talk," said Obed White. "We'll say to 'em: 'Come one, come all, this rock from its firm base may fly, but we're the boys who'll never say die.'"

They relapsed once more into silence. The rain had lightened a little, but the night was as dark as ever. The boy whom the man had called William Allen drew up by the side of Ned. They were of about the same height, and each was as tall and strong as a man.

"Have you any friends here with you?" asked Ned.

"All of them are my friends, but I made them in captivity. I came to Texas to find my fortune, and I found this."

The boy laughed, half in pity of himself, and half with genuine humor.

"But I ought not to complain," he added, "when we've been saved in the most wonderful way. How did you ever happen to do it?"

"We've been following you all the way from the other side of the Rio Grande, waiting a good chance. It came to-night with the darkness, the rain, and the carelessness of the Mexicans. I heard the man call you William Allen. My name is Fulton, Edward Fulton, Ned to my friends."

"And mine's Will to my friends."

"And you and I are going to be friends, that's sure."

"Nothing can be surer."

The hands of the two boys met in a strong grasp, signifying a friendship that was destined to endure.

The Panther and Obed now began to seek a place for a camp. They knew that too much haste would mean a breakdown, and they meant that the people whom they had rescued should have a rest. But it took a long time to find the trees which would furnish wood and partial shelter. It was Obed who made the happy discovery some time after midnight. Turning to their left, they entered a grove of dwarf oaks, covering a half acre or so, and with much labor and striving built a fire. They made it a big fire, too, and fed it until the flames roared and danced. Ned noticed that all the rescued prisoners crouched close to it, as if it were a giver of strength and courage as well as warmth, and now the light revealed their faces. He looked first at the crippled man, and the surprise that he had felt at his first glimpse of him increased.

The stranger was of a type uncommon on the border. His large features showed cultivation and the signs of habitual and deep thought. His thick white hair surmounted a broad brow. His clothing, although torn by thorns and briars, was of fine quality. Ned knew instinctively that it was a powerful face, one that seldom showed the emotions behind it. The rest, except the boy, were of the border, lean, sun-browned men, dressed in tanned deerskin.

The Panther and Obed also gazed at the crippled man with great curiosity. They knew the difference, and they were surprised to find such a man in such a situation. He did not seem to notice them at first, but from his seat on a log leaned over the fire warming his hands, which Ned saw were large, white and smooth. His legs lay loosely against the log, as if he were suffering from a species of paralysis. The others, soaked by the rain, which, however, now ceased, were also hovering over the fire which was giving new life to the blood in their veins. The man with the white hands turned presently and, speaking to Ned, Obed and the Panther, said:

"My name is Roylston, John Roylston."

Ned started.

"I see that you have heard of it," continued the stranger, but without vanity. "Yes, I am the merchant of New Orleans. I have lands and other property in this region for which I have paid fairly. I hold the deeds and they are also guaranteed to me by Santa Anna and the Mexican Congress. I was seized by this guerilla leader, Urrea. He knew who I was, and he sought to extract from me an order for a large sum of money lying in a European bank in the City of Mexico. There are various ways of procuring such orders, and he tried one of the most primitive methods. That is why I cannot walk without help. No, I will not tell what was done. It is not pleasant to hear. Let it pass. I shall walk again as well as ever in a month."

"Did he get the order?" asked Obed curiously.

Roylston laughed deep in his throat.

"He did not," he said. "It was not because I valued it so much, but my pride would not permit me to give way to such crude methods. I must say, however, that you three came just in time, and you have done a most marvelous piece of work."

Ned shuddered and walked a little space out on the plain to steady his nerves. He had never deceived himself about the dangers that the Texans were facing, but it seemed that they would have to fight every kind of ferocity. When he returned, Obed and the Panther were building the fire higher.

"We must get everybody good and dry," said the Panther. "Pursuit will come, but not to-night, an' we needn't worry about the blaze. We've food enough for all of you for a day, but we haven't the horses, an' for that I'm sorry. If we had them we could git away without a doubt to the Texan army."

"But not having them," said Obed, "we'll even do the best we can, if the Mexicans, having run away, come back to fight another day."

"So we will," said a stalwart Texan named Fields. "That Urrea don't get me again, and if I ain't mistook your friend here is Mr. Palmer, better known in our parts as the Ring Tailed Panther, ain't he?"

Ned saw the Panther's huge form swell. He still wore the great serape, which shone in the firelight with a deep blood-red tinge.

"I am the Ring Tailed Panther," he said proudly.

"Then lemme shake your hand. You an' your pards have done a job to-night that ain't had its like often, and me bein' one of them that's profited by it makes it look all the bigger to me."

The Panther graciously extended an enormous palm, and the great palm of Fields met it in a giant clasp. A smile lighted up the somber face of Mr. Roylston as he looked at them.

"Often we find powerful friends when we least expect them," he said.

"As you are the worst hurt of the lot," said the Panther, "we're going to make you a bed right here by the fire. No, it ain't any use sayin' you won't lay down on it. If you won't we'll jest have to put you down."

They spread a blanket, upon which the exhausted merchant lay, and they covered him with a serape. Soon he fell asleep, and then Fields said to Ned and his comrades:

"You fellows have done all the work, an' you've piled up such a mountain of debt against us that we can never wipe it out. Now you go to sleep and four of us will watch. And, knowin' what would happen to us if we were caught, we'll watch well. But nothing is to be expected to-night."

"Suits us," said Obed. "Some must watch while others sleep, so runs the world away. Bet you a dollar, Ned, that I'm off to Slumberland before you are."

"I don't take the bet," said Ned, "but I'll run you an even race."

In exactly five minutes the two, rolled in their own blankets, slept soundly. All the others soon followed, except four, who, unlike the Mexicans, kept a watch that missed nothing.

CHAPTER III.
THE FIGHT WITH URREA

Morning came. Up rose the sun, pouring a brilliant light over the desolate plains. Beads of water from the rain the night before sparkled a little while and then dried up. But the day was cold, nevertheless, and a sharp wind now began to search for the weakest point of every one. Ned, Obed and the Panther were up betimes, but some of the rescued still slept.

Ned, at the suggestion of the Panther, mounted one of the horses and rode out on the plain a half mile to the south. Those keen eyes of his were becoming all the keener from life upon the vast rolling plains. But no matter how he searched the horizon he saw only a lonesome cactus or two shivering in the wind. When he returned with his report the redoubtable Panther said:

"Then we'll just take our time. The pursuit's goin' to come, but since it ain't in sight we'll brace up these new friends of ours with hot coffee an' vittles. I guess we've got coffee enough left for all."

They lighted the fire anew and soon pleasant odors arose. The rescued prisoners ate and drank hungrily, and Mr. Roylston was able to limp a little. Now that Ned saw him in the full daylight he understood more clearly than ever that this was indeed a most uncommon man. The brow and eyes belonged to one who thought, planned and organized. He spoke little and made no complaint, but when he looked at Ned he said:

"You are young, my boy, to live among such dangers. Why do you not go north into the states where life is safe?"

"There are others as young as I, or younger, who have fought or will fight for Texas," said Ned. "I belong here and I've got powerful friends. Two of them have saved my life more than once and are likely to do so again."

He nodded toward Obed and the Panther, who were too far away to hear. Roylston smiled. The two men were in singular contrast, but each was striking in his way. Obed, of great height and very thin, but exceedingly strong, was like a steel lath. The Panther, huge in every aspect, reminded one, in his size and strength, of a buffalo bull.

"They are uncommon men, no doubt," said Roylston. "And you expect to remain with them?"

"I'd never leave them while this war lasts! Not under any circumstances!"

Ned spoke with great energy, and again Roylston smiled, but he said no more.

"It's time to start," said the Panther.

Roylston again mounted one of the horses. Ned saw that it hurt his pride to have to ride, but he saw also that he would not complain when complaints availed nothing. He felt an increasing interest in a man who seemed to have perfect command over himself.

The boy, Will Allen, was fresh and strong again. His youthful frame had recovered completely from all hardships, and now that he was free, armed, and in the company of true friends his face glowed with pleasure and enthusiasm. He was tall and strong, and now he carried a good rifle with a pistol also in his belt. He and Ned walked side by side, and each rejoiced in the companionship of one of his own age.

"How long have you been with them?" asked Will, looking at Obed and the Panther.

"I was first with Obed away down in Mexico. We were prisoners together in the submarine dungeon of San Juan de Ulua. I'd never have escaped without him. And I'd never have escaped a lot more things without him, either. Then we met the Panther. He's the greatest frontiersman in all the southwest, and we three somehow have become hooked together."

Will looked at Ned a little enviously.

"What comrades you three must be!" he said. "I have nobody."

"Are you going to fight for Texas?"

"I count on doing so."

"Then why don't you join us, and we three will turn into four?"

Will looked at Ned, and his eyes glistened.

"Do you mean that?" he asked.

"Do I mean it? I think I do. Ho, there, Panther! You and Obed, just a minute or two!"

The two turned back. Ned and Will were walking at the rear of the little company.

"I've asked Will to be one of us," said Ned, "to join our band and to share our fortunes, good or bad."

"Can he make all the signs, an' has he rid the goat?" asked the Panther solemnly.

"Does he hereby swear never to tell any secret of ours to Mexican or Indian?" asked Obed. "Does he swear to obey all our laws and by-laws wherever he may be, and whenever he is put to the test?"

"He swears to everything," replied Ned, "and I know that he is the kind to make a trusty comrade to the death."

"Then you are declared this minute a member of our company in good standin'," said the Panther to Will, "an' with this grip I give you welcome."

He crushed the boy's hand in a mighty grasp that made him wince, and Obed followed with one that was almost equally severe. But the boy did not mind the physical pain. Instead, his soul was uplifted. He was now the chosen comrade of these three paladins, and he was no longer alone in the world. But he merely said:

"I'll try to show myself worthy."

They were compelled to stop at noon for rather a long rest, as walking was tiresome. Fields, who was a good scout, went back and looked for pursuers, but announced that he saw none, and, after an hour, they started again.

"I'm thinkin'," said the Panther, "that Urrea has already organized the pursuit. Mebbe he has pow'ful glasses an' kin see us when we can't see him. He may mean to attack to-night. It's a lucky thing for us that we can find timber now an' then."

"It's likely that you're right about to-night," said Obed, "but there's no night so dark that it doesn't have its silver lining. I guess everybody in this little crowd is a good shot, unless maybe it's Mr. Roylston, and as we have about three guns apiece we can make it mighty hot for any force that Urrea may bring against us."

They began now to search for timber, looking especially for some clump of trees that also inclosed water. They did not anticipate any great difficulty in regard to the water, as the winter season and the heavy rains had filled the dry creek beds, and had sent torrents down the arroyos. Before dark they found a stream about a foot deep running over sand between banks seven or eight feet high toward the Rio Grande. A mile further on a small grove of myrtle oaks and pecans grew on its left bank, and there they made their camp.

Feeling that they must rely upon their valor and watchfulness, and not upon secrecy, they built a fire, and ate a good supper. Then they put out the fire and half of them remained on guard, the other half going to sleep, except Roylston, who sat with his back to a tree, his injured legs resting upon a bed of leaves which the boys had raked up for him. He had been riding Old Jack and the horse had seemed to take to him, but after the stop Ned himself had looked after his mount.

The boy allowed Old Jack to graze a while, and then he tethered him in the thickest of the woods just behind the sleeping man. He wished the horse to be as safe as possible in case bullets should be flying, and he could find no better place for him. But before going he stroked his nose and whispered in his ear.

"Good Old Jack! Brave fellow!" he said. "We are going to have troublous times, you and I, along with the others, but I think we are going to ride through them safely."

The horse whinnied ever so softly, and nuzzled Ned's arm. The understanding between them was complete. Then Ned left him, intending to take a position by the bank of the creek as he was on the early watch. On the way he passed Roylston, who regarded him attentively.

"I judge that your leader, Mr. Palmer, whom you generally call the Panther, is expecting an attack," said the merchant.

"He's the kind of man who tries to provide for everything," replied Ned.

"Of course, then," said Roylston, "he provides for the creek bed. The Mexican skirmishers can come up it and yet be protected by its banks."

"That is so," said the Panther, who had approached as he was speaking. "It's the one place that we've got to watch most, an' Ned an' me are goin' to sit there on the banks, always lookin'. I see that you've got the eye of a general, Mr. Roylston."

The merchant smiled.

"I'm afraid I don't count for much in battle," he said, "and least of all hampered as I am now. But if the worst comes to the worst I can sit here with my back to this tree and shoot. If you will kindly give me a rifle and ammunition I shall be ready for the emergency."

"But it is your time to sleep, Mr. Roylston," said the Panther.

"I don't think I can sleep, and as I cannot I might as well be of use."

The Panther brought him the rifle, powder and bullets, and Roylston, leaning against the tree, rifle across his knees, watched with bright eyes. Sentinels were placed at the edge of the grove, but the Panther and Ned, as arranged, were on the high bank overlooking the bed of the creek. Now and then they walked back and forth, meeting at intervals, but most of the time each kept to his own particular part of the ground.

Ned found an oak, blown down on the bank by some hurricane, and as there was a comfortable seat on a bough with the trunk as a rest for his back he remained there a long time. But his ease did not cause him to relax his vigilance. He was looking toward the north, and he could see two hundred yards or more up the creek bed to a point where it curved. The bed itself was about thirty feet wide, although the water did not have a width of more than ten feet.

Everything was now quite dry, as the wind had been blowing all day. But the breeze had died with the night, and the camp was so still that Ned could hear the faint trickle of the water over the sand. It was a fair night, with a cold moon and cold stars looking down. The air was full of chill, and Ned began to walk up and down again in order to keep warm. He noticed Roylston still sitting with eyes wide open and the rifle across his lap.

As Ned came near in his walk the merchant turned his bright eyes upon him.

"I hear," he said, "that you have seen Santa Anna."

"More than once. Several times when I was a prisoner in Mexico, and again when I was recaptured."

"What do you think of him?"

The gaze of the bright eyes fixed upon Ned became intense and concentrated.

"A great man! A wickedly great man!"

Roylston turned his look away, and interlaced his fingers thoughtfully.

"A good description, I think," he said. "You have chosen your words well. A singular compound is this Mexican, a mixture of greatness, vanity and evil. I may talk to you more of him some day. But I tell you now that I am particularly desirous of not being carried a prisoner to him."

He lifted the rifle, put its stock to his shoulder, and drew a bead.

"I think I could hit at forty or fifty yards in this good moonlight," he said.

He replaced the rifle across his knees and sighed. Ned was curious, but he would not ask questions, and he walked back to his old position by the bank. Here he made himself easy, and kept his eyes on the deep trench that had been cut by the stream. The shadows were dark against the bank, but it seemed to him that they were darker than they had been before.

Ned's blood turned a little colder, and his scalp tingled. He was startled but not afraid. He looked intently, and saw moving figures in the river bed, keeping close against the bank. He could not see faces, he could not even discern a clear outline of the figures, but he had no doubt that these were Urrea's Mexicans. He waited only a moment longer to assure himself that the dark moving line was fact and not fancy. Then, aiming his rifle at the foremost shape, he fired. While the echo of the sharp crack was yet speeding across the plain he cried:

"Up, men! up! Urrea is here!"

A volley came from the creek bed, but in an instant the Panther, Obed, Will and Fields were by Ned's side.

"Down on your faces," cried the Panther, "an' pot 'em as they run! So they thought to go aroun' the grove, come down from the north an' surprise us this way! Give it to 'em, boys!"

The rifles flashed and the dark line in the bed of the creek now broke into a huddle of flying forms. Three fell, but the rest ran, splashing through the sand and water, until they turned the curve and were protected from the deadly bullets. Then the Panther, calling to the others, rushed to the other side of the grove, where a second attack, led by Urrea in person, had been begun. Here men on horseback charged directly at the wood, but they were met by a fire which emptied more than one saddle.

Much of the charge was a blur to Ned, a medley of fire and smoke, of beating hoofs and of cries. But one thing he saw clearly and never forgot. It was the lame man with the thick white hair sitting with his back against a tree calmly firing a rifle at the Mexicans. Roylston had time for only two shots, but when he reloaded the second time he placed the rifle across his knees as before and smiled.

Most Mexican troops would have been content with a single charge, but these returned, encouraged by shouts and driven on by fierce commands. Ned saw a figure waving a sword. He believed it to be Urrea, and he fired, but he missed, and the next moment the horseman was lost in the shadows.

The second charge was beaten back like the first, and several skirmishers who tried to come anew down the bed of the creek were also put to flight. Two Mexicans got into the thickets and tried to stampede the horses, but the quickness of Obed and Fields defeated their aim. One of the Mexicans fell there, but the other escaped in the darkness.

When the second charge was driven back and the horses were quieted the Panther and Obed threshed up the woods, lest some Mexican musketeer should lie hidden there.

Nobody slept any more that night. Ned, Will and the Panther kept a sharp watch upon the bed of the creek, the moon and stars fortunately aiding them. But the Mexicans did not venture again by that perilous road, although toward morning they opened a scattering fire from the plain, many of their bullets whistling at random among the trees and thickets. Some of the Texans, crawling to the edge of the wood, replied, but they seemed to have little chance for a good shot, as the Mexicans lay behind a swell. The besiegers grew tired after a while and silence came again.

Three of the Texans had suffered slight wounds, but the Panther and Fields bound them up skillfully. It was still light enough for these tasks. Fields was particularly jubilant over their success, as he had a right to be. The day before he could look forward only to his own execution. Now he was free and victorious. Exultantly he hummed:

> You've heard, I s'pose, of New Orleans,
> It's famed for youth and beauty;
> There are girls of every hue, it seems,
> From snowy white to sooty.
> Now Packenham has made his brags,
> If he that day was lucky,
> He'd have the girls and cotton bags
> In spite of Old Kentucky.
> But Jackson, he was wide awake,
> And was not scared at trifles,
> For well he knew Kentucky's boys,
> With their death-dealing rifles.
> He led them down to cypress swamp,
> The ground was low and mucky;
> There stood John Bull in martial pomp,
> And here stood old Kentucky.

"Pretty good song, that of yours," said the Panther approvingly. "Where did you get it?"

"From my father," replied Fields. "He's a Kentuckian, an' he fit at New Orleans. He was always hummin' that song, an' it come back to me after we drove off the Mexicans. Struck me that it was right timely."

Ned and Will, on their own initiative, had been drawing all the fallen logs that they could find and move to the edge of the wood, and having finished the task they came back to the bed of the creek. Roylston, the rifle across his knees, was sitting with his eyes closed, but he opened them as they approached. They were uncommonly large and bright eyes, and they expressed pleasure.

"It gratifies me to see that neither of you is hurt," he said. "This has been a strange night for two who are as young as you are. And it is a strange night for me, too. I never before thought that I should be firing at any one with intent to kill. But events are often too powerful for us."

He closed his eyes again.

"I am going to sleep a little, if I can," he said.

But Ned and Will could not sleep. They went to Ned's old position at the edge of the creek bed, and together watched the opening dawn. They saw the bright sun rise over the great plains, and the dew sparkle for a little while on the brown grass. The day was cold, but apparently it had come with peace. They saw nothing on the plain, although they had no doubt that the Mexicans were waiting just beyond the first swell. But Ned and Will discerned three dark objects lying on the sand up the bed of the creek, and they knew that they were the men who had fallen in the first rush. Ned was glad that he could not see their faces.

At the suggestion of the Panther they lighted fires and had warm food and coffee again, thus putting heart into all the defenders. Then the Panther chose Ned for a little scouting work on horseback. Ned found Old Jack seeking blades of grass within the limits allowed by his lariat. But when the horse saw his master he stretched out his head and neighed.

"I think I understand you," said Ned. "Not enough food and no water. Well, I'll see that you get both later, but just now we're going on a little excursion."

The Panther and Ned rode boldly out of the trees, and advanced a short distance upon the plain. Two or three shots were fired from a point behind the first swell, but the bullets fell far short.

"I counted on that," said the Panther. "If a Mexican has a gun it's mighty hard for him to keep from firing it. All we wanted to do was to uncover their position an' we've done it. We'll go back now, an' wait fur them to make the first move."

But they did not go just yet. A man on horseback waving a large white handkerchief appeared on the crest of the swell and rode toward them. It was Urrea.

"He knows that he can trust us, while we don't know that we can trust him," said the Panther, "so we'll just wait here an' see what he has to say."

Urrea, looking fresh and spirited, came on with confidence and saluted in a light easy fashion. The two Americans did not return the salute, but waited gravely.

"We can be polite, even if we are enemies," said Urrea, "so I say good morning to you both, former friends of mine."

"I have no friendship with spies and traitors," growled the Panther.

"I serve my country in the way I think best," said Urrea, "and you must remember that in our view you two are rebels and traitors."

"We don't stab in the back," said the Panther.

Urrea flushed through his swarthy skin.

"We will not argue the point any further," he said, "but come at once to the business before us. First, I will admit several things. Your rescue of the prisoners was very clever. Also you beat us off last night, but I now have a hundred men with me and we have plenty of arms. We are bound to take you sooner or later."

"Then why talk to us about it?" said the Panther.

"Because I wish to save bloodshed."

"Wa'al, then, what do you have to say?"

"Give us the man, Roylston, and the rest of you can go free."

"Why are you so anxious to have Roylston?"

Ned eagerly awaited the answer. It was obvious that Roylston had rather minimized his own importance. Urrea flicked the mane of his mustang with a small whip and replied:

"Our President and General, the illustrious Santa Anna, is extremely anxious to see him. Secrets of state are not for me. I merely seek to do my work."

"Then you take this from me," said the Panther, a blunt frontiersman, "my comrades an' me ain't buyin' our lives at the price of nobody else's."

"You feel that way about it, do you?"

"That's just the way we feel, and I want to say, too, that I wouldn't take the word of either you or your Santa Anna. If we was to give up Mr. Roylston— which we don't dream of doin'—you'd be after us as hot an' strong as ever."

Urrea's swarthy cheeks flushed again.

"I shall not notice your insults," he said. "They are beneath me. I am a Mexican officer and gentleman, and you are mere riders of the plains."

"All the same," said the Panther grimly, "if you are goin' to talk you have to talk with us."

"That is true," said Urrea lightly, having regained complete control of his temper. "In war one cannot choose his enemies. I make you the proposition once more. Give us Roylston and go. If you do not accept we shall nevertheless take him and all of you who do not fall first. Remember that you are rebels and traitors and that you will surely be shot or hanged."

"I don't remember any of them things," said the Panther grimly. "What I do remember is that we are Texans fightin' fur our rights. To hang a man you've first got to catch him, an' to shoot him you've first got to hit him. An' since things are to be remembered, remember that what you are tryin' to do to us we may first do to you. An' with that I reckon we'll bid you good day, Mr. Urrea."

Urrea bowed, but said nothing. He rode back toward his men, and Ned and the Panther returned to the grove. Roylston was much better that morning and he was able to stand, leaning against a tree.

"May I ask the result of your conference," he said.

"There ain't no secret about it," replied the Panther, "but them Mexicans seem to be almighty fond of you, Mr. Roylston."

"In what way did they show it?"

"Urrea said that all of us could go if we would give up you."

"And your answer?"

The Panther leaned forward a little on his horse.

"You know something about the Texans, don't you, Mr. Roylston?"

"I have had much opportunity to observe and study them."

"Well, they've got plenty of faults, but you haven't heard of them buyin' their lives at the price of a comrade's, have you?"

"I have not, but I wish to say, Mr. Palmer, that I'm sorry you returned this answer. I should gladly take my chances if the rest of you could go."

"We'd never think of it," said the Panther. "Besides, them Mexicans wouldn't keep their word. They're goin' to besiege us here, hopin' maybe that starvation or thirst will make us give you up. Now the first thing for us to do is to get water for the horses."

This presented a problem, as the horses could not go down to the creek, owing to the steep high banks, but the Texans soon solved it. The cliff was soft and they quickly cut a smooth sloping path with their knives and hatchets. Old Jack was the first to walk down it and Ned led him. The horse hung back a little, but Ned patted his head and talked to him as a friend and equal. Under such persuasion Old Jack finally made the venture, and when he landed safely at the bottom he drank eagerly. Then the other two horses followed. Meanwhile two riflemen kept a keen watch up and down the creek bed for lurking Mexican sharpshooters.

But the watering of the horses was finished without incident, and they were tethered once more in the thicket. Fields and another man kept a watch upon the plain, and the rest conferred under the trees. The Panther announced that by a great reduction of rations the food could be made to last two days longer. It was not a cheerful statement, as the Mexicans must know the scanty nature of their supplies, and would wait with all the patience of Indians.

"All things, including starvation, come to him who waits long enough," said Obed White soberly.

"We'll jest set the day through," said the Panther, "an' see what turns up."

But the day was quite peaceful. It was warmer than usual and bright with sunshine. The Mexicans appeared on some of the knolls, seemingly near in the thin clear air, but far enough away to be out of rifle shot, and began to play cards or loll on their serapes. Several went to sleep.

"They mean to show us that they have all the time in the world," said Ned to Will, "and that they are willing to wait until we fall like ripe apples into their hands."

"Do you think they will get us again?" asked Will anxiously.

"I don't. We've got food for two days and I believe that something will happen in our favor within that time. Do you notice, Will, that it's beginning to cloud up again? In winter you can't depend upon bright sunshine to last always. I think we're going to have a dark night and it's given me an idea."

"What is it?"

"I won't tell you, because it may amount to nothing. It all depends upon what kind of night we have."

The sun did not return. The clouds banked up more heavily, and in the afternoon Ned went to the Panther. They talked together earnestly, looking frequently at the skies, and the faces of both expressed satisfaction. Then they entered the bed of the creek and examined it critically. Will was watching them. When the two separated and Ned came toward him, he said:

"I can guess your idea now. We mean to escape to-night up the bed of the creek."

Ned nodded.

"Your first guess is good," he said. "If the promise of a dark night keeps up we're going to try."

The promise was fulfilled. The Mexicans made no hostile movement throughout the afternoon, but they maintained a rigid watch.

When the sun had set and the thick night had come down the Panther told of the daring enterprise they were about to undertake, and all approved. By nine o'clock the darkness was complete, and the little band gathered at the point where the path was cut down into the bed of the creek. It was likely that Mexicans were on all sides of the grove, but the Panther did not believe that any of them, owing to bitter experience, would enter the cut made by the stream. But, as leader, he insisted upon the least possible noise. The greatest difficulty would be with the horses. Ned, at the head of Old Jack, led the way.

Old Jack made the descent without slipping and in a few minutes the entire force stood upon the sand. They had made no sound that any one could have heard thirty yards away.

"Now Mr. Roylston," whispered the Panther to the merchant, "you get on Ned's horse an' we'll be off."

Roylston sighed. It hurt his pride that he should be a burden, but he was a man of few words, and he mounted in silence. Then they moved slowly over the soft sand. They had loaded the extra rifles and muskets on the other two horses, but every man remained thoroughly armed and ready on the instant for any emergency.

The Panther and Obed led. Just behind them came Ned and Will. They went very slowly in order to keep the horses' feet from making any sound that listening Mexican sentinels might hear. They were fortunate in the sand, which was fine and soundless like a carpet. Ned thought that the Mexicans would not make any attempt upon the grove until late at night, and then only with skirmishers and snipers. Or they might not make any attempt at all, content with their cordon.

But it was thrilling work as they crept along on the soft sand in the darkness and between the high banks. Ned felt a prickling of the blood. An incautious footstep or a stumble by one of the horses might bring the whole Mexican force down upon them at any moment. But there was no incautious footstep. Nor did any horse stumble. The silent procession moved on, passed the curve in the bed of the creek and continued its course.

Urrea had surrounded the grove completely. His men were on both sides of the creek, but no sound came to them, and they had a healthy respect for the deadly Texan rifles. Their leader had certainly been wise in deciding to starve them out. Meanwhile the little procession in the bed of the creek increased its speed slightly.

The Texans were now a full four hundred yards from the grove, and their confidence was rising.

"If they don't discover our absence until morning," whispered Ned to Will, "we'll surely get away."

"Then I hope they won't discover it until then," said Will fervently. "I don't want to die in battle just now, nor do I want to be executed in Mexico for a rebel or for anything else."

They were now a full mile from the grove and the banks of the creek were decreasing in height. They did not rise anywhere more than three or four feet. But the water increased in depth and the margin of sand was narrower. The Panther called a halt and they listened. They heard no sound but the faint moaning of the wind among the dips and swells, and the long lone howl of a lonesome coyote.

"We've slipped through 'em! By the great horn spoon, we've slipped through 'em!" said the Panther exultantly. "Now, boys, we'll take to the water here to throw 'em off our track, when they try to follow it in the mornin'."

The creek was now about three feet in depth and flowing slowly like most streams in that region, but over a bed of hard sand, where the trace of a footstep would quickly vanish.

"The water is likely to be cold," said the Panther, "an' if any fellow is afraid of it he can stay behind and consort with the Mexicans who don't care much for water."

"Lead on, Macduff," said Obed, "and there's nobody who will cry 'hold, enough.'"

The Panther waded directly into the middle of the stream, and all the others followed. The horses, splashing the water, made some noise, but they were not so careful in that particular now since they had put a mile between themselves and the grove. In fact, the Panther urged them to greater speed, careless of the sounds, and they kept in the water for a full two miles further. Then they quit the stream at a point where the soil seemed least likely to leave traces of their footsteps, and stood for a little while upon the prairie, resting and shivering. Then they started at a rapid pace across the country, pushing for the Rio Grande until noon. Then Fields stalked and shot an antelope, with which they renewed their supply of food. In the afternoon it rained heavily, but by dark they reached the Rio Grande, across which they made a dangerous passage, as the waters had risen, and stood once more on the soil of Texas.

"Thank God!" said Will.

"Thank God!" repeated Ned.

Then they looked for shelter, which all felt they must have.

CHAPTER IV.
THE CABIN IN THE WOODS

It proved a difficult matter to find shelter. All the members of the little group were wet and cold, and a bitter wind with snow began to whistle once more across the plain. But every one strove to be cheerful and the relief that their escape had brought was still a tonic to their spirits. Yet they were not without comment upon their condition.

"I've seen hard winters in Maine," said Obed White, "but there you were ready for them. Here it tricks you with warm sunshine and then with snow. You suffer from surprise."

"We've got to find a cabin," said the Panther.

"Why not make it a whole city with a fine big hotel right in the center of it?" said Obed. "Seems to me there's about as much chance of one as the other."

"No, there ain't," said the Panther. "There ain't no town, but there are huts. I've rid over this country for twenty year an' I know somethin' about it. There are four or five settlers' cabins in the valleys of the creeks runnin' down to the Rio Grande. I had a mighty good dinner at one of 'em once. They're more'n likely to be abandoned now owin' to the war an' their exposed situation, but if the roofs haven't fell in any of 'em is good enough for us."

"Then you lead on," said Obed. "The quicker we get there the happier all of us will be."

"I may not lead straight, but I'll get you there," replied the Panther confidently.

Roylston, at his own urgent insistence, dismounted and walked a little while. When he betook himself again to the back of Old Jack he spoke with quiet confidence.

"I'm regaining my strength rapidly," he said. "In a week or two I shall be as good as I ever was. Meanwhile my debt to you, already great, is accumulating."

The Panther laughed.

"You don't owe us nothin'," he said. "Why, on this frontier it's one man's business to help another out of a scrape. If we didn't do that we couldn't live."

"Nevertheless, I shall try to pay it," said Roylston, in significant tones.

"For the moment we'll think of that hut we're lookin' for," said the Panther.

"It will be more than a hut," said Will, who was of a singularly cheerful nature. "I can see it now. It will be a gorgeous palace. Its name will be the Inn of the Panther. Menials in gorgeous livery will show us to our chambers, one for every man, where we will sleep between white sheets of the finest linen."

"I wonder if they will let us take our rifles to bed with us," said Ned, "because in this country I don't feel that I can part with mine, even for a moment."

"That is a mere detail which we will discuss with our host," said Obed. "Perhaps, after you have eaten of the chicken and drunk of the wine at this glorious Inn of the Panther, you will not be so particular about the company of your rifle, Mr. Fulton."

The Panther uttered a cry of joy.

"I've got my b'arin's exactly now," he said. "It ain't more'n four miles to a cabin that I know of, an' if raiders haven't smashed it it'll give us all the shelter we want."

"Then lead us swiftly," said Obed. "There's no sunset or anything to give me mystical lore, but the coming of that cabin casts its shadow before, or at least I want it to do it."

The Panther's announcement brought new courage to every one and they quickened their lagging footsteps. He led toward a dark line of timber which now began to show through the driving snow, and when they passed among the trees he announced once more and with exultation:

"Only a mile farther, boys, an' we'll be where the cabin stands, or stood. Don't git your feelin's too high, 'cause it may have been wiped off the face of the earth."

A little later he uttered another cry, and this was the most exultant of all.

"There she is," he said, pointing ahead. "She ain't been wiped away by nobody or nothin'. Don't you see her, that big, stout cabin ahead?"

"I do," said young Allen joyously, "and it's the Inn of the Panther as sure as you live."

"But I don't see any smoke coming out of the chimney," said Ned, "and there are no gorgeous menials standing on the doorstep waiting for us."

"It's been abandoned a long time," said the Panther. "I can tell that by its looks, but I'm thinkin' that it's good enough fur us an' mighty welcome. An' there's a shed behind the house that'll do for the horses. Boys, we're travelin' in tall luck."

The cabin, a large one, built of logs and adobe, was certainly a consoling sight. They had almost reached the limit of physical endurance, but they broke into a run to reach it. The Panther and Ned were the first to push open a heavy swinging door, and they entered side by side. It was dry within. The solid board roof did not seem to be damaged at all, and the floor of hard, packed earth was as dry as a bone also. At one end were a wide stone fireplace, cold long since, and a good chimney of mud and sticks. There were two windows, closed with heavy clapboard shutters.

There was no furniture in the cabin except two rough wooden benches. Evidently the original owners had prepared well for their flight, but it was likely that no one had come since. The lonely place among the trees had passed unobserved by raiders. The shed behind the cabin was also in good condition, and they tethered there the horses, which were glad enough to escape from the bitter wind and driving snow.

The whole party gathered in the cabin, and as they no longer feared pursuit it was agreed unanimously that they must have luxury. In this case a fire meant the greatest of all luxuries.

They gathered an abundance of fallen wood, knocked the snow from it and heaped it on either side of the fireplace. They cut with infinite difficulty dry shavings from the inside of the logs in the wall of the house, and after a full hour of hard work lighted a blaze with flint and steel. The rest was easy, and soon they had a roaring fire. They fastened the door with the wooden bar which stood in its place and let the windows remain shut. Although there was a lack of air, they did not yet feel it, and gave themselves up to the luxury of the glowing heat.

They took off their clothes and held them before the fire. When they were dry and warm they put them on again and felt like new beings. Strips of the antelope were fried on the ends of ramrods, and they ate plentifully. All the chill was driven from their bodies, and in its place came a deep pervading sense of comfort. The bitter wind yet howled without and they heard the snow driven against the door and windows. The sound heightened their feeling of luxury. They were like a troop of boys now, all of them—except Roylston. He sat on one of the piles of wood and his eyes gleamed as the others talked.

"I vote that we enlarge the name of our inn," said Allen. "Since our leader has black hair and black eyes, let's call it the Inn of the Black Panther. All in favor of that motion say 'Aye.'"

"Aye!" they roared.

"All against it say 'no.'"

Silence.

"The Inn of the Black Panther it is," said Will, "an' it is the most welcome inn that ever housed me."

The Panther smiled benevolently.

"I don't blame you boys for havin' a little fun," he said. "It does feel good to be here after all that we've been through."

The joy of the Texans was irrepressible. Fields began to pat and three or four of them danced up and down the earthen floor of the cabin. Will watched with dancing eyes. Ned, more sober, sat by his side.

However, the highest spirits must grow calm at last, and gradually the singing and dancing ceased. It had grown quite close in the cabin now, and one of the window shutters was thrown open, permitting a rush of cool, fresh air that was very welcome. Ned looked out. The wind was still whistling and moaning, and the snow, like a white veil, hid the trees.

The men one by one went to sleep on the floor. Obed and Fields kept watch at the window during the first half of the night, and the Panther and Ned relieved them for the second half. They heard nothing but the wind, and saw nothing but the snow. Day came with a hidden sun, and the fine snow still driven by the wind, but the Panther, a good judge of weather, predicted a cessation of the snow within an hour.

The men awoke and rose slowly from the floor. They were somewhat stiff, but no one had been overcome, and after a little stretching of the muscles all the soreness disappeared. The horses were within the shed, unharmed and warm, but hungry. They relighted the fire and broiled more strips of the antelope, but they saw that little would be left. The Panther turned to Roylston, who inspired respect in them all.

"Now, Mr. Roylston," he said, "we've got to agree upon some course of action an' we've got to put it to ourselves squar'ly. I take it that all of us want to serve Texas in one way or another, but we've got only three horses, we're about out of food, an' we're a long distance from the main Texas settlements. It ain't any use fur us to start to rippin' an' t'arin' unless we've got somethin' to rip an' t'ar with."

"Good words," said Obed White. "A speech in time saves errors nine."

"I am glad you have put the question, Mr. Palmer," said Roylston. "Our affairs have come to a crisis, and we must consider. I, too, wish to help Texas, but I can help it more by other ways than battle."

It did not occur to any of them to doubt him. He had already established over them the mental ascendency that comes from a great mind used to dealing with great affairs.

"But we are practically dismounted," he continued. "It is winter and we do not know what would happen to us if we undertook to roam over the prairies as we are. On the other hand, we have an abundance of arms and ammunition and a large and well-built cabin. I suggest that we supply ourselves with food, and stay here until we can acquire suitable mounts. We may also contrive to keep a watch upon any Mexican armies that may be marching north. I perhaps have more reason than any of you for hastening away, but I can spend the time profitably in regaining the use of my limbs."

"Your little talk sounds mighty good to me," said the Panther. "In fact, I don't see anything else to do. This cabin must have been built an' left here 'speshully fur us. We know, too, that the Texans have all gone home, thinkin' that the war is over, while we know different an' mebbe we can do more good here than anywhere else. What do you say, boys? Do we stay?"

"We stay," replied all together.

They went to work at once fitting up their house. More firewood was brought in. Fortunately the men had been provided with hatchets, in the frontier style, which their rescuers had not neglected to bring away, and they fixed wooden hooks in the walls for their extra arms and clothing. A half dozen scraped away a large area of the thin snow and enabled the horses to find grass. A fine spring two hundred yards away furnished a supply of water.

After the horses had eaten Obed, the Panther and Ned rode away in search of game, leaving Mr. Roylston in command at the cabin.

The snow was no longer falling, and that which lay on the ground was melting rapidly.

"I know this country," said the Panther, "an' we've got four chances for game. It may be buffalo, it may be deer, it may be antelope, and it may be wild turkeys. I think it most likely that we'll find buffalo. We're so fur west of the main settlements that they're apt to hang 'roun' here in the winter in the creek bottoms, an' if it snows they'll take to the timber fur shelter."

"And it has snowed," said Ned.

"Jest so, an' that bein' the case we'll search the timber. Of course big herds couldn't crowd in thar, but in this part of the country we gen'rally find the buffalo scattered in little bands."

They found patches of forest, generally dwarfed in character, and looked diligently for the great game. Once a deer sprang out of a thicket, but sped away so fast they did not get a chance for a shot. At length Obed saw large footprints in the thinning snow, and called the Panther's attention to them. The big man examined the traces critically.

"Not many hours old," he said. "I'm thinkin' that we'll have buffalo steak fur supper. We'll scout all along this timber. What we want is a young cow. Their meat is not tough."

They rode through the timber for about two hours, when Ned caught sight of moving figures on the far side of a thicket. He could just see the backs of large animals, and he knew that there were their buffalo. He pointed them out to the Panther, who nodded.

"We'll ride 'roun' the thicket as gently as possible," he said, "an' then open fire. Remember, we want a tender young cow, two of 'em if we can get 'em, an' don't fool with the bulls."

Ned's heart throbbed as Old Jack bore him around the thicket. He had fought with men, but he was not yet a buffalo hunter. Just as they turned the flank of the bushes a huge buffalo bull, catching their odor, raised his head and uttered a snort. The Panther promptly fired at a young cow just beyond him. The big bull, either frightened or angry, leaped head down at Old Jack. The horse was without experience with buffaloes, but he knew that those sharp horns meant no good to him, and he sprang aside with so much agility that Ned was almost unseated.

The big bull rushed on, and Ned, who had retained his hold upon his rifle, was tempted to take a shot at him for revenge, but, remembering the Panther's injunction, he controlled the impulse and fired at a young cow.

When the noise and confusion were over and the surviving buffaloes had lumbered away, they found that they had slain two of the young cows and that they had an ample supply of meat.

"Ned," said the Panther, "you know how to go back to the cabin, don't you?"

"I can go straight as an arrow."

"Then ride your own horse, lead the other two an' bring two men. We'll need 'em with the work here."

The Panther and Obed were already at work skinning the cows. Ned sprang upon Old Jack, and rode away at a trot, leading the other two horses by their lariats. The snow was gone now and the breeze was almost balmy. Ned felt that great rebound of the spirits of which the young are so capable. They had outwitted Urrea, they had taken his prisoners from him, and then had escaped across the Rio Grande. They had found shelter and now they had obtained a food supply. They were all good comrades together, and what more was to be asked?

He whistled as he rode along, but when he was half way back to the cabin he noticed something in a large tree that caused him to stop. He saw the outlines of great bronze birds, and he knew that they were wild turkeys. Wild turkeys would make a fine addition to their larder, and, halting Old Jack, he shot from his back, taking careful aim at the largest of the turkeys. The huge bird fell, and as the others flew away Ned was lucky enough to bring down a second with a pistol shot.

His trophies were indeed worth taking, and tying their legs together with a withe he hung them across his saddle bow. He calculated that the two together weighed nearly sixty pounds, and he rode triumphantly when he came in sight of the cabin.

Will saw him first and gave a shout that drew the other men.

"What luck?" hailed young Allen.

"Not much," replied Ned, "but I did get these sparrows."

He lifted the two great turkeys from his saddle and tossed them to Will. The boy caught them, but he was borne to his knees by their weight. The men looked at them and uttered approving words.

"What did you do with the Panther and Obed?" asked Fields.

"The last I saw of them they had been dismounted and were being chased over the plain by two big bull buffaloes. The horns of the buffaloes were then not more than a foot from the seats of their trousers. So I caught their horses, and I have brought them back to camp."

"I take it," said Fields, "that you've had good luck."

"We have had the finest of luck," replied Ned. "We ran into a group of fifteen or twenty buffaloes, and we brought down two fine, young cows. I came back for two more men to help with them, and on my way I shot these turkeys."

Fields and another man named Carter returned with Ned. Young Allen was extremely anxious to go, but the others were chosen on account of their experience with the work. They found that Obed and the Panther had already done the most of it, and when it was all finished Fields and Carter started back with the three horses, heavily laden. As the night promised to be mild, and the snow was gone, Ned, Obed and the Panther remained in the grove with the rest of their food supply.

They also wished to preserve the two buffalo robes, and they staked them out upon the ground, scraping them clean of flesh with their knives. Then they lighted a fire and cooked as much of the tender meat as they wished. By this time it was dark and they were quite ready to rest. They put out the fire and raked up the beds of leaves on which they would spread their blankets. But first they enjoyed the relaxation of the nerves and the easy talk that come after a day's work well done.

"It certainly has been a fine day for us," said Obed. "Sometimes I like to go through the bad days, because it makes the good days that follow all the better. Yesterday we were wandering around in the snow, and we had nothing, to-day we have a magnificent city home, that is to say, the cabin, and a beautiful country place, that is to say, this grove. I can add, too, that our nights in our country place are spent to the accompaniment of music. Listen to that beautiful song, won't you?"

A long, whining howl rose, sank and died. After an interval they heard its exact duplicate and the Panther remarked tersely:

"Wolves. Mighty hungry, too. They've smelled our buffalo meat and they want it. Guess from their big voices that they're timber wolves and not coyotes."

Ned knew that the timber wolf was a much larger and fiercer animal than his prairie brother, and he did not altogether like this whining sound which now rose and died for the third time.

"Must be a dozen or so," said the Panther, noticing the increasing volume of sound. "We'll light the fire again. Nothing is smarter than a wolf, an' I don't want one of those hulkin' brutes to slip up, seize a fine piece of buffalo and dash away with it. But fire will hold 'em. How a wolf does dread it! The little red flame is like a knife in his heart."

They lighted four small fires, making a rude ring which inclosed their leafy beds and the buffalo skins and meat. Before they finished the task they saw slim dusky figures among the trees and red eyes glaring at them. The Panther picked up a stick blazing like a torch, and made a sudden rush for one of the figures. There was a howl of terror and a sound of something rushing madly through the bushes.

The Panther flung his torch as far as he could in the direction of the sounds and returned, laughing deep in his throat.

"I think I came pretty near hittin' the master wolf with that," he said, "an' I guess he's good an' scared. But they'll come back after a while, an' don't you forget it. For that reason, I think we'd better keep a watch. We'll divide it into three hours apiece, an' we'll give you the first, Ned."

Ned was glad to have the opening watch, as it would soon be over and done with, and then he could sleep free from care about any watch to come. The Panther and Obed rolled in their blankets, found sleep almost instantly, and the boy, resolved not to be a careless sentinel, walked in a circle just outside the fires.

Sure enough, and just as the Panther had predicted, he saw the red eyes and dusky forms again. Now and then he heard a faint pad among the bushes, and he knew that a wolf had made it. He merely changed from the outside to the inside of the fire ring, and continued his walk. With the fire about him and his friends so near he was not afraid of wolves, no matter how big and numerous they might be.

Yet their presence in the bushes, the light shuffle of their feet and their fiery eyes had an uncanny effect. It was unpleasant to know that such fierce beasts were so near, and he gave himself a reassuring glance at the sleeping forms of his partners. By and by the red eyes melted away, and he heard another soft tread, but heavier than that of the wolves. With his rifle lying in the hollow of his arm and his finger on the trigger he looked cautiously about the circle of the forest.

Ned's gaze at last met that of a pair of red eyes, a little further apart than those of the wolves. He knew then that they belonged to a larger animal, and presently he caught a glimpse of the figure. He was sure that it was a puma or cougar, and so far as he could judge it was a big brute. It, too, must be very hungry, or it would not dare the fire and the human odor.

Ned felt tentatively of his rifle, but changed his mind. He remembered the Panther's exploit with the firebrand, and he decided to imitate it, but on a much larger scale. He laid down his rifle, but kept his left hand on the butt of the pistol in his belt. Then selecting the largest torch from the fire he made a rush straight for the blazing eyes, thrusting the flaming stick before him. There was a frightened roar, and then the sound of a heavy body crashing away through the undergrowth. Ned returned, satisfied that he had done as well as the Panther and better.

Both the Panther and Obed were awake and sitting up. They looked curiously at Ned, who still carried the flaming brand in his hand.

"A noise like the sound of thunder away off wakened me up," said the Panther. "Now, what have you been up to, young 'un?"

"Me?" said Ned lightly. "Oh, nothing important. I wanted to make some investigations in natural history out there in the bushes, and as I needed a light for the purpose I took it."

"An' if I'm not pressin' too much," said the Panther, in mock humility, "may I make so bold as to ask our young Solomon what is natural history?"

"Natural history is the study of animals. I saw a panther in the bushes and I went out there to examine him. I saw that he was a big fellow, but he ran away so fast I could tell no more about him."

"You scared him away with the torch instead of shooting," said Obed. "It was well done, but it took a stout heart. If he comes again tell him I won't wake up until it's time for my watch."

He was asleep again inside of a minute, and the Panther followed him quickly. Both men trusted Ned fully, treating him now as an experienced and skilled frontiersman. He knew it, and he felt proud and encouraged.

The panther did not come back, but the wolves did, although Ned now paid no attention to them. He was growing used to their company and the uncanny feeling departed. He merely replenished the fires and sat patiently until it was time for Obed to succeed him. Then he, too, wrapped himself in his blankets and slept a dreamless sleep until day.

The remainder of the buffalo meat was taken away the next day, but anticipating a long stay at the cabin they continued to hunt, both on horseback and on foot. Two more buffalo cows fell to their rifles. They also secured a deer, three antelope and a dozen wild turkeys.

Their hunting spread over two days, but when they were all assembled on the third night at the cabin general satisfaction prevailed. They had ranged over considerable country, and as game was plentiful and not afraid the Panther drew the logical conclusion that man had been scarce in that region.

"I take it," he said, "that the Mexicans are a good distance east, and that the Lipans and Comanches are another good distance west. Just the same, boys, we've got to keep a close watch, an' I think we've got more to fear from raidin' parties of the Indians than from the Mexicans. All the Mexicans are likely to be ridin' to some point on the Rio Grande to meet the forces of Santa Anna."

"I wish we had more horses," said Obed. "We'd go that way ourselves and see what's up."

"Well, maybe we'll get 'em," said the Panther. "Thar's a lot of horses on these plains, some of which ought to belong to us an' we may find a way of claimin' our rights."

They passed a number of pleasant days at the cabin and in hunting and foraging in the vicinity. They killed more big game and the dressed skins of buffalo, bear and deer were spread on the floor or were hung on the walls. Wild turkeys were numerous, and they had them for food every day. But they discovered no signs of man, white or red, and they would have been content to wait there had they not been so anxious to investigate the reported advance of Santa Anna on the Rio Grande.

Roylston was the most patient of them all, or at least he said the least.

"I think," he said about the fourth or fifth day, "that it does not hurt to linger here. The Mexican power has not yet gathered in full. As for me, personally, it suits me admirably. I can walk a full two hundred yards now, and next week I shall be able to walk a mile."

"When we are all ready to depart, which way do you intend to go Mr. Roylston?" asked Ned.

"I wish to go around the settlements and then to New Orleans," replied Roylston. "That city is my headquarters, but I also have establishments elsewhere, even as far north as New York. Are you sure, Ned, that you cannot go with me and bring your friend Allen, too? I could make men of you both in a vast commercial world. There have been great opportunities, and greater are coming. The development of this mighty southwest will call for large and bold schemes of organization. It is not money alone that I offer, but the risk, the hopes and rewards of a great game, in fact, the opening of a new world to civilization, for such this southwest is. It appeals to some deeper feeling than that which can be aroused by the mere making of money."

Ned, deeply interested, watched him intently as he spoke. He saw Roylston show emotion for the first time, and the mind of the boy responded to that of the man. He could understand this dream. The image of a great Texan republic was already in the minds of men. It possessed that of Ned. He did not believe that the Texans and Mexicans could ever get along together, and he was quite sure that Texas could never return to its original position as part of a Mexican state.

"You can do much for Texas there with me in New Orleans," said Roylston, as if he were making a final appeal to one whom he looked upon almost as a son. "Perhaps you could do more than you can here in Texas."

Ned shook his head a little sadly. He did not like to disappoint this man, but he could not leave the field. Young Allen also said that he would remain.

"Be it so," said Roylston. "It is young blood. Never was there a truer saying than 'Young men for war, old men for counsel.' But the time may come when you will need me. When it does come send the word."

Ned judged from Roylston's manner that dark days were ahead, but the merchant did not mention the subject again. At the end of a week, when they were amply supplied with everything except horses, the Panther decided to take Ned and Obed and go on a scout toward the Rio Grande. They started early in the morning and the horses, which had obtained plenty of grass, were full of life and vigor.

They soon left the narrow belt of forest far behind them, maintaining an almost direct course toward the southeast. The point on the river that they intended to reach was seventy or eighty miles away, and they did not expect to cover the distance in less than two days.

They rode all that day and did not see a trace of a human being, but they did see both buffalo and antelope in the distance.

"It shows what the war has done," said the Panther. "I rode over these same prairies about a year ago an' game was scarce, but there were some men. Now the men are all gone an' the game has come back. Cur'us how quick buffalo an' deer an' antelope learn about these things."

They slept the night through on the open prairie, keeping watch by turns. The weather was cold, but they had their good blankets with them and they took no discomfort. They rode forward again early in the morning, and about noon struck an old but broad trail. It was evident that many men and many wagons had passed here. There were deep ruts in the earth, cut by wheels, and the traces of footsteps showed over a belt a quarter of a mile wide.

"Well, Ned, I s'pose you can make a purty good guess what this means?" said the Panther.

"This was made weeks and weeks ago," replied Ned confidently, "and the men who made it were Mexicans. They were soldiers, the army of Cos, that we took at San Antonio, and which we allowed to retire on parole into Mexico."

"There's no doubt you're right," said the Panther. "There's no other force in this part of the world big enough to make such a wide an' lastin' trail. An' I think it's our business to follow these tracks. What do you say, Obed?"

"It's just the one thing in the world that we're here to do," said the Maine man. "Broad is the path and straight is the way that leads before us, and we follow on."

"Do we follow them down into Mexico?" said Ned.

"I don't think it likely that we'll have to do it," replied the Panther, glancing at Obed.

Ned caught the look and he understood.

"Do you mean," he asked, "that Cos, after taking his parole and pledging his word that he and his troops would not fight against us, would stop at the Rio Grande?"

"I mean that an' nothin' else," replied the Panther. "I ain't talkin' ag'in Mexicans in general. I've knowed some good men among them, but I wouldn't take the word of any of that crowd of generals, Santa Anna, Cos, Sesma, Urrea, Gaona, Castrillon, the Italian Filisola, or any of them."

"There's one I'd trust," said Ned, with grateful memory, "and that's Almonte."

"I've heard that he's of different stuff," said the Panther, "but it's best to keep out of their hands."

They were now riding swiftly almost due southward, having changed their course to follow the trail, and they kept a sharp watch ahead for Mexican scouts or skirmishers. But the bare country in its winter brown was lone and desolate. The trail led straight ahead, and it would have been obvious now to the most inexperienced eye that an army had passed that way. They saw remains of camp fires, now and then the skeleton of a horse or mule picked clean by buzzards, fragments of worn-out clothing that had been thrown aside, and once a broken-down wagon. Two or three times they saw little mounds of earth with rude wooden crosses stuck upon them, to mark where some of the wounded had died and had been buried.

They came at last to a bit of woodland growing about a spring that seemed to gush straight up from the earth. It was really an open grove with no underbrush, a splendid place for a camp. It was evident that Cos's force had put it to full use, as the earth nearly everywhere had been trodden by hundreds of feet, and the charred pieces of wood were innumerable. The Panther made a long and critical examination of everything.

"I'm thinkin'," he said, "that Cos stayed here three or four days. All the signs p'int that way. He was bound by the terms we gave him at San Antonio to go an' not fight ag'in, but he's shorely takin' his time about it. Look at these bones, will you? Now, Ned, you promisin' scout an' skirmisher, tell me what they are."

"Buffalo bones," replied Ned promptly.

"Right you are," replied the Panther, "an' when Cos left San Antonio he wasn't taking any buffaloes along with him to kill fur meat. They staid here so long that the hunters had time to go out an' shoot game."

"A long lane's the thief of time," said Obed, "and having a big march before him, Cos has concluded to walk instead of run."

"'Cause he was expectin' somethin' that would stop him," said the Panther angrily. "I hate liars an' traitors. Well, we'll soon see."

Their curiosity became so great that they rode at a swift trot on the great south trail, and not ten miles further they came upon the unmistakable evidences of another big camp that had lasted long.

"Slower an' slower," muttered the Panther. "They must have met a messenger. Wa'al, it's fur us to go slow now, too."

But he said aloud:

"Boys, it ain't more'n twenty miles now to the Rio Grande, an' we can hit it by dark. But I'm thinkin' that we'd better be mighty keerful now as we go on."

"I suppose it's because Mexican scouts and skirmishers may be watching," said Ned.

"Yes, an' 'specially that fellow Urrea. His uncle bein' one of Santa Anna's leadin' gen'rals, he's likely to have freer rein, an', as we know, he's clever an' active. I'd hate to fall into his hands again."

They rode more slowly, and three pairs of eyes continually searched the plain for an enemy. Ned's sight was uncommonly acute, and Obed and the Panther frequently appealed to him as a last resort. It flattered his pride and he strove to justify it.

Their pace became slower and slower, and presently the early twilight of winter was coming. A cold wind moaned, but the desolate plain was broken here and there by clumps of trees. At the suggestion of the Panther they rode to one of these and halted under cover of the timber.

"The river can't be much more than a mile ahead," said the Panther, "an' we might run into the Mexicans any minute. We're sheltered here, an' we'd better wait a while. Then I think we can do more stalkin'."

Obed and Ned were not at all averse, and dismounting they stretched themselves, easing their muscles. Old Jack hunted grass and, finding none, rubbed Ned's elbow with his nose suggestively.

"Never mind, old boy," said Ned, patting the glossy muzzle of his faithful comrade. "This is no time for feasting and banqueting. We are hunting Mexicans, you and I, and after that business is over we may consider our pleasures."

They remained several hours among the trees. They saw the last red glow that the sun leaves in the west die away. They saw the full darkness descend over the earth, and then the stars come trooping out. After that they saw a scarlet flush under the horizon which was not a part of the night and its progress. The Panther noted it, and his great face darkened. He turned to Ned.

"You see it, don't you? Now tell me what it is."

"That light, I should say, comes from the fires of an army. And it can be no other army than that of Cos."

"Right again, ain't he, Obed?"

"He surely is. Cos and his men are there. He who breaks his faith when he steals away will have to fight another day. How far off would you say that light is, Panther?"

"'Bout two miles, an' in an hour or so we'll ride fur it. The night will darken up more then, an' it will give us a better chance for lookin' an listenin'. I'll be mightily fooled if we don't find out a lot that's worth knowin'."

True to Obed's prediction, the night deepened somewhat within the hour. Many of the stars were hidden by floating wisps of cloud, and objects could not be seen far on the dusky surface of the plain. But the increased darkness only made the scarlet glow in the south deepen. It seemed, too, to spread far to right and left.

"That's a big force," said the Panther. "It'll take a lot of fires to make a blaze like that."

"I'm agreeing with you," said Obed. "I'm thinking that those are the camp fires of more men than Cos took from San Antonio with him."

"Which would mean," said Ned, "that another Mexican army had come north to join him."

"Anyhow, we'll soon see," said the Panther.

They mounted their horses and rode cautiously toward the light.

CHAPTER V.
SANTA ANNA'S ADVANCE

The three rode abreast, Ned in the center. The boy was on terms of perfect equality with Obed and the Panther. They treated him as a man among men, and respected his character, rather grave for one so young, and always keen to learn.

The land rolled away in swells as usual throughout a great part of Texas, but they were not of much elevation and the red glow in the south was always in sight, deepening fast as they advanced. They stopped at last on a little elevation within the shadow of some myrtle oaks, and saw the fires spread before them only four or five hundred yards away, and along a line of at least two miles. They heard the confused murmur of many men. The dark outlines of cannon were seen against the firelight, and now and then the musical note of a mandolin or guitar came to them.

"We was right in our guess," said the Panther. "It's a lot bigger force than the one that Cos led away from San Antonio, an' it will take a heap of rippin' an' t'arin' an' roarin' to turn it back. Our people don't know how much is comin' ag'in 'em."

The Panther spoke in a solemn tone. Ned saw that he was deeply impressed and that he feared for the future. Good cause had he. Squabbles among the Texan leaders had reduced their army to five or six hundred men.

"Don't you think," said Ned, "that we ought to find out just exactly what is here, and what this army intends?"

"Not a doubt of it," said Obed. "Those who have eyes to see should not go away without seeing."

The Panther nodded violently in assent.

"We must scout about the camp," he said. "Mebbe we'd better divide an' then we can all gather before day-break at the clump of trees back there."

He pointed to a little cluster of trees several hundred yards back of them, and Ned and Obed agreed. The Panther turned away to the right, Obed to the left and Ned took the center. Their plan of dividing their force had a great advantage. One man was much less likely than three to attract undue attention.

Ned went straight ahead a hundred yards or more, when he was stopped by an arroyo five or six feet wide and with very deep banks. He looked about, uncertain at first what to do. Obed and the Panther had already disappeared in the dusk. Before him glowed the red light, and he heard the distant sound of many voices.

Ned quickly decided. He remembered how they had escaped up the bed of the creek when they were besieged by Urrea, and if one could leave by an arroyo, one could also approach by it. He rode to the group of trees that had been designated as the place of meeting, and left his horse there. He noticed considerable grass within the ring of trunks, and he was quite confident that Old Jack would remain there until his return. But he addressed to him words of admonition:

"Be sure that you stay among these trees, old friend," he said, "because it's likely that when I want you I'll want you bad. Remain and attend to this grass."

Old Jack whinnied softly and, after his fashion, rubbed his nose gently against his master's arm. It was sufficient for Ned. He was sure that the horse understood, and leaving him he went back to the arroyo, which he entered without hesitation.

Ned was well armed, as every one then had full need to be. He wore a sombrero in the Mexican fashion, and flung over his shoulders was a great serape which he had found most useful in the winter. With his perfect knowledge of Spanish and its Mexican variants he believed that if surprised he could pass as a Mexican, particularly in the night and among so many.

The arroyo led straight down toward the plain upon which the Mexicans were encamped, and when he emerged from it he saw that the fires which at a distance looked like one continuous blaze were scores in number. Many of them were built of buffalo chips and others of light wood that burned fast. Sentinels were posted here and there, but they kept little watch. Why should they? Here was a great Mexican army, and there was certainly no foe amounting to more than a few men within a hundred miles.

Ned's heart sank as he beheld the evident extent of the Mexican array. The little Texan force left in the field could be no match for such an army as this.

Nevertheless, his resolution to go through the Mexican camp hardened. If he came back with a true and detailed tale of their numbers the Texans must believe and prepare. He drew the brim of his sombrero down a little further, and pulled his serape up to meet it. The habit the Mexicans had of wrapping their serapes so high that they were covered to the nose was fortunate at this time. He was now completely disguised, without the appearance of having taken any unusual precaution.

He walked forward boldly and sat down with a group beside a fire. He judged by the fact that they were awake so late that they had but little to do, and he saw at once also that they were Mexicans from the far south. They were small, dark men, rather amiable in appearance. Two began to play guitars and they sang a plaintive song to the music. The others, smoking cigarritos, listened attentively and luxuriously. Ned imitated them perfectly. He, too, lying upon his elbow before the pleasant fire, felt the influence of the music, so sweet, so murmurous, speaking so little of war. One of the men handed him a cigarrito, and, lighting it, he made pretense of smoking — he would not have seemed a Mexican had he not smoked the cigarrito.

Lying there, Ned saw many tents, evidence of a camp that was not for the day only, and he beheld officers in bright uniforms passing among them. His heart gave a great jump when he noticed among them a heavy-set, dark man. It was Cos, Cos the breaker of oaths. With him was another officer whose uniform indicated the general. Ned learned later that this was Sesma, who had been dispatched with a brigade by Santa Anna to meet Cos on the Rio Grande, where they were to remain until the dictator himself came with more troops.

The music ceased presently and one of the men said to Ned:

"What company?"

Ned had prepared himself for such questions, and he moved his hand vaguely toward the left.

"Over there," he said.

They were fully satisfied, and continued to puff their cigarritos, resting their heads with great content upon pillows made of their saddles and blankets. For a while they said nothing more, happily watching the rings of smoke from their cigarritos rise and melt into the air. Although small and short, they looked hardy and strong. Ned noticed the signs of bustle and expectancy about the camp. Usually Mexicans were asleep at this hour, and he wondered why they lingered. But he did not approach the subject directly.

"A hard march," he said, knowing that these men about him had come a vast distance.

"Aye, it was," said the man next on his right. "Santiago, but was it not, José?"

José, the second man on the right, replied in the affirmative and with emphasis:

"You speak the great truth, Carlos. Such another march I never wish to make. Think of the hundreds and hundreds of miles we have tramped from our warm lands far in the south across mountains, across bare and windy deserts, with the ice and the snow beating in our faces. How I shivered, Carlos, and how long I shivered! I thought I should continue shivering all my life even if I lived to be a hundred, no matter how warmly the sun might shine."

The others laughed, and seemed to Ned to snuggle a little closer to the fire, driven by the memory of the icy plains.

"But it was the will of the great Santa Anna, surely the mightiest man of our age," said Carlos. "They say that his wrath was terrible when he heard how the Texan bandits had taken San Antonio de Bexar. Truly, I am glad that I was not one of his officers, and that I was not in his presence at the time. After all, it is sometimes better to be a common soldier than to have command."

"Aye, truly," said Ned, and the others nodded in affirmation.

"But the great Santa Anna will finish it," continued Carlos, who seemed to have the sin of garrulity. "He has defeated all his enemies in Mexico, he has consolidated his power and now he advances with a mighty force to crush these insolent and miserable Texans. As I have said, he will finish it. The rope and the bullet will be busy. In six months there will be no Texans."

Ned shivered, and when he looked at the camp fires of the great army he saw that this peon was not talking foolishness. Nevertheless his mind returned to its original point of interest. Why did the Mexican army remain awake so late?

"Have you seen the President?" he asked of Carlos.

"Often," replied Carlos, with pride. "I fought under him in the great battle on the plain of Guadalupe less than two years ago, when we defeated Don Francisco Garcia, the governor of Zacatecas. Ah, it was a terrible battle, my friends! Thousands and thousands were killed and all Mexicans. Mexicans killing Mexicans. But who can prevail against the great Santa Anna? He routed the forces of Garcia, and the City of Zacatecas was given up to us to pillage. Many fine things I took that day from the houses of those who presumed to help the enemy of our leader. But now we care not to kill Mexicans, our own people. It is only the miserable Texans who are really Gringos."

Carlos, who had been the most amiable of men, basking in the firelight, now rose up a little and his eyes flashed. He had excited himself by his own tale of the battle and loot of Zacatecas and the coming slaughter of the Texans. That strain of cruelty, which in Ned's opinion always lay embedded in the Spanish character, was coming to the surface.

Ned made no comment. His serape, drawn up to his nose, almost met the brim of his sombrero and nobody suspected that the comrade who sat and chatted with them was a Gringo, but he shivered again, nevertheless.

"We shall have a great force when it is all gathered," he said at length.

"Seven thousand men or more," said José proudly, "and nearly all of them are veterans of the wars. We shall have ten times the numbers of the Texans, who are only hunters and rancheros."

"Have you heard when we march?" asked Ned, in a careless tone.

"As soon as the great Santa Anna arrives it will be decided, I doubt not," said José. "The general and his escort should be here by midnight."

Ned's heart gave a leap. So it was that for which they were waiting. Santa Anna himself would come in an hour or two. He was very glad that he had entered the Mexican camp. Bidding a courteous good night to the men about the fire, he rose and sauntered on. It was easy enough for him to do so without attracting attention, as many others were doing the same thing. Discipline seldom amounted to much in a Mexican army, and so confident were both officers and soldiers of an overwhelming victory that they preserved scarcely any at all. Yet the expectant feeling pervaded the whole camp, and now that he knew that Santa Anna was coming he understood.

Santa Anna was the greatest man in the world to these soldiers. He had triumphed over everything in their own country. He had exhibited qualities of daring and energy that seemed to them supreme, and his impression upon them was overwhelming. Ned felt once more that little shiver. They might be right in their view of the Texan war.

He strolled on from fire to fire, until his attention was arrested suddenly by one at which only officers sat. It was not so much the group as it was one among them who drew his notice so strongly. Urrea was sitting on the far side of the fire, every feature thrown into clear relief by the bright flames. The other officers were young men of about his own age and they were playing dice. They were evidently in high good humor, as they laughed frequently.

Ned lay down just within the shadow of a tent wall, drew his serape higher about his face, and rested his head upon his arm. He would have seemed sound asleep to an ordinary observer, but he was never more wide awake in his life. He was near enough to hear what Urrea and his friends were saying, and he intended to hear it. It was for such that he had come.

"You lose, Francisco," said one of the men as he made a throw of the dice and looked eagerly at the result. "What was it that you were saying about the general?"

"That I expect an early advance, Ramon," replied Urrea, "a brief campaign, and a complete victory. I hate these Texans. I shall be glad to see them annihilated."

The young officer whom he called Ramon laughed.

"If what I hear be true, Francisco," he said, "you have cause to hate them. There was a boy, Fulton, that wild buffalo of a man, whom they call the Panther, and another who defeated some of your finest plans."

Urrea flushed, but controlled his temper.

"It is true, Ramon," he replied. "The third man I can tell you is called Obed White, and they are a clever three. I hate them, but it hurts my pride less to be defeated by them than by any others whom I know."

"Well spoken, Urrea," said a third man, "but since these three are fighters and will stay to meet us, it is a certainty that our general will scoop them into his net. Then you can have all the revenge you wish."

"I count upon it, Ambrosio," said Urrea, smiling. "I also hope that we shall recapture the man Roylston. He has great sums of money in the foreign banks in our country, and we need them, but our illustrious president cannot get them without an order from Roylston. The general would rather have Roylston than a thousand Texan prisoners."

All of them laughed, and the laugh made Ned, lying in the shadow, shiver once more. Urrea glanced his way presently, but the recumbent figure did not claim his notice. The attention of his comrades and himself became absorbed in the dice again. They were throwing the little ivory cubes upon a blanket, and Ned could hear them click as they struck together. The sharp little sound began to flick his nerves. Not one to cherish resentment, he nevertheless began to hate Urrea, and he included in that hatred the young men with him. The Texans were so few and poor. The Mexicans were so many, and they had the resources of a nation more than two centuries old.

Ned rose by and by and walked on. He could imitate the Mexican gait perfectly, and no one paid any attention to him. They were absorbed, moreover, in something else, because now the light of torches could be seen dimly in the south. Officers threw down cards and dice. Men straightened their uniforms and Cos and Sesma began to form companies in line. More fuel was thrown on the fires, which sprang up, suffusing all the night with color and brightness. Ned with his rifle at salute fell into place at the end of one of the companies, and no one knew that he did not belong there. In the excitement of the moment he forgot all about the Panther and Obed.

A thrill seemed to run through the whole Mexican force. It was the most impressive scene that Ned had ever beheld. A leader, omnipotent in their eyes, was coming to these men, and he came at midnight out of the dark into the light.

The torches grew brighter. A trumpet pealed and a trumpet in the camp replied. The Mexican lines became silent save for a deep murmur. In the south they heard the rapid beat of hoofs, and then Santa Anna came, galloping at the head of fifty horsemen. Many of the younger officers ran forward, holding up torches, and the dictator rode in a blaze of light.

Ned looked once more upon that dark and singular face, a face daring and cruel, that might have belonged to one of the old conquistadores. In the saddle his lack of height was concealed, but on the great white horse that he rode Ned felt that he was an imposing, even a terrible, figure. His eyes were blazing with triumph as his army united with torches to do him honor. It was like Napoleon on the night before Austerlitz, and what was he but the Napoleon of the New World? His figure swelled and the gold braid on his cocked hat and gorgeous uniform reflected the beams of the firelight.

A mighty cheer from thousands of throats ran along the Mexican line, and the torches were waved until they looked like vast circles of fire. Santa Anna lifted his hat and bowed three times in salute. Again the Mexican cheer rolled to right and to left. Santa Anna, still sitting on his horse, spread out his hands. There was instant silence save for the deep breathing of the men.

"My children," he said, "I have come to sweep away these miserable Texans who have dared to raise the rebel flag against us. We will punish them all. Houston, Austin, Bowie and the rest of their leaders shall feel our justice. When we finish our march over their prairies it shall be as if a great fire had passed. I have said it. I am Santa Anna."

The thunderous cheer broke forth again. Ned had never before heard words so full of conceit and vainglory, yet the strength and menace were there. He felt it instinctively. Santa Anna believed himself to be the greatest man in the world, and he was certainly the greatest in Mexico. His belief in himself was based upon a deep well of energy and daring. Once more Ned felt a great and terrible fear for Texas, and the thin line of skin-clad hunters and ranchmen who were its sole defence. But the feeling passed as he watched Santa Anna. A young officer rushed forward and held his stirrup as the dictator dismounted. Then the generals, including those who had come with him, crowded around him. It was a brilliant company, including Sesma,

Cos, Duque, Castrillon, Tolsa, Gaona and others, among whom Ned noted a man of decidedly Italian appearance. This was General Vincente Filisola, an Italian officer who had received a huge grant of land in Texas, and who was now second in command to Santa Anna.

Ned watched them as they talked together and occasionally the crowd parted enough for him to see Santa Anna, who spoke and gesticulated with great energy. The soldiers had been drawn away by the minor officers, and were now dispersing to their places by the fires where they would seek sleep.

Ned noticed a trim, slender figure on the outer edge of the group around Santa Anna. It seemed familiar, and when the man turned he recognized the face of Almonte, the gallant young Mexican colonel who had been kind to him. He was sorry to see him there. He was sorry that he should have to fight against him.

Santa Anna went presently to a great marquée that had been prepared for him, and the other generals retired also to the tents that had been set about it. The dictator was tired from his long ride and must not be disturbed. Strict orders were given that there should be no noise in the camp, and it quickly sank into silence.

Ned lay down before one of the fires at the western end of the camp wrapped as before in his serape. He counterfeited sleep, but nothing was further from his mind. It seemed to him that he had done all he could do in the Mexican camp. He had seen the arrival of Santa Anna, but there was no way to learn when the general would order an advance. But he could infer from Santa Anna's well-known energy and ability that it would come quickly.

Between the slit left by the brim of his sombrero and his serape he watched the great fires die slowly. Most of the Mexicans were asleep now, and their figures were growing indistinct in the shadows. But Ned, rising, slouched forward, imitating the gait of the laziest of the Mexicans. Yet his eyes were always watching shrewdly through the slit. Very little escaped his notice. He went along the entire Mexican line and then back again. He had a good mathematical mind, and he saw that the estimate of 7,000 for the Mexican army was not too few. He also saw many cannon and the horses for a great cavalry force. He knew, too, that Santa Anna had with him the best regiments in the Mexican service.

On his last trip along the line Ned began to look for the Panther and Obed, but he saw no figures resembling theirs, although he was quite sure that he would know the Panther in any disguise owing to his great size. This circumstance would make it more dangerous for the Panther than for either

Obed or himself, as Urrea, if he should see so large a man, would suspect that it was none other than the redoubtable frontiersman.

Ned was thinking of this danger to the Panther when he came face to face with Urrea himself. The young Mexican captain was not lacking in vigilance and energy, and even at that late hour he was seeing that all was well in the camp of Santa Anna. Ned was truly thankful now that Mexican custom and the coldness of the night permitted him to cover his face with his serape and the brim of his sombrero.

"Why are you walking here?" demanded Urrea.

"I've just taken a message to General Castrillon," replied Ned.

He had learned already that Castrillon commanded the artillery, and as he was at least a mile away he thought this the safest reply.

"From whom?" asked Urrea shortly.

"Pardon, sir," replied Ned, in his best Spanish, disguising his voice as much as possible, "but I am not allowed to tell."

Ned's tone was courteous and apologetic, and in ninety-nine cases out of a hundred Urrea would have contented himself with an impatient word or two. But he was in a most vicious temper. Perhaps he had been rebuked by Santa Anna for allowing the rescue of Roylston.

"Why don't you speak up?" he exclaimed. "Why do you mumble your words, and why do you stand in such a slouching manner. Remember that a soldier should stand up straight."

"Yes, my captain," said Ned, but he did not change his attitude. The tone and manner of Urrea angered him. He forgot where he was and his danger.

Urrea's swarthy face flushed. He carried in his hand a small riding whip, which he switched occasionally across the tops of his tall, military boots.

"Lout!" he cried. "You hear me! Why do you not obey!"

Ned stood impassive. Certainly Urrea had had a bad half hour somewhere. His temper leaped beyond control.

"Idiot!" he exclaimed.

Then he suddenly lashed Ned across the face with the little riding whip. The blow fell on serape and sombrero and the flesh was not touched, but for a few moments Ned went mad. He dropped his rifle, leaped upon the astonished officer, wrenched the whip from his hands, slashed him across the cheeks with it until the blood ran in streams, then broke it in two and threw the pieces in his face. Ned's serape fell away. Urrea had clasped his hands to his cheeks that stung like fire, but now he recognized the boy.

"Fulton!" he cried.

The sharp exclamation brought Ned to a realization of his danger. He seized his rifle, pulled up the serape and sprang back. Already Mexican soldiers were gathering. It was truly fortunate for Ned that he was quick of thought, and that his thoughts came quickest when the danger was greatest. He knew that the cry of "Fulton!" was unintelligible to them, and he exclaimed:

"Save me, comrades! He tried to beat me without cause, and now he would kill me, as you see!"

Urrea had drawn a pistol and was shouting fiery Mexican oaths. The soldiers, some of them just awakened from sleep, and all of them dazed, had gathered in a huddle, but they opened to let Ned pass. Excessive and cruel punishment was common among them. A man might be flogged half to death at the whim of an officer, and instinctively they protected their comrade.

As the Mexican group closed up behind him, and between him and Urrea, Ned ran at top speed toward the west where the arroyo cut across the plain. More Mexicans were gathering, and there was great confusion. Everybody was asking what was the matter. The boy's quick wit did not desert him. There was safety in ignorance and the multitude.

He quickly dropped to a walk and he, too, began to ask of others what had caused the trouble. All the while he worked steadily toward the arroyo, and soon he left behind him the lights and the shouting. He now came into the dark, passed beyond the Mexican lines, and entered the cut in the earth down which he had come.

He was compelled to sit down on the sand and relax. He was exhausted by the great effort of both mind and body which had carried him through so much danger. His heart was beating heavily and he felt dizzy. But his eyes cleared presently and his strength came back. He considered himself safe. In the darkness it was not likely that any of the Mexicans would stumble upon him.

He thought of the Panther and Obed, but he could do nothing for them. He must trust to meeting them again at the place appointed. He looked at the Mexican camp. The fires had burned up again there for a minute or two, but as he looked they sank once more. The noise also decreased. Evidently they were giving up the pursuit.

Ned rose and walked slowly up the arroyo. He became aware that the night was very cold and it told on his relaxed frame. He pulled up the serape again, and now it was for warmth and not for disguise. He stopped at intervals to search the darkness with his eyes and to listen for noises. He might meet with an enemy or he might meet with one of his friends. He was prepared for either. He had regained control of himself both body and mind, and his ready rifle rested in the hollow of his arm.

He met neither. He heard nothing but the usual sighing of the prairie wind that ceased rarely, and he saw nothing but the faint glow on the southern horizon that marked the Mexican camp where he had met his enemy.

He left the arroyo, and saw a dark shadow on the plain, the figure of a man, rifle in hand, Ned instantly sprang back into the arroyo and the stranger did the same. A curve in the line of this cut in the earth now hid them from each other, and Ned, his body pressed against the bank, waited with beating heart. He had no doubt that it was a Mexican sentinel or scout more vigilant than the others, and he felt his danger.

Ned in this crisis used the utmost caution. He did not believe that any other would come, and it must be a test of patience between him and his enemy. Whoever showed his head first would be likely to lose in the duel for life. He pressed himself closer and closer against the bank, and sought to detect some movement of the stranger. He saw nothing and he did not hear a sound. It seemed that the man had absolutely vanished into space. It occurred to Ned that it might have been a mere figment of the dusk and his excited brain, but he quickly dismissed the idea. He had seen the man and he had seen him leap into the arroyo. There could be no doubt of it.

There was another long wait, and the suspense became acute. The man was surely on the other side of that curve waiting for him. He was held fast. He was almost as much a prisoner as if he lay bound in the Mexican camp. It seemed to him, too, that the darkness was thinning a little. It would soon be day and then he could not escape the notice of horsemen from Santa Anna's army. He decided that he must risk an advance and he began creeping forward cautiously. He remembered now what he had forgotten in the first moments of the meeting. He might yet, even before this sentinel or scout, pass as a Mexican.

He stopped suddenly when he heard a low whistle in front of him. While it could be heard but a short distance, it was singularly sweet. It formed the first bars of an old tune, "The World Turned Upside Down," and Ned promptly recognized it. The whistle stopped in a moment or two, but Ned took up the air and continued it for a few bars more. Then, all apprehension gone, he sprang out of the arroyo and stood upon the bank. Another figure was projected from the arroyo and stood upon the bank facing him, not more than twenty feet away.

Simultaneously Obed White and Edward Fulton advanced, shook hands and laughed.

"You kept me here waiting in this gully at least half an hour," said Obed. "Time and I waited long on you."

"But no longer than I waited on you," said Ned. "Why didn't you think of whistling the tune sooner?"

"Why didn't you?"

They laughed and shook hands again.

"At any rate, we're here together again, safe and unharmed," said Ned. "And now to see what has become of the Panther."

"You'd better be lookin' out for yourselves instead of the Panther," growled a voice, as a gigantic figure upheaved itself from the arroyo eight or ten yards behind them. "I could have picked you both off while you were standin' there shakin' hands, an' neither of you would never have knowed what struck him."

"The Panther!" they exclaimed joyously, and they shook hands with him also.

"An' now," said the Panther, "it will soon be day. We'd better make fur our horses an' then clear out. We kin tell 'bout what we've seen an' done when we're two or three miles away."

They found the horses safe in the brushwood, Old Jack welcoming Ned with a soft whinny. They were in the saddle at once, rode swiftly northward, and none of them spoke for a half hour. When a faint tinge of gray appeared on the eastern rim of the world the Panther said:

"My tale's short. I couldn't get into the camp, 'cause I'm too big. The very first fellow I saw looked at me with s'picion painted all over him. So I had to keep back in the darkness. But I saw it was a mighty big army. It can do a lot of rippin', an' t'arin', an' chawin'."

"I got into the camp," said Obed, after a minute of silence, "but as I'm not built much like a Mexican, being eight or ten inches too tall, men were looking at me as if I were a strange specimen. One touch of difference and all the world's staring at you. So I concluded that I'd better stay on the outside of the lines. I hung around, and I saw just what Panther saw, no more and no less. Then I started back and I struck the arroyo, which seemed to me a good way for leaving. But before I had gone far I concluded I was followed. So I watched the fellow who was following, and the fellow who was following watched me for about a year. The watch was just over when you came up, Panther. It was long, but it's a long watch that has no ending."

"And I," said Ned, after another wait of a minute, "being neither so tall as Obed nor so big around as the Panther, was able to go about in the Mexican camp without any notice being taken of me. I saw Santa Anna arrive to take the chief command."

"Santa Anna himself?" exclaimed the Panther.

"Yes, Santa Anna himself. They gave him a great reception. After a while I started to come away. I met Urrea. He took me for a peon, gave me an order, and when I didn't obey it tried to strike me across the face with a whip."

"And what did you do?" exclaimed the two men together.

"I took the whip away from him and lashed his cheeks with it. I was recognized, but in the turmoil and confusion I escaped. Then I had the encounter with Obed White, of which he has told already."

"Since Santa Anna has come," said the Panther, "they're likely to move at any moment. We'll ride straight for the cabin an' the boys."

CHAPTER VI.
FOR FREEDOM'S SAKE

Evidently the horses had found considerable grass through the night, as they were fresh and strong, and the miles fell fast behind them. At the gait at which they were going they would reach the cabin that night. Meanwhile they made plans. The little force would divide and messengers would go to San Antonio, Harrisburg and other points, with the news that Santa Anna was advancing with an immense force.

And every one of the three knew that the need was great. They knew how divided counsels had scattered the little Texan army. At San Antonio, the most important point of all, the town that they had triumphantly taken from a much greater force of Mexicans, there were practically no men, and that undoubtedly was Santa Anna's destination. Unconsciously they began to urge their horses to great and yet greater speed, until the Panther recalled them to prudence.

"Slower, boys! slower!" he said. "We mustn't run our horses out at the start."

"And there's a second reason for pulling down," said Ned, "since there's somebody else on the plain."

His uncommon eyesight had already detected before the others the strange presence. He pointed toward the East.

"Do you see that black speck there, where the sky touches the ground?" he said. "If you'll watch it you'll see that it's moving. And look! There's another! and another! and another!"

The Panther and Obed now saw the black specks also. The three stopped on the crest of a swell and watched them attentively.

"One! two! three! four! five! six! seven! eight! nine! ten! eleven! twelve! thirteen!" counted the far-sighted boy.

"An' them thirteen specks are thirteen men on horseback," continued the Panther, "an' now I wonder who in the name of the great horn spoon they are!"

"Suppose we see," said Obed. "All things are revealed to him who looks—at least most of the time. It is true that they are more than four to our one, but our horses are swift, and we can get away."

"That's right," said the Panther. "Still, we oughtn't to take the risk unless everybody is willin'. What do you say, Ned?"

"I reply 'yes,' of course," said the boy, "especially as I've an idea that those are not Mexicans. They look too big and tall, and they sit too straight up in their saddles for Mexicans."

"Them ideas of yours are ketchin'," said the Panther. "Them fellers may be Mexicans, but they don't look like Mexicans, they don't act like Mexicans, an' they ain't Mexicans."

"Take out what isn't, and you have left what is," said Obed.

"We'll soon see," said Ned.

A few minutes more and there could be no further doubt that the thirteen were Texans or Americans. One rode a little ahead of the others, who came on in an even line. They were mounted on large horses, but the man in front held Ned's attention.

The leader was tall and thin, but evidently muscular and powerful. His hair was straight and black like an Indian's. His features were angular and tanned by the winds of many years. His body was clothed completely in buckskin, and a raccoon skin cap was on his head. Across his shoulder lay a rifle with a barrel of unusual length.

"Never saw any of them before," said the Panther. "By the great horn spoon, who can that feller in front be? He looks like somebody."

The little band rode closer, and its leader held up his hand as a sign of amity.

"Good friends," he said, in a deep clear voice, "we don't have very close neighbors out here, and that makes a meeting all the pleasanter. You are Texans, I guess."

"You guess right," said the Panther, in the same friendly tone. "An' are you Texans, too?"

"That point might be debated," replied the man, in a whimsical tone, "and after a long dispute neither I nor my partners here could say which was right and which was wrong. But while we may not be Texans, yet we will be right away."

His eyes twinkled as he spoke, and Ned suddenly felt a strong liking for him. He was not young and, despite his buckskin dress and careless grammar, there was something of the man of the world about him. But he seemed to have a certain boyishness of spirit that appealed strongly to Ned.

"I s'pose," he continued, "that a baptism will make us genuine Texans, an' it 'pears likely to me that we'll get that most lastin' of all baptisms, a baptism of fire. But me an' Betsy here stand ready for it."

He patted lovingly the stock of his long rifle as he spoke the word "Betsy." It was the same word "Betsy" that gave Ned his sudden knowledge.

"I'm thinking that you are Davy Crockett," he said.

The man's face was illumined with an inimitable smile.

"Correct," he said. "No more and no less. Andy Jackson kept me from going back to Washington, an' so me an' these twelve good friends of mine, Tennesseans like myself, have come here to help free Texas."

He reached out his hand and Ned grasped it. The boy felt a thrill. The name of Davy Crockett was a great one in the southwest, and here he was, face to face, hands gripped with the great borderer.

"This is Mr. Palmer, known all over Texas as the Panther, and Mr. Obed White, once of Maine, but now a Texan," said Ned, introducing his friends.

Crockett and the Panther shook hands, and looked each other squarely in the eye.

"Seems to me," said Crockett, "that you're a man."

"I was jest thinkin' the same of you," said the Panther.

"An' you," said Crockett to Obed White, "are a man, too. But they certainly do grow tall where you come from."

"I'm not as wide as a barn door, but I may be long enough to reach the bottom of a well," said Obed modestly. "Anyway, I thank you for the compliment. Praise from Sir Davy is sweet music in my ear, indeed. And since we Texans have to stand together, and since to stand together we must know about one another, may I ask you, Mr. Crockett, which way you are going?"

"We had an idea that we would go to San Antonio," said Crockett, "but I'm never above changin' my opinion. If you think it better to go somewhere else, an' can prove it, why me an' Betsy an' the whole crowd are ready to go there instead."

"What would you say?" asked the Panther, "if we told you that Santa Anna an' 7,000 men were on the Rio Grande ready to march on San Antonio?"

"If you said it, I'd say it was true. I'd also say that it was a thing the Texans had better consider. If I was usin' adjectives I'd call it alarmin'.".

"An' what would you say if I told you there wasn't a hundred Texan soldiers in San Antonio to meet them seven thousand Mexicans comin' under Santa Anna?"

"If you told me that I'd say it was true. I'd say also, if I was usin' adjectives, that it was powerful alarmin'. For Heaven's sake, Mr. Panther, the state of affairs ain't so bad as that, is it?"

"It certainly is," replied the Panther. "Ned Fulton here was all through their camp last night. He can talk Mexican an' Spanish like lightnin' an' he makes up wonderful—an' he saw their whole army. He saw old Santa Anna, too, an' fifty or a hundred generals, all covered with gold lace. If we don't get a lot of fightin' men together an' get 'em quick, Texas will be swept clean by that Mexican army same as if a field had been crossed by millions of locusts."

It was obvious that Crockett was impressed deeply by these blunt statements.

"What do you wish us to do?" he asked the Panther.

"You an' your friends come with us. We've got some good men at a cabin in the woods that we can reach to-night. We'll join with them, raise as many more as we can, spread the alarm everywhere, an' do everything possible for the defence of San Antonio."

"A good plan, Mr. Panther," said Crocket. "You lead the way to this cabin of yours, an' remember that we're servin' under you for the time bein'."

The Panther rode on without another word and the party, now raised from three to sixteen, followed. Crockett fell in by the side of Ned, and soon showed that he was not averse to talking.

"A good country," he said, nodding at the landscape, "but it ain't like Tennessee. It would take me a long time to git used to the lack of hills an' runnin' water an' trees which just cover the state of Tennessee."

"We have them here, too," replied Ned, "though I'll admit they're scattered. But it's a grand country to fight for."

"An' as I see it we'll have a grand lot of fightin' to do," said Davy Crockett.

They continued at good speed until twilight, when they rested their horses and ate of the food that they carried. The night promised to be cold but clear, and the crisp air quickened their blood.

"How much further is it?" asked Crockett of Ned.

"Fifteen or eighteen miles, but at the rate we're going we should be there in three hours. We've got a roof. It isn't a big one, and we don't know who built it, but it will shelter us all."

"I ain't complainin' of that," rejoined Davy Crockett. "I'm a lover of fresh air an' outdoors, but I don't object to a roof in cold weather. Always take your comfort, boy, when it's offered to you. It saves wear an' tear."

A friendship like that between him and Bowie was established already between Ned and Crockett. Ned's grave and serious manner, the result of the sufferings through which he had gone, invariably attracted the attention and liking of those far older than himself.

"I'll remember your advice, Mr. Crockett," he said.

A rest of a half hour for the horses and they started riding rapidly. After a while they struck the belt of forest and soon the cabin was not more than a mile away. But the Panther, who was still in the lead, pulled up his horse suddenly.

"Boys," he exclaimed, "did you hear that?"

Every man stopped his horse also and with involuntary motion bent forward a little to listen. Then the sound that the Panther had heard came again. It was the faint ping of a rifle shot, muffled by the distance. In a moment they heard another and then two more. The sounds came from the direction of their cabin.

"The boys are attacked," said the Panther calmly, "an' it's just as well that we've come fast. But I can't think who is after 'em. There was certainly no Mexicans in these parts yesterday, an' Urrea could not possibly have got ahead of us with a raidin' band. But at any rate we'll ride on an' soon see."

They proceeded with the utmost caution, and they heard the faint ping of the rifles a half dozen times as they advanced. The nostrils of the Panther began to distend, and streaks of red appeared on his eyeballs. He was smelling the battle afar, and his soul rejoiced. He had spent his whole life amid scenes of danger, and this was nature to him. Crockett rode up by his side, and he, too, listened eagerly. He no longer carried Betsy over his shoulder but held the long rifle across the pommel of his saddle, his hand upon hammer and trigger.

"What do you think it is, Panther?" he asked. Already he had fallen into the easy familiarity of the frontier.

"I can't make it out yet," replied the Panther, "but them shots shorely came from the cabin an' places about it. Our fellows are besieged, but I've got to guess at the besiegers, an' then I'm likely to guess wrong."

They were riding very slowly, and presently they heard a dozen shots, coming very clearly now.

"I think we'd better stop here," said the Panther, "an' do a little scoutin'. If you like it, Mr. Crockett, you an' me an' Ned, here, will dismount, slip forward an' see what's the trouble. Obed will take Command of the others, an' wait in the bushes till we come back with the news, whatever it is."

"I'll go with you gladly," said Davy Crockett. "I'm not lookin' for trouble with a microscope, but if trouble gets right in my path I'm not dodgin' it. So I say once more, lead on, noble Mr. Panther, an' if Betsy here must talk she'll talk."

The Panther grinned in the dusk. He and Davy Crockett had instantly recognized congenial souls, each in the other.

"I can't promise you that thar'll be rippin' an' t'arin' an' roarin' an' chawin' all the time," he said, "but between you an' me, Davy Crockett, I've an' idee that we're not goin' to any sort of prayer meetin' this time of night."

"No, I'm thinkin' not," said Crockett, "but if there is a scene of turbulence before us lead on. I'm prepared for my share in it. The debate may be lively, but I've no doubt that I'll get my chance to speak. There are many ways to attract the attention of the Speaker. Pardon me, Mr. Panther, but I fall naturally into the phrases of legislative halls."

"I remember that you served two terms in Congress at Washington," said the Panther.

"An' I'd be there yet if it wasn't for Andy Jackson. I wanted my way in Tennessee politics an' he wanted his. He was so stubborn an' headstrong that here I am ready to become a statesman in this new Texas which is fightin' for its independence. An' what a change! From marble halls in Washington to a night in the brush on the frontier, an' with an unknown enemy before you."

They stopped talking now and, kneeling down in a thicket, began to creep forward. The cabin was not more than four or five hundred yards away, but a long silence had succeeded the latest shots, and after an advance of thirty or forty yards they lay still for a while. Then they heard two shots ahead of them, and saw little pink dots of flame from the exploding gunpowder.

"It cannot be Mexicans who are besieging the cabin," said Ned. "They would shout or make some kind of a noise. We have not heard a thing but the rifle shots."

"Your argyment is good," whispered the Panther. "Look! Did you see that figure passin' between us an' the cabin?"

"I saw it," said Davy Crockett, "an' although it was but a glimpse an' this is night it did not seem to me to be clad in full Christian raiment. I am quite sure it is not the kind of costume that would be admitted to the galleries of Congress."

"You're right, doubly right," said the Panther. "That was an Injun you saw, but whether a Comanche or a Lipan I couldn't tell. The boys are besieged not by Mexicans, but by Injuns. Hark to that!"

There was a flash from the cabin, a dusky figure in the woods leaped into the air, uttered a death cry, fell and lay still.

"An', as you see," continued the Panther, in his whisper, "the boys in the house are not asleep, dreamin' beautiful dreams. Looks to me as if they was watchin' mighty sharp for them fellers who have broke up their rest."

Crack! went a second shot from the house, but there was no answering cry, and they could not tell whether it hit anything. But they soon saw more dark figures flitting through the bushes, and their own position grew very precarious. If a band of the Indians stumbled upon them they might be annihilated before they gave their besieged comrades any help.

"I make the motion, Mr. Panther," said Crockett, "that you form a speedy plan of action for us, an' I trust that our young friend Ned here will second it."

"I second the motion," said Ned.

"It is carried unanimously. Now, Mr. Panther, we await your will."

"It's my will that we git back to the rest of the men as soon as we can. I reckon, Mr. Crockett, that them Tennesseans of yours wouldn't head in the other direction if a fight grew hot."

"I reckon that wild horses couldn't drag 'em away," said Crockett dryly.

"Then we'll go back an' j'in 'em."

"To hold a caucus, so to speak."

"I don't know what a cow-cuss is."

"It's Congressional for a conference. Don't mind these parliamentary expressions of mine, Mr. Panther. They give me pleasure an' they hurt nobody."

They reached the Tennesseans without interruption, and the Panther quickly laid his plan before them. They would advance within a quarter of a mile of the cabin, tie their horses in the thickest of the brush, leave four men to guard them, then the rest would go forward to help the besieged.

Crockett's eyes twinkled when the Panther announced the campaign in a few words.

"Very good; very good," he said. "A steering committee could not have done better. That also is parliamentary, but I think you understand it."

They heard detached shots again and then a long yell.

"They're Comanches," said the Panther. "I know their cry, an' I guess there's a lot of them."

Ned hoped that the shout did not mean the achieving of some triumph. They reached presently a dense growth of brush, and there the horses were tied. Four reluctant Tennesseans remained with them and the rest crept forward. They did not hear any shot after they left the horses until they were within three hundred yards of the house. Then an apparition caused all to stop simultaneously.

A streak of flame shot above the trees, curved and fell. It was followed by another and another. Ned was puzzled, but the Panther laughed low.

"This can't be fireworks on election night," said Davy Crockett. "It seems hardly the place for such a display."

"They're fireworks, all right," said the Panther, "but it's not election night. You're correct about that part of it. Look, there goes the fourth an' the fifth."

Two more streaks of flame curved and fell, and Ned and Crockett were still puzzled.

"Them's burnin' arrers," said the Panther. "It's an old trick of the Injuns. If they had time enough they'd be sure to set the cabin on fire, and then from ambush they'd shoot the people as they ran out. But what we're here for is to stop that little game of theirs. The flight of the arrers enables us to locate the spot from which they come an' there we'll find the Comanches."

They crept toward the point from which the lighted arrows were flying, and peering; from the thicket saw a score or more of Comanches gathered in the bushes and under the trees. One of the Tennesseans, seeking a better position, caused a loud rustling, and the alert Comanches, instantly taking alarm, turned their attention to the point from which the sound had come.

"Fire, boys! Fire at once!" cried the Panther.

A deadly volley was poured into the Comanche band. The Indians replied, but were soon compelled to give way. The Panther, raising his voice, shouted in tremendous tones:

"Rescue! Rescue! We're here, boys!"

The defenders of the cabin, hearing the volleys and the shouts of their friends, opened the door and rushed out of the cabin, rifle in hand. Caught between two forces, the Comanches gave up and rushed to the plain, where they had left their ponies. Jumping upon the backs of these, they fled like the wind.

The two victorious parties met and shook hands.

"We're mighty glad to see you, Panther," said Fields, grinning. "You don't look like an angel, but you act like one, an' I see you've brought a lot of new angels with you."

"Yes," replied the Panther, with some pride in his voice, "an' the first of the angels is Davy Crockett. Mr. Crockett, Mr. Fields."

The men crowded around to shake hands with the renowned Davy. Meanwhile a small party brought the four Tennesseans and the horses. Fortunately the Comanches had fled in the other direction. But it was not all joy in the Texan camp. Two silent figures covered with serapes were stretched on the floor in the cabin, and several others had wounds, although they had borne their part in the fighting.

"Tell us how it happened," said the Panther, after they had set sentinels in the forest.

"They attacked us about an hour after dark," replied Fields. "We knew that no Mexicans were near, but we never thought of Indians raiding this far to the eastward. Some of the men were outside looking after jerked meat when they suddenly opened fire from the brush. Two of the boys, Campbell and Hudson, were hurt so badly that they died after they were helped into the house by the others. The Comanches tried to rush in with our own men, but we drove them off and we could have held the cabin against 'em forever, if they hadn't begun to shoot the burning arrows. Then you came."

Campbell and Hudson were buried. Ned had been welcomed warmly by Allen, and the two boys compared notes. Will's face glowed when he heard of Ned's adventures within the Mexican lines.

"I could never have done it," he said. "I couldn't have kept steady enough when one crisis after another came along. I suppose this means, of course, that we must try to meet Santa Anna in some way. What do you think we can do, Ned?"

"I don't know, but just at present I'm going to sleep. The Panther, Davy Crockett and Obed will debate the plans."

Ned, who was becoming inured to war and danger, was soon asleep, but Will could not close his eyes. He had borne a gallant part in the defense, and the sounds of rifle shots and Indian yells still resounded in his excited ear. He remained awake long after he heard the heavy breathing of the men about him, but exhausted nerves gave way at last and he, too, slept.

The next morning their news was debated gravely by all. There was not one among them who did not understand its significance, but it was hard to agree upon a policy. Davy Crockett, who had just come, and who was practically a stranger to Texas, gave his opinions with hesitation.

"It's better for you, Mr. Panther, an' you, Mr. White, to make the motions," he said, "an' I an' my Tennesseans will endorse them. But it seems, boys, that if we came for a fight it is offered to us the moment we get here."

"Yes," said the twelve Tennesseans all together.

"I shall be compelled to leave you," said Roylston. "Pray, don't think it's because I'm afraid to fight the Mexicans. But, as I told you before, I can do far greater good for the Texan cause elsewhere. As I am now as well as ever, and I am able to take care of myself, I think I shall leave at once."

"I've known you only a few hours, Mr. Roylston," said Crockett, "but I've knocked around a hard world long enough to know a man when I see him. If you say you ought, you ought to go."

"That's so," said the Panther. "We've seen Mr. Roylston tried more than once, and nobody doubts his courage."

A good horse, saddled and bridled, and arms and ammunition, were given to Roylston. Then he bade them farewell. When he was about twenty yards away he beckoned to Ned. When the boy stood at his saddle bow he said very earnestly:

"If you fall again into the hands of Santa Anna, and are in danger of your life, use my name with him. It is perhaps a more potent weapon than you think. Do not forget."

"I will not," said Ned, "and I thank you very much, Mr. Roylston. But I hope that no such occasion will arise."

"So do I," said Roylston with emphasis. Then he rode away, a square, strong figure, and never looked back.

"What was he saying, Ned?" asked Will, when the boy returned.

"Merely promising help if we should need it, hereafter."

"He looks like a man who would give it."

After some further talk it was decided that Ned, Will, Obed and the Panther should ride south to watch the advance of Santa Anna, while Crockett, Fields and the remainder should go to San Antonio and raise such troops as they could.

"An' if you don't mind my sayin' it to you, Mr. Crockett," said the Panther, "keep tellin' 'em over an' over again that they have need to beware. Tell 'em that Santa Anna, with all the power of Mexico at his back, is comin'."

"Fear not, my good friend," said Davy Crockett. "I shall tell them every hour of the day. I shall never cease to bring the information before the full quorum of the House. Again I am parliamentary, but I think you understand, Mr. Panther."

"We all understan'," said the Panther, and then Crockett rode away at the head of the little troop which tacitly made him commander. Ned's eyes followed his figure as long as he was in sight. Little did he dream of what was to pass when they should meet again, scenes that one could never forget, though he lived a thousand years.

"A staunch man and true," said Obed. "He will be a great help to Texas."

Then they turned back to the cabin, the four of them, because they did not intend to go forth until night. They missed their comrades, but the cabin was a pleasant place, well stored now with meat of buffalo, deer and wild turkey. Floor and walls alike were covered with dressed skins.

"Why not fasten it up just as tightly as we can before we go away," said Allen. "The Comanches are not likely to come back, the war is swinging another way, and maybe we'll find it here handy for us again some day."

"You're talkin' sense, Will Allen," said the Panther. "It's been a shelter to us once, and it might be a shelter to us twice. The smell of the meat will, of course, draw wolves an' panthers, but we can fix it so they can't get in."

Taking sufficient provisions for themselves, they put the rest high up on the rafters. Then they secured the windows, and heaped logs before the door in such a manner that the smartest wolves and panthers in the world could not force an entrance. As they sat on their horses in the twilight preparatory to riding away, they regarded their work with great content.

"There it is, waiting for us when we come again," said Obed White. "It's a pleasant thing to have a castle for refuge when your enemies are making it too hot for you out in the open."

"So it is," said the Panther, "and a man finds that out more than once in his life."

Then they turned their horses and rode southward in the dusk. But before long they made an angle and turned almost due west. It was their intention to intersect the settlements that lay between the Rio Grande and San Antonio and give warning of the approach of Santa Anna.

They went on steadily over a rolling country, mostly bare, but with occasional clumps of trees.

CHAPTER VII.
THE HERALD OF ATTACK

About midnight they rode into the thickest part of the woods that they could find, and slept there until day. Then they continued their course toward the west, and before night they saw afar small bands of horsemen.

"What do you say they are?" asked the Panther of Ned when they beheld the first group. "Seems to me they are Mexican."

Ned looked long before returning an answer. Then he replied with confidence:

"Yes, they are Mexicans. The two men in the rear have lances, and no Texan ever carried such a weapon."

"Then," said Obed White, "it behooves us to have a care. We're scouts now and we're not looking for a battle. He who dodges the fight and runs away may live to scout another day."

The Mexican horsemen were on their right, and the four continued their steady course to the west. They were reassured by the fact that the Mexicans were likely to take them in the distance for other Mexicans. It became evident now that Santa Anna was taking every precaution. He was sending forward scouts and skirmishers in force, and the task of the four was likely to become one of great danger.

Toward night an uncommonly raw and cold wind began to blow. That winter was one of great severity in Northern Mexico and Southern Texas, noted also for its frequent Northers. Although the time for the Texan spring was near at hand, there was little sign of it. Not knowing what else to do they sought the shelter of timber again and remained there a while. By and by they saw for the second time a red glow in the south, and they knew that it came from the camp fires of Santa Anna. But it was now many miles north of the Rio Grande. Santa Anna was advancing.

"He's pressin' forward fast," said the Panther, "an' his skirmishers are scourin' the plain ahead of him. We've got to keep a sharp lookout, because we may run into 'em at any time. I think we'd better agree that if by any luck we get separated an' can't reunite, every fellow should ride hard for San Antonio with the news."

The plan seemed good to all, and, after a long wait, they rode to another clump of trees four or five hundred yards further south. Here they saw the red glow more plainly. It could not be more than two miles away, and they believed that to approach any nearer was to imperil their task. Before the first light appeared the next day they would turn back on San Antonio as the heralds of Santa Anna's advance.

The four sat on their horses among the trees, darker shadows in the shadow. Beyond the little grove they saw the plain rolling away on every side bare to the horizon, except in the south, where the red glow always threatened. Ned rode to the western edge of the grove in order to get a better view. He searched the plain carefully with his keen vision, but he could find no sign of life there in the west.

He turned Old Jack in order to rejoin his comrades, when he suddenly heard a low sound from the east. He listened a moment, and then, hearing it distinctly, he knew it. It was the thud of hoofs, and the horsemen were coming straight toward the grove, which was two or three hundred yards in width.

Owing to the darkness and the foliage Ned could not see his comrades, but he started toward them at once. Then came a sudden cry, the rapid beat of hoofs, the crack of shots, and a Mexican body of cavalry dashed into the wood directly between the boy and his comrades. He heard once the tremendous shout of the Panther and the wild Mexican yells. Two horsemen fired at him and a third rode at him with extended lance.

It was Old Jack that saved Ned's life. The boy was so startled that his brain was in a paralysis for a moment. But the horse shied suddenly away from the head of the lance, which was flashing in the moonlight. Ned retained both his seat and his rifle. He fired at the nearest of the Mexicans, who fell from his saddle, and then, seeing that but one alternative was left him he gave Old Jack the rein and galloped from the grove into the west.

Amid all the rush and terrific excitement of the moment, Ned thought of his comrades. It was not possible for him to join them now, but they were three together and they might escape. The Panther was a wonderful borderer, and Obed White was not far behind him. He turned his attention to his own escape. Two more shots were fired at him, but in both cases the bullets went wide. Then he heard only the thud of hoofs, but the pursuing horsemen were very near.

Something whizzed through the air and instinctively he bent forward almost flat on the neck of Old Jack. A coiling shape struck him on the head, slipped along his back, then along the quarters of his horse and fell to the ground. He felt as if a deadly snake had struck at him, and then had drawn its cold body across him. But he knew that it was a lasso. The Mexicans would wish to take him alive, as they might secure valuable information from him. Now he heard them shouting to one another, every one boasting that his would be the successful throw. As Ned's rifle was empty, and he could not reload it at such speed, they seemed to fear nothing for themselves.

He looked back. They numbered seven or eight, and they were certainly very near. They had spread out a little and whenever Old Jack veered a yard or two from the pursuers some one gained. He saw a coil of rope fly through the air and he bent forward again. It struck Old Jack on the saddle and fell to the ground. Ned wondered why they did not fire now, but he remembered that their rifles or muskets, too, might be empty, and suddenly he felt a strange exultation. He was still lying forward on his horse's neck, and now he began to talk to him.

"On! On! Old Jack," he said, "show 'em the cleanest heels that were ever seen in Texas! On! On! my beauty of a horse, my jewel of a horse! Would you let miserable Mexican ponies overtake you? You who were never beaten! Ah, now we gain! But faster! faster!"

It seemed that Old Jack understood. He stretched out his long neck and became a streak in the darkness. A third Mexican threw his lasso, but the noose only touched his flying tail. A fourth threw, and the noose did not reach him at all.

They were far out on the plain now, where the moonlight revealed everything, and the horse's sure instinct would guide. Ned felt Old Jack beneath him, running strong and true without a jar like the most perfect piece of machinery. He stole a glance over his shoulder. All the Mexicans were there, too far away now for a throw of the lasso, but several of them were trying to reload their weapons. Ned knew that if they succeeded he would be in great danger. No matter how badly they shot a chance bullet might hit him or his horse. And he could afford for neither himself nor Old Jack to be wounded.

Once more the boy leaned far over on his horse's neck and cried in his ear:

"On, Old Jack, on! Look, we gain now, but we must gain more. Show to them what a horse you are!"

And again the great horse responded. Fast as he was going it seemed to Ned that he now lengthened his stride. His long head was thrust out almost straight, and his great body fairly skimmed the earth. But the Mexicans hung on with grim tenacity. Their ponies were tough and enduring, and, spread out like the arc of a bow, they continually profited by some divergence that Old Jack made from the straight line. Aware of this danger Ned himself, nevertheless, was unable to tell whether the horse was going in a direct course, and he let him have his head.

"Crack!" went a musket, and a bullet sang past Ned's face. It grazed Old Jack's ear, drawing blood. The horse uttered an angry snort and fairly leaped forward. Ned looked back again. Another man had succeeded in loading his musket and was about to fire. Then the boy remembered the pistol at his belt. Snatching it out he fired at the fellow with the loaded musket.

The Mexican reeled forward on his horse's neck and his weapon dropped to the ground. Whether the man himself fell also Ned never knew, because he quickly thrust the pistol back in his belt and once more was looking straight ahead. Now confidence swelled again in his heart. He had escaped all their bullets so far, and he was still gaining. He would escape all the others and he would continue to gain.

He saw just ahead of him one of the clumps of trees that dotted the plain, but, although it might give momentary protection from the bullets he was afraid to gallop into it, lest he be swept from his horse's back by the boughs or bushes. But his direct course would run close to the left side of it, and once more he sought to urge Old Jack to greater speed.

The horse was still running without a jar. Ned could not feel a single rough movement in the perfect machinery beneath him. Unless wounded Old Jack would not fail him. He stole another of those fleeting glances backward.

Several of the Mexicans, their ponies spent, were dropping out of the race, but enough were left to make the odds far too great. Ned now skimmed along the edge of the grove, and when he passed it he turned his horse a little, so the trees were between him and his nearest pursuers. Then he urged Old Jack to his last ounce of speed. The plain raced behind him, and fortunate clouds, too, now came, veiling the moon and turning the dusk into deeper darkness. Ned heard one disappointed cry behind him, and then no sound but the flying beat of his own horse's hoofs.

When he pulled rein and brought Old Jack to a walk he could see or hear nothing of the Mexicans. The great horse was a lather of foam, his sides heaving and panting, and Ned sprang to the ground. He reloaded his rifle and pistol and then walked toward the west, leading Old Jack by the bridle. He reckoned that the Mexicans would go toward the north, thinking that he would naturally ride for San Antonio, and hence he chose the opposite direction.

He walked a long time and presently he felt the horse rubbing his nose gently against his arm. Ned stroked the soft muzzle.

"You've saved my life. Old Jack," he said, "and not for the first time. You responded to every call."

The horse whinnied ever so softly, and Ned felt that he was not alone. Now he threw the bridle reins back over the horse's head, and then the two walked on, side by side, man and beast.

They stopped at times, and it may be that the horse as well as the boy then looked and listened for a foe. But the Mexicans had melted away completely in the night. It was likely now that they were going in the opposite direction, and assured that he was safe from them for the time Ned collapsed, both physically and mentally. Such tremendous exertions and such terrible excitement were bound to bring reaction. He began to tremble violently, and he became so weak that he could scarcely stand. The horse seemed to be affected in much the same way and walked slowly and painfully.

Ned saw another little grove, and he and the horse walked straight toward it. It was fairly dense, and when he was in the center of it he wrapped his rifle and himself in his serape and lay down. The horse sank on his side near him. He did not care for anything now except to secure rest. Mexicans or Comanches or Lipans might be on the plain only a few hundred yards away. It did not matter to him. He responded to no emotion save the desire for rest, and in five minutes he was in a deep sleep.

Ned slept until long after daylight. He was so much exhausted that he scarcely moved during all that time. Nor did the horse. Old Jack had run his good race and won the victory, and he, too, cared for nothing but to rest.

Before morning some Lipan buffalo hunters passed, but they took no notice of the grove and soon disappeared in the west. After the dawn a detachment of Mexican lancers riding to the east to join the force of Santa Anna also passed the clump of trees, but the horse and man lay in the densest part of it, and no pair of Mexican eyes was keen enough to see them there. They were answering the call of Santa Anna, and they rode on at a trot, the grove soon sinking out of sight behind them.

Ned was awakened at last by the sun shining in his face. He stirred, recalled in a vague sort of way where he was and why he was there, and then rose slowly to his feet. His joints were stiff like those of an old man, and he rubbed them to acquire ease. A great bay horse, saddle on his back, was searching here and there for the young stems of grass. Ned rubbed his eyes.

It seemed to him that he knew that horse. And a fine big horse he was, too, worth knowing and owning. Yes, it was Old Jack, the horse that had carried him to safety.

His little store of provisions was still tied to the saddle and he ate hungrily. At the end of the grove was a small pool formed by the winter's rains, and though the water was far from clear he drank his fill. He flexed and tensed his muscles again until all the stiffness and soreness were gone. Then he made ready for his departure.

He could direct his course by the sun, and he intended to go straight to San Antonio. He only hoped that he might get there before the arrival of Santa Anna and his army. He could not spare the time to seek his comrades, and he felt much apprehension for them, but he yet had the utmost confidence in the skill of the Panther and Obed White.

It was about two hours before noon when Ned set out across the plain. Usually in this region antelope were to be seen on the horizon, but they were all gone now. The boy considered it a sure sign that Mexican detachments had passed that way. It was altogether likely, too, so he calculated, that the Mexican army was now nearer than he to San Antonio. His flight had taken him to the west while Santa Anna was moving straight toward the Texan outworks. But he believed that by steady riding he could reach San Antonio within twenty-four hours.

The afternoon passed without event. Ned saw neither human beings nor game on the vast prairie. He had hoped that by some chance he might meet with his comrades, but there was no sign of them, and he fell back on his belief that their skill and great courage had saved them. Seeking to dismiss them from his thoughts for the time in order that he might concentrate all his energies on San Antonio, he rode on. The horse had recovered completely from his great efforts of the preceding night, and once more that magnificent piece of machinery worked without a jar. Old Jack moved over the prairie with long, easy strides. It seemed to Ned that he could never grow weary. He patted the sinewy and powerful neck.

"Gallant comrade," he said, "you have done your duty and more. You, at least, will never fail."

Twilight came down, but Ned kept on. By and by he saw in the east, and for the third time, that fatal red glow extending far along the dusky horizon. All that he had feared of Santa Anna was true. The dictator was marching fast, whipping his army forward with the fierce energy that was a part of his nature. It was likely, too, that squadrons of his cavalry were much further on. A daring leader like Urrea would certainly be miles ahead of the main army, and it was more than probable that bands of Mexican horsemen were now directly between him and San Antonio.

Ned knew that he would need all his strength and courage to finish his task. So he gave Old Jack a little rest, although he did not seem to need it, and drew once more upon his rations.

When he remounted he was conscious that the air had grown much colder. A chill wind began to cut him across the cheek. Snow, rain and wind have played a great part in the fate of armies, and they had much to do with the struggle between Texas and Mexico in that fateful February. Ned's experience told him that another Norther was about to begin, and he was glad of it. One horseman could make much greater progress through it than an army.

The wind rose fast and then came hail and snow on its edge. The red glow in the east disappeared. But Ned knew that it was still there. The Norther had merely drawn an icy veil between. He shivered, and the horse under him shivered, too. Once more he wrapped around his body the grateful folds of the serape and he drew on a pair of buckskin gloves, a part of his winter equipment.

Then he rode on straight toward San Antonio as nearly as he could calculate. The Norther increased in ferocity. It brought rain, hail and snow, and the night darkened greatly. Ned began to fear that he would get lost. It was almost impossible to keep the true direction in such a driving storm. He had no moon and stars to guide him, and he was compelled to rely wholly upon instinct. Sometimes he was in woods, sometimes upon the plain, and once or twice he crossed creeks, the waters of which were swollen and muddy.

The Norther was not such a blessing after all. He might be going directly away from San Antonio, while Santa Anna, with innumerable guides, would easily reach there the next day. He longed for those faithful comrades of his. The four of them together could surely find a way out of this.

He prayed now that the Norther would cease, but his prayer was of no avail. It whistled and moaned about him, and snow and hail were continually driven in his face. Fortunately the brim of the sombrero protected his eyes. He floundered on until midnight. The Norther was blowing as fiercely as ever, and he and Old Jack were brought up by a thicket too dense for them to penetrate.

Ned understood now that he was lost. Instinct had failed absolutely. Brave and resourceful as he was he uttered a groan of despair. It was torture to be so near the end of his task and then to fail. But the despair lasted only a moment. The courage of a nature containing genuine greatness brought back hope.

He dismounted and led his horse around the thicket. Then they came to a part of the woods which seemed thinner, and not knowing anything else to do he went straight ahead. But he stopped abruptly when his feet sank in soft mud. He saw directly before him a stream yellow, swollen and flowing faster than usual.

Ned knew that it was the San Antonio River, and now he had a clue. By following its banks he would reach the town. The way might be long, but it must inevitably lead him to San Antonio, and he would take it.

He remounted and rode forward as fast as he could. The river curved and twisted, but he was far more cheerful now. The San Antonio was like a great coiling rope, but if he followed it long enough he would certainly come to the end that he wished. The Norther continued to blow. He and his horse were a huge moving shape of white. Now and then the snow, coating too thickly upon his serape, fell in lumps to the ground, but it was soon coated anew and as thick as ever. But whatever happened he never let the San Antonio get out of his sight.

He was compelled to stop at last under a thick cluster of oaks, where he was somewhat sheltered from the wind and snow. Here he dismounted again, stamped his feet vigorously for warmth and also brushed the snow from his faithful horse. Old Jack, as usual, rubbed his nose against the boy's arm.

The horse was a source of great comfort and strength to Ned. He always believed that he would have collapsed without him. As nearly as he could guess the time it was about halfway between midnight and morning, and in order to preserve his strength he forced himself to eat a little more.

A half hour's rest, and remounting he resumed his slow progress by the river. The rest had been good for both his horse and himself, and the blood felt warmer in his veins. He moved for some time among trees and thickets that lined the banks, and after a while he recognized familiar ground. He had been in some of these places in the course of the siege of San Antonio, and the town could not be far away.

It was probably two hours before daylight when he heard a sound which was not that of the Norther, a sound which he knew instantly. It was the dull clank of bronze against bronze. It could be made only by one cannon striking against another. Then Santa Anna, or one of his generals, despite the storm and the night, was advancing with his army, or a part of it. Ned shivered, and now not from the cold.

The Texans did not understand the fiery energy of this man. They would learn of it too late, unless he told them, and it might be too late even then.

He pressed on with as much increase of speed as the nature of the ground would allow. In another hour the snow and hail ceased, but the wind still blew fiercely, and it remained very cold.

The dawn began to show dimly through drifting clouds. Ned did not recall until long afterward that it was the birthday of the great Washington. By a singular coincidence Santa Anna appeared before Taylor with a vastly superior force on the same birthday eleven years later.

It was a hidden sun, and the day was bleak with clouds and driving winds. Nevertheless the snow that had fallen began to disappear. Ned and Old Jack still made their way forward, somewhat slowly now, as they were stiff and sore from the long night's fight with darkness and cold. On his right, only a few feet away, was the swollen current of the San Antonio. The stream looked deep to Ned, and it bore fragments of timber upon its muddy bosom. It seemed to him that the waters rippled angrily against the bank. His excited imagination—and full cause there was—gave a sinister meaning to everything.

A heavy fog began to rise from the river and wet earth. He could not see far in front of him, but he believed that the town was now only a mile or two away. Soon a low, heavy sound, a measured stroke, came out of the fog. It was the tolling of the church bell in San Antonio, and for some reason its impact upon Ned's ear was like the stroke of death. A strange chilly sensation ran down his spine.

He rode to the very edge of the stream and began to examine it for a possible ford. San Antonio was on the other side, and he must cross. But everywhere the dark, swollen waters threatened, and he continued his course along the bank.

A thick growth of bushes and a high portion of the bank caused him presently to turn away from the river until he could make a curve about the obstacles. The tolling of the bell had now ceased, and the fog was lifting a little. Out of it came only the low, angry murmur of the river's current.

As Ned turned the curve the wind grew much stronger. The bank of fog was split asunder and then floated swiftly away in patches and streamers. On his left beyond the river Ned saw the roofs of the town, now glistening in the clear morning air, and on his right, only four or five hundred yards away, he saw a numerous troop of Mexican cavalry. In the figure at the head of the horsemen he was sure that he recognized Urrea.

Ned's first emotion was a terrible sinking of the heart. After all that he had done, after all his great journeys, hardships and dangers, he was to fail with the towers and roofs of San Antonio in sight. It was the triumphant cry of the Mexicans that startled him into life again. They had seen the lone horseman by the river and they galloped at once toward him. Ned had made no mistake. It was Urrea, pressing forward ahead of the army, who led the troop, and it may be that he recognized the boy also.

With the cry of the Mexicans ringing in his ears, the boy shouted to Old Jack. The good horse, as always, made instant response, and began to race along the side of the river. But even his mighty frame had been weakened by so much strain. Ned noticed at once that the machinery jarred. The great horse was laboring hard and the Mexican cavalry, comparatively fresh, was coming on fast. It was evident that he would soon be overtaken, and so sure were the Mexicans of it that they did not fire.

There were deep reserves of courage and fortitude in this boy, deeper than even he himself suspected. When he saw that he could not escape by speed, the way out flashed upon him. To think was to do. He turned his horse without hesitation and urged him forward with a mighty cry.

Never had Old Jack made a more magnificent response. Ned felt the mighty mass of bone and muscle gather in a bunch beneath him. Then, ready to expand again with violent energy, it was released as if by the touch of a spring. The horse sprang from the high bank far out into the deep river.

Ned felt his serape fly from him and his rifle dropped from his hand. Then the yellow waters closed over both him and Old Jack. They came up again, Ned still on the horse's back, but with an icy chill through all his veins. He could not see for a moment or two, as the water was in his eyes, but he heard dimly the shouts of the Mexicans and several shots. Two or three bullets splashed the water around him and another struck his sombrero, which was floating away on the surface of the stream.

The horse, turning somewhat, swam powerfully in a diagonal course across the stream. Ned, dazed for the moment by the shock of the plunge from a height into the water, clung tightly to his back. He sat erect at first, and then remembering that he must evade the bullets leaned forward with the horse's neck between him and the Mexicans.

More shots were fired, but again he was untouched, and then the horse was feeling with his forefeet in the muddy bank for a hold. The next instant, with a powerful effort, he pulled himself upon the shore. The violent shock nearly threw Ned from his back, but the boy seized his mane and hung on.

The Mexicans shouted and fired anew, but Ned, now sitting erect, raced for San Antonio, only a mile away.

CHAPTER VIII.
IN THE ALAMO

Most of the people in San Antonio were asleep when the dripping figure of a half unconscious boy on a great horse galloped toward them in that momentous dawn. He was without hat or serape. He was bareheaded and his rifle was gone. He was shouting "Up! Up! Santa Anna and the Mexican army are at hand!" But his voice was so choked and hoarse that he could not be heard a hundred feet away.

Davy Crockett, James Bowie and a third man were standing in the Main Plaza. The third man, like the other two, was of commanding proportions. He was a full six feet in height, very erect and muscular, and with full face and red hair. He was younger than the others, not more than twenty-eight, but he was Colonel William Barrett Travis, a North Carolina lawyer, who was now in command of the few Texans in San Antonio.

The three men were talking very anxiously. Crockett had brought word that the army of Santa Anna was on the Texan side of the Rio Grande, but it had seemed impossible to rouse the Texans to a full sense of the impending danger. Many remained at their homes following their usu vocations. Mr. Austin was away in the states trying to raise money. Dissensions were numerous in the councils of the new government, and the leaders could agree upon nothing.

Travis, Bowie and Crockett were aware of the great danger, but even they did not believe it was so near. Nevertheless they were full of anxiety. Crockett, just come to Texas, took no command and sought to keep in the background, but he was too famous and experienced a man not to be taken at once by Travis and Bowie into their councils. They were discussing now the possibility of getting help.

"We might send messengers to the towns further east," said Travis, "and at least get a few men here in time."

"We need a good many," said Bowie. "According to Mr. Crockett the Mexican army is large, and the population here is unfriendly."

"That is so," said Travis, "and we have women and children of our own to protect."

It was when he spoke the last words that they heard the clatter of hoofs and saw Ned dashing down the narrow street toward the Main Plaza. They heard him trying to shout, but his voice was now so hoarse that he could not be understood.

But Ned, though growing weaker fast, knew two of the men. He could never forget the fair-haired Bowie nor the swarthy Crockett, and he galloped straight toward them. Then he pulled up his horse and half fell, half leaped to the ground. Holding by Old Jack's mane he pulled himself into an erect position. He was a singular sight The water still fell from his wet hair and dripped from his clothing. His face was plastered with mud.

"Santa Anna's army, five thousand strong, is not two miles away!" he said. "I tell you because I have seen it!"

"Good God!" cried Bowie. "It's the boy, Ned Fulton. I know him well. What he says must be truth."

"It is every word truth!" croaked Ned. "I was pursued by their vanguard! My horse swam the river with me! Up! Up! for Texas!"

Then he fainted dead away. Bowie seized him in his powerful arms and carried him into one of the houses occupied by the Texans, where men stripped him of his wet clothing and gave him restoratives. But Bowie himself hurried out into the Main Plaza. He had the most unlimited confidence in Ned's word and so had Crockett. They and Travis at once began to arrange the little garrison for defence.

Many of the Texans even yet would not believe. So great had been their confidence that they had sent out no scouting parties. Only a day or two before they had been enjoying themselves at a great dance. The boy who had come with the news that Santa Anna was at hand must be distraught. Certainly he had looked like a maniac.

A loud cry suddenly came from the roof of the church of San Fernando. Two sentinels posted there had seen the edge of a great army appear upon the plain and then spread rapidly over it. Santa Anna's army had come. The mad boy was right. Two horsemen sent out to reconnoiter had to race back for their lives. The flooded stream was now subsiding and only the depth of the water in the night had kept the Mexicans from taking cannon across and attacking.

Ned's faint was short. He remembered putting on clothing, securing a rifle and ammunition, and then he ran out into the square. From many windows he saw the triumphant faces of Mexicans looking out, but he paid no attention to them. He thought alone of the Texans, who were now displaying the greatest energy. In the face of the imminent and deadly peril Travis, Crockett, Bowie and the others were cool and were acting with rapidity. The order was swiftly given to cross to the Alamo, the old mission built like a fortress, and the Texans were gathering in a body. Ned saw a young lieutenant named Dickinson catch up his wife and child on a horse, and join the group of men. All the Texans had their long rifles, and there were also cannon.

As Ned took his place with the others a kindly hand fell upon his shoulder and a voice spoke in his ear.

"I was going to send for you, Ned," said Bowie, "but you've come. Perhaps it would have been better for you, though, if you had been left in San Antonio."

"Oh, no, Mr. Bowie!" cried Ned. "Don't say that. We can beat off any number of Mexicans!"

Bowie said nothing more. Much of Ned's courage and spirit returned, but he saw how pitifully small their numbers were. The little band that defiled across the plain toward the Alamo numbered less than one hundred and fifty men, and many of them were without experience.

They were not far upon the plain when Ned saw a great figure coming toward him. It was Old Jack, who had been forgotten in the haste and excitement. The saddle was still on his back and his bridle trailed on the ground. Ned met him and patted his faithful head. Already he had taken his resolution. There would be no place for Old Jack in the Alamo, but this good friend of his should not fall into the hands of the Mexicans.

He slipped off saddle and bridle, struck him smartly on the shoulder and exclaimed:

"Good-by, Old Jack, good-by! Keep away from our enemies and wait for me."

The horse looked a moment at his master, and, to Ned's excited eyes, it seemed for a moment that he wished to speak. Old Jack had never before been dismissed in this manner. Ned struck him again and yet more sharply.

"Go, old friend!" he cried.

The good horse trotted away across the plain. Once he looked back as if in reproach, but as Ned did not call him he kept on and disappeared over a swell. It was to Ned like the passing of a friend, but he knew that Old Jack would not allow the Mexicans to take him. He would fight with both teeth and hoofs against any such ignominious capture.

Then Ned turned his attention to the retreat. It was a little band that went toward the Alamo, and there were three women and three children in it, but since they knew definitely that Santa Anna and his great army had come there was not a Texan who shrank from his duty. They had been lax in their watch and careless of the future, faults frequent in irregular troops, but in the presence of overwhelming danger they showed not the least fear of death.

They reached the Alamo side of the river. Before them they saw the hewn stone walls of the mission rising up in the form of a cross and facing the river and the town. It certainly seemed welcome to a little band of desperate men who were going to fight against overwhelming odds. Ned also saw not far away the Mexican cavalry advancing in masses. The foremost groups were lancers, and the sun glittered on the blades of their long weapons.

Ned believed that Urrea was somewhere in one of these leading groups. Urrea he knew was full of skill and enterprise, but his heart filled with bitterness against him. He had tasted the Texan salt, he had broken bread with those faithful friends of his, the Panther and Obed White, and now he was at Santa Anna's right hand, seeking to destroy the Texans utterly.

"Looks as if I'd have a lot of use for Old Betsy," said a whimsical voice beside him. "Somebody said when I started away from Tennessee that I'd have nothing to do with it, might as well leave my rifle at home. But I 'low that Old Betsy is the most useful friend I could have just now."

It was, of course, Davy Crockett who spoke. He was as cool as a cake of ice. Old Betsy rested in the hollow of his arm, the long barrel projecting several feet. His raccoon skin cap was on the back of his head. His whole manner was that of one who was in the first stage of a most interesting event. But as Ned was looking at him a light suddenly leaped in the calm eye.

"Look there! look there!" said Davy Crockett, pointing a long finger. "We'll need food in that Alamo place, an' behold it on the hoof!"

About forty cattle had been grazing on the plain. They had suddenly gathered in a bunch, startled by the appearance of so many people, and of galloping horsemen.

"We'll take 'em with us! We'll need 'em! Say we can do it, Colonel!" shouted Crockett to Travis.

Travis nodded.

"Come on, Ned," cried Crockett, "an' come on the rest of you fleet-footed fellows! Every mother's son of you has driv' the cows home before in his time, an' now you kin do it again!"

A dozen swift Texans ran forward with shouts, Ned and Davy Crockett at their head. Crockett was right. This was work that every one of them knew how to do. In a flash they were driving the whole frightened herd in a run toward the gate that led into the great plaza of the Alamo. The swift motion, the sense of success in a sudden maneuver, thrilled Ned. He shouted at the cattle as he would have done when he was a small boy.

They were near the gate when he heard an ominous sound by his side. It was the cocking of Davy Crockett's rifle, and when he looked around he saw that Old Betsy was leveled, and that the sure eye of the Tennessean was looking down the sights.

Some of the Mexican skirmishers seeing the capture of the herd by the daring Texans were galloping forward to check it. Crockett's finger pressed the trigger. Old Betsy flashed and the foremost rider fell to the ground.

"I told that Mexican to come down off his horse, and he came down," chuckled Crockett.

The Mexicans drew back, because other Texan rifles, weapons that they had learned to dread, were raised. A second body of horsemen charged from a different angle, and Ned distinctly saw Urrea at their head. He fired, but the bullet missed the partisan leader and brought down another man behind him.

"There are good pickings here," said Davy Crockett, "but they'll soon be too many for us. Come on, Ned, boy! Our place is behind them walls!"

"Yes," repeated Bowie, who was near. "It's the Alamo or nothing. No matter how fast we fired our rifles we'd soon be trod under foot by the Mexicans."

They passed in, Bowie, Crockett and Ned forming the rear guard. The great gates of the Alamo were closed behind them and barred. For the moment they were safe, because these doors were made of very heavy oak, and it would require immense force to batter them in. It was evident that the Mexican horsemen on the plain did not intend to make any such attempt, as they drew off hastily, knowing that the deadly Texan rifles would man the walls at once.

"Well, here we are, Ned," said the cheerful voice of Davy Crockett, "an' if we want to win glory in fightin' it seems that we've got the biggest chance that was ever offered to anybody. I guess when old Santa Anna comes up he'll say: 'By nations right wheel; forward march the world.' Still these walls will help a little to make up the difference between fifty to one."

As he spoke he tapped the outer wall.

"No Mexican on earth," he said, "has got a tough enough head to butt through that. At least I think so. Now what do you think, Ned?"

His tone was so whimsical that Ned was compelled to laugh despite their terrible situation.

"It's a pity, though," continued Crockett, "that we've got such a big place here to defend. Sometimes you're the stronger the less ground you spread over."

Ned glanced around. He had paid the Alamo one hasty visit just after the capture of San Antonio by the Texans, but he took only a vague look then. Now it was to make upon his brain a photograph which nothing could remove as long as he lived.

He saw in a few minutes all the details of the Alamo. He knew already its history. This mission of deathless fame was even then more than a century old. Its name, the Alamo, signified "the Cottonwood tree," but that has long since been lost in another of imperishable grandeur.

The buildings of the mission were numerous, the whole arranged, according to custom, in the form of a cross. The church, which was now without a roof, faced town and river, but it contained arched rooms, and the sacristy had a solid roof of masonry. The windows, cut for the needs of an earlier time, were high and narrow, in order that attacking Indians might not pour in flights of arrows upon those who should be worshipping there. Over the heavy oaken doors were images and carvings in stone worn by time.

To the left of the church, beside the wing of the cross, was the plaza of the convent, about thirty yards square, with its separate walls more than fifteen feet high and nearly four feet thick.

Ned noted all these things rapidly and ineffaceably, as he and Crockett took a swift but complete survey of their fortress. He saw that the convent and hospital, each two stories in height, were made of adobe bricks, and he also noticed a sallyport, protected by a little redoubt, at the southeastern corner of the yard.

They saw beyond the convent yard the great plaza into which they had driven the cattle, a parallelogram covering nearly three acres, inclosed by a wall eight feet in height and three feet thick. Prisons, barracks and other buildings were scattered about. Beyond the walls was a small group of wretched jacals or huts in which some Mexicans lived. Water from the San Antonio flowed in ditches through the mission.

It was almost a town that they were called upon to defend, and Ned and Crockett, after their hasty look, came back to the church, the strongest of all the buildings, with walls of hewn stone five feet thick and nearly twenty-five feet high. They opened the heavy oaken doors, entered the building and looked up through the open roof at the sky. Then Crockett's eyes came back to the arched rooms and the covered sacristy.

"This is the real fort," he said, "an' we'll put our gunpowder in that sacristy. It looks like sacrilege to use a church for such a purpose, but, Ned, times are goin' to be very hot here, the hottest we ever saw, an' we must protect our powder."

He carried his suggestion to Travis, who adopted it at once, and the powder was quickly taken into the rooms. They also had fourteen pieces of cannon which they mounted on the walls of the church, at the stockade at the entrance to the plaza and at the redoubt. But the Texans, frontiersmen and not regular soldiers, did not place much reliance upon the cannon. Their favorite weapon was the rifle, with which they rarely missed even at long range.

It took the Texans but little time to arrange the defence, and then came a pause. Ned did not have any particular duty assigned to him, and went back to the church, which now bore so little resemblance to a house of worship. He gazed curiously at the battered carvings and images over the door. They looked almost grotesque to him now, and some of them threatened.

He went inside the church and looked around once more. It was old, very old. The grayness of age showed everywhere, and the silence of the defenders on the walls deepened its ancient aspect. But the Norther had ceased to blow, and the sun came down, bright and unclouded, through the open roof.

Ned climbed upon the wall. Bowie, who was behind one of the cannon, beckoned to him. Ned joined him and leaned upon the gun as Bowie pointed toward San Antonio.

"See the Mexican masses," he said. "Ned, you were a most timely herald. If it had not been for you our surprise would have been total. Look how they defile upon the plain."

The army of Santa Anna was entering San Antonio and it was spread out far and wide. The sun glittered on lances and rifles, and brightened the bronze barrels of cannon. The triumphant notes of a bugle came across the intervening space, and when the bugle ceased a Mexican band began to play.

It was fine music. The Mexicans had the Latin ear, the gift for melody, and the air they played was martial and inspiring. One could march readily to its beat. Bowie frowned.

"They think it nothing more than a parade," he said. "But when Santa Anna has taken us he will need a new census of his army."

He looked around at the strong stone walls, and then at the resolute faces of the men near him. But the garrison was small, pitifully small.

Ned left the walls and ate a little food that was cooked over a fire lighted in the convent plaza. Then he wandered about the place looking at the buildings and inclosures. The Alamo was so extensive that he knew Travis would be compelled to concentrate his defense about the church, but he wanted to examine all these places anyhow.

He wandered into one building that looked like a storehouse. The interior was dry and dusty. Cobwebs hung from the walls, and it was empty save for many old barrels that stood in the corner. Ned looked casually into the barrels and then he uttered a shout of joy. A score of so of them were full of shelled Indian corn in perfect condition, a hundred bushels at least. This was truly treasure trove, more valuable than if the barrels had been filled with coined gold.

He ran out of the house and the first man he met was Davy Crockett.

"Now what has disturbed you?" asked Crockett, in his drawling tone. "Haven't you seen Mexicans enough for one day? This ain't the time to see double."

"I wish I could see double in this case, Mr. Crockett," replied Ned, "because then the twenty barrels of corn that I've found would be forty."

He took Crockett triumphantly into the building and showed him the treasure, which was soon transferred to one of the arched rooms beside the entrance of the church. It was in truth one of the luckiest finds ever made. The cattle in the plaza would furnish meat for a long time, but they would need bread also. Again Ned felt that pleasant glow of triumph. It seemed that fortune was aiding them.

He went outside and stood by the ditch which led a shallow stream of water along the eastern side of the church. It was greenish in tint, but it was water, water which would keep the life in their bodies while they fought off the hosts of Santa Anna.

The sun was now past the zenith, and since the Norther had ceased to blow there was a spring warmth in the air. Ned, conscious now that he was stained with the dirt and dust of flight and haste, bathed his face and hands in the water of the ditch and combed his thick brown hair as well as he could with his fingers.

"Good work, my lad," said a hearty voice beside him. "It shows that you have a cool brain and an orderly mind."

Davy Crockett, who was always neat, also bathed his own face and hands in the ditch.

"Now I feel a lot better," he said, "and I want to tell you, Ned, that it's lucky the Spanish built so massively. Look at this church. It's got walls of hewn stone, five feet through, an' back in Tennessee we build 'em of planks a quarter of an inch thick. Why, these walls would turn the biggest cannon balls."

"It surely is mighty lucky," said Ned. "What are you going to do next, Mr. Crockett?"

"I don't know. I guess we'll wait on the Mexicans to open the battle. Thar, do you hear that trumpet blowin' ag'in? I reckon it means that they're up to somethin'."

"I think so, too," said Ned. "Let's go back upon the church walls, Mr. Crockett, and see for ourselves just what it means."

The two climbed upon the great stone wall, which was in reality a parapet. Travis and Bowie, who was second in command, were there already. Ned looked toward San Antonio, and he saw Mexicans everywhere. Mexican flags hoisted by the people were floating from the flat roofs of the houses, signs of their exultation at the coming of Santa Anna and the expulsion of the Texans.

The trumpet sounded again and they saw three officers detach themselves from the Mexican lines and ride forward under a white flag. Ned knew that one of them was the young Urrea.

"Now what in thunder can they want?" growled Davy Crockett. "There can be no talk or truce between us an' Santa Anna. If all that I've heard of him is true I'd never believe a word he says."

Travis called two of his officers, Major Morris and Captain Martin, and directed them to go out and see what the Mexicans wanted. Then, meeting Ned's eye, he recalled something.

"Ah, you speak Spanish and Mexican Spanish perfectly," he said. "Will you go along, too?"

"Gladly," said Ned.

"An', Ned," said Davy Crockett, in his whimsical tone, "if you don't tell me every word they said when you come back I'll keep you on bread an' water for a week. There are to be no secrets here from me."

"I promise, Mr. Crockett," said Ned.

The heavy oaken doors were thrown open and the three went out on foot to meet the Mexican officers who were riding slowly forward. The afternoon air was now soft and pleasant, and a light, soothing wind was blowing from the south. The sky was a vast dome of brilliant blue and gold. It was a picture that remained indelibly on Ned's mind like many others that were to come. They were etched in so deeply that neither the colors nor the order of their occurrence ever changed. An odor, a touch, or anything suggestive would make them return to his mind, unfaded and in proper sequence like the passing of moving pictures.

The Mexicans halted in the middle of the plain and the three Texans met them. The Mexicans did not dismount. Urrea was slightly in advance of the other two, who were older men in brilliant uniforms, generals at least. Ned saw at once that they meant to be haughty and arrogant to the last degree. They showed it in the first instance by not dismounting. It was evident that Urrea would be the chief spokesman, and his manner indicated that it was a part he liked. He, too, was in a fine uniform, irreproachably neat, and his handsome olive face was flushed.

"And so," he said, in an undertone and in Spanish to Ned, "we are here face to face again. You have chosen your own trap, the Alamo, and it is not in human power for you to escape it now."

His taunt stung, but Ned merely replied:

"We shall see."

Then Urrea said aloud, speaking in English, and addressing himself to the two officers:

"We have come by order of General Santa Anna, President of Mexico and Commander-in-Chief of her officers, to make a demand of you."

"A conference must proceed on the assumption that the two parties to it are on equal terms," said Major Morris, in civil tones.

"Under ordinary circumstances, yes," said Urrea, without abating his haughty manner one whit, "but this is a demand by a paramount authority upon rebels and traitors."

He paused that his words might sink home. All three of the Texans felt anger leap in their hearts, but they put restraint upon their words.

"What is it that you wish to say to us?" continued Major Morris. "If it is anything we should hear we are listening."

Urrea could not subdue his love of the grandiose and theatrical.

"As you may see for yourselves," he said, "General Santa Anna has returned to Texas with an overpowering force of brave Mexican troops. San

Antonio has fallen into his hands without a struggle. He can take the Alamo in a day. In a month not a man will be left in Texas able to dispute his authority."

"These are statements most of which can be disputed," said Major Morris. "What does General Santa Anna demand of us?"

His quiet manner had its effect upon Urrea.

"He demands your unconditional surrender," he said.

"And does he say nothing about our lives and good treatment?" continued the Major, in the same quiet tones.

"He does not," replied Urrea emphatically. "If you receive mercy it will be due solely to the clemency of General Santa Anna toward rebels."

Hot anger again made Ned's heart leap. The tone of Urrea was almost insufferable, but Major Morris, not he, was spokesman.

"I am not empowered to accept or reject anything," continued Major Morris. "Colonel Travis is the commander of our force, but I am quite positive in my belief that he will not surrender."

"We must carry back our answer in either the affirmative or the negative," said Urrea.

"You can do neither," said Major Morris, "but I promise you that if the answer is a refusal to surrender—and I know it will be such—a single cannon shot will be fired from the wall of the church."

"Very well," said Urrea, "and since that is your arrangement I see nothing more to be said."

"Nor do I," said Major Morris.

The Mexicans saluted in a perfunctory manner and rode toward San Antonio. The three Texans went slowly back to the Alamo. Ned walked behind the two men. He hoped that the confidence of Major Morris was justified. He knew Santa Anna too well. He believed that the Texans had more to fear from surrender than from defence.

They entered the Alamo and once more the great door was shut and barred heavily. They climbed upon the wall, and Major Morris and Captain Martin went toward Travis, Bowie and Crockett, who stood together waiting. Ned paused a little distance away. He saw them talking together earnestly, but he could not hear what they said. Far away he saw the three Mexicans riding slowly toward San Antonio.

Ned's eyes came back to the wall. He saw Bowie detach himself from the other two and advance toward the cannon. A moment later a flash came from its muzzle, a heavy report rolled over the plain, and then came back in faint echoes.

The Alamo had sent its answer. A deep cheer came from the Texans. Ned's heart thrilled. He had his wish.

The boy looked back toward San Antonio and his eyes were caught by something red on the tower of the Church of San Fernando. It rose, expanded swiftly, and then burst out in great folds. It was a blood-red flag, flying now in the wind, the flag of no quarter. No Texan would be spared, and Ned knew it. Nevertheless his heart thrilled again.

CHAPTER IX.
THE FLAG OF NO QUARTER

Ned gazed long at the great red flag as its folds waved in the wind. A chill ran down his spine, a strange, throbbing sensation, but not of fear. They were a tiny islet there amid a Mexican sea which threatened to roll over them. But the signal of the flag, he realized, merely told him that which he had expected all the time. He knew Santa Anna. He would show no quarter to those who had humbled Cos and his forces at San Antonio.

The boy was not assigned to the watch that night, but he could not sleep for a long time. Among these borderers there was discipline, but it was discipline of their own kind, not that of the military martinet. Ned was free to go about as he chose, and he went to the great plaza into which they had driven the cattle. Some supplies of hay had been gathered for them, and having eaten they were now all at rest in a herd, packed close against the western side of the wall.

Ned passed near them, but they paid no attention to him, and going on he climbed upon the portion of the wall which ran close to the river. Some distance to his right and an equal distance to his left were sentinels. But there was nothing to keep him from leaping down from the wall or the outside and disappearing. The Mexican investment was not yet complete. Yet no such thought ever entered Ned's head. His best friends, Will Allen, the Panther and Obed White, were out there somewhere, if they were still alive, but his heart was now here in the Alamo with the Texans.

He listened intently, but he heard no sound of any Mexican advance. It occurred to him that a formidable attack might be made here, particularly under the cover of darkness. A dashing leader like the younger Urrea might attempt a surprise.

He dropped back inside and went to one of the sentinels who was standing on an abutment with his head just showing above the wall. He was a young man, not more than two or three years older than Ned, and he was glad to have company.

"Have you heard or seen anything?" asked Ned.

"No," replied the sentinel, "but I've been looking for 'em down this way."

They waited a little longer and then Ned was quite sure that he saw a dim form in the darkness. He pointed toward it, but the sentinel could not see it at all, as Ned's eyes were much the keener: But the shape grew clearer and Ned's heart throbbed.

The figure was that of a great horse, and Ned recognized Old Jack. Nothing could have persuaded him that the faithful beast was not seeking his master, and he emitted a low soft whistle. The horse raised his head, listened and then trotted forward.

"He is mine," said Ned, "and he knows me."

"He won't be yours much longer," said the sentinel. "Look, there's a Mexican creeping along the ground after him."

Ned followed the pointing finger, and he now noticed the Mexican, a vaquero, who had been crouching so low that his figure blurred with the earth. Ned saw the coiled lariat hanging over his arm, and he knew that the man intended to capture Old Jack, a prize worth any effort.

"Do you think I ought to shoot him?" asked the sentinel.

"Not yet, at least," replied Ned. "I brought my horse into this danger, but I think that he'll take himself out of it."

Old Jack had paused, as if uncertain which way to go. But Ned felt sure that he was watching the Mexican out of the tail of his eye. The vaquero, emboldened by the prospect of such a splendid prize, crept closer and closer, and then suddenly threw the lasso. The horse's head ducked down swiftly, the coil of rope slipped back over his head, and he dashed at the Mexican.

The vaquero was barely in time to escape those terrible hoofs. But howling with terror he sprang clear and raced away in the darkness. The horse whinnied once or twice gently, waited, and, when no answer came to his calls, trotted off in the dusk.

"No Mexican will take your horse," said the sentinel.

"You're right when you say that," said Ned. "I don't think another will ever get so near him, but if he should you see that my horse knows how to take care of himself."

Ned wandered back toward the convent yard. It was now late, but a clear moon was shining. He saw the figures of the sentinels clearly on the walls, but he was confident that no attack would be made by the Mexicans that night. His great tension and excitement began to relax and he felt that he could sleep.

He decided that the old hospital would be a good place, and, taking his blankets, he entered the long room of that building. Only the moonlight shone there, but a friendly voice hailed him at once.

"It's time you were hunting rest, Ned," said Davy Crockett. "I saw you wanderin' 'roun' as if you was carryin' the world on your shoulders, but I didn't say anything. I knew that you would come to if left to yourself. There's a place over there by the wall where the floor seems to be a little softer than it is most everywhere else. Take it an' enjoy it."

Ned laughed and took the place to which Crockett was pointing. The hardness of a floor was nothing to him, and with one blanket under him and another over him he went to sleep quickly, sleeping the night through without a dream. He awoke early, took a breakfast of fresh beef with the men in the convent yard, and then, rifle in hand, he mounted the church wall.

All his intensity of feeling returned with the morning. He was eager to see what was passing beyond the Alamo, and the first object that caught his eye was the blood-red flag of no quarter hanging from the tower of the Church of San Fernando. No wind was blowing and it drooped in heavy scarlet folds like a pall.

Looking from the flag to the earth, he saw great activity in the Mexican lines. Three or four batteries were being placed in position, and Mexican officers, evidently messengers, were galloping about. The flat roofs of the houses in San Antonio were covered with people. Ned knew that they were there to see Santa Anna win a quick victory and take immediate vengeance upon the Texans. He recognized Santa Anna himself riding in his crouched attitude upon a great white horse, passing from battery to battery and hurrying the work. There was proof that his presence was effective, as the men always worked faster when he came.

Ned saw all the Texan leaders, Travis, Bowie, Crockett and Bonham, watching the batteries. The whole Texan force was now manning the walls and the heavy cedar palisade at many points, but Ned saw that for the present all their dealings would be with the cannon.

Earthworks had been thrown up to protect the Mexican batteries, and the Texan cannon were posted for reply, but Ned noticed that his comrades seemed to think little of the artillery. In this desperate crisis they fondled their rifles lovingly.

He was still watching the batteries, when a gush of smoke and flame came from one of the cannon. There was a great shout in the Mexican lines, but the round shot spent itself against the massive stone walls of the mission.

"They'll have to send out a stronger call than that," said Davy Crockett contemptuously, "before this 'coon comes down."

Travis went along the walls, saw that the Texans were sheltering themselves, and waited. There was another heavy report and a second round shot struck harmlessly upon the stone. Then the full bombardment began. A half dozen batteries rained shot and shell upon the Alamo. The roar was continuous like the steady roll of thunder, and it beat upon the drums of Ned's ears until he thought he would become deaf.

He was crouched behind the stone parapet, but he looked up often enough to see what was going on. He saw a vast cloud of smoke gathering over river and town, rent continually by flashes of fire from the muzzles of the cannon. The air was full of hissing metal, shot and shell poured in a storm upon the Alamo. Now and then the Texan cannon replied, but not often.

The cannon fire was so great that for a time it shook Ned's nerves. It seemed as if nothing could live under such a rain of missiles, but when he looked along the parapet and saw all the Texans unharmed his courage came back.

Many of the balls were falling inside the church, in the convent yard and in the plazas, but the Texans there were protected also, and as far as Ned could see not a single man had been wounded.

The cannonade continued for a full hour and then ceased abruptly. The great cloud of smoke began to lift, and the Alamo, river and town came again into the brilliant sunlight. The word passed swiftly among the defenders that their fortress was uninjured and not a man hurt.

As the smoke rose higher Ned saw Mexican officers with glasses examining the Alamo to see what damage their cannon had done. He hoped they would feel mortification when they found it was so little. Davy Crockett knelt near him on the parapet, and ran his hand lovingly along the barrel of Betsy, as one strokes the head of a child.

"Do you want some more rifles, Davy?" asked Bowie.

"Jest about a half dozen," replied Crockett. "I think I can use that many before they clear out."

Six of the long-barreled Texan rifles were laid at Crockett's feet. Ned watched with absorbed interest. Crockett's eye was on the nearest battery and he was slowly raising Betsy.

"Which is to be first, Davy?" asked Bowie.

"The one with the rammer in his hand."

Crockett took a single brief look down the sights and pulled the trigger. The man with the rammer dropped to the earth and the rammer fell beside him. He lay quite still. Crockett seized a second rifle and fired. A loader fell and he also lay still. A third rifle shot, almost as quick as a flash, and a gunner went down, a fourth and a man at a wheel fell, a fifth and the unerring bullet claimed a sponger, a sixth and a Mexican just springing to cover was wounded in the shoulder. Then Crockett remained with the seventh rifle still loaded in his hands, as there was nothing to shoot at, all the Mexicans now being hidden.

But Crockett, kneeling on the parapet, the rifle cocked and his finger on the trigger, watched in case any of the Mexicans should expose himself again. He presented to Ned the simile of some powerful animal about to spring. The lean, muscular figure was poised for instant action, and all the whimsicality and humor were gone from the eyes of the sharpshooter.

A mighty shout of triumph burst from the Texans. Many a good marksman was there, but never before had they seen such shooting. The great reputation of Davy Crockett, universal in the southwest, was justified fully. The crew of the gun had been annihilated in less than a minute.

For a while there was silence. Then the Mexicans, protected by the earthwork that they had thrown up, drew the battery back a hundred yards. Even in the farther batteries the men were very careful about exposing themselves. The Texans, seeing no sure target, held their fire. The Mexicans opened a new cannonade and for another half hour the roar of the great guns drowned all other sounds. But when it ceased and the smoke drifted away the Texans were still unharmed.

Ned was now by the side of Bowie, who showed great satisfaction.

"What will they do next?" asked Ned.

"I don't know, but you see now that it's not the biggest noise that hurts the most. They'll never get us with cannon fire. The only way they can do it is to attack the lowest part of our wall and make a bridge of their own bodies."

"They are doing something now," said Ned, whose far-sighted vision always served him well. "They are pulling down houses in the town next to the river."

"That's so," said Bowie, "but we won't have to wait long to see what they're about."

Hundreds of Mexicans with wrecking hooks had assailed three or four of the houses, which they quickly pulled to pieces. Others ran forward with the materials and began to build a bridge across the narrow San Antonio.

"They want to cross over on that bridge and get into a position at once closer and more sheltered," said Bowie, "but unless I make a big mistake those men at work there are already within range of our rifles. Shall we open fire, Colonel?"

He asked the question of Travis, who nodded. A picked band of Mexicans under General Castrillon were gathered in a mass and were rapidly fitting together the timbers of the houses to make the narrow bridge. But the reach of the Texan rifles was great, and Davy Crockett was merely the king among so many sharpshooters.

The rifles began to flash and crack. No man fired until he was sure of his aim, and no two picked the same target. The Mexicans fell fast. In five minutes thirty or forty were killed, some of them falling into the river, and the rest, dropping the timbers, fled with shouts of horror from the fatal spot. General Castrillon, a brave man, sought to drive them back, but neither blows nor oaths availed. Santa Anna himself came and made many threats, but the men would not stir. They preferred punishment to the sure death that awaited them from the muzzles of the Texan rifles.

The light puffs of rifle smoke were quickly gone, and once more the town with the people watching on the flat roofs came into full view. A wind burst out the folds of the red flag of no quarter on the tower of the church of San Fernando, but Ned paid no attention to it now. He was watching for Santa Anna's next move.

"That's a bridge that will never be built," said Davy Crockett. "'Live an' learn' is a good sayin', I suppose, but a lot of them Mexicans neither lived nor learned. It's been a great day for 'Betsy' here."

Travis, the commander, showed elation.

"I think Santa Anna will realize now," he said, "that he has neither a promenade nor a picnic before him. Oh, if we only had six or seven hundred men, instead of less than a hundred and fifty!"

"We must send for help," said Bowie. "The numbers of Santa Anna continually increase, but we are not yet entirely surrounded. If the Texans know that we are beleaguered here they will come to our help."

"I will send messengers to-morrow night," said Travis. "The Texans are much scattered, but it is likely that some will come."

It was strange, but it was characteristic of them, nevertheless, that no one made any mention of escape. Many could have stolen away in the night over the lower walls. Perhaps all could have done so, but not a single Texan ever spoke of such a thing, and not one ever attempted it.

Santa Anna moved some of his batteries and also erected two new ones. When the work on the latter was finished all opened in another tremendous cannonade, lasting for fully an hour. The bank of smoke was heavier than ever, and the roaring in Ned's ears was incessant, but he felt no awe now. He was growing used to the cannon fire, and as it did so little harm he felt no apprehension.

While the fire was at its height he went down in the church and cleaned his rifle, although he took the precaution to remain in one of the covered rooms by the doorway. Davy Crockett was also there busy with the same task. Before they finished a cannon ball dropped on the floor, bounded against the wall and rebounded several times until it finally lay at rest.

"Somethin' laid a big egg then," said Crockett. "It's jest as well to keep a stone roof over your head when you're under fire of a few dozen cannon. Never take foolish risks, Ned, for the sake of showin' off. That's the advice of an old man."

Crockett spoke very earnestly, and Ned remembered his words. Bonham called to them a few minutes later that the Mexicans seemed to be meditating some movement on the lower wall around the grand plaza.

"Like as not you're right," said Crockett. "It would be the time to try it while our attention was attracted by the big cannonade."

Crockett himself was detailed to meet the new movement, and he led fifty sharpshooters. Ned was with him, his brain throbbing with the certainty that he was going into action once more. Great quantities of smoke hung over the Alamo and had penetrated every part of it. It crept into Ned's throat, and it also stung his eyes. It inflamed his brain and increased his desire for combat. They reached the low wall on a run, and found that Bonham was right. A large force of Mexicans was approaching from that side, evidently expecting to make an opening under cover of the smoke.

The assailants were already within range, and the deadly Texan rifles began to crack at once from the wall. The whole front line of the Mexican column was quickly burned away. The return fire of the Mexicans was hasty and irregular and they soon broke and ran.

"An' that's over," said Crockett, as he sent a parting shot. "It was easy, an' bein' sheltered not a man of ours was hurt. But, Ned, don't let the idea that we have a picnic here run away with you. We've got to watch an' watch an' fight an' fight all the time, an' every day more Mexicans will come."

"I understand, Mr. Crockett," said Ned. "You know that we may never get out of here alive, and I know it, too."

"You speak truth, lad," said Crockett, very soberly. "But remember that it's a chance we take every day here in the southwest. An' it's pleasant to know that they're all brave men here together. You haven't seen any flinchin' on the part of anybody an' I don't think you ever will."

"What are you going to do now?" asked Ned.

"I'm goin' to eat dinner, an' after that I'll take a nap. My advice to you is to do the same, 'cause you'll be on watch to-night."

"I know I can eat," said Ned, "and I'll try to sleep."

He found that his appetite was all right, and after dinner he lay down in the long room of the hospital. Here he heard the cannon of Santa Anna still thundering, but the walls softened the sound somewhat and made it seem much more distant. In a way it was soothing and Ned, although sure that he could not sleep, slept. All that afternoon he was rocked into deeper slumber by the continuous roar of the Mexican guns. Smoke floated over the convent yard and through all the buildings, but it did not disturb him. Now and then a flash of rifle fire came from the Texans on the walls, but that did not disturb him, either.

Nature was paying its debt. The boy lying on his blankets breathed deeply and regularly as he slept. The hours of the afternoon passed one by one, and it was dark when he awoke. The fire of the cannon had now ceased and two or three lights were burning in the hospital. Crockett was already up, and with some of the other men was eating beefsteak at a table.

"You said you'd try to sleep, Ned," he exclaimed, "an' you must have made a big try, 'cause you snored so loud we couldn't hear Santa Anna's cannon."

"Why, I'm sure I don't snore, Mr. Crockett," said Ned, red in the face.

"No, you don't snore, I'll take that back," said Davy Crockett, when the laugh subsided, "but I never saw a young man sleep more beautifully an' skillfully. Why, the risin' an' fallin' of your chest was as reg'lar as the tickin' of a clock."

Ned joined them at the table. He did not mind the jests of those men, as they did not mind the jests of one another. They were now like close blood-kin. They were a band of brethren, bound together by the unbreakable tie of mortal danger.

Ned spent two-thirds of the night on the church wall. The Mexicans let the cannon rest in the darkness, and only a few rifle shots were fired. But there were many lights in San Antonio, and on the outskirts two great bonfires burned. Santa Anna and his generals, feeling that their prey could not escape from the trap, and caring little for the peons who had been slain, were making a festival. It is even said that Santa Anna on this campaign, although he left a wife in the city of Mexico, exercised the privileges of an Oriental ruler and married another amid great rejoicings.

Ned slept soundly when his watch was finished, and he awoke again the next day to the thunder of the cannonade, which continued almost without cessation throughout the day, but in the afternoon Travis wrote a letter, a noble appeal to the people of Texas for help. He stated that they had been under a continual bombardment for more than twenty-four hours, but not a man had yet been hurt. "I shall never surrender or retreat," he said. "Then I call on you in the name of liberty, of patriotism, and of everything dear to the American character, to come to our aid with all dispatch." He closed with the three words, "Victory or death," not written in any vainglory or with any melodramatic appeal, but with the full consciousness of the desperate crisis, and a quiet resolution to do as he said.

The heroic letter is now in the possession of the State of Texas. Most of the men in the Alamo knew its contents, and they approved of it. When it was fully dark Travis gave it to Albert Martin. Then he looked around for another messenger.

"Two should go together in case of mishap," he said.

His eye fell upon Ned.

"If you wish to go I will send you," he said, "but I leave it to your choice. If you prefer to stay, you stay."

Ned's first impulse was to go. He might find Obed White, Will Allen and the Panther out there and bring them back with him, but his second impulse told him that it was only a chance, and he would abide with Crockett and Bowie.

"I thank you for the offer, but I think, sir, that I'll stay," he said.

He saw Crockett give him a swift approving glance. Another was quickly chosen in his stead, and Ned was in the grand plaza when they dropped over the low wall and disappeared in the darkness. His comrades and he listened attentively a long time, but as they heard no sound of shots they were sure that they were now safe beyond the Mexican lines.

"I don't want to discourage anybody," said Bowie, "but I'm not hoping much from the messengers. The Texans are scattered too widely."

"No, they can't bring many," said Crockett, "but every man counts. Sometimes it takes mighty little to turn the tale, and they may turn it."

"I hope so," said Bowie.

The Mexican cannon were silent that night and Ned slept deeply, awaking only when the dawn of a clear day came. He was astonished at the quickness with which he grew used to a state of siege and imminent danger. All the habits of life now went on as usual. He ate breakfast with as good an appetite as if he had been out on the prairie with his friends, and he talked with his new comrades as if Santa Anna and his army were a thousand miles away.

But when he did go upon the church wall he saw that Santa Anna had begun work again and at a new place. The Mexican general, having seen that his artillery was doing no damage, was making a great effort to get within much closer range where the balls would count. Men protected by heavy planking or advancing along trenches were seeking to erect a battery within less than three hundred yards of the entrance to the main plaza. They had already thrown up a part of a breastwork. Meanwhile the Texan sharpshooters were waiting for a chance.

Ned took no part in it except that of a spectator. But Crockett, Bowie and a dozen others were crouched on the wall with their rifles. Presently an incautious Mexican showed above the earthwork. It was Crockett who slew him, but Bowie took the next. Then the other rifles flashed fast, eight or ten Mexicans were slain, and the rest fled. Once more the deadly Texan rifles had triumphed.

Ned wondered why Santa Anna had endeavored to place the battery there in the daytime. It could be done at night, when it was impossible for the Texans to aim their rifles so well. He did not know that the pride of Santa Anna, unable to brook delay in the face of so small a force, had pushed him forward.

Knowing now what might be done at night, Ned passed the day in anxiety, and with the coming of the twilight his anxiety increased.

CHAPTER X.
CROCKETT AND BOWIE

Unluckily for the Texans, the night was the darkest of the month. No bonfires burned in San Antonio, and there were no sounds of music. It seemed to Ned that the silence and darkness were sure indications of action on the part of the foe.

He felt more lonely and depressed than at any other time hitherto in the siege, and he was glad when Crockett and a young Tennesseean whom he called the Bee-Hunter joined him. Crockett had not lost any of his whimsical good humor, and when Ned suggested that Santa Anna was likely to profit by the dark he replied:

"If he is the general I take him to be he will, or at least try, but meanwhile we'll just wait, an' look, an' listen. That's the way to find out if things are goin' to happen. Don't turn little troubles into big ones. You don't need a cowskin for a calf. We'll jest rest easy. I'm mighty nigh old enough to be your grandfather, Ned, an' I've learned to take things as they come. I guess men of my age were talkin' this same way five thousand years ago."

"You've seen a lot in your life, Mr. Crockett," said Ned, to whom the Tennesseean was a great hero.

Crockett laughed low, but deep in his throat, and with much pleasure.

"So I have! So I have!" he replied, "an', by the blue blazes, I can say it without braggin'. I've seen a lot of water go by since I was runnin' 'roun' a bare-footed boy in Tennessee. I've ranged pretty far from east to west, an' all the way from Boston in the north to this old mission, an' that must be some thousands of miles. An' I've had some big times in New York, too."

"You've been in New York," said Ned, with quick interest. "It must be a great town."

"It is. It's certainly a bulger of a place. There are thousands an' thousands of houses, an' you can't count the sails in the bay. I saw the City Hall an' it's a mighty fine buildin', too. It's all marble on the side looking south, an' plain stone on the side lookin' north. I asked why, an' they said all the poor people lived to the north of it. That's the way things often happen, Ned. An' I saw the great, big hotel John Jacob Astor was beginnin' to build on Broadway just below the City Hall. They said it would cost seven hundred thousand dollars, which is an all-fired lot of money, that it would cover mighty nigh a whole block, an' that there would be nothin' else in America comin' up to it."

"I'd like to see that town," said Ned.

"Maybe you will some day," said Crockett, "'cause you're young. You don't know how young you look to me. I heard a lot there, Ned, about that rich man, Mr. Astor. He got his start as a fur trader. I guess he was about the biggest fur trader that ever was. He was so active that all them animals that wore furs on their backs concluded they might as well give up. I heard one story there about an otter an' a beaver talkin'. Says the otter to the beaver, when he was tellin' the beaver good-by after a visit: 'Farewell, I never expect to see you again, my dear old friend.' 'Don't be too much distressed,' replies the beaver, 'you an' I, old comrade, will soon meet at the hat store.'"

Ned and the Bee-Hunter laughed, and Crockett delved again into his past life and his experiences in the great city, relatively as great then to the whole country as it is now.

"I saw a heap of New York," he continued, "an' one of the things I liked best in it was the theaters. Lad, I saw the great Fanny Kemble play there, an' she shorely was one of the finest women that ever walked this troubled earth. I saw her first as Portia in that play of Shakespeare's called, called, called——"

"'The Merchant of Venice,'" suggested Ned.

"Yes, that's it, 'The Merchant of Venice,' where she was the woman lawyer. She was fine to see, an' the way she could change her voice an' looks was clean mirac'lous. If ever I need a lawyer I want her to act for me. She had me mad, an' then she had me laughin', an' then she had the water startin' in my eyes. Whatever she wanted me to see I saw, an' whatever she wanted me to think I thought. An' then, too, she was many kinds of a woman, different in turn. In fact, Ned, she was just like a handsome piece of changeable silk—first one color an' then another, but always clean."

He paused and the others did not interrupt him.

"I don't like cities," he resumed presently. "They crowd me up too much, but I do like the theater. It makes you see so many things an' so many kinds of people that you wouldn't have time to see if you had to travel for 'em. We don't have much chance to travel right now, do we, Bee-Hunter?"

"A few hundred yards only for our bodies," replied the young Tennesseean, "but our spirits soar far;

"'Up with your banner, Freedom,
Thy champions cling to thee,
They'll follow where'er you lead them
To death or victory.
Up with your banner, Freedom.'"

He merely hummed the words, but Ned caught his spirit and he repeated to himself: "Up with your banner, Freedom."

"I guess you've heard enough tales from an old fellow like me," said Crockett. "At least you won't have time to hear any more 'cause the Mexicans must be moving out there. Do you hear anything, Ned?"

"Nothing but a little wind."

"Then my ears must be deceivin' me. I've used 'em such a long time that I guess they feel they've got a right to trick me once in a while."

But Ned was thinking just then of the great city which he wanted to see some day as Crockett had seen it. But it seemed to him at that moment as far away as the moon. Would his comrades and he ever escape from those walls?

His mind came back with a jerk. He did hear something on the plain. Crockett was right. He heard the tread of horses and the sound of wheels moving. He called the attention of Crockett to the noises.

"I think I know what causes them," said Crockett. "Santa Anna is planting his battery under the cover of the night an' I don't see, boys, how we're goin' to keep him from doin' it."

The best of the Texan sharpshooters lined the walls, and they fired occasionally at indistinct and flitting figures, but they were quite certain that they did no execution. The darkness was too great. Travis, Bowie and Crockett considered the possibility of a sortie, but they decided that it had no chance of success. The few score Texans would be overwhelmed in the open plain by the thousands of Mexicans.

But all the leaders were uneasy. If the Mexican batteries were brought much closer, and were protected by earthworks and other fortifications, the Alamo would be much less defensible. It was decided to send another messenger for help, and Ned saw Bonham drop over the rear wall and slip away in the darkness. He was to go to Goliad, where Fannin had 300 men and four guns, and bring them in haste.

When Bonham was gone Ned returned to his place on the wall. For hours he heard the noises without, the distant sound of voices, the heavy clank of metal against metal, and he knew full well that Santa Anna was planting his batteries. At last he went to his place in the long room of the hospital and slept.

When dawn came he sprang up and rushed to the wall. There was the battery of Santa Anna only three hundred yards from the entrance to the main plaza and to the southeast, but little further away, was another. The Mexicans had worked well during the night.

"They're creepin' closer, Ned. They're creepin' closer," said Crockett, who had come to the wall before him, "but even at that range I don't think their cannon will do us much harm. Duck, boy, duck! They're goin' to fire!"

The two batteries opened at the same time, and the Mexican masses in the rear, out of range, began a tremendous cheering. Many of the balls and shells now fell inside the mission, but the Texans stayed well under cover and they still escaped without harm. The Mexican gunners, in their turn, kept so well protected that the Texan riflemen had little chance.

The great bombardment lasted an hour, but when it ceased, and the smoke lifted, Ned saw a heavy mass of Mexican cavalry on the eastern road.

Both Ned and Crockett took a long look at the cavalry, a fine body of men, some carrying lances and others muskets. Ned believed that he recognized Urrea in the figure of their leader, but the distance was too great for certainty. But when he spoke of it to Crockett the Tenesseean borrowed Travis' field glasses.

"Take these," he said, "an' if it's that beloved enemy of yours you can soon tell."

The boy, with the aid of the glasses, recognized Urrea at once. The young leader in the uniform of a Mexican captain and with a cocked and plumed hat upon his head sat his horse haughtily. Ned knew that he was swelling with pride and that he, like Santa Anna, expected the trap to shut down on the little band of Texans in a day or two. He felt some bitterness that fate should have done so much for Urrea.

"I judge by your face," said Crockett whimsically, "that it is Urrea. But remember, Ned, that you can still be hated and live long."

"It is indeed Urrea," said Ned. "Now what are they gathering cavalry out there for? They can't expect to gallop over our walls."

"Guess they've an idea that we're goin' to try to slip out an' they're shuttin' up that road of escape. Seems to me, Ned, they're comin' so close that it's an insult to us."

"They're almost within rifle shot."

"Then these bad little Mexican boys must have their faces scorched as a lesson. Just you wait here, Ned, till I have a talk with Travis an' Bowie."

It was obvious to Ned that Crockett's talk with the commander and his second was satisfactory, because when he returned his face was in a broad grin. Bowie, moreover, came with him, and his blue eyes were lighted up with the fire of battle.

"We're goin' to teach 'em the lesson, Ned, beginnin' with a b c," said Crockett, "an' Jim here, who has had a lot of experience in Texas, will lead us. Come along, I'll watch over you."

A force of seventy or eighty was formed quickly, and hidden from the view of the Mexicans, they rushed down the plaza, climbed the low walls and dropped down upon the plain. The Mexican cavalry outnumbered them four or five to one, but the Texans cared little for such odds.

"Now, boys, up with your rifles!" cried Bowie. "Pump it into 'em!"

Bowie was a product of the border, hard and desperate, a man of many fierce encounters, but throughout the siege he had been singularly gentle and considerate in his dealings with his brother Texans. Now he was all warrior again, his eyes blazing with blue fire while he shouted vehement words of command to his men.

The sudden appearance of the Texan riflemen outside the Alamo look Urrea by surprise, but he was quick of perception and action, and his cavalrymen were the best in the Mexican army. He wheeled them into line with a few words of command and shouted to them to charge. Bowie's men instantly stopped, forming a rough line, and up went their rifles. Urrea's soldiers who carried rifles or muskets opened a hasty and excited fire at some distance.

Ned heard the bullets singing over his head or saw them kicking up dust in front of the Texans, but only one of the Texans fell and but few were wounded. The Mexican rifles or muskets were now empty, but the Mexican lancers came on in good order and in an almost solid group, the yellow sunlight flashing across the long blades of their lances.

It takes a great will to face sharp steel in the hands of horsemen thundering down upon you, and Ned was quite willing to own afterward that every nerve in him was jumping, but he stood. All stood, and at the command of Bowie their rifles flashed together in one tremendous explosion.

The rifles discharged, the Texans instantly snatched out their pistols, ready for anything that might come galloping through the smoke. But nothing came. When the smoke lifted they saw that the entire front of the Mexican column was gone. Fallen men and horses were thick on the plain and long lances lay across them. Other horses, riderless, were galloping away to right and left, and unhorsed men were running to the rear. But Urrea had escaped unharmed. Ned saw him trying to reform his shattered force.

"Reload your rifles, men!" shouted Bowie. "You can be ready for them before they come again!"

These were skilled sharpshooters, and they rammed the loads home with startling rapidity. Every rifle was loaded and a finger was on every trigger when the second charge of Urrea swept down upon them. No need of a command from Bowie now. The Texans picked their targets and fired straight into the dense group. Once more the front of the Mexican column was shot away, and the lances fell clattering on the plain.

"At 'em, boys, with your pistols!" shouted Bowie. "Don't give 'em a second chance!"

The Texans rushed forward, firing their pistols. Ned in the smoke became separated from his comrades, and when he could see more clearly he beheld but a single horseman. The man was Urrea.

The two recognized each other instantly. The Mexican had the advantage. He was on horseback and the smoke was in Ned's eyes, not his own. With a shout of triumph, he rode straight at the boy and made a fierce sweep with his cavalry saber. It was fortunate for Ned that he was agile of both body and mind. He ducked and leaped to one side. He felt the swish of the heavy steel over his head, but as he came up again he fired.

Urrea was protected largely by his horse's neck, and Ned fired at the horse instead, although he would have greatly preferred Urrea as a target. The bullet struck true and the horse fell, but the rider leaped clear and, still holding the saber, sprang at his adversary. Ned snatched up his rifle, which lay on the ground at his feet, and received the slash of the sword upon its barrel. The blade broke in two, and then, clubbing his rifle, Ned struck.

It was fortunate for Urrea, too, that he was agile of mind and body. He sprang back quickly, but the butt of the rifle grazed his head and drew blood. The next moment other combatants came between, and Urrea dashed away in search of a fresh horse. Ned, his blood on fire, was rushing after him, when Bowie seized his arm and pulled him back.

"No further, Ned!" he cried. "We've scattered their cavalry and we must get back into the Alamo or the whole Mexican army will be upon us!"

Ned heard far away the beat of flying hoofs. It was made by the horses of the Mexican cavalry fleeing for their lives. Bowie quickly gathered together his men, and carrying with them two who had been slain in the fight they retreated rapidly to the Alamo, the Texan cannon firing over their heads at the advancing Mexican infantry. In three or four minutes they were inside the walls again and with their comrades.

The Mexican cavalry did not reappear upon the eastern road, and the Texans were exultant, yet they had lost two good men and their joy soon gave way to more solemn feelings. It was decided to bury the slain at once in the plaza, and a common grave was made for them. They were the first of the Texans to fall in the defence, and their fate made a deep impression upon everybody.

It took only a few minutes to dig the grave, and the men, laid side by side, were covered with their cloaks. While the spades were yet at work the Mexican cannon opened anew upon the Alamo. A ball and a bomb fell in the plaza. The shell burst, but fortunately too far away to hurt anybody. Neither the bursting of the shell nor any other part of the cannonade interrupted the burial.

Crockett, a public man and an orator, said a few words. They were sympathetic and well chosen. He spoke of the two men as dying for Texas. Others, too, would fall in the defence of the Alamo, but their blood would water the tree of freedom. Then they threw in the dirt. While Crockett was speaking the cannon still thundered without, but every word could be heard distinctly.

When Ned walked away he felt to the full the deep solemnity of the moment. Hitherto they had fought without loss to themselves. The death of the two men now cast an ominous light over the situation. The Mexican lines were being drawn closer and closer about the Alamo, and he was compelled to realize the slenderness of their chances.

The boy resumed his place on the wall, remaining throughout the afternoon, and watched the coming of the night. Crockett joined him, and together they saw troops of Mexicans marching away from the main body, some to right and some to left.

"Stretchin' their lines," said Crockett. "Santa Anna means to close us in entirely after a while. Now, by the blue blazes, that was a close shave!"

A bullet sang by his head and flattened against the wall. He and Ned dropped down just in time. Other bullets thudded against the stone. Nevertheless, Ned lifted his head above the edge of the parapet and took a look. His eyes swept a circle and he saw little puffs of smoke coming from the roofs and windows of the jacals or Mexican huts on their side of the river. He knew at once that the best of the Mexican sharpshooters had hidden themselves there, and had opened fire not with muskets, but with improved rifles. He called Crockett's attention to this point of danger and the frontiersman grew very serious.

"We've got to get 'em out some way or other," he said. "As I said before, the cannon balls make a big fuss, but they don't come so often an' they come at random. It's the little bullets that have the sting of the wasp, an' when a man looks down the sights, draws a bead on you, an' sends one of them lead pellets at you, he gen'rally gets you. Ned, we've got to drive them fellers out of there some way or other."

The bullets from the jacals now swept the walls and the truth of Crockett's words became painfully evident. The Texan cannon fired upon the huts, but the balls went through the soft adobe and seemed to do no harm. It was like firing into a great sponge. Triumphant shouts came from the Mexicans. Their own batteries resumed the cannonade, while their sheltered riflemen sent in the bullets faster and faster.

Crockett tapped the barrel of Betsy significantly.

"The work has got to be done with this old lady an' others like her," he said. "We must get rid of them jacals."

"How?" asked Ned.

"You come along with me an' I'll show you," said Crockett. "I'm goin' to have a talk with Travis, an' if he agrees with me we'll soon wipe out that wasps' nest."

Crockett briefly announced his plan, which was bold in the extreme. Sixty picked riflemen, twenty of whom bore torches also, would rush out at one of the side gates, storm the jacals, set fire to them, and then rush back to the Alamo.

Travis hesitated. The plan seemed impossible of execution in face of the great Mexican force. But Bowie warmly seconded Crockett, and at last the commander gave his consent. Ned at once asked to go with the daring troop, and secured permission. The band gathered in a close body by one of the gates. The torches were long sticks lighted at the end and burning strongly. The men had already cocked their rifles, but knowing the immense risk they were about to take they were very quiet. Ned was pale, and his heart beat painfully, but his hand did not shake.

The Texan cannon, to cover the movement, opened fire from the walls, and the riflemen, posted at various points, helped also. The Mexican cannonade increased. When the thunder and crash were at their height the gate was suddenly thrown open and the sixty dashed out. Fortunately the drifting smoke hid them partially, and they were almost upon the jacals before they were discovered.

A great shout came from the Mexicans when they saw the daring Texans outside, and bullets from the jacals began to knock up grass and dust about them. But Crockett himself, waving a torch, led them on, shouting:

"It's only a step, boys! It's only a step! Now, let 'em have it!"

The Texans fired as they rushed, but they took care to secure good aim. The Mexicans were driven from the roofs and the windows and then the Texans carrying the torches dashed inside. Every house contained something inflammable, which was quickly set on fire, and two or three huts made of wood were lighted in a dozen places.

The dry materials blazed up fast. A light wind fanned the flames, which joined together and leaped up, a roaring pyramid. The Mexicans, who had lately occupied them, were scuttling like rabbits toward their main force, and the Texan bullets made them jump higher and faster.

Crockett, with a shout of triumph, flung down his torch.

"Now, boys," he cried. "Here's the end of them jacals. Nothin' on earth can put out that fire, but if we don't make a foot race back to the Alamo the end of us will be here, too, in a minute."

The little band wheeled for its homeward rush. Ned heard a great shout of rage from the Mexicans, and then the hissing and singing of shells and cannon balls over his head. He saw Mexicans running across the plain to cut them off, but his comrades and he had reloaded their rifles, and as they ran they sent a shower of bullets that drove back their foe.

Ned's heart was pumping frightfully, and myriads of black specks danced before his eyes, but he remembered afterward that he calculated how far they were from the Alamo, and how far the Mexicans were from them. A number of his comrades had been wounded, but nobody had fallen and they still raced in a close group for the gate, which seemed to recede as they rushed on.

"A few more steps, Ned," cried Crockett, "an' we're in! Ah, there go our friends!"

The Texan cannon over their heads now fired into the pursuing Mexican masses, and the sharpshooters on the walls also poured in a deadly hail. The Mexicans recoiled once more and then Crockett's party made good the gate.

"All here!" cried Crockett, as those inside held up torches. He ran over the list rapidly himself and counted them all, but his face fell when he saw his young friend the Bee-Hunter stagger. Crockett caught him in his arms and bore him into the hospital. He and Ned watched by his side until he died, which was very soon. Before he became unconscious he murmured some lines from an old Scotch poem:

"But hame came the saddle, all bluidy to see.
And hame came the steed, but never hame came he."

They buried him that night beside the other two, and Ned was more solemn than ever when he sought his usual place in the hospital by the wall. It had been a day of victory for the Texans, but the omens, nevertheless, seemed to him to be bad.

The next day he saw the Mexicans spreading further and further about the Alamo, and they were in such strong force that the Texans could not now afford to go out and attack any of these bands. A light cold rain fell, and as he was not on duty he went back to the hospital, where he sat in silence.

He was deeply depressed and the thunder of the Mexican cannon beat upon his ears like the voice of doom. He felt a strange annoyance at the reports of the guns. His nerves jumped, and he became angry with himself at what he considered a childish weakness.

Now, and for the first time, he felt despair. He borrowed a pencil and a sheet of paper torn from an old memorandum book and made his will. His possessions were singularly few, and the most valuable at hand was his fine long-barreled rifle, which he left to his faithful friend, Obed White. He bequeathed his pistol and knife to the Panther, and his clothes to Will Allen. He was compelled to smile at himself when he had finished his page of writing. Was it likely that his friends would ever find this paper, or, if finding it, was it likely that any one of them could ever obtain his inheritance? But it was a relief to his feelings and, folding the paper, he put it in the inside pocket of his hunting shirt.

The bombardment was renewed in the afternoon, but Ned stayed in his place in the hospital. After a while Davy Crockett and several others joined him there. Crockett as usual was jocular, and told more stories of his trips to the large eastern cities. He had just finished an anecdote of Philadelphia, when he turned suddenly to Ned.

"Boy," he said, "you and I have fought together more than once now, an' I like you. You are brave an' you've a head full of sense. When you grow older you'll be worth a lot to Texas. They'll need you in the council. No, don't protest. This is the time when we can say what is in us. The Mexican circle around the Alamo is almost complete. Isn't that so, boys?"

"It is."

"Then I'll say what we all know. Three or four days from now the chances will be a hundred to one against any of us ever gettin' out of here. An' you're the youngest of the defence, Ned, so I want you to slip out to-night while there's yet time. Mebbe you can get up a big lot of men to come to our help."

Ned looked straight at Crockett, and the veteran's eyes wavered.

"It's a little scheme you have," said Ned, "to get me out of the way. You think because I'm the youngest I ought to go off alone at night and save my own life. Well, I'm not going. I intend to stay here and fight it out with the rest of you."

"I meant for the best, boy, I meant for the best," said Crockett. "I'm an old fellow an' I've had a terrible lot of fun in my time. About as much, I guess, as one man is entitled to, but you've got all your life before you."

"Couldn't think of it," said Ned lightly; "besides, I've got a password in case I'm taken by Santa Anna."

"What's that?" asked Crockett curiously.

"It's the single word 'Roylston.' Mr. Roylston told me if I were taken by Santa Anna to mention his name to him."

"That's queer, an' then maybe it ain't," said Crockett musingly. "I've heard a lot of John Roylston. He's about the biggest trader in the southwest. I guess he must have some sort of a financial hold on Santa Anna, who is always wantin' money. Ned, if the time should ever come, don't you forget to use that password."

The next night was dark and chilly with gusts of rain. In the afternoon the Mexican cannonade waned, and at night it ceased entirely. The Alamo itself, except for a few small lights within the buildings, was kept entirely dark in order that skulking sharpshooters without might not find a target.

Ned was on watch near one of the lower walls about the plaza. He wrapped his useful serape closely about his body and the lower part of his face in order to protect himself from the cold and wet, and the broad brim of his sombrero was drawn down to meet it. The other Texans on guard were protected in similar fashion, and in the flitting glimpses that Ned caught of them they looked to him like men in disguise.

The time went on very slowly. In the look backward every hour in the Alamo seemed to him as ten. He walked back and forth a long time, occasionally meeting other sentinels, and exchanging a few words with them. Once he glanced at their cattle, which were packed closely under a rough shed, where they lay, groaning with content. Then he went back to the wall and noticed the dim figure of one of the sentinels going toward the convent yard and the church.

Ned took only a single glance at the man, but he rather envied him. The man was going off duty early, and he would soon be asleep in a warm place under a roof. He did not think of him again until a full hour later, when he, too, going off duty, saw a figure hidden in serape and sombrero passing along the inner edge of the plaza. The walk and figure reminded him of the man whom he had seen an hour before, and he wondered why any one who could have been asleep under shelter should have returned to the cold and rain.

He decided to follow, but the figure flitted away before him down the plaza and toward the lowest part of the wall. This was doubly curious. Moreover, it was ground for great suspicion. Ned followed swiftly. He saw the figure mounting the wall, as if to take position there as a sentinel, and then the truth came to him in a flash. It was Urrea playing the congenial role of spy.

Ned rushed forward, shouting. Urrea turned, snatched a pistol and fired. The bullet whistled past Ned's head. The next moment Urrea dropped over the wall and fled away in the darkness. The other sentinels were not able to obtain a shot at him.

CHAPTER XI.
THE DESPERATE DEFENCE

Ned's report created some alarm among the defenders of the Alamo, but it passed quickly.

"I don't see just how it can help 'em," said Crockett. "He's found out that we're few in number. They already knew that. He's learned that the Alamo is made up of a church an' other buildings with walls 'roun' them. They already knew that, too, an' so here we all are, Texans an' Mexicans, just where we stood before."

Nevertheless, the bombardment rose to a fiercer pitch of intensity the next day. The Mexicans seemed to have an unlimited supply of ammunition, and they rained balls and shells on the Alamo. Many of the shells did not burst, and the damage done was small. The Texans did not reply from the shelter of their walls for a long time. At last the Mexicans came closer, emboldened perhaps by the thought that resistance was crushed, and then the Texan sharpshooters opened fire with their long-barreled rifles.

The Texans had two or three rifles apiece, and they poured in a fast and deadly fire. So many of the Mexicans fell that the remainder retreated with speed, leaving the fallen behind them. But when the smoke lifted others came forward under a white flag, and the Texans allowed them to take away their dead.

The cannonade now became spasmodic. All the Mexican cannon would fire continuously for a half hour or so, and then would ensue a silence of perhaps an hour.

In the afternoon Bowie was taken very ill, owing to his great exertions, and a bed was made for him in the hospital. Ned sat there with him a while. The gentle mood that had distinguished the Georgian throughout the siege was even more marked now.

"Ned," he said, "you ought to have gone out the other night when we wanted you to go. Fannin may come to our help or he may not, but even if he should come I don't think his force is sufficient. It would merely increase the number of Texans in the trap."

"I've quite made up my mind that I won't go," said Ned.

"I'm sorry," said Bowie. "As for me, it's different. I'm a man of violence, Ned. I don't deny it. There's human blood on my hands, and some of it is that of my own countrymen. I've done things that I'd like to call back, and so I'm glad to be here, one of a forlorn hope, fighting for Texas. It's a sort of atonement, and if I fall I think it will be remembered in my favor."

Ned was singularly impressed. Crockett had talked in much the same way. Could these men, heroes of a thousand dangers, have really given up? Not to give up in the sense of surrender, but to expect death fighting? But for himself he could not believe such a thing possible. Youth was too strong in him.

He was on the watch again for part of the next night, and he and Crockett were together. They heard sounds made by the besiegers on every side of them. Mexicans were calling to Mexicans. Bridle bits rattled, and metal clanked against metal.

"I suppose the circle is complete," said Ned.

"Looks like it," said Crockett, "but we've got our cattle to eat an' water to drink an' only a direct attack in force can take us. They can bang away with their cannon till next Christmas an' they won't shake our grip on the Alamo."

The night was fairly dark, and an hour later Ned heard a whistle. Crockett heard it, too, and stiffened instantly into attention.

"Did that sound to you like a Mexican whistling?" he asked.

"No, I'd say it came from American lips, and I'd take it also for a signal."

"An' so it is. It's just such a whistle as hunters use when they want to talk to one another without words. I've whistled to my pardners that way in the woods hundreds of times. I think, Ned, that some Texans are at hand waitin' a chance to slip in."

Crockett emitted a whistle, low but clear and penetrating, almost like the song of a night bird, and in a half minute came the rejoinder. He replied to it briefly, and then they waited. Others had gathered at the low plaza wall with them. Hidden to the eyes, they peered over the parapet.

They heard soft footsteps in the darkness, and then dim forms emerged. Despite the darkness they knew them to be Texans, and Crockett spoke low:

"Here we are, boys, waitin' for you! This way an' in a half minute you're in the Alamo!"

The men ran forward, scaled the wall and were quickly inside. They were only thirty-two. Ned had thought that the Panther, Obed, and Will Allen might be among them, but they were not there. The new men were shaking hands with the others and were explaining that they had come from Gonzales with Captain Smith at their head. They were all well armed, carried much ammunition, and were sure that other parties would arrive from different points.

The thirty-two were full of rejoicings over their successful entry, but they were worn, nevertheless, and they were taken into one of the buildings, where food and water were set before them. Ned stood by, an eager auditor, as they told of their adventures.

"We had a hard time to get in here to you," said Captain Smith, "and from the looks of things I reckon we'll have as hard a time to get out. There must be a million Mexicans around the Alamo. We tried to get up a bigger force, but we couldn't gather any more without waiting, and we thought if you needed us at all you needed us in a hurry."

"Reckon you're right about the need of bein' in a hurry," said Crockett. "When you want help you want it right then an' there."

"So you do," said Smith, as he took a fresh piece or steak, "and we had it in mind all the time. The wind was blowing our way, and in the afternoon we heard the roaring of cannon a long distance off. Then as we came closer we heard Mexicans buzzing all around the main swarm, scouts and skirmishers everywhere.

"We hid in an arroyo and waited until dark. Then we rode closer and found that there would never be any chance to get into the Alamo on horseback. We took the saddles and bridles off our horses, and turned them loose on the prairie. Then we undertook to get in here, but it was touch and go. I tell you it was touch and go. We wheeled and twisted and curved and doubled, until our heads got dizzy. Wherever we went we found Mexicans, thousands of 'em."

"We've noticed a few ourselves," said Crockett.

"It was pretty late when we struck an opening, and then not being sure we whistled. When we heard you whistle back we made straight for the wall, and here we are."

"We're mighty glad to see you," said Crockett, "but we ain't welcomin' you to no picnic, I reckon you understand that, don't you, Jim Smith?"

"We understand it, every one of us," replied Smith gravely. "We heard before we started, and now we've seen. We know that Santa Anna himself is out there, and that the Mexicans have got a big army. That's the reason we came, Davy Crockett, because the odds are so heavy against you."

"You're a true man," said Crockett, "and so is every one of these with you."

The new force was small—merely a few more for the trap—but they brought with them encouragement. Ned shared in the general mental uplift. These new faces were very welcome, indeed. They gave fresh vigor to the little garrison, and they brought news of that outside world from which he seemed to have been shut off so long. They told of numerous parties sure to come to their relief, but he soon noticed that they did not particularize. He felt with certainty that the Alamo now had all the defenders that it would ever have.

Repeated examinations from the walls of the church confirmed Ned in his belief. The Mexican circle was complete, and their sheltered batteries were so near that they dropped balls and shells whenever they pleased inside the Alamo. Duels between the cannon and the Texan sharpshooters were frequent. The gunners as they worked their guns were forced to show themselves at times, and every exposure was instantly the signal for a Texan bullet which rarely missed. But the Mexicans kept on. It seemed that they intended to wear out the defenders by the sheer persistency of their cannon fire.

Ned became so hardened to the bombardment that he paid little attention to it. Even when a ball fell inside the Alamo the chances were several hundred to one that it would not hit him. He had amused himself with a mathematical calculation of the amount of space he occupied compared with the amount of space in the Alamo. Thus he arrived at the result, which indicated comparatively little risk for himself.

The shrewdest calculations are often wrong. As he passed through the convent yard he met Crockett, and the two walked on together. But before they had gone half a dozen steps a bomb hissed through the air, fell and rolled to their feet. It was still hissing and smoking, but Ned, driven by some unknown impulse, seized it and with a mighty effort hurled it over the wall, where it burst. Then he stood licking his burned fingers and looking rather confusedly at Crockett. He felt a certain shyness over what he had done.

The veteran frontiersman had already formed a great affection for the boy. He knew that Ned's impulse had come from a brave heart and a quick mind, and that he had probably saved both their lives. He took a great resolution that this boy, the youngest of all the defenders, should be saved.

"That was done well, Ned," he said quietly. "I'm glad, boy, that I've known you. I'd be proud if you were a son of mine. We can talk plainly here with death all around us. You've got a lot in that head of yours. You ought to make a great man, a great man for Texas. Won't you do what I say and slip out of the Alamo while there's still a chance?"

Ned was much moved, but he kept his resolution as he had kept it before. He shook his head.

"You are all very good to me here," he said. "Mr. Bowie, too, has asked me to go, but if I should do so and the rest of you were to fall I'd be ashamed of myself all the rest of my life. I'm a Texan now, and I'm going to see it through with the rest of you."

"All right," said Crockett lightly. "I've heard that you can lead a horse to the water, but you can't make him drink, an' if a boy don't want to go you can't make him go. So we'll just go into this little improvised armory of ours, an' you an' I will put in our time moldin' bullets."

They entered one of the adobe buildings. A fire had been built on the hearth, and a half dozen Texans were already busy there. But they quickly made room for Crockett and Ned. Crockett did not tell Ned that their supplies of powder and lead were running low, and that they must reduce their fire from the walls in order that they might have sufficient to meet an attack in force.

But it was a cheerful little party that occupied itself with molding bullets. Ned put a bar of lead into a ladle, and held it over the fire until the bar became molten. Then he poured it into the mold until it was full, closed it, and when he opened it again a shining bullet dropped out. He worked hour after hour. His face became flushed with the heat, but with pride he watched his heap of bullets grow.

Crockett at last said they had done enough for one day, and Ned was glad when they went outside and breathed the fresh air again. There was no firing at that time, and they climbed once more upon the church wall. Ned looked out upon the scene, every detail of which was so familiar to him now. But conspicuous, and seeming to dominate all, was the blood-red flag of no quarter floating from the tower of the church of San Fernando. Wind and rain had not dimmed its bright color. The menace in its most vivid hue was always there.

Travis, who was further along the wall with a pair of strong field glasses, came back and joined Ned and Crockett.

"If you would like to see Santa Anna you can," he said to Ned. "He is on the church of San Fernando now with his generals looking at us. Take these glasses and your gaze may meet his."

Ned took the glasses, and there was Santa Anna standing directly under the folds of the banner with his own glasses to his eyes, studying the Alamo and its defenders. About him stood a half dozen generals. Ned's heart swelled with anger. The charm and genius of Santa Anna made him all the more repellent now. Ned knew that he would break any promise if it suited him, and that cunning and treachery were his most potent tools.

Santa Anna, at that very moment, was discussing with Sesma, Cos, Gaona and others the question of an immediate assault with his whole army upon the Alamo. They had heard rumors of an advance by Fannin with help for the Texans, but, while some of the younger spirits wished prompt attack, Santa Anna decided on delay.

The dictator doubted whether Fannin would come up, and if he did he would merely put so many more rats in the trap. Santa Anna felt secure in his vast preponderance of numbers. He would take the Texans in his own good time, that is, whenever he felt like it. He did not care to hurry, because he was enjoying himself greatly in San Antonio. Capable of tremendous energy at times, he gave himself up at other times to Babylonian revels.

Ned handed the glasses to Crockett, who also took a long look.

"I've heard a lot of Santa Anna," he said, "an' maybe I'll yet meet him eye to eye."

"It's possible," said Travis, "but, Davy, we've got to wait on the Mexicans. It's always for them to make the move, and then we'll meet it if we can. I wish we could hear from Bonham. I'm afraid he's been taken."

"Not likely," said Crockett. "One man, all alone, an' as quick of eye an' foot as Bonham, would be pretty sure to make his way safely."

"I certainly hope so," said Travis. "At any rate, I intend to send out another letter soon. If the Texans are made to realize our situation they will surely come, no matter how far away they may be."

"I hope they will," said Crockett. But Ned noticed that he did not seem to speak with any great amount of confidence. Balancing everything as well as he could, he did not see how much help could be expected. The Texan towns were tiny. The whole fringe of Texan settlements was small. The Texans were but fifty or sixty thousands against the seven or eight millions of Mexico, and now that they knew a great Mexican army was in Texas the scattered borderers would be hard put to it to defend themselves. He did not believe that in any event they could gather a force great enough to cut its way through the coil of Santa Anna's multitude.

But Travis' faith in Bonham, at least, was justified. The next night, about halfway between midnight and morning, in the darkest hour, a man scaled the wall and dropped inside the plaza. It proved to be Bonham himself, pale, worn, covered with mud and dust, but bringing glad tidings. Ned was present when he came into the church and was met by Travis. Bowie, Crockett and Smith. Only a single torch lighted up the grim little group.

"Fannin has left Goliad with 300 men and four cannon to join us," Bonham said. "He started five days ago, and he should be here soon. With his rifles and big guns he'll be able to cut his way through the Mexicans and enter the Alamo."

"I think so, too," said Travis, with enthusiasm.

But Ned steadily watched Bowie and Crockett. They were the men of experience, and in matters such as these they had minds of uncommon penetration. He noticed that neither of them said anything, and that they showed no elation.

Everybody in the Alamo knew the next day that Bonham had come from Fannin, and the whole place was filled with new hope. As Ned reckoned, it was about one hundred and fifty miles from San Antonio de Bexar to Goliad; but, according to Bonham, Fannin had already been five days on the way, and they should hear soon the welcome thunder of his guns. He eagerly scanned the southeast, in which direction lay Goliad, but the only human beings he saw were Mexicans. No sound came to his ears but the note of a Mexican trumpet or the crack of a vaquero's whip.

He was not the only one who looked and listened. They watched that day and the next through all the bombardment and the more dangerous rifle fire. But they never saw on the horizon the welcome flash from any of Fannin's guns. No sound that was made by a friend reached their ears. The only flashes of fire they saw outside were those that came from the mouths of Mexican cannon, and the only sounds they heard beyond the Alamo were made by the foe. The sun, huge, red and vivid, sank in the prairie and, as the shadows thickened over the Alamo, Ned was sure in his heart that Fannin would never come.

A few days before the defenders of the Alamo had begun to scan the southeast for help a body of 300 men were marching toward San Antonio de Bexar. They were clad in buckskin and they were on horseback. Their faces were tanned and bore all the signs of hardship. Near the middle of the column four cannon drawn by oxen rumbled along, and behind them came a heavy wagon loaded with ammunition.

It was raining, and the rain was the raw cold rain of early spring in the southwest. The men, protecting themselves as well as they could with cloaks and serapes, rarely spoke. The wheels of the cannon cut great ruts in the prairie, and the feet of the horses sank deep in the mud.

Two men and a boy rode near the head of the column. One of these would have attracted attention anywhere by his gigantic size. He was dressed completely in buckskin, save for the raccoon skin cap that crowned his thick black hair. The rider on his right hand was long and thin with the calm countenance of a philosopher, and the one on his left was an eager and impatient boy.

"I wish this rain would stop," said the Panther, his ensanguined eye expressing impatience and anger. "I don't mind gettin' cold an' I don't mind gettin' wet, but there is nothin' stickier or harder to plough through than the Texas mud. An' every minute counts. Them boys in that Alamo can't fight off thousands of Mexicans forever. Look at them steers! Did you ever see anything go as slow as they do?"

"I'd like to see Ned again," said Will Allen. "I'd be willing to take my chance with him there."

"That boy of ours is surely with Crockett and Bowie and Travis and the others, helping to fight off Santa Anna and his horde," said Obed White. "Bonham couldn't have made any mistake about him. If we had seen Bonham himself we could have gone with him to the Alamo."

"But he gave Ned's name to Colonel Fannin," said Will, "and so it's sure to be he."

"Our comrade is certainly there," said Obed White, "and we've got to help rescue him as well as help rescue the others. It's hard not to hurry on by ourselves, but we can be of most help by trying to push on this force, although it seems as if everything had conspired against us."

"It shorely looks as if things was tryin' to keep us back," exclaimed the Panther angrily. "We've had such a hard time gettin' these men together, an' look at this rain an' this mud! We ought to be at Bexar right now, a-roarin', an' a-t'arin', an' a-rippin', an' a-chawin' among them Mexicans!"

"Patience! Patience!" said Obed White soothingly. "Sometimes the more haste the oftener you trip."

"Patience on our part ain't much good to men sixty or eighty miles away, who need us yelling' an' shootin' for them this very minute."

"I'm bound to own that what you say is so," said Obed White.

They relapsed into silence. The pace of the column grew slower. The men were compelled to adapt themselves to the cannon and ammunition wagon, which were now almost mired. The face of the Panther grew black as thunder with impatience and anger, but he forced himself into silence.

They stopped a little while at noon and scanty rations were doled out. They had started in such haste that they had only a little rice and dried beef, and there was no time to hunt game.

They started again in a half hour, creeping along through the mud, and the Panther was not the only man who uttered hot words of impatience under his breath. They were nearing the San Antonio River now, and Fannin began to show anxiety about the fort. But the Panther was watching the ammunition wagon, which was sinking deeper and deeper into the mire. It seemed to him that it was groaning and creaking too much even for the deep mud through which it was passing.

The driver of the ammunition wagon cracked his long whip over the oxen and they tugged at the yoke. The wheels were now down to the hub, and the wagon ceased to move. The driver cracked his whip again and again, and the oxen threw their full weight into the effort. The wheels slowly rose from their sticky bed, but then something cracked with a report like a pistol shot. The Panther groaned aloud, because he knew what had happened.

The axle of the wagon had broken, and it was useless. They distributed the ammunition, including the cannon balls, which they put in sacks, as well as they could, among the horsemen, and went on. They did not complain, but every one knew that it was a heavy blow. In two more hours they came to the banks of the muddy San Antonio, and stared in dismay at the swollen current. It was evident at once to everybody that the passage would be most difficult for the cannon, which, like the ammunition wagon, were drawn by oxen.

The river was running deep, with muddy banks, and a muddy bottom, and, taking the lightest of the guns, they tried first to get it across. Many of the men waded neck deep into the water and strove at the wheels. But the stream went completely over the cannon, which also sank deeper and deeper in the oozy bottom. It then became an effort to save the gun. The Panther put all his strength at the wheel, and, a dozen others helping, they at last got it back to the bank from which they had started.

Fannin, not a man of great decision, looked deeply discouraged, but the Panther and others urged him on to new attempts. The Panther, himself, as he talked, bore the aspect of a huge river god. Yellow water streamed from his hair, beard, and clothing, and formed a little pool about him. But he noticed it not at all, urging the men on with all the fiery energy which a dauntless mind had stored in a frame so great and capable.

"If it can be done the Panther will get the guns across," said Will to Obed.

"That's so," said Obed, "but who'd have thought of this? When we started out we expected to have our big fight with an army and not with a river."

They took the cannon into the water a second time, but the result was the same. They could not get it across, and with infinite exertion they dragged it back to the bank. Then they looked at one another in despair. They could ford the river, but it seemed madness to go on without the cannon. While they debated there, a messenger came with news that the investment of the Alamo by Santa Anna was now complete. He gave what rumor said, and rumor told that the Mexican army numbered ten or twelve thousand men with fifty or sixty guns. Santa Anna's force was so great that already he was sending off large bodies to the eastward to attack Texan detachments wherever they could be found.

Fannin held an anxious council with his officers. It was an open talk on the open prairie, and anybody who chose could listen. Will Allen and Obed White said nothing, but the Panther was vehement.

"We've got to get there!" he exclaimed. "We can't leave our people to die in the Alamo! We've got to cut our way through, an', if the worst comes to the worst, die with them!"

"That would benefit nobody," said Fannin. "We've made every human effort to get our cannon across the river, and we have failed. It would not profit Texas for us to ride on with our rifles merely to be slaughtered. There will be other battles and other sieges, and we shall be needed."

"Does that mean we're not goin' on?" asked the Panther.

"We can't go on."

Fannin waved his hand at the yellow and swollen river.

"We must return to Goliad," he said, "I have decided. Besides, there is nothing else for us to do. About face, men, and take up the march."

The men turned slowly and reluctantly, and the cannon began to plough the mud on the road to Goliad, from which they had come.

The Panther had remounted, and he drew to one side with Will and Obed, who were also on their horses. His face was glowing with anger. Never had he looked more tremendous as he sat on his horse, with the water still flowing from him.

"Colonel Fannin," he called out, "you can go back to Goliad, but as for me an' my pardners, Obed White an' Will Allen, we're goin' to Bexar, an' the Alamo."

"I have no control over you," said Fannin, "but it would be much better for you three to keep with us."

"No," said the Panther firmly. "We hear the Alamo callin'. Into the river, boys, but keep your weapons an' ammunition dry."

Their horses, urged into the water, swam to the other bank, and, without looking back the three rode for San Antonio de Bexar.

While the Panther, Obed White and Will Allen were riding over the prairie, Ned Fulton sat once more with his friend. Davy Crockett, in one of the adobe buildings. Night had come, and they heard outside the fitful crackle of rifle fire, but they paid no attention to it. Travis, at a table with a small tallow candle at his elbow, was writing his last message.

Ned was watching the commander as he wrote. But he saw no expression of despair or even discouragement on Travis' fine face. The letter, which a messenger succeeded in carrying through the lines that night, breathed a noble and lofty courage. He was telling again how few were his men, and how the balls and bombs had rained almost continuously for days upon the Alamo. Even as his pen was poised they heard the heavy thud of a cannon, but the pen descended steadily and he wrote:

"I shall continue to hold it until I get relief from my countrymen, or perish in its defence."

He wrote on a little longer and once more came the heavy thud of a great gun. Then the pen wrote:

"Again I feel confident that the determined spirit and desperate courage heretofore exhibited by my men will not fail them in the last struggle, and, although they may be sacrificed to the vengeance of a Gothic enemy, the victory will cost that enemy so dear that it will be worse than a defeat."

"Worse than a defeat!" Travis never knew how significant were the words that he penned then. A minute or two later the sharp crack of a half dozen rifles came to them, and Travis wrote:

"A blood-red flag waves from the church of Bexar and in the camp above us, in token that the war is one of vengeance against rebels."

They heard the third heavy thud of a cannon, and a shell, falling in the court outside, burst with a great crash. Ned went out and returned with a report of no damage. Travis had continued his letter, and now he wrote:

"These threats have no influence upon my men, but to make all fight with desperation, and with that high-souled courage which characterizes the patriot who is willing to die in defence of his country, liberty and his own honor, God and Texas.

"Victory or death."

He closed the letter and addressed it. An hour later the messenger was beyond the Mexican lines with it, but Travis sat for a long time at the table, unmoving and silent. Perhaps he was blaming himself for not having been more watchful, for not having discovered the advance of Santa Anna. But he was neither a soldier nor a frontiersman, and since the retreat into the Alamo he had done all that man could do.

He rose at last and went out. Then Crockett said to Ned, knowing that it was now time to speak the full truth:

"He has given up all hope of help."

"So have I," said Ned.

"But we can still fight," said Crockett.

The day that followed was always like a dream to Ned, vivid in some ways, and vague in others. He felt that the coil around the Alamo had tightened. Neither he nor any one else expected aid now, and they spoke of it freely one to another. Several who could obtain paper wrote, as Ned had done, brief wills, which they put in the inside pockets of their coats. Always they spoke very gently to one another, these wild spirits of the border. The strange and softening shadow which Ned had noticed before was deepening over them all.

Bowie was again in the hospital, having been bruised severely in a fall from one of the walls, but his spirit was as dauntless as ever.

"The assault by the Mexicans in full force cannot be delayed much longer," he said to Ned. "Santa Anna is impatient and energetic, and he surely has brought up all his forces by this time."

"Do you think we can beat them off?" asked Ned.

Bowie hesitated a little, and then he replied frankly:

"I do not. We have only one hundred and seventy or eighty men to guard the great space that we have here. But in falling we will light such a flame that it will never go out until Texas is free."

Ned talked with him a little longer, and always Bowie spoke as if the time were at hand when he should die for Texas. The man of wild and desperate life seemed at this moment to be clothed about with the mantle of the seer.

The Mexican batteries fired very little that day, and Santa Anna's soldiers kept well out of range. They had learned a deep and lasting respect for the Texan rifles. Hundreds had fallen already before them, and now they kept under cover.

The silence seemed ominous and brooding to Ned. The day was bright, and the flag of no quarter burned a spot of blood-red against the blue sky. Ned saw Mexican officers occasionally on the roofs of the higher buildings, but he took little notice of them. He felt instinctively that the supreme crisis had not yet come. They were all waiting, waiting.

The afternoon drew its slow length away in almost dead silence, and the night came on rather blacker than usual. Then the word was passed for all to assemble in the courtyard. They gathered there, Bowie dragging his sick body with the rest. Every defender of the Alamo was present. The cannon and the walls were for a moment deserted, but the Mexicans without did not know it.

There are ineffaceable scenes in the life of every one, scenes which, after the lapse of many years, are as vivid as of yesterday. Such, the last meeting of the Texans, always remained in the mind of Ned. They stood in a group, strong, wiry men, but worn now by the eternal vigilance and danger of the siege. One man held a small torch, which cast but a dim light over the brown faces.

Travis stood before them and spoke to them.

"Men," he said, "all of you know what I know, that we stand alone. No help is coming for us. The Texans cannot send it or it would have come. For ten days we have beaten off every attack of a large army. But another assault in much greater force is at hand. It is not likely that we can repel it. You have seen the red flag of no quarter flying day after day over the church, and you know what it means. Santa Anna never gives mercy. It is likely that we shall all fall, but, if any man wishes to go, I, your leader, do not order him to stay. You have all done your duty ten times over. There is just a chance to escape over the walls and in the darkness. Now go and save your lives if you can."

"We stay," came the deep rumble of many voices together. One man slipped quietly away a little later, but he was the only one. Save for him, there was no thought of flight in the minds of that heroic band.

Ned's heart thrilled and the blood pounded in his ears. Life was precious, doubly so, because he was so young, but he felt a strange exaltation in the face of death, an exaltation that left no room for fear.

The eyes of Travis glistened when he heard the reply.

"It is what I expected," he said. "I knew that every one of you was willing to die for Texas. Now, lads, we will go back to the walls and wait for Santa Anna."

CHAPTER XII.
BEFORE THE DICTATOR

Ned's feeling of exaltation lasted. The long siege, the incessant danger and excitement, and the wonderful way in which the little band of Texans had kept a whole army at bay had keyed him up to a pitch in which he was not himself, in which he was something a little more than human. Such extraordinary moments come to few people, and his vivid, imaginative mind was thrilled to the utmost.

He was on the early watch, and he mounted the wall of the church. The deep silence which marked the beginning of the night still prevailed. They had not heard any shots, and for that reason they all felt that the messenger had got through with Travis' last letter.

It was very dark that night and Ned could not see the red flag on the tower of the church of San Fernando. But he knew it was there, waving a little in the soft wind which blew out of the southwest, herald of spring. Nothing broke the silence. After so much noise, it was ominous, oppressive, surcharged with threats. Fewer lights than usual burned in the town and in the Mexican camp. All this stillness portended to Ned the coming storm, and he was right.

His was a short watch, and at 11 o'clock he went off duty. It was silent and dark in the convent yard, and he sought his usual place for sleep in the hospital, where many of the Texans had been compelled to go, not merely to sleep, but because they were really ill, worn out by so many alarms, so much fighting and so much watching. But they were all now asleep, overpowered by exhaustion. Ned crept into his own dark little corner, and he, too, was soon asleep.

But he was awakened about four hours later by some one pulling hard at his shoulder. He opened his eyes, and stared sleepily. It was Crockett bending over him, and, Bowie lying on his sick bed ten feet away, had raised himself on his elbow. The light was so faint that Ned could scarcely see Crockett's face, but it looked very tense and eager.

"Get up, Ned! Get up!" said Crockett, shaking him again. "There's great work for you to do!"

"Why, what is it?" exclaimed the boy, springing to his feet.

"It's your friends, Roylston, an' that man, the Panther, you've been tellin' me about," replied Crockett in quick tones. "While you were asleep a Mexican, friendly to us, sneaked a message over the wall, sayin' that Roylston, the Panther, an' others were layin' to the east with a big force not more'n twenty miles away—not Fannin's crowd, but another one that's come down from the north. They don't know whether we're holdin' out yet or not, an' o' course they don't want to risk destruction by tryin' to cut through the Mexican army to reach us when we ain't here. The Mexican dassent go out of San Antonio. He won't try it, 'cause, as he says, it's sure death for him, an' so somebody must go to Roylston with the news that we're still alive, fightin' an' kickin'. Colonel Travis has chose you, an' you've got to go. No, there's no letter. You're just to tell Roylston by word of mouth to come on with his men."

The words came forth popping like pistol shots. Ned was swept off his feet. He did not have time to argue or ask questions. Bowie also added a fresh impetus. "Go, Ned, go at once!" he said. "You are chosen for a great service. It's an honor to anybody!"

"A service of great danger, requirin' great skill," said Crockett, "but you can do it, Ned, you can do it."

Ned flushed. This was, in truth, a great trust. He might, indeed, bring the help they needed so sorely.

"Here's your rifle an' other weapons an' ammunition," said Crockett. "The night's at its darkest an' you ain't got any time to waste. Come on!"

So swift was Crockett that Ned was ready almost before he knew it. The Tennesseean never ceased hurrying him. But as he started, Bowie called to him:

"Good-by, Ned!"

The boy turned back and offered his hand. The Georgian shook it with unusual warmth, and then lay back calmly on his blankets.

"Good-by, Ned," he repeated, "and if we don't meet again I hope you'll forget the dark things in my life, and remember me as one who was doing his best for Texas."

"But we will meet again," said Ned. "The relieving force will be here in two or three days and I'll come with it."

"Out with you!" said Crockett. "That's talk enough. What you want to do now is to put on your invisible cap an' your seven league boots an' go like lightnin' through the Mexican camp. Remember that you can talk their lingo like a native, an' don't forget, neither, to keep always about you a great big piece of presence of mind that you can use on a moment's notice."

Ned wore his serape and he carried a pair of small, light but very warm blankets, strapped in a pack on his back. His haversack contained bread and dried beef, and, with his smaller weapons in his belt, and his rifle over his shoulder, he was equipped fully for a long and dangerous journey.

Crockett and the boy passed into the convent yard.

The soft wind from the southwest blew upon their faces, and from the high wall of the church a sentinel called: "All's well!" Ned felt an extraordinary shiver, a premonition, but it passed, unexplained. He and Crockett went into the main plaza and reached the lowest part of the wall.

"Ought I to see Colonel Travis?" asked Ned, as they were on the way.

"No, he asked me to see to it, 'cause there ain't no time to waste. It's about three o'clock in the mornin' now, an' you've got to slip through in two or three hours, 'cause the light will be showin' then. Now, Ned, up with you an' over."

Ned climbed to the summit of the wall. Beyond lay heavy darkness, and he neither saw nor heard any human being. He looked back, and extended his hand to Crockett as he had to Bowie.

"Good-by, Mr. Crockett," he said, "you've been very good to me."

The great brown hand of the frontiersman clasped his almost convulsively.

"Aye, Ned," he said, "we've cottoned to each other from the first. I haven't knowed you long, but you've been like a son to me. Now go, an' God speed you!"

Ned recalled afterward that he did not say anything about Roylston's relieving force. What he thought of then was the deep feeling in Crockett's words.

"I'm coming back," he said, "and I hope to hunt buffalo with you over the plains of a free Texas."

"Go! go! Hurry, Ned!" said Crockett.

"Good-by," said Ned, and he dropped lightly to the ground.

He was outside the Alamo after eleven days inside, that seemed in the retrospect almost as many months. He flattened himself against the wall, and stood there for a minute or two, looking and listening. He thought he might hear Crockett again inside, but evidently the Tennesseean had gone back at once. In front of him was only the darkness, pierced by a single light off toward the west.

Ned hesitated. It was hard for him to leave the Alamo and the friends who had been knitted to him by so many common dangers, yet his errand was one of high importance—it might save them all—and he must do it. Strengthening his resolution he started across an open space, walking lightly. As Crockett had truly said, with his perfect knowledge of the language he might pass for a Mexican. He had done so before, and he did not doubt his ability to do so again.

He resolved to assume the character of a Mexican scout, looking into the secrets of the Alamo, and going back to report to Santa Anna. As he advanced he heard voices and saw earthworks from which the muzzles of four cannon protruded. Behind the earthwork was a small fire, and he knew that men would be sitting about it. He turned aside, not wishing to come too much into the light, but a soldier near the earthwork hailed him, and Ned, according to his plan, replied briefly that he was on his way to General Santa Anna in San Antonio.

But the man was talkative.

"What is your name?" he asked.

"Pedro Miguel Alvarado," replied Ned on the spur of the moment.

"Well, friend, it is a noble name, that of Alvarado."

"But it is not a noble who bears it. Though a descendant of the great Alvarado, who fought by the side of the glorious and mighty conquistador, Hernando Cortez, I am but a poor peasant offering my life daily for bread in the army of General Santa Anna."

The man laughed.

"You are as well off as I am," he said. "But what of the wicked Texans? Are they yet ready to surrender their throats to our knives? The dogs hold us over long. It is said that they number scarce two hundred within the mission. Truly they fight hard, and well they may, knowing that death only is at the end."

Ned shuddered. The man seemed to take it all so lightly. But he replied in a firm voice:

"I learned little of them save that they still fight. I took care not to put myself before the muzzle of any of their rifles."

The Mexican laughed again.

"A lad of wisdom, you," he said. "They are demons with their rifles. When the great assault is made, many a good man will speed to his long home before the Alamo is taken."

So, they had already decided upon the assault. The premonition within the Alamo was not wrong. It occurred to Ned that he might learn more, and he paused.

"Has it been finally settled?" he asked. "We attack about three days from now, do we not?"

"Earlier than that," replied the Mexican. "I know that the time has been chosen, and I think it is to-morrow morning."

Ned's heart beat heavily. To-morrow morning! Even if he got through, how could he ever bring Roylston and the relief force in time?

"I thank you," he said, "but I must hurry with my report."

"Adios, Señor," said the man politely, and Ned repeated his "Adios" in the same tone. Then he hurried forward, continually turning in toward the east, hoping to find a passage where the Mexican line was thinnest. But the circle of the invaders was complete, and he saw that he must rely upon his impersonation of a Mexican to take him through.

He was in a fever of haste, knowing now that the great assault was to come so soon, and he made for a point between two smoldering camp fires fifty or sixty yards apart. Boldness only would now avail, and with the brim of his sombrero pulled well down over his face he walked confidently forward, coming fully within the light of the fire on his left.

A number of Mexican soldiers were asleep around the fire, but at least a half dozen men were awake. They called to Ned as he passed and he responded readily, but Fortune, which had been so kind to him for a long time, all at once turned her back upon him. When he spoke, a man in officer's uniform who had been sitting by the fire rose quickly.

"Your name?" he cried.

"Pedro Miguel Alvarado," replied Ned instantly. At the same moment he recognized Urrea.

"It is not so!" cried Urrea. "You are one of the Texans, young Fulton. I know your voice. Upon him, men! Seize him!"

His action and the leap of the Mexicans were so sudden that Ned did not have time to aim his rifle. But he struck one a short-arm blow with the butt of it that sent him down with a broken head, and he snatched at his pistol as three or four others threw themselves upon him. Ned was uncommonly strong and agile, and he threw off two of the men, but the others pressed him to the ground, until, at Urrea's command, his arms were bound and he was allowed to rise.

Ned was in despair, not so much for himself but because there was no longer a chance that he could get through to Roylston. It was a deep mortification, moreover, to be taken by Urrea. But he faced the Mexican with an appearance of calmness.

"Well," he said, "I am your prisoner."

"You are," said Urrea, "and you might have passed, if I had not known your voice. But I remind you that you come from the Alamo. You see our flag, and you know its meaning."

The black eyes of the Mexican regarded Ned malignantly. The boy knew that the soul of Urrea was full of wicked triumph. The officer could shoot him down at that moment, and be entirely within orders. But Ned recalled the words of Roylston. The merchant had told him to use his name if he should ever fall again into the hands of Santa Anna.

"I am your prisoner," he repeated, "and I demand to be taken before General Santa Anna. Whatever your red flag may mean, there are reasons why he will spare me. Go with me and you will see."

He spoke with such boldness and directness that Urrea was impressed.

"I shall take you to the general," he said, "not because you demand it, but because I think it well to do so. It is likely that he will want to examine you, and I believe that in his presence you will tell all you know. But it is not yet 4 o'clock in the morning, and I cannot awaken him now. You will stay here until after daylight."

"Very well," said Ned, trying to be calm as possible. "As you have bound me I cannot walk, but if you'll put me on a blanket there by the fire I'll sleep until you want me."

"We won't deny you that comfort," replied Urrea grimly.

When Ned was stretched on his blanket he was fairly easy so far as the body was concerned. They had bound him securely, but not painfully. His agony of mind, though, was great. Nevertheless he fell asleep, and slept in a restless way for three or four hours, until Urrea awoke him, and told him they were going to Santa Anna.

It was a clear, crisp dawn and Ned saw the town, the river, and the Alamo. There, only a short distance away, stood the dark fortress, from which he had slipped but a few hours before with such high hopes. He even saw the figures of the sentinels, moving slowly on the church walls, and his heart grew heavy within him. He wished now that he was back with the defenders. Even if he should escape it would be too late. At Urrea's orders he was unbound.

"There is no danger of your escaping now," said the young Mexican. "Several of my men are excellent marksmen, and they will fire at the first step you take in flight. And even should they miss, what chance do you think you have here?"

He swept his right hand in a circle, and, in the clear morning air, Ned saw batteries and troops everywhere. He knew that the circle of steel about the Alamo was complete. Perhaps he would have failed in his errand even had he got by. It would require an unusually strong force to cut through an army as large as that of Santa Anna, and he did not know where Roylston could have found it. He started, as a sudden suspicion smote him. He remembered Crockett's hurried manner, and his lack of explanation. But he put it aside. It could not be true.

"I see that you look at the Alamo," said Urrea ironically. "Well, the rebel flag is still there, but it will not remain much longer. The trap is about ready to shut down."

Ned's color rose.

"It may be so," he said, "but for every Texan who falls the price will be five Mexicans."

"But they will fall, nevertheless," said Urrea. "Here is food for you. Eat, and I will take you to the general."

They offered him Mexican food, but he had no appetite, and he ate little. He stretched and tensed his limbs in order to restore the full flood of circulation, and announced that he was ready. Urrea led the way, and Ned followed with a guard of four men about him.

The boy had eyes and ears for everything around him, but he looked most toward the Alamo. He could not, at the distance, recognize the figures on the wall, but all those men were his friends, and his eyes filled with tears at their desperate case. Out here with the Mexicans, where he could see all their overwhelming force and their extensive preparations, the chances of the Texans looked worse than they did inside the Alamo.

They entered the town and passed through the same streets, along which Ned had advanced with the conquering army of the Texans a few months before. Many evidences of the siege remained. There were tunnels, wrecked houses and masses of stone and adobe. The appearance of the young prisoner aroused the greatest curiosity among both soldiers and people. He heard often the word "Texano." Women frequently looked down at him from the flat roofs, and some spoke in pity.

Ned was silent. He was resolved not to ask Urrea any questions or to give him a chance to show triumph. He noticed that they were advancing toward the plaza, and then they turned into the Veramendi house, which he had cause to remember so well.

"This was the home of the Vice-Governor," said Urrea, "and General Santa Anna is here."

"I know the place," said Ned. "I am proud to have been one of the Texans who took it on a former occasion."

"We lost it then, but we have it now and we'll keep it," said Urrea. "My men will wait with you here in the courtyard, and I'll see if our illustrious general is ready to receive you."

Ned waited patiently. Urrea was gone a full half hour, and, when he returned, he said:

"The general was at breakfast with his staff. He had not quite finished, but he is ready to receive you now."

Then Urrea led the way into the Veramendi house. Luxurious fittings had been put in, but many of the rents and scars from the old combat were yet visible. They entered the great dining room, and, once more, Ned stood face to face with the most glorious general, the most illustrious dictator, Don Antonio Lopez de Santa Anna. But Ned alone stood. The dictator sat at the head of the table, about which were Castrillon, Sesma, Cos, Gaona, the Italian, Filisola and others. It seemed to Ned that he had come not only upon a breakfast but upon a conference as well.

The soldiers who had guarded Ned stepped back, Urrea stood by the wall, and the boy was left to meet the fixed gaze of Santa Anna. The dictator wore a splendid uniform, as usual. His face seemed to Ned fuller and more flushed than when they had last met in Mexico. The marks of dissipation were there. Ned saw him slip a little silver box from the pocket of his waistcoat and take from it a pinch of a dark drug, which he ate. It was opium, but the Mexican generals seemed to take no note of it.

Santa Anna's gaze was fixed and piercing, as if he would shoot terror into the soul of his enemy—a favorite device of his—but Ned withstood it. Then Santa Anna, removing his stare from his face, looked him slowly up and down. The generals said nothing, waiting upon their leader, who could give life or death as he chose. Ned was sure that Santa Anna remembered him, and, in a moment, he knew that he was right.

"It is young Fulton, who made the daring and ingenious escape from our hospitality in the capital," he said, "and who also departed in an unexpected manner from one of the submarine dungeons of our castle of San Juan de Ulua. Fate does not seem to reward your courage and enterprise as they deserve, since you are in our hands again."

The dictator laughed and his generals laughed obediently also. Ned said nothing.

"I am informed by that most meritorious young officer, Captain Urrea," continued Santa Anna, "that you were captured about three o'clock this morning trying to escape from the Alamo."

"That is correct," said Ned.

"Why were you running away in the dark?"

Ned flushed, but, knowing that it was an unworthy and untruthful taunt, he remained silent.

"You do not choose to answer," said Santa Anna, "but I tell you that you are the rat fleeing from the sinking ship. Our cannon have wrecked the interior of the Alamo. Half of your men are dead, and the rest would gladly surrender if I should give them the promise of life."

"It is not true!" exclaimed Ned with heat. "Despite all your fire the defenders of the Alamo have lost but a few men. You offer no quarter and they ask none. They are ready to fight to the last."

There was a murmur among the generals, but Santa Anna raised his hand and they were silent again.

"I cannot believe all that you say," he continued. "It is a boast. The Texans are braggarts. To-morrow they die, every one of them. But tell us the exact condition of everything inside the Alamo, and perhaps I may spare your life."

Ned shut his teeth so hard that they hurt. A deep flush surged into the dark face of Santa Anna.

"You are stubborn. All the Texans are stubborn. But I do not need any information from you. I shall crush the Alamo, as my fingers would smash an eggshell."

"But your fingers will be pierced deep," Ned could not keep from replying. "They will run blood."

"Be that as it may," said Santa Anna, who, great in some things, was little enough to taunt an enemy in his power, "you will not live to see it. I am about to give orders to have you shot within an hour."

His lips wrinkled away from his white teeth like those of a great cat about to spring, and his cruel eyes contracted. Holding all the power of Mexico in his hands he was indeed something to be dreaded. The generals about the table never spoke. But Ned remembered the words of Roylston.

"A great merchant named John Roylston has been a good friend to me," he said. "He told me that if I should ever fall into your hands I was to mention his name to you, and to say that he considered my life of value."

The expression of the dictator changed. He frowned, and then regarded Ned intently, as if he would read some secret that the boy was trying to hide.

"And so you know John Roylston," he said at length, "and he wishes you to say to me that your life is of value."

Ned saw the truth at once. He had a talisman and that talisman was the name of Roylston. He did not know why it was so, but it was a wonderful talisman nevertheless, because it was going to save his life for the time being, at least. He glanced at the generals, and he saw a look of curiosity on the face of every one of them.

"I know Roylston," said Santa Anna slowly, "and there are some matters between us. It may be to my advantage to spare you for a while."

Ned's heart sprang up. Life was sweet. Since he was to be spared for a while it must mean ultimately exchange or escape. Santa Anna, a reader of the human face, saw what was in his mind.

"Be not too sanguine," he said, "because I have changed my mind once it does not mean that you are to be free now or ever. I shall keep you here, and you shall see your comrades fall."

A sudden smile, offspring of a quick thought and satanic in its nature, passed over his face.

"I will make you a spectator of the defeat of the Texans," he said. "A great event needs a witness, and since you cannot be a combatant you can serve in that capacity. We attack at dawn to-morrow, and you shall miss nothing of it."

The wicked smile passed over his face again. It had occurred to Ned, a student of history, that the gladiatorial cruelty of the ancient Romans had descended to the Spaniards instead of the Italians. Now he was convinced that it was so.

"You shall be kept a prisoner in one of our strongest houses," said Santa Anna, "and Captain Urrea, whose vigilance prevented your escape, will keep guard over you. I fancy it is a task that he does not hate."

Santa Anna had also read the mind of the young Mexican. Urrea smiled. He liked this duty. He hated Ned and he, too, was not above taunting a prisoner. He advanced, and put a hand upon Ned's shoulder, but the boy shook it off.

"Don't touch me," said Ned. "I'll follow without resistance."

Santa Anna laughed.

"Let him have his way for the present, Captain Urrea," he said. "But remember that it is due to your gentleness and mercy. Adios, Señor Fulton, we meet again to-morrow morning, and if you survive I shall report to Mr. Roylston the manner in which you may bear yourself."

"Good-day," said Ned, resolved not to be outdone, even in ironical courtesy. "And now, Captain Urrea, if you will lead the way, I'll follow."

Urrea and his soldiers took Ned from the Veramendi house and across the street to a large and strong stone building.

"You are fortunate," said Urrea, "to have escaped immediate death. I do not know why the name of Roylston was so powerful with our general, but I saw that it was."

"It seemed to have its effect," said Ned.

Urrea led the way to the flat roof of the house, a space reached by a single narrow stairway.

"I shall leave you here with two guards," he said. "I shall give them instructions to fire upon you at the slightest attempt on your part to escape, but I fancy that you will have sense enough not to make any such attempt."

Urrea departed, but the two sentinels sat by the entrance to the stairway, musket in hand. He had not the faintest chance to get by them, and knowing it he sat down on the low stone coping of the roof. He wondered why Urrea had brought him there instead of locking him up in a room. Perhaps it was to mock him with the sight of freedom so near and yet unattainable.

His gaze turned instinctively to the Alamo like the magnet to the pole. There was the fortress, gray and grim in the sunshine, with the dim figures of the watchers on the walls. What were they doing inside now? How were Crockett and Bowie? His heart filled with grief that he had failed them. But had he failed them? Neither Urrea nor any other Mexican had spoken of the approach of a relieving force under Roylston. There was no sign that the Mexicans were sending any part of their army to meet it.

The heavy thud of a great gun drew his attention, and he saw the black smoke from the discharge rising over the plain. A second, a third and a fourth cannon shot were fired, but no answer came from the walls of the Alamo. At length he saw one of the men in the nearest battery to the Alamo expose himself above the earthwork. There was a flash from the wall of the church, a little puff of smoke, and Ned saw the man fall as only dead men fall. Perhaps it was Davy Crockett, the great marksman, who had fired that shot. He liked to think that it was so, and he rejoiced also at this certain evidence that the little garrison was as dauntless as ever. He watched the Alamo for nearly an hour, and he saw that the firing was desultory. Not more than a dozen cannon shots were fired during that time, and only three or four rifles replied from the Alamo. Toward noon the firing ceased entirely, and Ned knew that this was in very fact and truth the lull before the storm.

His attention wandered to his guards. They were mere peons, but, although watchful, they were taking their ease. Evidently they liked their task. They were resting with the complete relaxation of the body that only the Southern races know. Both had lighted cigarritos, and were puffing at them contentedly. It had been a long time since Ned had seen such a picture of lazy ease.

"You like it here?" he said to the nearest.

The man took the cigarrito from his mouth, emitted smoke from his nose and replied politely:

"It is better to be here lying in the sun than out there on the grass with a Texan bullet through one's body. Is it not so, Fernando?"

"Aye, it is so," replied his comrade. "I like not the Texan bullets. I am glad to be here where they cannot reach me. It is said that Satan sights their rifles for them, because they do not miss. They will die hard to-morrow. They will die like the bear in its den, fighting the hunters, when our army is poured upon them. That will be an end to all the Texans, and we will go back to the warm south."

"But are you sure," asked Ned, "that it will be an end of the Texans? Not all the Texans are shut up in the Alamo."

"What matters it?" replied Fernando, lightly. "It may be delayed, but the end will be the same. Nothing can resist the great, the powerful, the most illustrious Santa Anna. He is always able to dig graves for his enemies."

The men talked further. Ned gathered from them that the whole force of Santa Anna was now present. Some of his officers wanted him to wait for siege artillery of the heaviest caliber that would batter down the walls of the Alamo, but the dictator himself was impatient for the assault. It would certainly take place the next morning.

"And why is the young señor here?" asked Fernando. "The order has been issued that no Texan shall be spared, and do you not see the red flag waving there close by us?"

Ned looked up. The red flag now flaunted its folds very near to him. He could not repress a shiver.

"I am here," he replied, "because some one who has power has told General Santa Anna that I am not to be put to death."

"It is well for you, then," said Fernando, "that you have a friend of such weight. It is a pity to die when one is so young and so straight and strong as you. Ah, my young señor, the world is beautiful. Look how green is the grass there by the river, and how the sun lies like gold across it!"

Ned had noticed before the love of beauty that the humblest peon sometimes had, and there was a certain touch of brotherly feeling between him and this man, his jailer.

"The world is beautiful," said the boy, "and I am willing to tell you that I have no wish to leave it."

"Nor I," said Fernando. "Why are the Texans so foolish as to oppose the great Santa Anna, the most illustrious and powerful of all generals and rulers? Did they not know that he would come and crush them, every one?"

Ned did not reply. The peon, in repose at least, had a gentle heart, and the boy knew that Santa Anna was to him omnipotent and omniscient. He turned his attention anew to the Alamo, that magnet of his thoughts. It was standing quiet in the sun now. The defiant flag of the defenders, upon which they had embroidered the word "Texas," hung lazily from the staff.

The guards in the afternoon gave him some food and a jug of water, and they also ate and drank upon the roof. They were yet amply content with their task and their position there. No bullets could reach them. The sunshine was golden and pleasant. They had established friendly relations with the prisoner. He had not given them the slightest trouble, and, before and about them, was spread the theater upon which a mighty drama was passing, all for them to see. What more could be asked by two simple peasants of small wants?

Ned was glad that they let him remain upon the roof. The Alamo drew his gaze with a power that he could not break if he would. Since he was no longer among the defenders he was eager to see every detail in the vast drama that was now unfolding.

But the afternoon passed in inaction. The sun was brilliant and toward evening turned to a deep, glowing red. It lighted up for the last time the dim figures that stood on the walls of the Alamo. Ned choked as he saw them there. He felt the premonition.

Urrea came upon the roof shortly before twilight. He was not sneering or ironical, and Ned, who had no wish to quarrel at such a time, was glad of it.

"As General Santa Anna told you," said Urrea, "the assault is to be made in overwhelming force early in the morning. It will succeed, of course. Nothing can prevent it. Through the man Roylston, you have some claim upon the general, but it may not be strong enough to save you long. A service now might make his pardon permanent."

"What do you mean by a service now?"

"A few words as to the weaker points of the Alamo, the best places for our troops to attack. You cannot do anything for the defenders. You cannot alter their fate in any particular, but you might do something for yourself."

Ned did not wish to appear dramatic. He merely turned his back upon the young Mexican.

"Very well," said Urrea, "I made you the offer. It was for you to accept it or not as you wish."

He left him upon the roof, and Ned saw the last rim of the red sun sink in the plain. He saw the twilight come, and the Alamo fade into a dim black bulk in the darkness. He thought once that he heard a cry of a sentinel from its walls, "All's well," but he knew that it was only fancy. The distance was far too great. Besides, all was not well.

When the darkness had fully come, he descended with his two benevolent jailers to a lower part of the house, where he was assigned to a small room, with a single barred window and without the possibility of escape. His guards, after bringing him food and water, gave him a polite good night and went outside. He knew that they would remain on watch in the hall.

Ned could eat and drink but little. Nor could he yet sleep. The night was far too heavy upon him for slumber. Besides, it had brought many noises, significant noises that he knew. He heard the rumble of cannon wheels over the rough pavements, and the shouts of men to the horses or mules. He heard troops passing, now infantry, and then cavalry, the hoofs of their horses grinding upon the stones.

He pressed his face against the barred window. He was eager to hear and yet more eager to see. He caught glimpses only of horse and foot as they passed, but he knew what all those sights and sounds portended. In the night the steel coil of the Mexicans was being drawn closer and closer about the Alamo.

Brave and resolute, he was only a boy after all. He felt deserted of all men. He wanted to be back there with Crockett and Bowie and Travis and the others. The water came into his eyes, and unconsciously he pulled hard at the iron bars.

He remained there a long time, listening to the sounds. Once he heard a trumpet, and its note in the night was singularly piercing. He knew that it was a signal, probably for the moving of a regiment still closer to the Alamo. But there were no shots from either the Mexicans or the mission. The night was clear with many stars.

After two or three hours at the window Ned tried to sleep. There was a narrow bed against the wall, and he lay upon it, full length, but he did not even close his eyes. He became so restless that at last he rose and went to the window again. It must have been then past midnight. The noises had ceased. Evidently the Mexicans had everything ready. The wind blew cold upon his face, but it brought him no news of what was passing without.

He went back to the bed, and by and by he sank into a heavy slumber.

CHAPTER XIII.
TO THE LAST MAN

Ned awoke after a feverish night, when there was yet but a strip of gray in the east. It was Sunday morning, but he had lost count of time, and did not know it. He had not undressed at all when he lay down, and now he stood by the window, seeking to see and hear. But the light was yet dim and the sounds were few. Nevertheless the great pulse in his throat began to leap. The attack was at hand.

The door of the room was unlocked and the two peons who had guarded him upon the roof came for him. Ned saw in the half gloom that they were very grave of countenance.

"We are to take you to the noble Captain Urrea, who is waiting for you," said Fernando.

"Very well," said Ned. "I am ready. You have been kind to me, and I hope that we shall meet again after to-day."

Both men shook their heads.

"We fear that is not to be," said Fernando.

They found Urrea and another young officer waiting at the door of the house. Urrea was in his best uniform and his eyes were very bright. He was no coward, and Ned knew that the gleam was in anticipation of the coming attack.

"The time is at hand," he said, "and it will be your wonderful fortune to see how Mexico strikes down her foe."

His voice, pitched high, showed excitement, and a sense of the dramatic. Ned said nothing, and his own pulses began to leap again. The strip of gray in the east was broadening, and he now saw that the whole town was awake, although it was not yet full daylight. Santa Anna had been at work in the night, while he lay in that feverish sleep. He heard everywhere now the sound of voices, the clank of arms and the beat of horses' hoofs. The flat roofs were crowded with the Mexican people. Ned saw Mexican women there in their dresses of bright colors, like Roman women in the Colosseum, awaiting the battle of the gladiators. The atmosphere was surcharged with excitement, and the sense of coming triumph.

Ned's breath seemed to choke in his throat and his heart beat painfully. Once more he wished with all his soul that he was with his friends, that he was in the Alamo. He belonged with them there, and he would rather face death with those familiar faces around him than be here, safe perhaps, but only a looker-on. It was with him now a matter of the emotions, and not of reasoned intellect. Once more he looked toward the old mission, and saw the dim outline of the buildings, with the dominating walls of the church. He could not see whether anyone watched on the walls, but he knew that the sentinels were there. Perhaps Crockett, himself, stood among them now, looking at the great Mexican coil of steel that was wrapping itself tighter and tighter around the Alamo. Despite himself, Ned uttered a sigh.

"What is the matter with you?" asked Urrea, sharply. "Are you already weeping for the conquered?"

"You know that I am not," replied Ned. "You need not believe me, but I regret that I am not in the Alamo with my friends."

"It's an idle wish," said Urrea, "but I am taking you now to General Santa Anna. Then I leave, and I go there! Look, the horsemen!"

He extended his hand, and Ned saw his eyes kindling. The Mexican cavalry were filing out in the dim dawn, troop after troop, the early light falling across the blades of the lances, spurs and bridles jingling. All rode well, and they made a thrilling picture, as they rode steadily on, curving about the old fortress.

"I shall soon be with them," said Urrea in a tone of pride. "We shall see that not a single one of your Texans escapes from the Alamo."

Ned felt that choking in his throat again, but he deemed it wiser to keep silent. They were going toward the main plaza now, and he saw masses of troops gathered in the streets. These men were generally silent, and he noticed that their faces expressed no elation. He divined at once that they were intended for the assault, and they had no cause for joy. They knew that they must face the deadly Texan rifles.

Urrea led the way to a fortified battery standing in front of the main plaza. A brilliant group stood behind an earthen wall, and Ned saw Santa Anna among them.

"I have brought the prisoner," said Urrea, saluting.

"Very good," replied the dictator, "and now, Captain Urrea, you can join your command. You have served me well, and you shall have your share in the glory of this day."

Urrea flushed with pride at the compliment, and bowed low. Then he hurried away to join the horse. Santa Anna turned his attention.

"I have brought you here at this moment," he said, "to give you a last chance. It is not due to any mercy for you, a rebel, but it is because you have been so long in the Alamo that you must know it well. Point out to us its weakest places, and you shall be free. You shall go north in safety. I promise it here, in the presence of my generals."

"I have nothing to tell," replied Ned.

"Are you sure?"

"Absolutely sure."

"Then it merely means a little more effusion of blood. You may stay with us and see the result."

All the ancient, inherited cruelty now shone in Santa Anna's eyes. It was the strange satanic streak in him that made him keep his captive there in order that he might see the fall of his own comrades. A half dozen guards stood near the person of the dictator, and he said to them:

"If the prisoner seeks to leave us, shoot him at once."

The manner of Santa Anna was arrogant to the last degree, but Ned was glad to stay. He was eager to see the great panorama which was about to be unrolled before him. He was completely absorbed in the Alamo, and he utterly forgot himself. Black specks were dancing before his eyes, and the blood was pounding in his ears, but he took no notice of such things.

The gray bar in the east broadened. A thin streak of shining silver cut through it, and touched for a moment the town, the river, the army and the Alamo. Ned leaned against an edge of the earthwork, and breathed heavily and painfully. He had not known that his heart could beat so hard.

The same portentous silence prevailed everywhere. The men and women on the roofs of the houses were absolutely still. The cavalry, their line now drawn completely about the mission, were motionless. Ned, straining his eyes toward the Alamo, could see nothing there. Suddenly he put up his hand and wiped his forehead. His fingers came away wet. His blood prickled in his veins like salt. He became impatient, angry. If the mine was ready, why did they not set the match? Such waiting was the pitch of cruelty.

"Cos, my brother," said Santa Anna to the swart general, "take your command. It was here that the Texan rebels humiliated you, and it is here that you shall have full vengeance."

Cos saluted, and strode away. He was to lead one of the attacking columns.

"Colonel Duque," said Santa Anna to another officer, "you are one of the bravest of the brave. You are to direct the attack on the northern wall, and may quick success go with you."

Duque glowed at the compliment, and he, too, strode away to the head of his column.

"Colonel Romero," said Santa Anna, "the third column is yours, and the fourth is yours, Colonel Morales. Take your places and, at the signal agreed, the four columns will charge with all their strength. Let us see which will be the first in the Alamo."

The two colonels saluted as the others had done, and joined their columns.

The bar of gray in the east was still broadening, but the sun itself did not yet show. The walls of the Alamo were still dim, and Ned could not see whether any figures were there. Santa Anna had put a pair of powerful glasses to his eyes, but when he took them down he said nothing of what he had seen.

"Are all the columns provided?" he said to General Sesma, who stood beside him.

"They have everything," replied Sesma, "crowbars, axes, scaling ladders. Sir, they cannot fail!"

"No, they cannot," said Santa Anna exultantly. "These Texan rebels fight like demons, but we have now a net through which they cannot break. General Gaona, see that the bands are ready and direct them to play the Deguelo when the signal for the charge is given."

Ned shivered again. The "Deguelo" meant the "cutting-of-throats," and it, too, was to be the signal of no quarter. He remembered the red flag, and he looked up. It hung, as ever, on the tower of the church of San Fernando, and its scarlet folds moved slowly in the light morning breeze. General Gaona returned.

"The bands are ready, general," he said, "and when the signal is given they will play the air that you have chosen."

A Mexican, trumpet in hand, was standing near. Santa Anna turned and said to him the single word:

"Blow!"

The man lifted the trumpet to his lips, and blew a long note that swelled to its fullest pitch, then died away in a soft echo.

It was the signal. A tremendous cry burst from the vast ring of the thousands, and it was taken up by the shrill voices of the women on the flat roofs of the houses. The great circle of cavalrymen shook their lances and sabers until they glittered.

When the last echo of the trumpet's dying note was gone the bands began to play with their utmost vigor the murderous tune that Santa Anna had chosen. Then four columns of picked Mexican troops, three thousand strong, rushed toward the Alamo. Santa Anna and the generals around him were tremendously excited. Their manner made no impression upon Ned then, but he recalled the fact afterward.

The boy became quickly unconscious of everything except the charge of the Mexicans and the Alamo. He no longer remembered that he was a prisoner. He no longer remembered anything about himself. The cruel throb of that murderous tune, the Deguelo, beat upon the drums of his ears, and mingled with it came the sound of the charging Mexicans, the beat of their feet, the clank of their arms, and the shouts of their officers.

Whatever may be said of the herded masses of the Mexican troops, the Mexican officers were full of courage. They were always in advance, waving their swords and shouting to their men to come on. Another silver gleam flashed through the gray light of the early morning, ran along the edges of swords and lances, and lingered for a moment over the dark walls of the Alamo.

No sound came from the mission, not a shot, not a cry. Were they asleep? Was it possible that every man, overpowered by fatigue, had fallen into slumber at such a moment? Could such as Crockett and Bowie and Travis be blind to their danger? Such painful questions raced through Ned's mind. He felt a chill run down his spine. Yet his breath was like fire to his lips.

"Nothing will stop them!" cried Santa Anna. "The Texans cower before such a splendid force! They will lay down their arms!"

Ned felt his body growing colder and colder, and there was a strange tingling at the roots of the hair. Now the people upon the roofs were shouting their utmost, and the voices of many women united in one shrill, piercing cry. But he never turned to look at them. His eyes were always on the charging host which converged so fast upon the Alamo.

The trumpet blew another signal, and there was a crash so loud that it made Ned jump. All the Mexican batteries had fired at once over the heads of their own troops at the Alamo. While the gunners reloaded the smoke of the discharge drifted away and the Alamo still stood silent. But over it yet hung a banner on which was written in great letters the word, "Texas."

The Mexican troops were coming close now. The bands playing the Deguelo swelled to greater volume and the ground shook again as the Mexican artillery fired its second volley. When the smoke drifted away again the Alamo itself suddenly burst into flame. The Texan cannon at close range poured their shot and shell into the dense ranks of the Mexicans. But piercing through the heavy thud of the cannon came the shriller and more deadly crackle of the rifles. The Texans were there, every one of them, on the walls. He might have known it. Nothing on earth could catch them asleep, nor could anything on earth or under it frighten them into laying down their arms.

Ned began to shout, but only hoarse cries came from a dry throat through dry lips. The great pulses in his throat were leaping again, and he was saying: "The Texans! The Texans! Oh, the brave Texans!"

But nobody heard him. Santa Anna, Filisola, Castrillon, Tolsa, Gaona and the other generals were leaning against the earthwork, absorbed in the tremendous spectacle that was passing before them. The soldiers who were to guard the prisoner forgot him and they, too, were engrossed in the terrible and thrilling panorama of war. Ned might have walked away, no one noticing, but he, too, had but one thought, and that was the Alamo.

He saw the Mexican columns shiver when the first volley was poured upon them from the walls. In a single glance aside he beheld the exultant look on the faces of Santa Anna and his generals die away, and he suddenly became conscious that the shrill shouting on the flat roofs of the houses had ceased. But the Mexican cannon still poured a cloud of shot and shell over the heads of their men at the Alamo, and the troops went on.

Ned, keen of ear and so intent that he missed nothing, could now separate the two fires. The crackle of the rifles which came from the Alamo dominated. Rapid, steady, incessant, it beat heavily upon the hearing and nerves. Pyramids and spires of smoke arose, drifted and arose again. In the intervals he saw the walls of the church a sheet of flame, and he saw the Mexicans falling by dozens and scores upon the plain. He knew that at the short range the Texan rifles never missed, and that the hail of their bullets was cutting through the Mexican ranks like a fire through dry grass.

"God, how they fight!" he heard one of the generals—he never knew which—exclaim.

Then he saw the officers rushing about, shouting to the men, striking them with the flats of their swords and urging them on. The Mexican army responded to the appeal, lifted itself up and continued its rush. The fire from the Alamo seemed to Ned to increase. The fortress was a living flame. He had not thought that men could fire so fast, but they had three or four rifles apiece.

The silence which had replaced the shrill shouting in the town continued. All the crash was now in front of them, and where they stood the sound of the human voice would carry. In a dim far-away manner Ned heard the guards talking to one another. Their words showed uneasiness. It was not the swift triumphal rush into the Alamo that they had expected. Great swaths had been cut through the Mexican army. Santa Anna paled more than once when he saw his men falling so fast.

"They cannot recoil! They cannot!" he cried.

But they did. The column led by Colonel Duque, a brave man, was now at the northern wall, and the men were rushing forward with the crowbars, axes and scaling ladders. The Texan rifles, never more deadly, sent down a storm of bullets upon them. A score of men fell all at once. Among them was Duque, wounded terribly. The whole column broke and reeled away, carrying Duque with them.

Ned saw the face of Santa Anna turn purple with rage. He struck the earthwork furiously with the flat of his sword.

"Go! Go!" he cried to Gaona and Tolsa. "Rally them! See that they do not run!"

The two generals sprang from the battery and rushed to their task. The Mexican cannon had ceased firing, for fear of shooting down their own men, and the smoke was drifting away from the field. The morning was also growing much lighter. The gray dawn had turned to silver, and the sun's red rim was just showing above the eastern horizon.

The Texan cannon were silent, too. The rifles were now doing all the work. The volume of their fire never diminished. Ned saw the field covered with slain, and many wounded were drifting back to the shelter of the earthworks and the town.

Duque's column was rallied, but the column on the east and the column on the west were also driven back, and Santa Anna rushed messenger after messenger, hurrying up fresh men, still driving the whole Mexican army against the Alamo. He shouted orders incessantly, although he remained safe within the shelter of the battery.

Ned felt an immense joy. He had seen the attack beaten off at three points. A force of twenty to one had been compelled to recoil. His heart swelled with pride in those friends of his. But they were so few in number! Even now the Mexican masses were reforming. The officers were among them, driving them forward with threats and blows. The great ring of Mexican cavalry, intended to keep any of the Texans from escaping, also closed in, driving their own infantry forward to the assault.

Ned's heart sank as the whole Mexican army, gathering now at the northern or lower wall, rushed straight at the barrier. But the deadly fire of the rifles flashed from it, and their front line went down. Again they recoiled, and again the cavalry closed in, holding them to the task.

There was a pause of a few moments. The town had been silent for a long time, and the Mexican soldiers themselves ceased to shout. Clouds of smoke eddied and drifted about the buildings. The light of the morning, first gray, then silver, turned to gold. The sun, now high above the earth's rim, poured down a flood of rays.

Everything stood out sharp and clear. Ned saw the buildings of the Alamo dark against the sun, and he saw men on the walls. He saw the Mexican columns pressed together in one great force, and he even saw the still faces of many who lay silent on the plain.

He knew that the Mexicans were about to charge again, and his feeling of exultation passed. He no longer had hope that the defenders of the Alamo could beat back so many. He thought again how few, how very few, were the Texans.

The silence endured but a moment or two. Then the Mexicans rushed forward in a mighty mass at the low northern wall, the front lines firing as they went. Flame burst from the wall, and Ned heard once more the deadly crackle of the Texan rifles. The ground was littered by the trail of the Mexican fallen, but, driven by their officers, they went on.

Ned saw them reach the wall and plant the scaling ladders, many of them. Scores of men swarmed up the ladders and over the wall. A heavy division forced its way into the redoubt through the sallyport, and as Ned saw he uttered a deep gasp. He knew that the Alamo was doomed. And the Mexicans knew it, too. The shrill screaming of the women began again from the flat roofs of the houses, and shouts burst from the army also.

"We have them! We have them!" cried Santa Anna, exultant and excited.

Sheets of flame still burst from the Alamo, and the rifles still poured bullets on the swarming Mexican forces, but the breach had been made. The Mexicans went over the low wall in an unbroken stream, and they crowded through the sallyport by hundreds. They were inside now, rushing with the overwhelming weight of twenty to one upon the little garrison. They seized the Texan guns, cutting down the gunners with lances and sabers, and they turned the captured cannon upon the defenders.

Some of the buildings inside the walls were of adobe, and they were soon shattered by the cannon balls. The Texans, covered with smoke and dust and the sweat of battle, were forced back by the press of numbers into the convent yard, and then into the church and hospital. Here the cannon and rifles in hundreds were turned upon them, but they still fought. Often, with no time to reload their rifles, they clubbed them, and drove back the Mexican rush.

The Alamo was a huge volcano of fire and smoke, of shouting and death. Those who looked on became silent again, appalled at the sights and sounds. The smoke rose far above the mission, and caught by a light wind drifted away to the east. The Mexican generals brought up fresh forces and drove them at the fortress. A heavy column, attacking on the south side, where no defenders were now left, poured over a stockade and crowded into the mission. The circle of cavalry about the Alamo again drew closer, lest any Texan should escape. But it was a useless precaution. None sought flight.

In very truth, the last hope of the Alamo was gone, and perhaps there was none among the defenders who did not know it. There were a few wild and desperate characters of the border, whom nothing in life became so much as their manner of leaving it. In the culminating moment of the great tragedy they bore themselves as well as the best.

Travis, the commander, and Bonham stood in the long room of the hospital with a little group around them, most of them wounded, the faces of all black with powder smoke. But they fought on. Whenever a Mexican appeared at the door an unerring rifle bullet struck him down. Fifty fell at that single spot before the rifles, yet they succeeded in dragging up a cannon, thrust its muzzle in at the door and fired it twice loaded with grape shot into the room.

The Texans were cut down by the shower of missiles, and the whole place was filled with smoke. Then the Mexicans rushed in and the few Texans who had survived the grape shot fell fighting to the last with their clubbed rifles. Here lay Travis of the white soul and beside him fell the brave Bonham, who had gone out for help, and who had returned to die with his comrades. The Texans who had defended the room against so many were only fifteen in number, and they were all silent now. Now the whole attack converged on the church, the strongest part of the Alamo, where the Texans were making their last stand. The place was seething with fire and smoke, but above it still floated the banner upon which was written in great letters the word, "Texas."

The Mexicans, pressing forward in dense masses, poured in cannon balls and musket balls at every opening. Half the Texans were gone, but the others never ceased to fire with their rifles. Within that raging inferno they could hardly see one another for the smoke, but they were all animated by the same purpose, to fight to the death and to carry as many of their foes with them as they could.

Evans, who had commanded the cannon, rushed for the magazine to blow up the building. They had agreed that if all hope were lost he should do so, but he was killed on his way by a bullet, and the others went on with the combat.

Near the entrance to the church stood a great figure swinging a clubbed rifle. His raccoon skin cap was lost, and his eyes burned like coals of fire in his swarthy face. It was Crockett, gone mad with battle, and the Mexicans who pressed in recoiled before the deadly sweep of the clubbed rifle. Some were awed by the terrific figure, dripping blood, and wholly unconscious of danger.

"Forward!" cried a Mexican officer, and one of his men went down with a shattered skull. The others shrank back again, but a new figure pressed into the ring. It was that of the younger Urrea. At the last moment he had left the cavalry and joined in the assault.

"Don't come within reach of his blows!" he cried. "Shoot him! Shoot him!"

He snatched a double-barreled pistol from his own belt and fired twice straight at Crockett's breast. The great Tennesseean staggered, dropped his rifle and the flame died from his eyes. With a howl of triumph his foes rushed upon him, plunged their swords and bayonets into his body, and he fell dead with a heap of the Mexican slain about him.

A bullet whistled past Urrea's face and killed a man beyond him. He sprang back. Bowie, still suffering severe injuries from a fall from a platform, was lying on a cot in the arched room to the left of the entrance. Unable to walk, he had received at his request two pistols, and now he was firing them as fast as he could pull the triggers and reload.

"Shoot him! Shoot him at once!" cried Urrea.

His own pistol was empty now, but a dozen musket balls were fired into the room. Bowie, hit twice, nevertheless raised himself upon his elbow, aimed a pistol with a clear eye and a steady hand, and pulled the trigger. A Mexican fell, shot through the heart, but another volley of musket balls was discharged at the Georgian. Struck in both head and heart he suddenly straightened out and lay still upon the cot. Thus died the famous Bowie.

Mrs. Dickinson and her baby had been hidden in the arched room on the other side for protection. The Mexicans killed a Texan named Walters at the entrance, and, wild with ferocity, raised his body upon a half dozen bayonets while the blood ran down in a dreadful stream upon those who held it aloft.

Urrea rushed into the room and found the cowering woman and her baby. The Mexicans followed, and were about to slay them, too, when a gallant figure rushed between. It was the brave and humane Almonte. Sword in hand, he faced the savage horde. He uttered words that made Urrea turn dark with shame and leave the room. The soldiers were glad to follow.

At the far end of the church a few Texans were left, still fighting with clubbed rifles. The Mexicans drew back a little, raised their muskets and fired an immense shattering volley. When the smoke cleared away not a single Texan was standing, and then the troops rushed in with sword and bayonet.

It was nine o'clock in the morning, and the Alamo had fallen. The defenders were less than nine score, and they had died to the last man. A messenger rushed away at once to Santa Anna with the news of the triumph, and he came from the shelter, glorying, exulting and crying that he had destroyed the Texans.

Ned followed the dictator. He never knew exactly why, because many of those moments were dim, like the scenes of a dream, and there was so much noise, excitement and confusion that no one paid any attention to him. But an overwhelming power drew him on to the Alamo, and he rushed in with the Mexican spectators.

Ned passed through the sallyport and he reeled back aghast for a moment. The Mexican dead, not yet picked up, were strewn everywhere. They had fallen in scores. The lighter buildings were smashed by cannon balls and shells. The earth was gulleyed and torn. The smoke from so much firing drifted about in banks and clouds, and it gave forth the pungent odor of burned gunpowder.

The boy knew not only that the Alamo had fallen, but that all of its defenders had fallen with it. The knowledge was instinctive. He had been with those men almost to the last day of the siege, and he had understood their spirit.

He was not noticed in the crush. Santa Anna and the generals were running into the church, and he followed them. Here he saw the Texan dead, and he saw also a curious crowd standing around a fallen form. He pressed into the ring and his heart gave a great throb of grief.

It was Crockett, lying upon his back, his body pierced by many wounds. Ned had known that he would find him thus, but the shock, nevertheless, was terrible. Yet Crockett's countenance was calm. He bore no wounds in the face, and he lay almost as if he had died in his bed. It seemed to Ned even in his grief that no more fitting death could have come to the old hero.

Then, following another crowd, he saw Bowie, also lying peacefully in death upon his cot. He felt the same grief for him that he had felt for Crockett, but it soon passed in both cases. A strange mood of exaltation took its place. They had died as one might wish to die, since death must come to all. It was glorious that these defenders of the Alamo, comrades of his, should have fallen to the last man. The full splendor of their achievement suddenly burst in a dazzling vision before him. Texans who furnished such valor could not be conquered. Santa Anna might have twenty to one or fifty to one or a hundred to one, in the end it would not matter.

The mood endured. He looked upon the dead faces of Travis and Bonham also, and he was not shaken. He saw others, dozens and dozens whom he knew, and the faces of all of them seemed peaceful to him. The shouting and cheering and vast chatter of the Mexicans did not disturb him. His mood was so high that all these things passed as nothing.

Ned made no attempt to escape. He knew that while he might go about almost as he chose in this crowd of soldiers, now disorganized, the ring of cavalry beyond would hold him. The thought of escape, however, was but little in his mind just then. He was absorbed in the great tomb of the Alamo. Here, despite the recent work of the cannon, all things looked familiar. He could mark the very spots where he had stood and talked with Crockett or Bowie. He knew how the story of the immortal defence would spread like fire throughout Texas and beyond. When he should tell how he had seen the faces of the heroes, every heart must leap.

He wandered back to the church, where the curious still crowded. Many people from the town, influential Mexicans, wished to see the terrible Texans, who yet lay as they had fallen. Some spoke scornful words, but most regarded them with awe. Ned looked at Crockett for the second time, and a hand touched him on the shoulder. It was Urrea.

"Where are your Texans now?" he asked.

"They are gone," replied Ned, "but they will never be forgotten." And then he added in a flash of anger. "Five or six times as many Mexicans have gone with them."

"It is true," said the young Mexican thoughtfully. "They fought like cornered mountain wolves. We admit it. And this one, Crockett you call him, was perhaps the most terrible of them all. He swung his clubbed rifle so fiercely that none dared come within its reach. I slew him."

"You?" exclaimed Ned.

"Yes, I! Why should I not? I fired two pistol bullets into him and he fell."

He spoke with a certain pride. Ned said nothing, but he pressed his teeth together savagely and his heart swelled with hate of the sleek and triumphant Urrea.

"General Santa Anna, engrossed in much more important matters, has doubtless forgotten you," continued the Mexican, "but I will see that you do not escape. Why he spares you I know not, but it is his wish."

He called to two soldiers, whom he detailed to follow Ned and see that he made no attempt to escape. The boy was yet so deeply absorbed in the Alamo that no room was left in his mind for anything else. Nor did he care to talk further with Urrea, who he knew was not above aiming a shaft or two at an enemy in his power. He remained in the crowd until Santa Anna ordered that all but the troops be cleared from the Alamo.

Then, at the order of the dictator, the bodies of the Texans were taken without. A number of them were spread upon the ground, and were covered with a thick layer of dry wood and brush. Then more bodies of men and heaps of dry wood were spread in alternate layers until the funeral pile was complete.

Young Urrea set the torch, while the Mexican army and population looked on. The dry wood flamed up rapidly and the whole was soon a pyramid of fire and smoke. Ned was not shocked at this end, even of the bodies of brave men. He recalled the stories of ancient heroes, the bodies of whom had been consumed on just such pyres as this, and he was willing that his comrades should go to join Hercules, Hector, Achilles and the rest.

The flames roared and devoured the great pyramid, which sank lower, and at last Ned turned away. His mood of exaltation was passing. No one could remain keyed to that pitch many hours. Overwhelming grief and despair came in its place. His mind raged against everything, against the cruelty of Santa Anna, who had hoisted the red flag of no quarter, against fate, that had allowed so many brave men to perish, and against the overwhelming numbers that the Mexicans could always bring against the Texans.

He walked gloomily toward the town, the two soldiers who had been detailed as guards following close behind him. He looked back, saw the sinking blaze of the funeral pyre, shuddered and walked on.

San Antonio de Bexar was rejoicing. Most of its people, Mexican to the core, shared in the triumph of Santa Anna. The terrible Texans were gone, annihilated, and Santa Anna was irresistible. The conquest of Texas was easy now. No, it was achieved already. They had the dictator's own word for it that the rest was a mere matter of gathering up the fragments.

Some of the graver and more kindly Mexican officers thought of their own losses. The brave and humane Almonte walked through the courts and buildings of the Alamo, and his face blanched when he reckoned their losses. A thousand men killed or wounded was a great price to pay for the nine score Texans who were sped. But no such thoughts troubled Santa Anna. All the vainglory of his nature was aflame. They were decorating the town with all the flags and banners and streamers they could find, and he knew that it was for him. At night they would illuminate in his honor. He stretched out his arm toward the north and west, and murmured that it was all his. He would be the ruler of an empire half the size of Europe. The scattered and miserable Texans could set no bounds to his ambition. He had proved it.

He would waste no more time in that empty land of prairies and plains. He sent glowing dispatches about his victory to the City of Mexico and announced that he would soon come. His subordinates would destroy the wandering bands of Texans. Then he did another thing that appealed to his vanity. He wrote a proclamation to the Texans announcing the fall of the Alamo, and directing them to submit at once, on pain of death, to his authority. He called for Mrs. Dickinson, the young wife, now widow, whom the gallantry of Almonte had saved from massacre in the Alamo. He directed her to take his threat to the Texans at Gonzales, and she willingly accepted. Mounting a horse and alone save for the baby in her arms, she rode away from San Antonio, shuddering at the sight of the Mexicans, and passed out upon the desolate and dangerous prairies.

The dictator was so absorbed in his triumph and his plans for his greater glory that for the time he forgot all about Ned Fulton, his youthful prisoner, who had crossed the stream and who was now in the town, attended by the two peons whom Urrea had detailed as his guards. But Ned had come out of his daze, and his mind was as keen and alert as ever. The effects of the great shock of horror remained. His was not a bitter nature, but he could not help feeling an intense hatred of the Mexicans. He was on the battle line, and he saw what they were doing. He resolved that now was his time to escape, and in the great turmoil caused by the excitement and rejoicing in San Antonio he did not believe that it would be difficult.

He carefully cultivated the good graces of the two soldiers who were guarding him. He bought for them mescal and other fiery drinks which were now being sold in view of the coming festival. Their good nature increased and also their desire to get rid of a task that had been imposed upon them. Why should they guard a boy when everybody else was getting ready to be merry?

They went toward the Main Plaza, and came to the Zambrano Row, where the Texans had fought their way when they took San Antonio months before. Ned looked up at the buildings. They were still dismantled. Great holes were in the walls and the empty windows were like blind eyes. He saw at once that their former inhabitants had not yet returned to them, and here he believed was his chance.

When they stood beside the first house he called the attention of his guards to some Mexican women who were decorating a doorway across the street. When they looked he darted into the first of the houses in the Zambrano Row. He entered a large room and at the corner saw a stairway. He knew this place. He had been here in the siege of San Antonio by the Texans, and now he had the advantage over his guards, who were probably strangers.

He rushed for the staircase and, just as he reached the top, one of the guards, who had followed as soon as they noticed the flight of the prisoner, fired his musket. The discharge roared in the room, but the bullet struck the wall fully a foot away from the target. Ned was on the second floor, and out of range the next moment. He knew that the soldiers would follow him, and he passed through the great hole, broken by the Texans, into the next house.

Here he paused to listen, and he heard the two soldiers muttering and breathing heavily. The distaste which they already felt for their task had become a deep disgust. Why should they be deprived of their part in the festival to follow up a prisoner? What did a single captive amount to, anyhow? Even if he escaped now the great, the illustrious Santa Anna, whose eyes saw all things, would capture him later on when he swept all the scattered Texans into his basket.

Ned went from house to house through the holes broken in the party walls, and occasionally he heard his pursuers slouching along and grumbling. At the fourth house he slipped out upon the roof, and lay flat near the stone coping.

He knew that if the soldiers came upon the roof they would find him, but he relied upon the mescal and their lack of zeal. He heard them once tramping about in the room below him, and then he heard them no more.

Ned remained all the rest of the afternoon upon the roof, not daring to leave his cramped position against the coping. He felt absolutely safe there from observation, Mexicans would not be prowling through dismantled and abandoned houses at such a time. Now and then gay shouts came from the streets below. The Mexicans of Bexar were disturbed little by the great numbers of their people who had fallen at the Alamo. The dead were from the far valleys of Mexico, and were strangers.

Ned afterward thought that he must have slept a little toward twilight, but he was never sure of it. He saw the sun set, and the gray and silent Alamo sink away into the darkness. Then he slipped from the roof, anxious to be away before the town was illuminated. He had no difficulty at all in passing unnoticed through the streets, and he made his way straight for the Alamo.

He was reckoning very shrewdly now. He knew that the superstitious Mexicans would avoid the mission at night as a place thronged with ghosts, and that Santa Anna would not need to post any guard within those walls. He would pass through the inclosures, then over the lower barriers by which the Mexicans had entered, and thence into the darkness beyond.

It seemed to him the best road to escape, and he had another object also in entering the Alamo. The defenders had had three or four rifles apiece, and he was convinced that somewhere in the rooms he would find a good one, with sufficient ammunition.

It was with shudders that he entered the Alamo, and the shudders came again when he looked about the bloodstained courts and rooms, lately the scene of such terrible strife, but now so silent. In a recess of the church which had been used as a little storage place by himself and Crockett he found an excellent rifle of the long-barreled Western pattern, a large horn of powder and a pouch full of bullets. There was also a supply of dried beef, which he took, too.

Now he felt himself a man again. He would find the Texans and then they would seek vengeance for the Alamo. He crossed the Main Plaza, dropped over the low wall and quickly disappeared in the dusk.

CHAPTER XIV.
THE NEWS OF THE FALL

Five days before the fall of the Alamo a little group of men began to gather at the village of Washington, on the Brazos river in Texas. The name of the little town indicated well whence its people had come. All the houses were new, mostly of unpainted wood, and they contained some of the furniture of necessity, none of luxury. The first and most important article was the rifle which the Texans never needed more than they did now.

But this new and little Washington was seething with excitement and suspense, and its population was now more than triple the normal. News had come that the Alamo was beleaguered by a force many times as numerous as its defenders, and that Crockett, Bowie, Travis and other famous men were inside. They had heard also that Santa Anna had hoisted the red flag of no quarter, and that Texans everywhere, if taken, would be slaughtered as traitors. The people of Washington had full cause for their excitement and suspense.

The little town also had the unique distinction of being a capital for a day or two. The Texans felt, with the news that Santa Anna had enveloped the Alamo, that they must take decisive action. They believed that the Mexicans had broken every promise to the Texans. They knew that not only their liberty and property, but their lives, also, were in peril. Despite the great disparity of numbers it must be a fight to the death between Texas and Mexico. The Texans were now gathering at Washington.

One man who inspired courage wherever he went had come already. Sam Houston had ridden into town, calm, confident and talking only of victory. He was dressed with a neatness and care unusual on the border, wearing a fine black suit, while his face was shaded by the wide brim of a white sombrero. The famous scouts, "Deaf" Smith and Henry Karnes, and young Zavala, whom Ned had known in Mexico, were there also.

Fifty-eight delegates representing Texas gathered in the largest room of a frame building. "Deaf" Smith and Henry Karnes came in and sat with their rifles across their knees. While some of the delegates were talking Houston signaled to the two, and they went outside.

"What do you hear from the Alamo, Smith?" asked Houston.

"Travis has fought off all the attacks of the Mexicans," replied the great borderer, "but when Santa Anna brings up his whole force an' makes a resolute assault it's bound to go under. The mission is too big an' scattered to be held by Travis an' his men against forty or fifty times their number."

"I fear so. I fear so," said Houston sadly, "and we can't get together enough men for its relief. All this quarreling and temporizing are our ruin. Heavens, what a time for disagreements!"

"There couldn't be a worse time, general," said Henry Karnes. "Me an' 'Deaf' would like mighty well to march to the Alamo. A lot of our friends are in there an' I reckon we've seen them for the last time."

The fine face of Houston grew dark with melancholy.

"Have you been anywhere near San Antonio?" he asked Smith.

"Not nearer than thirty miles," replied Smith, "but over at Goliad I saw a force under Colonel Fannin that was gettin' ready to start to the relief of Travis. With it were some friends of mine. There was Palmer, him they call the Panther, the biggest and strongest man in Texas; Obed White, a New Englander, an' a boy, Will Allen. I've knowed 'em well for some time, and there was another that belonged to their little band. But he's in the Alamo now, an' they was wild to rescue him."

"Do you think Fannin will get through?" asked Houston.

"I don't," replied Smith decidedly, "an' if he did it would just mean the loss of more good men for us. What do you think about it, Hank?"

"The same that you do," replied Karnes.

Houston pondered over their words a long time. He knew that they were thoroughly acquainted with Texas and the temper of its people, and he relied greatly on their judgment. When he went back in the room which was used as a convention hall Smith and Karnes remained outside.

Smith sat down on the grass, lighted a pipe and began to smoke deliberately. Karnes also sat down on the grass, lighted his own pipe and smoked with equal deliberation. Each man rested his rifle across his knees.

"Looks bad," said Smith.

"Powerful bad."

"Almighty bad."

"Talkin's no good when the enemy's shootin'."

"Reckon there's nothin' left for us but this," tapping the barrel of his rifle significantly.

"Only tool that's left for us to use."

"Reckon we'll soon have as many chances as we want to use it, an' more."

"Reckon you're Almighty right."

"An' we'll be there every time."

The two men reached over and shook hands deliberately. Houston by and by came out again, and saw them sitting there smoking, two images of patience and quiet.

"Boys," he said, "you're not taking much part in the proceedings."

"Not much, just yet, Colonel Sam," replied Smith, "but we're waitin'. I reckon that to-morrow you'll declare Texas free an' independent, a great an' good republic. An' as there ain't sixty of you to declare it, mebbe you'll need the help of some fellows like Hank an' me to make them resolutions come true."

"We will," said Houston, "and we know that we can rely upon you."

He was about to pass on, but he changed his mind and sat down with the men. Houston was a singular character. He had been governor of an important state, and he had lived as a savage among savages. He could adapt himself to any company.

"Boys," he said, "you know a merchant, John Roylston, who has headquarters in New Orleans, and also offices in St. Louis and Cincinnati?"

"We do," said Smith, "an' we've seen him, too, more than once. He's been in these parts not so long ago."

"He's in New Orleans now," said Houston. "He's the biggest trader along the coast. Has dealings with Santa Anna himself, but he's a friend of Texas, a powerful one. Boys, I've in my pocket now an order from him good for a hundred thousand dollars. It's to be spent buying arms and ammunition for us. And when the time comes there's more coming from the same place. We've got friends, but keep this to yourselves."

He walked on and the two took a long and meditative pull at their pipes.

"I reckon Roylston may not shoot as straight as we can," said Smith, "but mebbe at as long range as New Orleans he can do more harm to the Mexicans than we can."

"Looks like it. I ain't much of a hand at money, but I like the looks of that man Roylston, an' I reckon the more rifles and the more ammunition we have the fewer Mexicans will be left."

The two scouts, having smoked as long as they wished, went to their quarters and slept soundly through the night. But Houston and the leading Texans with him hardly slept at all. There was but one course to choose, and they were fully aware of its gravity, Houston perhaps more so than the rest, as he had seen more of the world. They worked nearly all night in the bare room, and when Houston sought his room he was exhausted.

Houston's room was a bare little place, lighted by a tallow candle, and although it was not long until day he sat there a while before lying down. A man of wide experience, he alone, with the exception of Roylston, knew how desperate was the situation of the Texans. In truth, it was the money of Roylston sent from New Orleans that had caused him to hazard the chance. He knew, too, that, in time, more help would arrive from the same source, and he believed there would be a chance against the Mexicans, a fighting chance, it is true, but men who were willing to die for a cause seldom failed to win. He blew out the candle, got in bed and slept soundly.

"Deaf" Smith and Henry Karnes were up early—they seldom slept late— and saw the sun rise out of the prairie. They were in a house which had a small porch, looking toward the Brazos. After breakfast they lighted their cob pipes again, smoked and meditated.

"Reckon somethin' was done by our leadin' statesmen last night," said Smith.

"Reckon there was," said Karnes.

"Reckon I can guess what it was."

"Reckon I can, too."

"Reckon I'll wait to hear it offish-ul-ly before I speak."

"Reckon I will, too. Lots of time wasted talkin'."

"Reckon you're right."

They sat in silence for a full two hours. They smoked the first hour, and they passed the second in their chairs without moving. They had mastered the borderer's art of doing nothing thoroughly, when nothing was to be done. Then a man came upon the porch and spoke to them. His name was Burnet, David G. Burnet.

"Good mornin'. How is the new republic?" said "Deaf" Smith.

"So you know," said Burnet.

"We don't know, but we've guessed, Hank an' me. We saw things as they was comin'."

"I reckon, too," said Karnes, "that we ain't a part of Mexico any more."

"No, we're a free an' independent republic. It was so decided last night, and we've got nothing more to do now but to whip a nation of eight millions, the fifty thousand of us."

"Well," said Smith philosophically, "it's a tough job, but it might be did. I've heard tell that them old Greeks whipped the Persians when the odds were powerful high against them."

"That is true," said Burnet, "and we can at least try. We give the reason for declaring our independence. We assert to the world that the Mexican republic has become a military despotism, that our agents carrying petitions have been thrown in dungeons in the City of Mexico, that we have been ordered to give up the arms necessary for our defence against the savages, and that we have been deprived of every right guaranteed to us when we settled here."

"We're glad it's done, although we knew it would be done," said Smith. "We ain't much on talkin', Mr. President, Hank an' me, but we can shoot pretty straight, an' we're at your call."

"I know that, God bless you both," said Burnet. "The talking is over. It's rifles that we need and plenty of them. Now I've to see Houston. We're to talk over ways and means."

He hurried away, and the two, settling back into their chairs on the porch, relighted their pipes and smoked calmly.

"Reckon there'll be nothin' doin' for a day or two, Hank," said Smith.

"Reckon not, but we'll have to be doin' a powerful lot later, or be hoofin' it for the tall timber a thousand miles north."

"You always was full of sense, Hank. Now there goes Sam Houston. Queer stories about his leavin' Tennessee and his life in the Indian Territory."

"That's so, but he's an honest man, looks far ahead, an' 'tween you an' me, 'Deaf,' it's a thousand to one that he's to lead us in the war."

"Reckon you're guessin' good."

Houston, who had just awakened and dressed, was walking across the grass and weeds to meet Burnet. Not even he, when he looked at the tiny village and the wilderness spreading about it, foresaw how mighty a state was to rise from beginnings so humble and so small. He and Burnet went back into the convention hall, and he wrote a fiery appeal to the people. He said that the Alamo was beleaguered and "the citizens of Texas must rally to the aid of our army or it will perish."

Smith and Karnes remained while the convention continued its work. They did little ostensibly but smoke their cob pipes, but they observed everything and thought deeply. On Sunday morning, five days after the men had gathered at Washington, as they stood at the edge of the little town they saw a man galloping over the prairie. Neither spoke, but watched him for a while, as the unknown came on, lashing a tired horse.

"'Pears to be in a hurry," said Smith.

"An' to be in a hurry generally means somethin' in these parts," said Karnes.

"I'm makin' 'a guess."

"So am I, an' yours is the same as mine. He comes from the Alamo."

Others now saw the man, and there was a rush toward him. His horse fell at the edge of the town, but the rider sprang to his feet and came toward the group, which included both Houston and Burnet. He was a wild figure, face and clothing covered with dust. But he recognized Houston and turned to him at once.

"You're General Houston, and I'm from the Alamo," he said. "I bring a message from Colonel Travis."

There was a sudden and heavy intake of breath in the whole group.

"Then the Alamo has not fallen?" said Houston.

"Not when I left, but that was three days ago. Here is the letter."

It was the last letter of Travis, concluding with the words: "God and Texas; victory or death." But when the messenger put the letter into the hands of Houston the Alamo had fallen two hours before.

The letter was laid before the convention, and the excitement was great and irrepressible. The feelings of these stern men were moved deeply. Many wished to adjourn at once and march to the relief of the Alamo, but the eloquence of Houston, who had been reelected Commander-in-chief, prevailed against the suggestion. Then, with two or three men, he departed for Gonzales to raise a force, while the others elected Burnet President of the new Texas, and departed for Harrisburg on Buffalo Bayou.

"Deaf" Smith and Henry Karnes did not go just then with Houston. They were scouts, hunters and rough riders, and they could do as they pleased. They notified General Sam Houston, commander-in-chief of the Texan armies, that they would come on later, and he was content.

When the Texan government and the Texan army, numbering combined about a hundred men, followed by most of the population, numbering fifty or sixty more, filed off for Gonzales, the two sat once more on the same porch, smoking their cob pipes. They were not ordinary men. They were not ordinary scouts and borderers. One from the north and one from the south, they were much alike in their mental processes, their faculties of keen observation and deep reasoning. Both were now stirred to the core, but neither showed a trace of it on his face. They watched the little file pass away over the prairie until it was lost to sight behind the swells, and then Smith spoke:

"I reckon you an' me, Hank, will ride toward the Alamo."

"I reckon we will, Deaf, and that right away."

Inside of five minutes they were on the road, armed and provisioned, the best two borderers, with the single exception of the Panther, in all the southwest. They were mounted on powerful mustangs, which, with proper handling and judicious rests, could go on forever. But they pushed them a little that afternoon, stopped for two hours after sundown, and then went on again. They crossed the Colorado River in the night, swimming their horses, and about a mile further on stopped in dense chaparral. They tethered the mustangs near them, and spread out their blankets.

"If anything comes the horses will wake us," said Smith.

"I reckon they will," said Karnes.

Both were fast asleep in a few minutes, but they awoke shortly after sunrise. They made a frugal breakfast, while the mustangs had cropped short grass in the night. Both horses and men, as tough and wiry as they ever become, were again as fresh as the dawn, and, with not more than a dozen words spoken, the two mounted and rode anew on their quest. Always chary of speech, they became almost silence itself as they drew nearer to San Antonio de Bexar. In the heart of each was a knowledge of the great tragedy, not surmise, but the certainty that acute intelligence deduces from facts.

They rode on until, by a simultaneous impulse, the two reined their horses back into a cypress thicket and waited. They had seen three horsemen on the sky line, coming, in the main, in their direction. Their trained eyes noticed at once that the strangers were of varying figure. The foremost, even at the distance, seemed to be gigantic, the second was very long and thin, and the third was normal. Smith and Karnes watched them a little while, and then Karnes spoke in words of true conviction.

"It would be hard, Deaf, for even a bad eye to mistake the foremost."

"Right you are, Hank. You might comb Texas with a fine-tooth comb an' you'd never rake out such another."

"If that ain't Mart Palmer, the Ring Tailed Panther, I'll go straight to Santa Anna an' ask him to shoot me as a fool."

"You won't have to go to Santa Anna."

Smith rode from the covert, put his curved hand to his mouth, and uttered a long piercing cry. The three horsemen stopped at once, and the giant in the lead gave back the signal in the same fashion. Then the two little parties rode rapidly toward each other. While they were yet fifty yards apart they uttered words of hail and good fellowship, and when they met they shook hands with the friendship that has been sealed by common hardships and dangers.

"You're goin' toward the Alamo?" said Smith.

"Yes," replied the Panther. "We started that way several days ago, but we've been delayed. We had a brush with one little party of Mexicans, and we had to dodge another that was too big for us. I take it that you ride for the same place."

"We do. Were you with Fannin?"

The dark face of the Panther grew darker.

"We were," he replied. "He started to the relief of the Alamo, but the ammunition wagon broke down, an' they couldn't get the cannon across the San Antonio River. So me an' Obed White an' Will Allen here have come on alone."

"News for news," said Smith dryly. "Texas has just been made a free an' independent republic, an' Sam Houston has been made commander-in-chief of all its mighty armies, horse, foot an' cannon. We saw all them things done back there at Washington settlement, an' we, bein' a part of the army, are ridin' to-the relief of the Alamo."

"We j'in you, then," said the Panther, "an' Texas raises two armies of the strength of three an' two to one of five. Oh, if only all the Texans had come what a roarin' an' rippin' an' t'arin' and chawin' there would have been when we struck Santa Anna's army, no matter how big it might be."

"But they didn't come," said Smith grimly, "an' as far as I know we five are all the Texans that are ridin' toward San Antonio de Bexar an' the Alamo."

"But bein' only five won't keep us from ridin' on," said the Panther.

"And things are not always as bad as they look," said Obed White, after he had heard of the messenger who had come to Houston and Unmet. "It's never too late to hope."

The five rode fast the remainder of the day. They passed through a silent and desolate land. They saw a few cabins, but every one was abandoned. The deep sense of tragedy was over them all, even over young Will Allen. They rarely spoke, and they rode along in silence, save for the beat of their horses' hoofs. Shortly before night they met a lone buffalo hunter whom the Panther knew.

"Have you been close to San Antonio, Simpson?" asked the Panther, after the greeting.

"I've been three or four days hangin' 'roun' the neighborhood," replied the hunter. "I came down from the northwest when I heard that Santa Anna was advancing an' once I thought I'd make a break an' try to get into the Alamo, but the Mexican lines was drawed too thick an' close."

"Have you heard anything about the men inside?" asked the Panther eagerly.

"Not a thing. But I've noticed this. A mornin' an' evenin' gun was fired from the fortress every day until yesterday, Sunday, an' since then—nothin'."

The silence in the little band was as ominous as the silence of the morning and evening gun. Simpson shook his head sadly.

"Boys," he said, "I'm goin' to ride for Gonzales an' join Houston. I don't think it's any use for me to be hangin' aroun' San Antonio de Bexar any longer. I wish you luck in whatever you're tryin' to do."

He rode away, but the five friends continued their course toward the Alamo, without hope now, but resolved to see for themselves. Deep in the night, which fortunately for their purpose was dark, heavy clouds shutting out the moon and stars, they approached San Antonio from the east. They saw lights, which they knew were those of the town, but there was darkness only where they knew the Alamo stood.

They tethered their horses in some bushes and crept closer, until they could see the dim bulk of the Alamo. No light shone there. They listened long and intently, but not a single sound came from the great hecatomb. Again they crept nearer. There were no Mexican guards anywhere. A little further and they stood by the low northern wall.

"Boys," said the Panther, "I can't stand it any longer. Queer feelin's are runnin' all over me. No, I'm goin' to take the risk, if there is any, all alone. You wait for me here, an' if I don't come back in an hour then you can hunt for me."

The Panther climbed over the wall and disappeared. The others remained in the deepest shadow waiting and silent. They were oppressed by the heavy gloom that hung over the Alamo. It was terrifying to young Will Allen, not the terror that is caused by the fear of men, but the terror that comes from some tragic mystery that is more than half guessed.

Nearly an hour passed, when a great figure leaped lightly from the wall and joined them. The swarthy face of the Panther was as white as chalk, and he was shivering.

"Boys," he whispered, "I've seen what I never want to see ag'in. I've seen red, red everywhere. I've been through the rooms of the Alamo, an' they're red, splashed with the red blood of men. The water in the ditch was stained with red, an' the earth all about was soaked with it. Somethin' awful must have happened in the Alamo. There must have been a terrible fight, an' I'm thinkin' that most of our fellows must have died before it was took. But it's give me the creeps, boys, an' I think we'd better get away."

"We can't leave any too quick to please me," said Will Alien. "I'm seeing ghosts all the time."

"Now that we know for sure the Alamo has fallen," said Smith, "nothin' is to be gained by stayin' here. It's for Sam Houston to lead us to revenge, and the more men he has the better. I vote we ride for Gonzales."

"Seein' what we can see as we go," said Karnes. "The more information we can pick up on the way about the march of the Mexicans the better it will be for Houston."

"No doubt of that," said the Panther. "When we go to roarin' an' rippin' an' t'arin' we must know what we're about. But come on, boys, all that red in the Alamo gives me conniption fits."

They rode toward the east for a long time until they thought they were beyond the reach of Mexican skirmishing parties, and then they slept in a cypress thicket, Smith and Karnes standing guard by turns. As everybody needed rest they did not resume their journey the next day until nearly noon, and they spent most of the afternoon watching for Mexican scouts, although they saw none. They had a full rest that night and the next day they rode slowly toward Gonzales.

About the middle of the afternoon, as they reached the crest of a swell, Will Allen uttered an exclamation, and pointed toward the eastern horizon. There they saw a single figure on horseback, and another walking beside it. The afternoon sun was very bright, casting a glow over the distant figures, and, shading their eyes with their hands, they gazed at them a long time.

"It's a woman that's ridin'," said Smith at last, "an' she's carryin' some sort of a bundle before her."

"You're shorely right, Deaf," said Karnes, "an' I think the one walkin' is a black fellow. Looks like it from here."

"I'm your way of thinkin'," said the Panther, "an' the woman on the horse is American, or I'm mightily fooled in my guess. S'pose we ride ahead faster an' see for shore."

They increased the speed of their mustangs to a gallop and rapidly overhauled the little party. They saw the woman trying to urge her horse to greater speed. But the poor beast, evidently exhausted, made no response. The woman, turning in the saddle, looked back at her pursuers.

"By all that's wonderful!" exclaimed Obed White, "the bundle that she's carrying is a baby!"

"It's so," said Smith, "an' you can see well enough now that she's one of our own people. We must show her that she's got nothin' to fear from us."

He shouted through his arched hands in tremendous tones that they were Texans and friends. The woman stopped, and as they galloped up she would have fallen from her horse had not Obed White promptly seized her and, dismounting, lifted her and the baby tenderly to the ground. The colored boy who had been walking stood by and did not say anything aloud, but muttered rapidly: "Thank the Lord! Thank the Lord!"

Three of the five were veteran hunters, but they had never before found such a singular party on the prairie. The woman sat down on the ground, still holding the baby tightly in her arms, and shivered all over. The Texans regarded her in pitying silence for a few minutes, and then Obed White said in gentle tones:

"We are friends, ready to take you to safety. Tell us who you are."

"I am Mrs. Dickinson," she replied.

"Deaf" Smith looked startled.

"There was a Lieutenant Dickinson in the Alamo," he said.

"I am his wife," she replied, "and this is our child."

"And where is——" Smith stopped suddenly, knowing what the answer must be.

"He is dead," she replied. "He fell in the defence of the Alamo."

"Might he not be among the prisoners?" suggested Obed White gently.

"Prisoners!" she replied. "There were no prisoners. They fought to the last. Every man who was in the Alamo died in its defence."

The five stared at her in amazement, and for a little while none spoke.

"Do you mean to say," asked Obed White, "that none of the Texans survived the fall of the Alamo?"

"None," she replied.

"How do you know?"

Her pale face filled with color. It seemed that she, too, at that moment felt some of the glow that the fall of the Alamo was to suffuse through Texas.

"Because I saw," she replied. "I was in one of the arched rooms of the church, where they made the last stand. I saw Crockett fall and I saw the death of Bowie, too. I saw Santa Anna exult, but many, many Mexicans fell also. It was a terrible struggle. I shall see it again every day of my life, even if I live to be a hundred."

She covered her face with her hands, as if she would cut out the sight of that last inferno in the church. The others were silent, stunned for the time.

"All gone," said Obed White, at last. "When the news is spread that every man stood firm to the last I think it will light such a fire in Texas that Santa Anna and all his armies cannot put it out."

"Did you see a boy called Ned Fulton in the Alamo, a tall, handsome fellow with brown hair and gray eyes?" asked Obed White.

"Often," replied Mrs. Dickinson. "He was with Crockett and Bowie a great deal."

"And none escaped?" said Will Allen.

"Not one," she repeated, "I did not see him in the church in the final assault. He doubtless fell in the hospital or in the convent yard. Ah, he was a friend of yours! I am sorry."

"Yes, he was a friend of ours," said the Panther. "He was more than that to me. I loved that boy like a son, an' me an' my comrades here mean to see that the Mexicans pay a high price for his death. An' may I ask, ma'am, how you come to be here?"

She told him how Santa Anna had provided her with the horse, and had sent her alone with the proclamation to the Texans. At the Salado Creek she had come upon the negro servant of Travis, who had escaped from San Antonio, and he was helping her on the way.

"An' now, ma'am," said "Deaf" Smith, "we'll guard you the rest of the way to Gonzales."

The two little groups, now fused into one, resumed their journey over the prairie.

CHAPTER XV.
IN ANOTHER TRAP

When Ned Fulton scaled the lowest wall of the Alamo and dropped into the darkness he ran for a long time. He scarcely knew in what direction he was going, but he was anxious to get away from that terrible town of San Antonio de Bexar. He was filled with grief for his friends and anger against Santa Anna and his people. He had passed through an event so tremendous in its nature, so intense and fiery in its results, that his whole character underwent a sudden change. But a boy in years, the man nevertheless replaced the boy in his mind. He had looked upon the face of awful things, so awful that few men could bear to behold them.

There was a certain hardening of his nature now. As he ran, and while the feeling of horror was still upon him, the thought of vengeance swelled into a passion. The Texans must strike back for what had been done in the Alamo. Surely all would come when they heard the news that he was bringing.

He believed that the Texans, and they must be assembled in force somewhere, would be toward the east or the southeast, at Harrisburg or Goliad or some other place. He would join them as soon as he could, and he slackened his pace to a walk. He was too good a borderer now to exhaust himself in the beginning.

He was overpowered after a while by an immense lethargy. A great collapse, both physical and mental, came after so much exhaustion. He felt that he must rest or die. The night was mild, as the spring was now well advanced in Texas, and he sought a dense thicket in which he might lie for a while. But there was no scrub or chaparral within easy reach, and his feeling of lassitude became so great that he stopped when he came to a huge oak and lay down under the branches, which spread far and low.

He judged that he was about six miles from San Antonio, a reasonably safe distance for the night, and, relaxing completely, he fell asleep. Then nature began her great work. The pulses which were beating so fast and hard in the hoy's body grew slower and more regular, and at last became normal.

The blood flowed in a fresh and strong current through his veins. The great physician, minute by minute, was building up his system again.

Ned's collapse had been so complete that he did not stir for hours. The day came and the sun rose brilliant in red and gold. The boy did not stir, but not far away a large animal moved. Ned's tree was at the edge of a little grassy plain, and upon this the animal stood, with a head held high and upturned nose sniffing the breeze that came from the direction of the sleeper.

It was in truth a great animal, one with tremendous teeth, and after hesitating a while it walked toward the tree under which the boy lay. Here it paused and again sniffed the air, which was now strong with the human odor. It remained there a while, staring with great eyes at the sleeping form, and then went back to the grassy little meadow. It revisited the boy at intervals, but never disturbed him, and Ned slept peacefully on.

It was nearly noon when Ned awoke, and he might not have awakened then had not the sun from its new position sent a shaft of light directly into his eyes. He saw that his precious rifle was still lying by his side, and then he sprang to his feet, startled to find by the sun that it was so late. He heard a loud joyous neigh, and a great bay horse trotted toward him.

It was Old Jack, the faithful dumb brute, of which he had thought so rarely during all those tense days in the Alamo. The Mexicans had not taken him. He was here, and happy chance had brought him and his master together again. It was so keen a joy to see a friend again, even an animal, that Ned put his arm around Old Jack's neck, and for the first time tears came to his eyes.

"Good Old Jack!" he said, patting his horse's nose. "You must have been waiting here all the time for me. And you must have fared well, too. I never before saw you looking so fat and saucy."

The finding of the horse simplified Ned's problem somewhat. He had neither saddle nor bridle, but Old Jack always obeyed him beautifully. He believed that if it came to the pinch, and it became necessary for him to ride for his life, he could guide him in the Indian fashion with the pressure of the knees.

He made a sort of halter of withes which he fastened on Old Jack's head, and then he sprang upon his bare back, feeling equal to almost anything. He rode west by south now, his course taking him toward Goliad, and he went on at a good gait until twilight. A little later he made out the shapes of wild turkeys, then very numerous in Texas among the boughs of the trees, and he brought a fine fat one down at the first shot. After some difficulty he lighted a fire with the flint and steel, which the Mexicans fortunately had not taken from him, toasted great strips over the coals, and ate hungrily of juicy and tender wild turkey.

He was all the time aware that his fire might bring danger down upon him, but he was willing to chance it. After he had eaten enough he took the remainder of his turkey and rode on. It was a clear, starry night and, as he had been awake only since noon, he continued until about ten o'clock, when he again took the turf under a tree for a couch. He slipped the rude halter from Old Jack, patted him on the head and said:

"Old Jack, after the lofty way in which you have behaved I wouldn't disgrace you by tying you up for the night. Moreover, I know that you're the best guard I could possibly have, and so, trusting you implicitly, I shall go to sleep."

His confidence was justified, and the next morning they were away again over the prairie. Ned was sure that he would meet roving Texans or Mexicans before noon, but he saw neither. He surmised that the news of Santa Anna's great force had sent all the Texans eastward, but the loneliness and desolation nevertheless weighed upon him.

He crossed several streams, all of them swollen and deep from spring rains, and every time he came to one he returned thanks again because he had found Old Jack. The great horse always took the flood without hesitation, and would come promptly to the other bank.

He saw many deer, and started up several flights of wild turkeys, but he did not disturb them. He was a soldier now, not a hunter, and he sought men, not animals. Another night came and found him still alone on the prairie. As before, he slept undisturbed under the boughs of a tree, and he awoke the next morning thoroughly sound in body and much refreshed in mind. But the feeling of hardness, the desire for revenge, remained. He was continually seeing the merciless face of Santa Anna and the sanguinary interior of the Alamo. The imaginative quality of his mind and his sensitiveness to cruelty had heightened the effect produced upon him.

He continued to ride through desolate country for several days, living on the game that his rifle brought. He slept one night in an abandoned cabin, with Old Jack resting in the grass that was now growing rankly at the door. He came the next day to a great trail, so great in truth that he believed it to have been made by Mexicans. He did not believe that there was anywhere a Texan force sufficient to tread out so broad a road.

He noticed, too, that the hoofs of the horses were turned in the general direction of Goliad or Victoria, nearer the sea, and he concluded that this was another strong Mexican army intended to complete the ruin of infant Texas.

He decided to follow, and near nightfall he saw the camp fires of a numerous force. He rode as near as he dared and reckoned that there were twelve or fifteen hundred men in the camp. He was sure that it was no part of the army with which Santa Anna had taken the Alamo.

Ned rode a wide circuit around the camp and continued his ride in the night. He was forced to rest and sleep a while toward morning, but shortly after daylight he went forward again to warn he knew not whom. Two or three hours later he saw two horsemen on the horizon, and he rode toward them. He knew that if they should prove to be Mexicans Old Jack was swift enough to carry him out of reach. But he soon saw that they were Texans, and he hailed them.

The two men stopped and watched him as he approached. The fact that he rode a horse without saddle or bridle was sufficient to attract their attention, and they saw, too, that he was wild in appearance, with long, uncombed hair and torn clothing. They were hunters who had come out from the little town of Refugio.

Ned hailed them again when he came closer.

"You are Texans and friends?" he said.

"Yes, we are Texans and friends," replied the older of the two men. "Who are you?"

"My name is Fulton, Edward Fulton, and I come from the Alamo."

"The Alamo? How could that be? How could you get out?"

"I was sent out on an errand by Colonel Crockett, a fictitious errand for the purpose of saving me, I now believe. But I fell at once into the hands of Santa Anna. The next morning the Alamo was taken by storm, but every Texan in it died in its defence. I saw it done."

Then he told to them the same tale that Mrs. Dickinson had told to the Panther and his little party, adding also that a large Mexican force was undoubtedly very near.

"Then you've come just in time," said the older man. "We've heard that a big force under General Urrea was heading for the settlements near the coast, and Captain King and twenty-five or thirty men are now at Refugio to take the people away. We'll hurry there with your news and we'll try to get you a saddle and bridle, too."

"For which I'll be thankful," said Ned.

But he was really more thankful for human companionship than anything else. He tingled with joy to be with the Texans again, and during the hours that they were riding to Refugio he willingly answered the ceaseless questions of the two men, Oldham and Jackson, who wanted to know everything that had happened at the Alamo. When they reached Refugio they found there Captain King with less than thirty men who had been sent by Fannin, as Jackson had said, to bring away the people.

Ned was taken at once to King, who had gathered his men in the little plaza. He saw that the soldiers were not Texans, that is, men who had long lived in Texas, but fresh recruits from the United States, wholly unfamiliar with border ways and border methods of fighting. The town itself was an old Mexican settlement with an ancient stone church or mission, after the fashion of the Alamo, only smaller.

"You say that you were in the Alamo, and that all the defenders have fallen except you?" said the Captain, looking curiously at Ned.

"Yes," replied the boy.

"And that the Mexican force dispatched against the Eastern settlements is much nearer than was supposed?"

"Yes," replied Ned, "and as proof of my words there it is now."

He had suddenly caught the gleam of lances in a wood a little distance to the west of the town, and he knew that the Mexican cavalry, riding ahead of the main army, was at hand. It was a large force, too, one with which the little band of recruits could not possibly cope in the open. Captain King seemed dazed, but Ned, glancing at the church, remembered the Alamo. Every Spanish church or mission was more or less of a fortress, and he exclaimed:

"The church, Captain, the church! We can hold it against the cavalry!"

"Good!" cried the Captain. "An excellent idea!"

They rushed for the church and Ned followed. Old Jack did not get the saddle and bridle that had been promised to him. When the boy leaped from his back he snatched off the halter of withes and shouted loudly to him: "Go!"

It pained him to abandon his horse a second time under compulsion, but there was no choice. Old Jack galloped away as if he knew what he ought to do, and then Ned, running into the church with the others, helped them to bar the doors.

The church was a solid building of stone with a flat roof, and with many loopholes made long ago as a defence against the Indians. Ned heard the cavalry thundering into the village as they barred the doors, and then he and half a dozen men ran to the roof. Lying down there, they took aim at the charging horsemen.

These were raw recruits, but they knew how to shoot. Their rifles flashed and four or five saddles were emptied. The men below were also firing from the loopholes, and the front rank of the Mexican cavalry was cut down by the bullets. The whole force turned at a shout from an officer, and galloped to the shelter of some buildings. Ned estimated that they were two hundred in number, and he surmised that young Urrea led them.

He descended from the roof and talked with King. The men understood their situation, but they were exultant. They had beaten off the enemy's cavalry, and they felt that the final victory must be theirs. But Ned had been in the Alamo, and he knew that the horsemen had merely hoped to surprise and overtake them with a dash. Stone fortresses are not taken by cavalry. He was sure that the present force would remain under cover until the main army came up with cannon. He suggested to Captain King that he send a messenger to Fannin for help.

King thought wisely of the suggestion and chose Jackson, who slipped out of the church, escaped through an oak forest and disappeared. Ned then made a careful examination of the church, which was quite a strong building with a supply of water inside and some dried corn. The men had brought rations also with them, and they were amply supplied for a siege of several days. But Ned, already become an expert in this kind of war, judged that it would not last so long. He believed that the Mexicans, flushed by the taking of the Alamo, would push matters.

King, lacking experience, leaned greatly on young Fulton. The men, who believed implicitly every word that he had said, regarded him almost with superstition. He alone of the defenders had come alive out of that terrible charnel house, the Alamo.

"I suspect," said King, "that the division you saw is under General Urrea."

"Very probably," said Ned. "Of course, Santa Anna, no longer having any use for his army in San Antonio, can send large numbers of troops eastward."

"Which means that we'll have a hard time defending this place," said King gloomily.

"Unless Fannin sends a big force to our help."

"I'm not so sure that he'll send enough," said King. "His men are nearly all fresh from the States, and they know nothing of the country. It's hard for him to tell what to do. We started once to the relief of the Alamo, but our ammunition wagon broke down and we could not get our cannon across the San Antonio River. Things don't seem to be going right with us."

Ned was silent. His thoughts turned back to the Alamo. And so Fannin and his men had started but had never come! Truly "things were going wrong!" But perhaps it was just as well. The victims would have only been more numerous, and Fannin's men were saved to fight elsewhere for Texas.

He heard a rattle of musketry, and through one of the loopholes he saw that the Mexican cavalry in the wood had opened a distant fire. Only a few of the bullets reached the church, and they fell spent against the stones. Ned saw that very little harm was likely to come from such a fire, but he believed it would be wise to show the Mexicans that the defenders were fully awake.

"Have you any specially good riflemen?" he asked King.

"Several."

"Suppose you put them at the loopholes and see if they can't pick off some of those Mexican horsemen. It would have a most healthy effect."

Six young men came forward, took aim with their long barreled rifles, and at King's command fired. Three of the saddles were emptied, and there was a rapid movement of the Mexicans, who withdrew further into the wood. The defenders reloaded and waited.

Ned knew better than Captain King or any of his men the extremely dangerous nature of their position. Since the vanguard was already here the Mexican army must be coming on rapidly, and this was no Alamo. Nor were these raw recruits defenders of an Alamo.

He saw presently a man, holding a white handkerchief on the end of a lance, ride out from the wood. Ned recognized him at once. It was young Urrea. As Ned had suspected, he was the leader of the cavalry for his uncle, the general.

"What do you think he wants?" asked King.

"He will demand our surrender, but even if we were to yield it is likely that we should be put to death afterward."

"I have no idea of surrendering under any circumstances. Do you speak Spanish?"

"Oh, yes," said Ned, seizing the opportunity.

"Then, as I can't, you do the talking for us, and tell it to him straight and hard that we're going to fight."

Ned climbed upon the roof, and sat with only his head showing above the parapet, while Urrea rode slowly forward, carrying the lance and the white flag jauntily. Ned could not keep from admiring his courage, as the white flag, even, in such a war as this might prove no protection. He stopped at a distance of about thirty yards and called loudly in Spanish:

"Within the church there! I wish to speak to you!"

Ned stood up, his entire figure now being revealed, and replied:

"I have been appointed spokesman for our company. What do you want?"

Urrea started slightly in his saddle, and then regarded Ned with a look of mingled irony and hatred.

"And so," he said, "our paths cross again. You escaped us at the Alamo. Why General Santa Anna spared you then I do not know, but he is not here to give new orders concerning you!"

"What do you want?" repeated Ned.

"We want the church, yourself and all the other bandits who are within it."

Ned's face flushed at Urrea's contemptuous words and manner, and his heart hardened into a yet deeper hatred of the Mexicans. But he controlled his voice and replied evenly.

"And if we should surrender, what then?"

"The mercy of the illustrious General Santa Anna, whatever it may be."

"I saw his mercy at the Alamo," replied Ned, "and we want none of it. Nor would we surrender, even if we could trust your most illustrious General Santa Anna."

"Then take your fate," said Urrea. "Since you were at the Alamo you know what befell the defenders there, and this place, mostly in ruins, is not nearly so strong. Adios!"

"Adios!" said Ned, speaking in a firm tone. But he felt that there was truth in Urrea's words. Little was left of the mission but its strong walls. Nevertheless, they might hold them.

"What did he say?" asked King.

"He demanded our surrender."

"On what terms?"

"Whatever Santa Anna might decree, and if you had seen the red flag of no quarter waving in sight of the Alamo you would know his decree."

"And your reply?"

"I told him that we meant to hold the place."

THE TEXAN SCOUTS A Story Of The Alamo And Goliad | 193

"Good enough," said King. "Now we will go back to business. I wish that we had more ammunition."

"Fannin's men may bring plenty," said Ned. "And now, if you don't mind, Captain King, I'm going to sleep down there at the foot of the wall, and to-night I'll join the guard."

"Do as you wish," said King, "you know more about Texas and these Mexicans than any of us."

"I'd suggest a very thorough watch when night comes. Wake me up about midnight, won't you?"

Ned lay down in the place that he had chosen. It was only the middle of the afternoon, but he had become so inured to hardship that he slept quickly. Several shots were fired before twilight came, but they did not awaken him. At midnight King, according to his request, took him by the shoulder and he stood up.

"Nothing of importance has happened," said King.

"You can see the camp fires of the Mexicans in the wood, but as far as we can tell they are not making any movement."

"Probably they are content to wait for the main force," said Ned.

"Looks like it," said King.

"If you have no objection, Captain," said Ned, "I think I'll go outside and scout about a little."

"Good idea, I think," said King.

They opened the door a moment and Ned slipped forth. The night was quite dark and, with the experience of border work that he was rapidly acquiring, he had little fear of being caught by the Mexicans. He kept his eye on the light burning in the wood and curved in a half circle to the right. The few houses that made up the village were all dark, but his business was with none of them. He intended to see, if he could, whether the main Mexican force was approaching. If it should prove to be at hand with the heavy cannon there would be no possible chance of holding the mission, and they must get away.

He continued in his wide curve, knowing that in this case the longest way around was the best and safest, and he gradually passed into a stretch of chaparral beyond the town. Crossing it, he came into a meadow, and then he suddenly heard the soft pad of feet. He sought to spring back into the chaparral, but a huge dim figure bore down upon him, and then his heart recovered its normal beat when he saw that it was only Old Jack.

Ned stroked the great muzzle affectionately, but he was compelled to put away his friend.

"No, faithful comrade," he said. "I can't take you with me. I'd like to do it, but there's no room in a church for a horse as big as you are. Go now! Go at once, or the Mexicans will get you!"

He struck the horse smartly on the jaw. Old Jack looked at him reproachfully, but turned and trotted away from the town. Ned continued his scout. This proof of affection from a dumb brute cheered him.

An hour's cautious work brought him to the far side of the wood. As well as he could judge, nearly all the Mexican troopers were asleep around two fires, but they had posted sentinels who walked back and forth, calling at intervals "Sentinela alerte" to one another. Obviously there had been no increase in their force. They were sufficient to maintain a blockade of the church, but too few to surround it completely.

He went two or three miles to the west and, seeing no evidence that the main force was approaching, he decided to return to the church. His original curve had taken him by the south side of the wood, and he would return by the north side in order that his examination might be complete.

He walked rapidly, as the night was far advanced, and the sky was very clear, with bright stars twinkling in myriads. He did not wish day to catch him outside the mission. It was a prairie country, with patches of forest here and there, and as he crossed from one wood to another he was wholly without cover.

He was within a mile of the mission when he heard the faint tread of horses' hoofs, and he concluded that Old Jack, contrary to orders, was coming forward to meet him again. He paused, but the faint tread suddenly became rapid and heavy. A half dozen horsemen who had ridden into the prairie had caught sight of him and now they were galloping toward him. The brightness of the night showed Ned at once that they were Mexican cavalrymen, and as he was on foot he was at a great disadvantage.

He ran at full speed for the nearest grove. The Mexicans fired several musket shots at him, but the bullets all went wild. He did not undertake a reply, as he was straining every effort to reach the trees. Several pistols also were emptied at him, but he yet remained unhurt.

Nevertheless, the horsemen were coming alarmingly near.

He heard the thunder of hoofs in his ears, and he heard also a quick hiss like that of a snake.

Ned knew that the hissing sound was made by a lasso, and as he dodged he felt the coil, thrown in vain, slipping from his shoulders. He whirled about and fired at the man who had thrown the lasso. The rider uttered a cry, fell backward on his horse, and then to the ground.

As Ned turned for the shot he saw that Urrea was the leader of the horsemen. Whether Urrea had recognized him or not he did not know, but the fact that he was there increased his apprehension. He made a mighty effort and leaped the next instant into the protection of the trees and thickets. Fortune favored him now. A wood alone would not have protected him, but here were vines and bushes also.

He turned off at a sharp angle and ran as swiftly and with as little noise as he could. He heard the horses floundering in the forest, and the curses of their riders. He ran a hundred yards further and, coming to a little gully, lay down in it and reloaded his rifle. Then he stayed there until he could regain his breath and strength. While he lay he heard the Mexicans beating up the thickets, and Urrea giving sharp orders.

Ned knew that his hiding place must soon be discovered, and he began to consider what would be the best movement to make next. His heart had now returned to its normal beat, and he felt that he was good for another fine burst of speed.

He heard the trampling of the horses approaching, and then the voice of Urrea telling the others that he was going straight ahead and to follow him. Evidently they had beaten up the rest of the forest, and now they were bound to come upon him. Ned sprang from the gully, ran from the wood and darted across the prairie toward the next little grove.

He was halfway toward the coveted shelter when Urrea caught sight of him, gave a shout, and fired his pistol. Ned, filled with hatred of Urrea, fired in return. But the bullet, instead of striking the horseman, struck the horse squarely in the head. The horse fell instantly, and Urrea, hurled violently over his head, lay still.

Ned caught it all in a fleeting glance, and in a few more steps he gained the second wood. He did not know how much Urrea was hurt, nor did he care. He had paid back a little, too. He was sure, also, that the pursuit would be less vigorous, now that its leader was disabled.

The second grove did not contain so many vines and bushes, but, hiding behind a tree there, Ned saw the horsemen hold off. Without Urrea to urge them on they were afraid of the rifle that the fugitive used so well. Two, also, had stopped to tend Urrea, and Ned decided that the others would not now enter the grove.

He was right in his surmise. The horsemen rode about at a safe distance from the trees. Ned, taking his time, reloaded his rifle again and departed for the mission. There was now fairly good cover all the way, but he heard other troops of Mexicans riding about, and blowing trumpets as signals. No doubt the shots had been heard at the main camp, and many men were seeking their cause.

But Ned, fortunately for himself, was now like the needle in the haystack. While the trumpets signaled and the groups of Mexican horsemen rode into one another he stole back to the old mission and knocked upon the door with the butt of his rifle. Answering King's questions through the loophole, he was admitted quickly.

"The main army hasn't come up yet," he said, in reply to the eager inquiries of the defenders. "Fannin's men may get here in time, and if they are in sufficient force to beat off the cavalry detachment I suggest that we abandon the mission before we are caught in a trap, and retreat toward Fannin. If we linger the whole Mexican army will be around us."

"Sounds right," said King, "but we've got to hear from Fannin first. Now you look pretty tired, Fulton. Suppose you roll up in some blankets there by the wall and take a nap."

"I don't want to sleep now," said Ned. "You remember that I slept until nearly midnight. But I would like to stretch out a while. It's not very restful to be hunted through woods by Mexicans, even if you do get away."

Ned lay by the wall upon the blankets and watched the sun go slowly up the arch of the heavens. It seemed a hard fate to him that he should again be trapped thus in an old mission. Nor did he have here the strength and support of the great borderers like Bowie and Crockett. He missed them most of all now.

The day passed slowly and with an occasional exchange of shots that did little harm. Toward the twilight one of the sentinels on the wall uttered a great and joyous shout.

"The reinforcements!" he cried. "See, our friends are coming!"

Ned climbed upon the wall and saw a force of more than a hundred men, obviously Texans, approaching. They answered the hail of the sentinel and came on more swiftly. His eyes turned to the wood, in which the Mexican camp yet lay. Their cavalry would still outnumber the Texan force two or three to one, but the Mexicans invariably demanded greater odds than that before they would attack the Texans. Ned saw no stir in the wood. Not a shot was fired as the new men came forward and were joyously admitted to the church.

The men were one hundred and twenty in number, led by Colonel Ward, who by virtue of his rank now commanded all the defenders. As soon as they had eaten and rested a council, at which Ned was present, was held. King had already told the story of young Fulton to Ward, and that officer looked very curiously at Ned as he came forward. He asked him briefly about the Alamo, and Ned gave him the usual replies. Then he told of what he had seen before he joined King.

"How large do you think this force was?" asked Ward.

"About fifteen hundred men."

"And we've a hundred and fifty here. You were not much more than a hundred and fifty in the Alamo, and you held it two weeks against thousands. Why should we retreat?"

"But the Alamo fell at last," said Ned, "and this Refugio mission is not so defensible as the Alamo was."

"You think, then, we should retreat?"

"I do. I'm sure the place cannot be held against a large army."

There was much discussion. Ned saw that all the men of the new force were raw recruits from the States like King's. Many of them were mere boys, drawn to Texas by the love of adventure. They showed more curiosity than alarm, and it was evident to Ned that they felt able to defeat any number of Mexicans.

Ned, called upon again for his opinion, urged that they withdraw from the church and the town at once, but neither Ward nor King was willing to make a retreat in the night. They did not seem especially anxious to withdraw at all, but finally agreed to do so in the morning.

Ned left the council, depressed and uneasy. He felt that his countrymen held the Mexicans too lightly. Were other tragedies to be added to that of the Alamo? He was no egotist, but he was conscious of his superiority to all those present in the grave affairs with which they were now dealing.

He took his rifle and went upon the wall, where he resolved to watch all through the night. He saw the lights in the wood where the Mexicans were camped, but darkness and silence prevailed everywhere else. He had no doubt that young Urrea had sent messengers back to hurry up the main force. He smiled to himself at the thought of Urrea. He was sure that the young Mexican had sustained no fatal injury, but he must have painful wounds. And Ned, with the Alamo as vivid as ever in his mind, was glad that he had inflicted them.

Midnight came, and Ward told Ned that he need not watch any longer when the second relay of sentinels appeared. But the boy desired to remain and Ward had no objection.

"But you'll be sleepy," he said, in a good-humored tone, "when we start at the break of day, and you won't have much chance to rest on a long march."

"I'll have to take the risk," said Ned. "I feel that I ought to be watching."

Toward morning the men in the mission were awakened and began to prepare for the march. They made considerable noise as they talked and adjusted their packs, but Ned paid no attention to them. He was listening instead to a faint sound approaching the town from the south. No one in the church or on the walls heard it but himself, but he knew that it was steadily growing louder.

Ned, moreover, could tell the nature of that sound, and as it swelled his heart sank within him. The first spear of light, herald of dawn, appeared in the east and Ward called out cheerfully:

"Well, we are all ready to go now."

"It is too late," said Ned. "The whole Mexican army is here."

CHAPTER XVI.
FANNIN'S CAMP

When Ned made his startling announcement he leaped down lightly from the wall.

"If you will look through the loophole there," he said to Colonel Ward, "you will see a great force only a few hundred yards away. The man on the large horse in front is General Urrea, who commands them. He is one of Santa Anna's most trusted generals. His nephew, Captain Urrea, led the cavalry who besieged us yesterday and last night."

Captain Ward looked, but the Mexicans turned into the wood and were hidden from sight. Then the belief became strong among the recruits that Ned was mistaken. This was only a little force that had come, and Ward and King shared their faith. Ward, against Ned's protest, sent King and thirteen men out to scout.

Ned sadly watched them go. He was one of the youngest present, but he was first in experience, and he knew that he had seen aright. General Urrea and the main army were certainly at hand. But he deemed it wiser to say nothing more. Instead, he resumed his place on the wall, and kept sharp watch on the point where he thought the Mexican force lay. King and his scouts were already out of sight.

Ned suddenly heard the sound of shots, and he saw puffs of smoke from the wood. Then a great shout arose and Mexican cavalry dashed from the edge of the forest. Some of the other watchers thought the mission was about to be attacked, but the horsemen bore down upon another point to the northward. Ned divined instantly that they had discovered King and his men and were surrounding them.

He leaped once more from the wall and shouted the alarm to Ward.

"The men out there are surrounded," he cried. "They will have no chance without help!"

Ward was brave enough, and his men, though lacking skill, were brave enough, too. At his command they threw open the gate of the mission and rushed out to the relief of their comrades. Ned was by the side of Ward, near the front. As they appeared in the opening they heard a great shouting, and a powerful detachment of cavalry galloped toward their right, while an equally strong force of infantry moved on their left. The recruits were outnumbered at least five to one, but in such a desperate situation they did not blench.

"Take good aim with your rifles," shouted Ward. And they did. A shower of bullets cut gaps in the Mexican line, both horse and foot. Many riderless horses galloped through the ranks of the foe, adding to the confusion. But the Mexican numbers were so great that they continued to press the Texans. Young Urrea, his head in thick bandages, was again with the cavalry, and animated by more than one furious impulse he drove them on.

It became evident now even to the rawest that the whole Mexican army was present. It spread out to a great distance, and enfolded the Texans on three sides, firing hundreds of muskets and keeping up a great shouting, Ned's keen ear also detected other firing off to the right, and he knew that it was King and his men making a hopeless defence against overpowering numbers.

"We cannot reach King," groaned Ward.

"We have no earthly chance of doing so," said Ned, "and I think, Colonel, that your own force will have a hard fight to get back inside the mission."

The truth of Ned's words was soon evident to everyone. It was only the deadly Texan rifles that kept the Mexican cavalry from galloping over them and crushing them at once. The Mexican fire itself, coming from muskets of shorter range, did little damage. Yet the Texans were compelled to load and pull trigger very fast, as they retreated slowly upon the mission.

At last they reached the great door and began to pass rapidly inside. Now the Mexicans pressed closer, firing heavy volleys.

A score of the best Texan marksmen whirled and sent their bullets at the pursuing Mexicans with such good aim that a dozen saddles were emptied, and the whole force reeled back. Then all the Texans darted inside, and the great door was closed and barricaded. Many of the men sank down, breathless from their exertions, regardless of the Mexican bullets that were pattering upon the church. Ward leaned against the wall, and wiped the perspiration from his face.

"My God!" he exclaimed. "What has become of King?"

There was no answer. The Mexicans ceased to fire and shout, and retreated toward the wood. Ward was destined never to know what had become of King and his men, but Ned soon learned the terrible facts, and they only hardened him still further. The thirteen had been compelled to surrender to overwhelming numbers. Then they were immediately tied to trees and killed, where their skeletons remained upright until the Texans found them.

"You were right, Fulton," said Ward, after a long silence. "The Mexican army was there, as we have plenty of evidence to show."

He smiled sadly, as he wiped the smoke and perspiration from his face. Ned did not reply, but watched through a loophole. He had seen a glint of bronze in the wood, and presently he saw the Mexicans pushing a cannon from cover.

"They have artillery," he said to Ward. "See the gun. But I don't think it can damage our walls greatly. They never did much with the cannon at the Alamo. When they came too close there, we shot down all their cannoneers, and we can do the same here."

Ward chose the best sharpshooters, posting them at the loopholes and on the walls. They quickly slew the Mexicans who tried to man the gun, and General Urrea was forced to withdraw it to such a distance that its balls and shells had no effect whatever upon the strong walls of the church.

There was another period of silence, but the watchers in the old mission saw that much movement was going on in the wood and presently they beheld the result. The Mexican army charged directly upon the church, carrying in its center men with heavy bars of wood to be used in smashing in the door. But they yielded once more to the rapid fire of the Texan rifles, and did not succeed in reaching the building. Those who bore the logs and bars dropped them, and fled out of range.

A great cheer burst from the young recruits. They thought victory complete already, but Ned knew that the Mexicans would not abandon the enterprise. General Urrea, after another futile charge, repulsed in the same deadly manner, withdrew some distance, but posted a strong line of sentinels about the church.

Having much food and water the recruits rejoiced again and thought themselves secure, but Ned noticed a look of consternation on the face of Ward, and he divined the cause.

"It must be the ammunition, Colonel," he said in a whisper.

"It is," replied Ward. "We have only three or four rounds left. We could not possibly repel another attack."

"Then," said young Fulton, "there is nothing to do but for us to slip out at night, and try to cut our way through."

"That is so," said Ward. "The Mexican general doubtless will not expect any such move on our part, and we may get away."

He said nothing of his plan to the recruits until the darkness came, and then the state of the powder horns and the bullet pouches was announced. Most of the men had supposed that they alone were suffering from the shortage, and something like despair came over them when they found that they were practically without weapons. They were more than willing to leave the church, as soon as the night deepened, and seek refuge over the prairie.

"You think that we can break through?" said Ward to Ned.

"I have no doubt of it," replied Ned, "but in any event it seems to me, Colonel, that we ought to try it. All the valor and devotion of the men in the Alamo did not suffice to save them. We cannot hold the place against a determined assault."

"That is undoubtedly true," said Ward, "and flushed by the success that they have had elsewhere it seems likely to me that the Mexicans will make such an attack very soon."

"In any event," said Ned, "we are isolated here, cut off from Fannin, and exposed to imminent destruction."

"We start at midnight," said Ward.

Ned climbed upon the walls, and examined all the surrounding country. He saw lights in the wood, and now and then he discerned the figures of Mexican horsemen, riding in a circle about the church, members of the patrol that had been left by General Urrea. He did not think it a difficult thing to cut through this patrol, but the Texans, in their flight, must become disorganized to a certain extent. Nevertheless it was the only alternative.

The men were drawn up at the appointed time, and Ward told them briefly what they were to do. They must keep as well together as possible, and the plan was to make their way to Victoria, where they expected to rejoin Fannin. They gave calabashes of water and provisions to several men too badly wounded to move, and left them to the mercy of the Mexicans, a mercy that did not exist, as Urrea's troops massacred them the moment they entered the church.

Luckily it was a dark night, and Ned believed that they had more than half a chance of getting away. The great door was thrown silently open, and, with a moving farewell to their wounded and disabled comrades, they filed silently out, leaving the door open behind them.

Then the column of nearly one hundred and fifty men slipped away, every man treading softly. They had chosen a course that lay directly away from the Mexican army, but they did not expect to escape without an alarm, and it came in five minutes. A Mexican horseman, one of the patrol, saw the dark file, fired a shot and gave an alarm. In an instant all the sentinels were firing and shouting, and Urrea's army in the wood was awakening.

But the Texans now pressed forward rapidly. Their rifles cracked, quickly cutting a path through the patrol, and before Urrea could get up his main force they were gone through the forest and over the prairie.

Knowing that the whole country was swarming with the Mexican forces, they chose a circuitous course through forests and swamps and pressed on until daylight. Some of the Mexicans on horseback followed them for a while, but a dozen of the best Texan shots were told off to halt them. When three or four saddles were emptied the remainder of the Mexicans disappeared and they pursued their flight in peace.

Morning found them in woods and thickets by the banks of a little creek of clear water. They drank from the stream, ate of their cold food, and rested. Ned and some others left the wood and scouted upon the prairie. They saw no human being and returned to their own people, feeling sure that they were safe from pursuit for the present.

Yet the Texans felt no exultation. They had been compelled to retreat before the Mexicans, and they could not forget King and his men, and those whom they had left behind in the church. Ned, in his heart, knowing the Mexicans so well, did not believe that a single one of them had been saved.

They walked the whole day, making for the town of Victoria, where they expected to meet Fannin, and shortly before night they stopped in a wood, footsore and exhausted. Again their camp was pitched on the banks of a little creek and some of the hunters shot two fine fat deer further up the stream.

Seeking as much cheer as they could they built fires, and roasted the deer. The spirits of the young recruits rose. They would meet Fannin to-morrow or the next day and they would avenge the insult that the Mexicans had put upon them. They were eager for a new action in which the odds should not be so great against them, and they felt sure of victory. Then, posting their sentinels, they slept soundly.

But Ned did not feel so confident. Toward morning he rose from his blankets. Yet he saw nothing. The prairie was bare. There was not a single sign of pursuit. He was surprised. He believed that at least the younger Urrea with the cavalry would follow.

Ned now surmised the plan that the enemy had carried out. Instead of following the Texans through the forests and swamps they had gone straight to Victoria, knowing that the fugitives would make for that point. Where

Fannin was he could not even guess, but it was certain that Ward and his men were left practically without ammunition to defend themselves as best they could against a horde of foes.

The hunted Texans sought the swamps of the Guadalupe, where Mexican cavalry could not follow them, but where they were soon overtaken by skirmishers. Hope was now oozing from the raw recruits. There seemed to be no place in the world for them. Hunted here and there they never found rest. But the most terrible fact of all was the lack of ammunition. Only a single round for every man was left, and they replied sparingly to the Mexican skirmishers.

They lay now in miry woods, and on the other side of them flowed the wide and yellow river. The men sought, often in vain, for firm spots on which they might rest. The food, like the ammunition, was all gone, and they were famished and weak. The scouts reported that the Mexicans were increasing every hour.

It was obvious to Ned that Ward must surrender. What could men without ammunition do against many times their number, well armed? He resolved that he would not be taken with them, and shortly before day he pulled through the mud to the edge of the Guadalupe. He undressed and made his clothes and rifle into a bundle. He had been very careful of his own ammunition, and he had a half dozen rounds left, which he also tied into the bundle.

Then shoving a fallen log into the water he bestrode it, holding his precious pack high and dry. Paddling with one hand he was able to direct the log in a diagonal course across the stream. He toiled through another swamp on that shore, and, coming out upon a little prairie, dressed again.

He looked back toward the swamp in which the Texans lay, but he saw no lights and he heard no sounds there. He knew that within a short time they would be prisoners of the Mexicans. Everything seemed to be working for the benefit of Santa Anna. The indecision of the Texans and the scattering of their forces enabled the Mexicans to present overwhelming forces at all points. It seemed to Ned that fortune, which had worked in their favor until the capture of San Antonio, was now working against them steadily and with overwhelming power.

He gathered himself together as best he could, and began his journey southward. He believed that Fannin would be at Goliad or near it. Once more that feeling of vengeance hardened within him. The tremendous impression of the Alamo had not faded a particle, and now the incident of Ward, Refugio and the swamps of the Guadalupe was cumulative. Remembering what he had seen he did not believe that a single one of Ward's men would be spared when they were taken as they surely would be. There were humane men among the Mexicans, like Almonte, but the ruthless policy of Santa Anna was to spare no one, and Santa Anna held all the power.

He held on toward Goliad, passing through alternate regions of forest and prairie, and he maintained a fair pace until night. He had not eaten since morning, and all his venison was gone, but strangely enough he was not hungry. When the darkness was coming he sat down in one of the little groves so frequent in that region, and he was conscious of a great weariness. His bones ached. But it was not the ache that comes from exertion. It seemed to go to the very marrow. It became a pain rather than exhaustion.

He noticed that everything about him appeared unreal. The trees and the earth itself wavered. His head began to ache and his stomach was weak. Had the finest of food been presented to him he could not have eaten it. He had an extraordinary feeling of depression and despair.

Ned knew what was the matter with him. He was suffering either from overwhelming nervous and physical exhaustion, or he had contracted malaria in the swamps of the Guadalupe. Despite every effort of the will, he began to shake with cold, and he knew that a chill was coming. He had retained his blankets, his frontiersman's foresight not deserting him, and now, knowing that he could not continue his flight for the present, he sought the deepest part of the thicket. He crept into a place so dense that it would have been suited for an animal's den, and lying down there he wrapped the blankets tightly about himself, his rifle and his ammunition.

In spite of his clothing and the warm blankets he grew colder and colder. His teeth chattered and he shivered all over. He would not have minded that so much, but his head ached with great violence, and the least light hurt his eyes. It seemed to him the culmination. Never had he been more miserable, more lost of both body and soul. The pain in his head was so violent that life was scarcely worth the price.

He sank by and by into a stupor. He was remotely conscious that he was lying in a thicket, somewhere in boundless Texas, but it did not really matter. Cougars or bears might come there to find him, but he was too sick to raise a hand against them. Besides, he did not care. A million Mexicans might be beating up those thickets for him, and they would be sure to find him. Well, what of it? They would shoot him, and he would merely go at once to some other planet, where he would be better off than he was now.

It seems that fate reserves her severest ordeals for the strong and the daring, as if she would respond to the challenges they give. It seems also that often she brings them through the test, as if she likes the courage and enterprise that dare her, the all-powerful, to combat. Ned's intense chill abated. He ceased to shake so violently, and after a while he did not shake at all. Then fever came. Intolerable heat flowed through every vein, and his head was ready to burst. After a while violent perspiration broke out all over him, and then he became unconscious.

Ned lay all night in the thicket, wrapped in the blankets, and breathing heavily. Once or twice he half awoke, and remembered things dimly, but these periods were very brief and he sank back into stupor. When he awoke to stay awake the day was far advanced, and he felt an overwhelming lassitude. He slowly unwound himself from his blankets and looked at his hand. It was uncommonly white, and it seemed to him to be as weak as that of a child.

He crept out of the thicket and rose to his feet. He was attacked by dizziness and clutched a bush for support. His head still ached, though not with the violence of the night before, but he was conscious that he had become a very weak and poor specimen of the human being. Everything seemed very far away, impossible to be reached.

He gathered strength enough to roll up his blankets and shoulder his rifle. Then he looked about a little. There was the same alternation of woods and prairie, devoid of any human being. He did not expect to see any Texans, unless, by chance, Fannin came marching that way, but a detachment of Mexican lancers might stumble upon him at any moment. The thought, however, caused him no alarm. He felt so much weakness and depression that the possibility of capture or death could not add to it.

Young Fulton was not hungry,—the chill and following fever had taken his appetite away so thoroughly,—but he felt that he must eat. He found some early berries in the thickets and they restored his strength a little, but the fare was so thin and unsubstantial that he decided to look for game. He could never reach Fannin or anybody else in his present reduced condition.

He saw a line of oaks, which he knew indicated the presence of a water-course, probably one of the shallow creeks, so numerous in Eastern Texas, and he walked toward it, still dizzy and his footsteps dragging. His head was yet aching, and the sun, which was now out in full brightness, made it worse, but he persisted, and, after an interminable time, he reached the shade of the oaks, which, as he surmised, lined both sides of a creek.

He drank of the water, rested a while, and then began a search of the oaks. He was looking for squirrels, which he knew abounded in these trees, and, after much slow and painful walking, he shot a fine fat one among the boughs. Then followed the yet more mighty task of kindling a fire with sticks and tinder, but just when he was completely exhausted, and felt that he must fail, the spark leaped up, set fire to the white ash that he had scraped with his knife, and in a minute later a good fire was blazing.

He cooked the tenderest parts of the squirrel and ate, still forcing his appetite. Then he carefully put out the fire and went a mile further up the creek. He felt stronger, but he knew that he was not yet in any condition for a long journey. He was most intent now upon guarding against a return of the chill. It was not the right time for one to be ill. Again he sought a place in a thicket, like an animal going to its den, and, wrapping himself tightly in the blankets, lay down.

He watched with anxiety for the first shiver of the dreaded chill. Once or twice imagination made him feel sure that it had come, but it always passed quickly. His body remained warm, and, while he was still watching for the chill, he fell asleep, and slept soundly all through the night.

The break of day aroused him. He felt strong and well, and he was in a pleasant glow, because he knew now that the chill would not come. It had been due to overtaxed nerves, and there was no malaria in his system.

He hunted again among the big trees until he found a squirrel on one of the high boughs. He fired at it and missed. He found another soon and killed it at the first shot. But the miss had been a grave matter. He had only four bullets left. He took them out and looked at them, little shining pellets of lead. His life depended upon these four, and he must not miss again.

It took him an hour to start his fire, and he ate only half of the squirrel, putting the remainder into his bullet pouch for future needs. Then, much invigorated, he resumed his vague journey. But he was compelled very soon to go slowly and with the utmost caution. There were even times when he had to stop and hide. Mexican cavalry appeared upon the prairies, first in small groups and then in a detachment of about three hundred. Their course and Ned's was the same, and he knew then that he was going in the right direction. Fannin was surely somewhere ahead.

But it was most troublesome traveling for Ned. If they saw him they could easily ride him down, and what chance would he have with only four bullets in his pouch? Or rather, what chance would he have if the pouch contained a hundred?

The only thing that favored him was the creek which ran in the way that he wanted to go. He kept in the timber that lined its banks, and, so long as he had this refuge, he felt comparatively safe, since the Mexicans, obviously, were not looking for him. Yet they often came perilously near. Once, a large band rode down to the creek to water their horses, when Ned was not fifty feet distant. He instantly lay flat among some bushes, and did not move. He could hear the horses blowing the water back with their noses, as they drank.

When the horses were satisfied, the cavalrymen turned and rode away, passing so near that it seemed to him they had only to look down and see him lying among the bushes. But they went on, and, when they were out of sight, he rose and continued his flight through the timber.

But this alternate fleeing and dodging was most exhausting work, and before the day was very old he decided that he would lie down in a thicket, and postpone further flight until night. Just when he had found such a place he heard the faint sound of distant firing. He put his ear to the earth, and then the crackle of rifles came more distinctly. His ear, experienced now, told him that many men must be engaged, and he was sure that Fannin and the Mexican army had come into contact.

Young Fulton's heart began to throb. The dark vision of the Alamo came before him again. All the hate that he felt for the Mexicans flamed up. He must be there with Fannin, fighting against the hordes of Santa Anna. He rose and ran toward the firing. He saw from the crest of a hillock a wide plain with timber on one side and a creek on the other. The center of the plain was a shallow valley, and there the firing was heavy. Ned saw many flashes and puffs of smoke, and presently he heard the thud of cannon. Then he saw near him Mexican cavalry galloping through the timber. He could not doubt any longer that a battle was in progress. His excitement increased, and he ran at full speed through the bushes and grass into the plain, which he now saw took the shape of a shallow saucer. The firing indicated that the defensive force stood in the center of the saucer, that is, in the lowest and worst place.

A terrible fear assailed young Fulton, as he ran. Could it be possible that Fannin also was caught in a trap, here on the open prairie, with the Mexicans in vastly superior numbers on the high ground around him? He remembered, too, that Fannin's men were raw recruits like those with Ward, and his fear, which was not for himself, increased as he ran.

He noticed that there was no firing from one segment of the ring in the saucer, and he directed his course toward it. As soon as he saw horses and men moving he threw up his hands and cried loudly over and over again: "I'm a friend! Do not shoot!" He saw a rifle raised and aimed at him, but a hand struck it down. A few minutes later he sprang breathless into the camp, and friendly hands held him up as he was about to pitch forward with exhaustion.

His breath and poise came back in a few moments, and he looked about him. He had made no mistake. He was with Fannin's force, and it was already pressed hard by Urrea's army. Even as he drew fresh, deep breaths he saw a heavy mass of Mexican cavalry gallop from the wood, wheel and form a line between Fannin and the creek, the only place where the besieged force could obtain water.

"Who are you?" asked an officer, advancing toward Ned.

Young Fulton instantly recognized Fannin.

"My name is Edward Fulton, you will recall me, Colonel," he replied. "I was in the Alamo, but went out the day before it fell. I was taken by the Mexicans, but escaped, fled across the prairie, and was in the mission at Refugio when some of your men under Colonel Ward came to the help of King."

"I have heard that the church was abandoned, but where is Ward, and where are his men?"

Ned hesitated and Fannin read the answer in his eyes.

"You cannot tell me so!" he exclaimed.

"I'm afraid that they will all be taken," said Ned. "They had no ammunition when I slipped away, and the Mexicans were following them. There was no possibility of escape."

Fannin paled. But he pressed his lips firmly together for a moment and then said to Ned:

"Keep this to yourself, will you? Our troops are young and without experience. It would discourage them too much."

"Of course," said Ned. "But meanwhile I wish to fight with you."

"There will be plenty of chance," said Fannin. "Hark to it!"

The sound of firing swelled on all sides of them, and above it rose the triumphant shouts of the Mexicans.

—

CHAPTER XVII.
THE SAD SURRENDER

Ned took another look at the beleaguered force, and what he saw did not encourage him. The men, crowded together, were standing in a depression seven or eight feet below the surface of the surrounding prairie. Near by was an ammunition wagon with a broken axle. The men themselves, three ranks deep, were in a hollow square, with the cannon at the angles and the supply wagons in the center. Every face looked worn and anxious, but they did not seem to have lost heart.

Yet, as Ned had foreseen, this was quite a different force from that which had held the Alamo so long, and against so many. Most of the young faces were not yet browned by the burning sun of Texas. Drawn by the reports of great adventure they had come from far places, and each little company had its own name. There were the "Grays" from New Orleans, the "Mustangs" from Kentucky, the "Red Rovers" from Alabama and others with fancy names, but altogether they numbered, with the small reinforcements that had been received, only three hundred and fifty men.

Ned could have shed tears, when he looked upon the force. He felt himself a veteran beside them. Yet there was no lack of courage among them. They did not flinch, as the fire grew heavier, and the cannon balls whistled over their heads. Ned was sure now that General Urrea was around them with his whole army. The presence of the cannon indicated it, and he saw enough to know that the Mexican force outnumbered the Texan four or five to one.

He heard the Mexican trumpets pealing presently, and then he saw their infantry advancing in dark masses with heavy squadrons of cavalry on either flank. But as soon as they came within range, they were swept by the deadly fire of the Texan rifles and were driven back in confusion. Ned noticed that this always happened. The Mexicans could never carry a Texan position by a frontal attack. The Texans, or those who were called the Texans, shot straight and together so fast that no Mexican column could withstand their hail of bullets.

A second time the Mexicans charged, and a second time they were driven back in the same manner. Exultation spread among the recruits standing in the hollow, but they were still surrounded. The Mexicans merely drew out of range and waited. Then they attacked a third time, and, from all sides, charging very close, infantry and cavalry. The men in the hollow were well supplied with rifles, and their square fairly blazed. Yet the Mexicans pressed home the charge with a courage and tenacity that Ned had never seen among them before. These were Mexico's best troops, and, even when the men faltered, the officers drove them on again with the point of the sword. General Urrea himself led the cavalry, and the Mexicans pressed so close that the recruits saw both lance and bayonet points shining in their faces.

The hollow in which the Texans stood was a huge cloud of flame and smoke. Ned was loading and firing so fast that the barrel of his rifle grew hot to the touch. He stood with two youths but little older than himself, and the comradeship of battle had already made them friends. But they scarcely saw the faces of one another. The little valley was filled with the smoke of their firing. They breathed it and tasted it, and it inflamed their brains.

Ned's experience had made him a veteran, and when he heard the thunder of the horse's hoofs and saw the lance points so near he knew that the crisis had come.

"One more volley. One for your lives!" he cried to those around him.

The volley was forthcoming. The rifles were discharged at the range of only a few yards into the mass of Mexican cavalry. Horses and men fell headlong, some pitching to the very feet of the Texans and then one of the cannon poured a shower of grape shot into the midst of the wavering square. It broke and ran, bearing its general away with it, and leaving the ground cumbered with fallen men and horses.

The Mexican infantry was also driven back at every point, and retreated rapidly until they were out of range. Under the cloud of smoke wounded men crept away. But when the cloud was wholly gone, it disclosed those who would move no more, lying on every side. The defenders had suffered also. Fannin lay upon the ground, while two of his men bound up a severe wound in the thigh that he had sustained from a Mexican bullet. Many others had been wounded and some had been killed. Most alarming of all was the announcement that the cannon could be fired only a few times more, as there was no water for the sponges when they became heated and clogged. But this discouraged only the leaders, not the recruits themselves, who had ultimate faith in their rifles.

Ned felt an extreme dizziness. All his old strength had not yet returned, and after such furious action and so much excitement there was a temporary collapse. He lay back on the grass, closed his eyes, and waited for the weakness to pass. He heard around him the talk and murmur of the men, and the sounds of new preparations. He heard the recruits telling one another that they had repulsed four Mexican attacks, and that they could repulse four more. Yet the amount of talking was not great. The fighting had been too severe and continuous to encourage volubility. Most of them reloaded in silence and waited.

Ned felt that his weakness had passed, opened his eyes, and sat up again. He saw that the Mexicans had drawn a circle of horsemen about them, but well beyond range. Behind the horsemen their army waited. Fannin's men were rimmed in by steel, and Ned believed that Urrea, after his great losses in the charges, would now wait.

Ned stretched himself and felt his muscles. He was strong once more and his head was clear. He did not believe that the weakness and dizziness would come again. But his tongue and throat were dry, and one of the youths who had stood with him gave him a drink from his canteen. Ned would gladly have made the drink a deep one, but he denied himself, and, when he returned the canteen, its supply was diminished but little. He knew better than the giver how precious the water would become.

Ned was standing at the edge of the hollow, and his head was just about on a level with the surrounding prairie. After his look at the Mexican circle, something whistled by his ear. It was an unpleasant sound that he knew well, one marking the passage of a bullet, and he dropped down instantly. Then he cautiously raised himself up again, and, a half dozen others who had heard the shot did the same. One rose a little higher than the rest and he fell back with a cry, a bullet in his shoulder.

Ned was surprised and puzzled. Whence had come these shots? There was the line of Mexican cavalry, well out of range, and, beyond the horsemen, were the infantry. He could see nothing, but the wounded shoulder was positive proof that some enemy was near.

There was a third crack, and a man fell to the bottom of the hollow, where he lay still. The bullet had gone through his head. Ned saw a wreath of smoke rising from a tiny hillock, a hundred yards away, and then he saw lifted for only a moment a coppery face with high cheek bones and coarse black hair. An Indian! No one could ever mistake that face for a white man's. Many more shots were fired and he caught glimpses of other faces, Indian in type like the first.

Every hillock or other inequality of the earth seemed to spout bullets, which were now striking among the Texans, cooped up in the hollow, killing and wounding. But the circle of Mexican horsemen did not stir.

"What are they?" called Fannin, who was lying upon a pallet, suffering greatly from his wound.

"Indians," replied Ned.

"Indians!" exclaimed Fannin in surprise. "I did not know that there were any in this part of the country."

"Nor did I," replied Ned, "but they are surely here, Colonel, and if I may make a suggestion, suppose we pick sharp-shooters to meet them."

"It is the only thing to do," said Fannin, and immediately the best men with the rifle were placed along the edge of the hollow. It was full time, as the fire of the red sharpshooters was creeping closer, and was doing much harm. They were Campeachy Indians, whom the Mexicans had brought with them from their far country and, splendid stalkers and skirmishers, they were now proving their worth. Better marksmen than the Mexicans, naked to the waist, their dark faces inflamed with the rage to kill, they wormed themselves forward like snakes, flattened against the ground, taking advantage of every hillock or ridge, and finding many a victim in the hollow. Far back, the Mexican officers sitting on their horses watched their work with delighted approval.

Ned was not a sharpshooter like the Panther or Davy Crockett, but he was a sharpshooter nevertheless, and, driven by the sternest of all needs, he was growing better all the time. He saw another black head raised for a moment above a hillock, and a muzzle thrust forward, but he fired first. The head dropped back, but the rifle fell from the arms and lay across the hillock. Ned knew that his bullet had sped true, and he felt a savage joy.

The other sharpshooters around him were also finding targets. The Indian bullets still crashed into the crowded ranks in the hollow, but the white marksmen picked off one after another in the grass. The moment a red face showed itself a bullet that rarely missed was sent toward it. Here was no indiscriminate shooting. No man pulled the trigger until he saw his target. Ned had now fired four times, and he knew that he had not missed once. The consuming rage still possessed him, but it was for the Mexicans rather than the Indians against whom he was sending his bullets. Surely they were numerous enough to fight the Texans. They ought to be satisfied with ten to one in their favor, without bringing Indians also against the tiny settlements! The fire mounted to his brain, and he looked eagerly for a fifth head.

It was a singular duel between invisible antagonists. Never was an entire body seen, but the crackling fire and the spurts of flame and smoke were incessant. After a while the line of fire and smoke on the prairie began to retreat slowly. The fire of the white sharpshooters had grown too hot and the Indians were creeping away, leaving their dead in the grass. Presently their fire ceased entirely and then that of the white marksmen ceased also.

No sounds came from the Mexicans, who were all out of range. In the hollow the wounded, who now numbered one-fifth of the whole, suppressed their groans, and their comrades, who bound up their hurts or gave them water, said but little. Ned's own throat had become parched again, but he would not ask for another drop of water.

The Texans had used oxen to drag their cannon and wagons, and most of them now lay dead about the rim of the shallow crater, slain by the Mexican and Indian bullets. The others had been tied to the wagons to keep them, when maddened by the firing, from trampling down the Texans themselves. Now they still shivered with fear, and pulled at their ropes. Ned felt sorry for the poor brutes. Full cause had they for fright.

The afternoon was waning, and he ate a little supper, followed by a single drink of water. Every man received a similar drink and no more from the canteens. The coming twilight brought a coolness that was refreshing, but the Indians, taking advantage of the dusk, crept forward, and began to fire again at the Texans cooped up in the crater. These red sharpshooters had the advantage of always knowing the position of their enemy, while they could shift their own as they saw fit.

The Texan marksmen, worn and weary though they were, returned to their task. They could not see the Indians, but they used an old device, often successful in border warfare. Whenever an Indian fired a spurt of smoke shot up from his rifle's muzzle. A Texan instantly pulled trigger at the base of the smoke, and oftener than not the bullet hit his dusky foe.

This new duel in the dark went on for two hours. The Indians could fire at the mass in the hollow, while the Texans steadily picked out their more difficult targets. The frightened oxen uttered terrified lowings and the Indians, now and then aiming at the sounds, killed or wounded more of the animals. The Texans themselves slew those that were wounded, unwilling to see them suffer so much.

The skill of the Texans with the rifle was so great that gradually they prevailed over the Indians a second time in the trial of sharpshooting. The warriors were driven back on the Mexican cavalry, and abandoned the combat. The night was much darker than usual, and a heavy fog, rising from the plain, added to its density and dampness. The skies were invisible, hidden by heavy masses of floating clouds and fog.

Ned saw a circle of lights spring up around them. They were the camp fires of the Mexican army, and he knew that the troops were comfortable there before the blaze. His heart filled with bitterness. He had expected so much of Fannin's men, and Crockett and Bowie before him had expected so much! Yet here they were, beleaguered as the Texans had been beleaguered in the Alamo, and there were no walls behind which they could fight. It seemed to Ned that the hand of fate itself had resolved to strike down the Texans. He knew that Urrea, one of Santa Anna's ablest and most tenacious generals, would never relax the watch for an instant. In the darkness he could hear the Mexican sentinels calling to one another: "Sentinela Alerte!"

The cold damp allayed the thirst of the young recruits, but the crater was the scene of gloom. They did not dare to light a fire, knowing it would draw the Indian bullets at once, or perhaps cannon shots. The wounded in their blankets lay on the ground. A few of the unhurt slept, but most of them sat in silence looking somberly at one another.

Fannin lay against the breech of one of the cannon, blankets having been folded between to make his position easy. His wound was severe and he was suffering greatly, but he uttered no complaint. He had not shown great skill or judgment as a leader, but he was cool and undaunted in action. Now he was calling a council to see what they could do to release themselves from their desperate case. Officers and men alike attended it freely.

"Boys," said Fannin, speaking in a firm voice despite his weakness and pain, "we are trapped here in this hole in the prairie, but if you are trapped it does not follow that you have to stay trapped. I don't seek to conceal anything from you. Our position could not well be worse. We have cannon, but we cannot use them any longer because they are choked and clogged from former firing, and we have no water to wash them out. Shortly we will not have a drop to drink. But you are brave, and you can still shoot. I know that we can break through the Mexican lines to-night and reach the Coleto, the water and the timber. Shall we do it?"

Many replied yes, but then a voice spoke out of the darkness:

"What of the wounded, Colonel? We have sixty men who can't move."

There was an instant's silence, and then a hundred voices said in the darkness:

"We'll never leave them. We'll stay here and fight again!"

Ned was standing with those nearest Fannin, and although the darkness was great his eyes had become so used to it that he could see the pale face of the leader. Fannin's eyes lighted up at the words of his men, and a little color came into his cheeks.

"You speak like brave men rather than wise men," he said, "but I cannot blame you. It is a hard thing to leave wounded comrades to a foe such as the one who faces us. If you wish to stay here, then I say stay. Do you wish it?"

"We do!" thundered scores of voices, and Fannin, moving a little to make himself easier, said simply:

"Then fortify as best you can."

They brought spades and shovels from the wagons, and began to throw up an earthwork, toiling in the almost pitchy darkness. They reinforced it with the bodies of the slain oxen, and, while they toiled, they saw the fires where the Mexican officers rested, sure that their prey could not break from the trap. The Texans worked on. At midnight they were still working, and when they rested a while there was neither food nor drink for them. Every drop of water was gone long since, and they had eaten their last food at supper. They could have neither food nor drink nor sleep.

Ned had escaped from many dangers, but it is truth that this time he felt despair. His feeling about the hand of fate striking them down became an obsession. What chance had men without an ounce of food or a drop of water to withstand a siege?

But he communicated his fears to no one. Two or three hours before day, he became so sore and weary from work with the spade that he crawled into one of the half-wrecked wagons, and tried to go to sleep. But his nerves were drawn to too high a pitch. After a quarter of an hour's vain effort he got out of the wagon and stood by the wheel. The sky was still black, and the heavy clouds of fog and vapor rolled steadily past him. It seemed to him that everything was closing on them, even the skies, and the air was so heavy that he found it hard to breathe.

He would have returned to work, but he knew that he would overtask his worn frame, and he wanted to be in condition for the battle that he believed was coming with the morrow. They had not tried to cut out at night, then they must do it by day, or die where they stood of thirst.

He sat down at last on the ground, and leaned against a wagon wheel, drawing a blanket over his shoulders for warmth. He found that he could rest better here than inside the wagon, and, in an hour or two, he dozed a little, but when he awoke the night was still very dark.

The men finished their toil at the breastwork just before day and then, laying aside their shovels and picks and taking up their rifles, they watched for the first shoot of dawn in the east. It came presently, disclosing the long lines of Mexican sentinels and behind them the army. The enemy was on watch and soon a terrible rumor, that was true, spread among the Texans. They were caught like the men of Refugio. Only three or four rounds of ammunition were left. It was bad enough to be without food and water, but without powder and bullets either they were no army. Now Ned knew that his presages were true. They were doomed.

The sun rose higher, pouring a golden light upon the plain. The distance to the Mexican lines was in appearance reduced half by the vivid light. Then Ned of the keen eye saw a dark line far off to their right on the prairie. He watched them a little, and saw that they were Mexican cavalry, coming to swell still further Urrea's swollen force. He also saw two cannon drawn by mules.

Ned pointed out the column to Wallace, a Major among the Texans, and then Wallace used a pair of glasses.

"You are right," he said. "They are Mexicans and they have two pieces of artillery. Oh, if we could only use our own guns!"

But the Texan cannon stood as worthless as if they had been spiked, and the Texans were compelled to remain silent and helpless, while the Mexicans put their new guns in position, and took aim with deliberation, as if all the time in the world was theirs. Ned tried to console himself with the reflection that Mexican gunners were not often accurate, but the first thud and puff of smoke showed that these were better than usual.

A shower of grape shot coming from a superior height swept their camp, killing two or three of the remaining oxen, smashing the wagons to pieces, and wounding more men. Another shower from the second gun struck among them with like result, and the case of the Texans grew more desperate.

They tried to reach the gunners with their rifles, but the range was too great, and, after having thrown away nearly all the ammunition that was left, they were forced to stand idly and receive the Mexican fire. The Mexicans must have divined the Texan situation, as a great cheer rose from their lines. It became evident to Ned that the shallow crater would soon be raked through and through by the Mexican artillery.

Fannin, lying upon his pallet, was already calling a council of his officers, to which anyone who chose might listen. The wounded leader was still resolute for battle, saying that they might yet cut their way through the Mexicans. But the others had no hope. They pointed to the increased numbers of the foe, and the exhausted condition of their own men, who had not now tasted food or water for many hours. If Urrea offered them good terms they must surrender.

Ned stood on one side, saying nothing, although his experience was perhaps greater than that of anybody else present. But he had seen the inevitable. Either they must yield to the Mexicans or rush boldly on the foe and die to the last man, as the defenders of the Alamo had done. Yet Fannin still opposed.

"We whipped them off yesterday, and we can do it again to-day," he said.

But he was willing to leave it to the others, and, as they agreed that there was no chance to hold out any longer, they decided to parley with the Mexicans. A white cloth was hoisted on the muzzle of a rifle. The Mexican fire ceased, and they saw officers coming forward. The sight was almost more than Ned could stand. Here was a new defeat, a new tragedy.

"I shall meet them myself," said Fannin, as he rose painfully. "You come with me. Major Wallace, but we do not speak Spanish, either of us."

His eye roved over the recruits, and caught Ned's glance.

"I have been much in Mexico," said Ned. "I speak Spanish and also several Mexican variations of it."

"Good," said Fannin, "then you come with us, and you, too, Durangue. We may need you both."

The two officers and the two interpreters walked out of the hollow, passing the barricade of earth and dead oxen that had been of no avail, and saw four Mexican officers coming toward them. A silk handkerchief about the head of one was hidden partly by a cocked hat, and Ned at once saw that it was Urrea, the younger. His heart swelled with rage and mortification. It was another grievous pang that Urrea should be there to exult.

They met about midway between the camps, and Urrea stepped forward. He gave Ned only a single glance, but it made the boy writhe inwardly. The young Mexican was now all smoothness and courtesy, although Ned was sure that the cruel Spanish strain was there, hidden under his smiling air, but ready to flame up at provocation.

"I salute you as gallant foes," said Urrea in good English, taking off his hat. "My comrades and associates here are Colonel Salas, Lieutenant Colonel Holzinger and Lieutenant Gonzales, who are sent with myself by my uncle, General Urrea, to inquire into the meaning of the white flag that you have hoisted."

Each of the Mexican officers, as his name was called, took off his hat and bowed.

"I am Colonel Fannin," began the Texan leader.

All four Mexicans instantly bowed again.

"And you are wounded," said Urrea. "It shows the valor of the Texans, when their commander himself shares their utmost dangers."

Fannin smiled rather grimly.

"There was no way to escape the dangers," he said. "Your fire was heavy."

Urrea smiled in a gratified way, and then waited politely for Fannin to continue. The leader at once began to treat with the Mexican officers. Ned, Durangue and Urrea translated, and the boy did not miss a word that was said. It was agreed that the Texans should surrender, and that they should be treated as prisoners of war in the manner of civilized nations. Prompt and special attention would be given to the wounded.

Then the Mexican officers saluted courteously and went back toward their own ranks. It had all seemed very easy, very simple, but Ned did not like this velvet smoothness, this willingness of the Mexicans to agree to the most generous terms. Fannin, however, was elated. He had won no victories, but he had saved the lives of his men.

Their own return was slow, as Fannin's wound oppressed him, but when they reached their camp, and told what had been done, the recruits began silently to stack their arms, half in gladness and half in sorrow. More Mexican officers came presently and still treated them with that same smooth and silky courtesy. Colonel Holzinger received the surrendered arms, and, as he did so, he said to Ned, who stood by:

"Well, it's liberty and home in ten days for all you gentlemen."

"I hope so," said Ned gravely, although he had no home.

The Mexican courtesy went so far that the arms of the officers were nailed up in a box, with the statement that they would be given back to them as soon as they were released.

"I am sorry that we cannot consider you an officer, Señor Fulton," said young Urrea to Ned, "then you would get back your rifle and pistols."

"You need not bother about it," said Ned. "I am willing to let them go. I dare say that when I need them I can get others."

"Then you still mean to fight against us?" said Urrea.

"If I can get an exchange, and I suppose I can."

"You are not content even yet! You saw what happened at the Alamo. You survived that by a miracle, but where are all your companions in that siege? Dead. You escaped and joined the Texans at Refugio. Where are the defenders of Refugio? In the swamps of the Guadalupe, and we have only to put forth our hands and take them. You escaped from Refugio to find Fannin and his men. Where are Fannin and his men now? Prisoners in our hands. How many of the Texans are left? There is no place in all Texas so far that the arm of the great Santa Anna cannot reach it."

Ned was stung by his taunts and replied:

"You forget Houston."

Urrea laughed.

"Houston! Houston!" he said. "He does nothing. And your so-called government does nothing, but talk. They, too, will soon feel the might and wrath of Santa Anna. Nothing can save them but a swift flight to the States."

"We shall see," said Ned, although at that moment he was far from confident. "Remember how our men died at the Alamo. The Texans cannot be conquered."

Urrea said nothing further, as if he would not exult over a fallen enemy, although Ned knew that he was swelling with triumph, and went back to his uncle's camp. The Texan arms were taken ahead on some wagons, and then the dreary procession of the Texans themselves marched out of the hollow. They were all on foot and without arms. Those hurt worst were sustained by their comrades, and, thus, they marched into the Mexican camp, where they expected food and water, but General Urrea directed them to walk on to Goliad.

Fainting from hunger and thirst, they took up their march again. The Mexican cavalry rode on either side of them, and many of the horsemen were not above uttering taunts which, fortunately, few of the prisoners could understand. Young Urrea was in command of this guard and he rode near the head of the column where Ned could see him. Now and then a Mexican vaquero cracked his long whip, and every report made Ned start and redden with anger.

Some of the recruits were cheerful, talked of being exchanged and of fighting again in the war, but the great majority marched in silence and gloom. They felt that they had wasted themselves. They had marched into a trap, which the Mexicans were able to close upon them before they could strike a single blow for Texas. Now they were herded like cattle being driven to a stable.

They reached the town of Goliad, and the Mexican women and children, rejoicing in the triumph of their men, came out to meet them, uttering many shrill cries as they chattered to one another. Ned understood them, but he was glad that the others did not. Young Urrea rode up by the side of him and said:

"Well, you and your comrades have now arrived at our good town of Goliad. You should be glad that your lives have been spared, because you are rebels and you deserve death. But great is the magnanimity of our most illustrious president and general, Antonio Lopez de Santa Anna."

Ned looked up quickly. He thought he had caught a note of cruelty in that soft, measured voice. He never trusted Urrea, nor did he ever trust Santa Anna.

"I believe it is customary in civilized warfare to spare the lives of prisoners," he said.

"But rebels are rebels, and freebooters are freebooters," said Urrea.

It seemed to Ned that the young Mexican wanted to draw him into some sort of controversy, and he refused to continue. He felt that there was something sinister about Urrea, or that he represented something sinister, and he resolved to watch rather than talk. So, gazing straight ahead, he walked on in silence. Urrea, waiting for an answer, and seeing that he would get none, smiled ironically, and, turning his horse, galloped away.

The prisoners were marched through the town, and to the church. All the old Spanish or Mexican towns of Texas contained great stone churches, which were also fortresses, and Goliad was no exception. This was of limestone, vaulted and somber, and it was choked to overflowing with the prisoners, who could not get half enough air through the narrow windows. The surgeons, for lack of bandages and medicines, could not attend the wounded, who lay upon the floor.

Where were the fair Mexican promises, in accordance with which they had yielded? Many of the unwounded became so weak from hunger and thirst that they, too, were forced to lie upon the floor. Ned had reserves of strength that came to his aid. He leaned against the wall and breathed the foul air of the old church, which was breathed over and over again by nearly four hundred men.

The heavy doors were unbarred an hour later, and food and water were brought to them, but how little! There was a single drink and a quarter of a pound of meat for each man. It was but a taste after their long fast, and soon they were as hungry and thirsty as ever. It was a hideous night. There was not room for them all to sleep on the floor, and Ned dozed for a while leaning against the wall.

Food and water were brought to them in the same small quantities in the morning, but there was no word from the Mexicans concerning the promises of good treatment and parole that had been made when they surrendered.

Ned was surprised at nothing. He knew that Santa Anna dominated all Mexico, and he knew Santa Anna. Promises were nothing to him, if it served him better to break them. Fannin demanded writing materials and wrote a note to General Urrea protesting strongly against the violation of faith. But General Urrea was gone after Ward's men, who were surrounded in the marshes of the Guadalupe, leaving Colonel Portilla in command. Portilla, meanwhile, was dominated by the younger Urrea, a man of force and audacity, whom he knew to be high in the favor of Santa Anna.

Captain Urrea did not believe in showing any kindness to the men imprisoned in the church. They were rebels or filibusters. They had killed many good Mexicans, and they should be made to suffer for it. No answer was returned to Fannin's letter, and the men in the somber old limestone building became depressed and gloomy.

Ned, who was surprised at nothing, also hoped for nothing, but he sought to preserve his strength, believing that he would soon have full need of it. He stretched and tensed his muscles in order to keep the stiffness from coming into them, and he slept whenever he could.

Two or three days passed and the Mexican officer, Holzinger, came for Fannin, who was now recovered largely from his wound. The two went away to Copano on the coast to look for a vessel that would carry the prisoners to New Orleans. They returned soon, and Fannin and all his men were in high hopes.

Meanwhile a new group of prisoners were thrust into the church. They were the survivors of Ward's men, whom General Urrea had taken in the swamps of the Guadalupe. Then came another squad, eighty-two young Tennesseeans, who, reaching Texas by water, had been surrounded and captured by an overwhelming force the moment they landed. A piece of white cloth had been tied around the arms of every one of these men to distinguish them from the others.

But they were very cheerful over the news that Fannin had brought. There was much bustle among the Mexicans, and it seemed to be the bustle of preparation. The prisoners expected confidently that within another day they would be on the march to the coast and to freedom.

There was a singular scene in the old church. A boy from Kentucky had brought a flute with him which the Mexicans had permitted him to retain. Now sitting in Turkish fashion in the center of the floor he was playing:

"Home, Sweet Home." Either he played well or their situation deepened to an extraordinary pitch the haunting quality of the air.

Despite every effort tears rose to Ned's eyes. Others made no attempt to hide theirs. Why should they? They were but inexperienced boys in prison, many hundreds of miles from the places where they were born.

They sang to the air of the flute, and all through the evening they sang that and other songs. They were happier than they had been in many days. Ned alone was gloomy and silent. Knowing that Santa Anna was now the fountain head of all things Mexican he could not yet trust.

CHAPTER XVIII.
THE BLACK TRAGEDY

While the raw recruits crowded one another for breath in the dark vaulted church of Goliad, a little swarthy man in a gorgeous uniform sat dining luxuriously in the best house in San Antonio, far to the northwest. Some of his favorite generals were around him, Castrillon, Gaona, Almonte, and the Italian Filisola.

The "Napoleon of the West" was happy. His stay in San Antonio, after the fall of the Alamo, had been a continuous triumph, with much feasting and drinking and music. He had received messages from the City of Mexico, his capital, and all things there went well. Everybody obeyed his orders, although they were sent from the distant and barbarous land of Texas.

While they dined, a herald, a Mexican cavalrymen who had ridden far, stopped at the door and handed a letter to the officer on guard:

"For the most illustrious president, General Santa Anna," he said.

The officer went within and, waiting an opportune moment, handed the letter to Santa Anna.

"The messenger came from General Urrea," he said.

Santa Anna, with a word of apology, because he loved the surface forms of politeness, opened and read the letter. Then he uttered a cry of joy.

"We have all the Texans now!" he exclaimed. "General Urrea has taken Fannin and his men. There is nothing left in Texas to oppose us."

The generals uttered joyful shouts and drank again to their illustrious leader. The banquet lasted long, but after it was over Santa Anna withdrew to his own room and dictated a letter to his secretary. It was sealed carefully and given to a chosen messenger, a heavy-browed and powerful Mexican.

"Ride fast to Goliad with that letter," said Santa Anna.

The messenger departed at once. He rode a strong horse, and he would find fresh mounts on the way. He obeyed the orders of the general literally. He soon left San Antonio far behind, and went on hour after hour, straight toward Goliad. Now and then he felt the inside of his tunic where the letter lay, but it was always safe. Three or four times he met parties of Mexicans, and he replied briefly to their questions that he rode on the business of the most illustrious president, General Antonio Lopez de Santa Anna. Once, on the second day, he saw two horsemen, whom his trained eyes told him to be Texan hunters.

The messenger sheered off into a patch of timber, and waited until the hunters passed out of sight. Had they seen him much might have changed, a terrible story might have been different, but, at that period, the stars in their courses were working against the Texans. Every accident, every chance, turned to the advantage of their enemies.

The messenger emerged from the timber, and went on at the same steady gait toward Goliad. He was riding his fourth horse now, having changed every time he met a Mexican detachment, and the animal was fresh and strong. The rider himself, powerful by nature and trained to a life in the saddle, felt no weariness.

The scattered houses of Goliad came into view, by and by, and the messenger, giving the magic name of Santa Anna, rode through the lines. He inquired for General Urrea, the commander, but the general having gone to Victoria he was directed to Colonel Portilla, who commanded in his absence. He found Portilla sitting in a patio with Colonel Garay, the younger Urrea and several other Mexican officers. The messenger saluted, drew the letter from his pocket and presented it to Colonel Portilla.

"From the most illustrious president and commander-in-chief, General Santa Anna," he said.

Portilla broke the seal and read. As his eyes went down the lines, a deep flush crept through the tan of his face, and the paper trembled in his hands.

"I cannot do it! I cannot do it! Read, gentlemen, read!" he cried.

Urrea took the extended letter from his hand and read it aloud. Neither his voice nor his hand quivered as he read, and when he finished he said in a firm voice:

"The orders of the president must be obeyed, and you, Colonel Portilla, must carry them out at once. All of us know that General Santa Anna does not wish to repeat his commands, and that his wrath is terrible."

"It is so! It is so!" said Portilla hopelessly, and Garay also spoke words of grief. But Urrea, although younger and lower in rank, was firm, even exultant. His aggressive will dominated the others, and his assertion that the wrath of Santa Anna was terrible was no vain warning. The others began to look upon him as Santa Anna's messenger, the guardian of his thunderbolts, and they did not dare to meet his eye.

"We will go outside and talk about it," said Portilla, still much agitated.

When they left the patio their steps inevitably took them toward the church. The high note of a flute playing a wailing air came to them through the narrow windows. It was "Home, Sweet Home," played by a boy in prison. The Mexicans did not know the song, but its solemn note was not without an appeal to Portilla and Garay. Portilla wiped the perspiration from his face.

"Come away," he said. "We can talk better elsewhere."

They turned in the opposite direction, but Urrea did not remain with them long. Making some excuse for leaving them he went rapidly to the church. He knew that his rank and authority would secure him prompt admission from the guards, but he stopped, a moment, at the door. The prisoners were now singing. Three or four hundred voices were joined in some hymn of the north that he did not know, some song of the English-speaking people. The great volume of sound floated out, and was heard everywhere in the little town.

Urrea was not moved at all. "Rebels and filibusters!" he said in Spanish, under his breath, but fiercely. Then he ordered the door unbarred, and went in. Two soldiers went with him and held torches aloft.

The singing ceased when Urrea entered. Ned was standing against the wall, and the young Mexican instinctively turned toward him, because he knew Ned best. There was much of the tiger cat in Urrea. He had the same feline grace and power, the same smoothness and quiet before going into action.

"You sing, you are happy," he said to Ned, although he meant them all. "It is well. You of the north bear misfortune well."

"We do the best we can wherever we are," replied young Fulton, dryly.

"The saints themselves could do no more," said the Mexican.

Urrea was speaking in English, and his manner was so friendly and gentle that the recruits crowded around him.

"When are we to be released? When do we get our parole?" they asked.

Urrea smiled and held up his hands. He was all sympathy and generosity.

"All your troubles will be over to-morrow," he said, "and it is fitting that they should end on such a day, because it is Palm Sunday."

The recruits gave a cheer.

"Do we go down to the coast?" one of them asked.

Urrea smiled with his whole face, and with the gesture of his hands, too. But he shook his head.

"I can say no more," he replied. "I am not the general, and perhaps I have said too much already, but be assured, brave foes, that to-morrow will end your troubles. You fought us gallantly. You fought against great odds, and you have my sympathy."

Ned had said no more. He was looking at Urrea intently. He was trying, with all the power of his own mind and soul, to read this man's mind and soul. He was trying to pierce through that Spanish armor of smiles and gestures and silky tones and see what lay beneath. He sought to read the real meaning of all these polite phrases. His long and powerful gaze finally drew Urrea's own.

A little look of fear crept into Urrea's eyes, as the two antagonists stared at each other. But it was only for a few minutes. Then he looked away with a shrug and a laugh.

"Now I leave you," he said to the men, "and may the saints bring you much happiness. Do not forget that to-morrow is Palm Sunday, and that it is a good omen."

He went out, taking the torchbearers with him, and although it was dark again in the vaulted church, the recruits sang a long time. Ned sat down with his back against the wall, and he did not share in the general joy. He remembered the look that had come into Urrea's eyes, when they met the accusing gaze of his own.

After a while the singing ceased, and one by one the recruits fell asleep in the close, stifling air of the place. Ned dozed an hour or two, but awoke before dawn. He was oppressed by a deep and unaccountable gloom, and it was not lifted when, in the dusk, he looked at the rows of sleeping figures, crowded so close together that no part of the floor was visible.

He saw the first light appear in the east, and then spread like the slow opening of a fan. The recruits began to awaken by and by, and their good spirits had carried over from the night before. Soon the old church was filled with talk and laughter.

The day came fully, and then the guards brought food and water, not enough to satisfy hunger and thirst, but enough to keep them alive. They did not complain, as they would soon be free men, able to obtain all that they wanted. Presently the doors of the church were thrown open, and the officers and many soldiers appeared. Young Urrea was foremost among the officers, and, in a loud voice, he ordered all the prisoners to come out, an order that they obeyed with alacrity and pleasure.

Ned marched forth with the rest, although he did not speak to any of those about him. He looked first at Urrea, whose manner was polite and smiling, as it had been the night before, and then his glance shifted to the other officers, older men, and evidently higher in rank. He saw that two, Colonels by their uniforms, were quite pale, and that one of them was biting savagely at his mustache. It all seemed sinister to Ned. Why was Urrea doing everything, and why were his superiors standing by, evidently a prey to some great nervous strain?

The recruits, under Urrea's orders, were formed into three columns. One was to take the road toward San Antonio, the second would march toward San Patricio, and the third to Copano. The three columns shouted good-by, but the recruits assured one another that they would soon meet again. Urrea told one column that it was going to be sent home immediately, another that it was going outside the town, where it was to help in killing cattle for beef which they would eat, and the third that it was leaving the church in a hurry to make room for Santa Anna's own troops, who would reach the town in an hour.

Ned was in the largest column, near the head of it, and he watched everything with a wary eye. He noticed that the Mexican colonels still left all the arrangements to Urrea, and that they remained extremely nervous. Their hands were never quiet for a moment.

The column filed down through the town, and Ned saw the Mexican women looking at them. He heard two or three of them say "pobrecitos" (poor fellows), and their use of the word struck upon his ear with an ominous sound. He glanced back. Close behind the mass of prisoners rode a strong squadron of cavalry with young Urrea at their head. Ned could not see Urrea's face, which was hidden partly by a cocked and plumed hat, but he noticed that the young Mexican sat very upright, as if he felt the pride of authority. One hand held the reins, and the other rested on the silver hilt of a small sword at his side.

A column of Mexican infantry marched on either side of the prisoners, and only a few yards away. It seemed to Ned that they were holding the Texans very close for men whom they were to release in a few hours. Trusting the Mexicans in nothing, he was suspicious of everything, and he watched with a gaze that missed no detail. But he seemed to be alone in such thoughts. The recruits, enjoying the fresh air and the prospect of speedy freedom, were talking much, and exchanging many jests.

They passed out of the little town, and the last Ned saw of it was the Mexican women standing in the doorways and watching. They continued along the road in double file, with the Mexican infantry still on either side, and the Mexican cavalry in the rear. A half mile from the town, and Urrea gave an order. The whole procession stopped, and the column of Mexican infantry on the left passed around, joining their comrades on the right. The recruits paid no attention to the movement, but Ned looked instantly at Urrea. He saw the man rise now in his saddle, his whole face aflame. In a flash he divined everything. His heart leaped and he shouted:

"Boys, they are going to kill us!"

The startled recruits did not have time to think, because the next instant Urrea, rising to his full height in his stirrups, cried:

"Fire!"

The double line of Mexicans, at a range of a few yards, fired in an instant into the column of unarmed prisoners. There was a great blaze, a spurt of smoke and a tremendous crash. It seemed to Ned that he could fairly hear the thudding of bullets upon bodies, and the breaking of bones beneath the sudden fierce impact of the leaden hail. An awful strangled cry broke from the poor recruits, half of whom were already down. The Mexicans, reloading swiftly, poured in another volley, and the prisoners fell in heaps. Then Urrea and the cavalry, with swords and lances, charged directly upon them, the hoofs of their horses treading upon wounded and unwounded alike.

Ned could never remember clearly the next few moments in that red and awful scene. It seemed to him afterward that he went mad for the time. He was conscious of groans and cries, of the fierce shouting of the Mexicans, wild with the taste of blood, of the incessant crackling of the rifles and muskets, and of falling bodies. He saw gathering over himself and his slaughtered comrades a great column of smoke, pierced by innumerable jets of fire, and he caught glimpses of the swart faces of the Mexicans as they pulled triggers. From right and left came the crash of heavy but distant volleys, showing that the other two columns were being massacred in the same way.

He felt the thunder of hoofs and a horse was almost upon him, while the rider, leaning from the saddle, cut at him with a saber. Ned, driven by instinct rather than reason, sprang to one side the next instant, and then the horseman was lost in the smoke. He dashed against a figure, and was about to strike with his fist, the only weapon that he now had, when he saw that he had collided with a Texan, unwounded like himself. Then he, too, was lost in the smoke.

A consuming rage and horror seized Ned. Why he was not killed he never knew. The cloud over the place where the slaughtered recruits lay thickened, but the Mexicans never ceased to fire into it with their rifles and muskets. The crackling of the weapons beat incessantly upon the drums of his ears.

Mingled with it were the cries and groans of the victims, now fast growing fewer. But it was all a blurred and red vision to Ned. While he was in that deadly volcano he moved by instinct and impulse and not by reason.

A few of the unwounded had already dashed from the smoke and had undertaken flight across the plain, away from the Mexican infantry, where they were slain by the lances or muskets of the cavalry under Urrea. Ned followed them. A lancer thrust so savagely at him that when the boy sprang aside the lance was hurled from his hand. Ned's foot struck against the weapon, and instantly he picked it up. A horseman on his right was aiming a musket at him, and, using the lance as a long club, he struck furiously at the Mexican. The heavy butt landed squarely upon the man's head, and shattered it like an eggshell. Youthful and humane, Ned nevertheless felt a savage joy when the man's skull crashed beneath his blow.

It is true that he was quite mad for the moment. His rage and horror caused every nerve and muscle within him to swell. His brain was a mass of fire. His strength was superhuman. Whirling the great lance in club fashion about his head he struck another Mexican across the shoulders, and sent him with a howl of pain from the saddle. He next struck a horse across the forehead, and so great was the impact that the animal went down. A cavalryman at a range of ten yards fired at him and missed. He never fired again, as the heavy butt of the lance caught him the next instant on the side of the head, and he went to join his comrade.

All the while Ned was running for the timber. A certain reason was appearing in his actions, and he was beginning to think clearly. He curved about as he ran, knowing that it would disturb the aim of the Mexicans, who were not good shots, and instinctively he held on to the lance, whirling it about his head, and from time to time uttering fierce shouts like an Indian warrior wild with battle. More than one Mexican horseman sheered away from the formidable figure with the formidable weapon.

Ned saw other figures, unarmed, running for the wood. A few reached it, but most were cut down before they had gone half way. Behind him the firing and shouting of the Mexicans did not seem to decrease, but no more groans or cries reached him from the bank of smoke that hung over the place where the murdered recruits lay. But the crash of the fire, directed on the other columns to right and left, still came to him.

Ned saw the wood not far away now. Twenty or thirty shots had been fired at him, but all missed except two, which merely grazed him. He was not hurt and the superhuman strength, born of events so extraordinary, still bore him up. The trees looked very green. They seemed to hold out sheltering arms, and there was dense underbrush through which the cavalry could not dash.

He came yet nearer, and then a horseman, rifle raised to his shoulder, dashed in between. Sparks danced before Ned's eyes. Throat and mouth, lips and his whole face burned with smoke and fever, but all the heat seemed to drive him into fiercer action. He struck at horse and horseman so savagely that the two went down together, and the lance broke in his hands. Then with a cry of triumph that his parched throat could scarcely utter, he leaped into the timber.

Having reached the shelter of the trees, Ned ran on for a long time, and finally came into the belt of forest along the San Antonio River. Twenty-six others escaped in the same way on that day, which witnessed the most dreadful deed ever done on the soil of North America, but nearly four hundred were murdered in obedience to the letter sent by Antonio Lopez de Santa Anna. Fannin and Ward, themselves, were shot through the head, and their bodies were thrown into the common heap of the slain.

Ned did not see any of the other fugitives among the trees. He may have passed them, but his brain was still on fire, and he beheld nothing but that terrible scene behind him, the falling recruits, the fire and the smoke and the charging horsemen. He could scarcely believe that it was real. The supreme power would not permit such things. Already the Alamo had lighted a fire in his soul, and Goliad now turned it into a roaring flame. He hated Urrea, who had rejoiced in it, and he hated Santa Anna who, he dimly felt, had been responsible for this massacre. Every element in his being was turned for the time into passion and hatred. As he wandered on, he murmured unintelligible but angry words through his burning lips.

He knew nothing about the passage of time, but after many hours he realized that it was night, and that he had come to the banks of a river. It was the San Antonio, and he swam it, wishing to put the stream between himself and the Mexicans. Then he sat down in the thick timber, and the collapse from such intense emotions and such great exertions came quickly. He seemed to go to pieces all in a breath. His head fell forward and he became unconscious.

CHAPTER XIX.
THE RACE FOR THE BOAT

Five men, or rather four men and a boy, rode down the banks of the San Antonio, always taking care to keep well in the shelter of the timber. All the men were remarkable in figure, and at least three of them were of a fame that had spread to every corner of Texas.

The one who rode slightly in advance was of gigantic build, enormously thick through the shoulders and chest. He was dressed in brightly dyed deerskin, and there were many fanciful touches about his border costume. The others also wore deerskin, but theirs was of soberer hue. The man was Martin Palmer, far better known as the Panther, or, as he loved to call himself, the Ring Tailed Panther. His comrades were "Deaf" Smith, Henry Karnes, Obed White and Will Allen.

They were not a very cheerful five. Riding as free lances, because there was now practically no organized authority among the Texans, they had been scouting the day before toward Goliad. They had learned that Fannin and his men had been taken, and they had sought also to discover what the Mexican generals meant to do with the troops. But the Mexican patrols had been so numerous and strong that they could not get close enough to Goliad. Early in the morning while in the timber by the river they had heard the sound of heavy firing near Goliad, which continued for some time, but they had not been able to fathom its meaning. They concluded finally that a portion of Fannin's men must have been still holding out in some old building of Goliad, and that this was the last stand.

They made another effort to get closer to the town, but they were soon compelled to turn back, and, again they sought the thickest timber along the river. Now they were riding back, in the hope of finding some Texan detachment with which they could coöperate.

"If we keep huntin' we ought to find somebody who can tell us somethin'," said the Panther.

"It's a long lane that has no news at the end," said Obed White, with an attempt at buoyancy.

"That's so," said "Deaf" Smith. "We're bound to hit a trail somehow an' somewhere. We heard that Fannin's men had surrendered an' then we heard that firin'. But I guess that they wouldn't give up, without makin' good terms for themselves, else they would have held out as the boys did in the Alamo."

"Ah, the Alamo!" said Obed White. His face clouded at the words. He was thinking then of the gallant youth who had escaped with him from the dungeon under the sea in the castle of San Juan de Ulua, and who had been his comrade in the long and perilous flight through Mexico into Texas. The heart of the Maine man, alone in the world, had turned strongly to Ned Fulton, and mourning him as one dead he also mourned him as a son. But as he rarely talked of the things that affected him most, he seldom mentioned Ned. The Panther was less restrained.

"We've got a big score to settle for the Alamo," he said. "Some good friends of mine went down forever in that old mission an' there was that boy, Ned Fulton. I s'pose it ain't so bad to be cut off when you're old, an' you've had most of your life, but it does look bad for a strong, fine boy just turnin' into a man to come straight up ag'inst the dead wall."

Will Allen said nothing, but unbidden water forced itself to his eyes. He and Ned had become the strongest of friends and comrades.

"After all that's been done to our people," said the Panther, "I feel like rippin' an' r'arin' an' chawin' the rest of my life."

"We'll have the chance to do all of it we want, judgin' from the way things are goin'," said "Deaf" Smith.

Then they relapsed into silence, and rode on through the timber, going slowly as they were compelled to pick their way in the underbrush. It was now nearly noon, and a brilliant sun shone overhead, but the foliage of young spring was heavy on trees and bushes, and it gave them at the same time shade and shelter.

As they rode they watched everywhere for a trail. If either Texans or Mexicans had passed they wanted to know why, and when. They came at last to hoofprints in the soft bank of the river, indicating that horses—undoubtedly with men on their backs—had crossed here. The skilled trailers calculated the number at more than fifteen, perhaps more than twenty, and they followed their path across the timber and out upon the prairie.

When the hoofprints were more clearly discernible in the grass they saw that they had been made by unshod feet, and they were mystified, but they followed cautiously or, for two or three miles, when "Deaf" Smith saw something gleaming by the track. He alighted and picked up a painted feather.

"It's simple now," he said. "We've been followin' the trail of Indians. They wouldn't be in this part of the country, 'less they were helpin' the Mexicans, an' I guess they were at Goliad, leavin' after the business there was finished."

"You're right, Deaf," said Karnes. "That 'counts for the unshod hoofs. It ain't worth while for us to follow them any longer, so I guess we'd better turn back to the timber."

Safety obviously demanded this course, and soon they were again in the forest, riding near the San Antonio and down its stream. They struck the trail of a bear, then they roused up a deer in the thickets, but big game had no attraction for them now, and they went on, leaving bear and deer in peace. Then the sharp eyes of the Panther saw the print of a human foot on the river bank. He soon saw three or four more such traces leading into the forest, where the trail was lost.

The five gathered around the imprints in the earth, and debated their meaning. It was evident even to Will Allen that some one without a horse had swum the river at that point and had climbed up the bank. They could see the traces lower down, where he had emerged from the water.

"I figger it this way," said the Panther. "People don't go travelin' through this country except on horses, an' this fellow, whoever he is, didn't have any horse, as we all can see as plain as day."

"An' in such times as these," said "Deaf" Smith, "fellers don't go swimmin' rivers just for fun. The one that made these tracks was in a hurry. Ain't that so, Hank?"

"'Course he was," replied Karnes. "He was gettin' away from somewhere an' from somebody. That's why he swam the river; he wanted the San Antonio to separate him from them somebodies."

"And putting two and two and then two more together," said Obed White, "we draw the conclusion that it is a fugitive, probably one of our own Texans, who has escaped in some manner from his prison at Goliad."

"It's what we all think," said the Panther, "an' now we'll beat up these thickets till we find him. He's sure to keep movin' away from Goliad, an' he's got sense to stay in the cover of the timber."

The forest here ran back from the river three or four hundred yards, and the five, separating and moving up the stream, searched thoroughly. The hunt presently brought the Panther and Obed White together again, and they expressed their disappointment at finding nothing. Then they heard a cry from Will Allen, who came galloping through the thickets, his face white and his eyes starting.

THE TEXAN SCOUTS A Story Of The Alamo And Goliad | 235

"I've found Ned Fulton!" he cried. "He's lying here dead in the bushes!"

The Panther and Obed stared in amazement.

"Will," exclaimed the Panther, "have you gone plum' crazy? Ned was killed at the Alamo!"

"I tell you he is here!" cried the boy, who was shaking with excitement. "I have just seen him! He was lying on his back in the bushes, and he did not move!"

"Lead on! Let's see what you have seen!" said Obed, who began to share in the boy's excitement.

The Panther whistled, and Smith and Karnes joined them. Then, led by Will Allen, they rode swiftly through the bushes, coming, forty or fifty yards away, into a tiny grassy glade. It was either Ned Fulton or his ghost, and the Panther, remembering the Alamo, took it for the latter. He uttered a cry of astonishment and reined in his horse. But Obed White leaped to the ground, and ran to the prostrate figure.

"A miracle!" he exclaimed. "It's Ned Fulton! And he's alive!"

The others also sprang from their horses, and crowded around their youthful comrade, whom they had considered among the fallen of the Alamo. Ned was unconscious, his face was hot with fever, and his breathing was hard and irregular.

"How he escaped from the Alamo and how he came here we don't know," said Obed White solemnly, "but there are lots of strange things in heaven and earth, as old Shakespeare said, and this is one of the strangest of them all."

"However, it's happened we're glad to get him back," said the Panther. "And now we must go to work. You can tell by lookin' at him that he's been through all kinds of trouble, an' a powerful lot of it."

These skilled borderers knew that Ned was suffering from exhaustion. They forced open his mouth, poured a drink down his throat from a flask that Karnes carried, and rubbed his hands vigorously. Ned, after a while, opened his eyes and looked at them dimly. He knew in a vague way that these were familiar faces, but he remembered nothing, and he felt no surprise.

"Ned! Ned! Don't; you know us?" said Will Allen. "We're your friends, and we found you lying here in the bush!"

The clouds slowly cleared away from Ned's mind and it all came back, the terrible and treacherous slaughter of his unarmed comrades, his own flight through the timber his swimming of the river, and then the blank. But these were his best friends. It was no fantasy. How and when they had come he did not know, but here they were in the flesh, the Panther, Obed White, Will Allen, "Deaf" Smith and Henry Karnes.

"Boys," he asked weakly, "how did you find me?"

"Now don't you try to talk yet a while, Ned," said Obed White, veiling his feeling under a whimsical tone. "When people come back from the dead they don't always stay, and we want to keep you, as you're an enrolled member of this party. The news of your trip into the beyond and back again will keep, until we fix up something for you that will make you feel a lot stronger."

These frontiersmen never rode without an outfit, and Smith produced a small skillet from his kit. The Panther lighted a fire, Karnes chipped off some dried beef, and in a few minutes they had a fine soup, which Ned ate with relish. He sat with his back against a tree and his strength returned rapidly.

"I guess you can talk now, Ned," said Obed White. "You can tell us how you got away from the Alamo, and where you've been all the time."

Young Fulton's face clouded and Obed White saw his hands tremble.

"It isn't the Alamo," he said. "They died fighting there. It was Goliad."

"Goliad?" exclaimed "Deaf" Smith. "What do you mean?"

"I mean the slaughter, the massacre. All our men were led out. They were told that they were to go on parole. Then the whole Mexican army opened fire upon us at a range of only a few yards and the cavalry trod us down. We had no arms. We could not fight back. It was awful. I did not dream that such things could be. None of you will ever see what I've seen, and none of you will ever go through what I've gone through."

"Ned, you've had fever. It's a dream," said Obed White, incredulous.

"It is no dream. I broke through somehow, and got to the timber. Maybe a few others escaped in the same way, but all the rest were murdered in cold blood. I know that Santa Anna ordered it."

They knew perfectly well that Ned was telling the full truth, and the faces of all of them darkened. The same thought was in the heart of every one, vengeance for the deed, but however intense was the thought it did not approach the feeling of Ned, who had seen it all, and who had been through it all.

"I guess that was the firing we heard," said Smith, "when we thought it was the boys making a last stand at Goliad. I tell you, comrades, this means the freedom of Texas. No matter how the quarrel came about no people can stand such things."

"It's so," said the others together.

They did not declaim. They were of a tribe that was not given much to words, but they felt sure that their own resolve to fight until no Mexicans were left in Texas would now be shared by every Texan.

After Ned rested a while longer and ate more of the good soup, he told the full story of the great and tragic scenes through which he had passed since he became separated from them. Seasoned as they were, these men hung with breathless interest on every detail. He told them everything that had passed in the Alamo during the long days of the siege. He told of Crockett and Bowie and Travis and of the final assault.

The Panther drew a deep breath, when he finished that part of the story.

"They were certainly great men in the Alamo, them fellers," he said, "and when my time comes to die I believe I'd rather die that way than any other."

Ned did not linger long over the tale of Goliad. He could not yet bear the detailed repetition.

"I think we'd better make for the coast," said "Deaf" Smith, when he had finished. "Our forces in the field are about wiped out, an' we've got to raise a new army of some kind. We can look for our government, too. It's wanderin' aroun', tryin' to keep out of the hands of Santa Anna. We haven't any horse for you now, Ned, but you can ride behind Will Allen. Maybe we can get you a mount before long."

They remained in the timber the rest of the day, in order that Ned might recover sufficiently for the journey. About the middle of the afternoon they saw a dozen Mexican cavalrymen on the plain, and they hoped that they would invade the timber. They were keyed to such a pitch of anger and hate that they would have welcomed a fight, and they were more than confident of victory, but the Mexicans disappeared beyond the swells, and every one of the men was disappointed.

At night they began their march toward the north, and continued almost until morning. Ned, riding behind Will Allen, scarcely spoke. Obed White, then and afterward, observed a great change in him. He seemed to have matured suddenly far beyond his years, and Obed always felt that he had some unchanging purpose that had little to do with gentleness or mercy.

They slept in the timber until about 10 o'clock, and then resumed their ride northward, still holding to the opinion that the peripatetic Texan government would be found at Harrisburg, or somewhere in its vicinity. In the afternoon they encountered a Mexican force of eight mounted men, and attacked with such vigor that Ned and Will, riding double, were never able to get into the fight. Two of the Mexicans fell, and the rest got away. The Texans were unharmed.

The Panther, after a chase, captured one of the horses, and brought him back for Ned. They also secured the arms of the fallen Mexicans, one of these weapons being an American rifle, which Ned was quite sure had belonged to a slaughtered recruit at Goliad. They also found a letter in one of the Mexican haversacks. It was from General Urrea to General Santa Anna, and the Panther and his comrades inferred from the direction in which its bearer had been riding that the dictator himself had left San Antonio, and was marching eastward with the main Mexican army.

"I have to inform you," ran a part of the letter, "that your orders in regard to the rebels at Goliad were carried out, in my absence, by the brave and most excellent Colonel Portilla. They were all executed, except a few who escaped under cover of the smoke to the timber, but our cavalrymen are sure to find in time every one of these, and inflict upon them the justice that you have ordered.

"I shall march north, expecting to meet your excellency, and I trust that I shall have further good news to report to you. There are now no rebel forces worthy of the name. We shall sweep the country clean. I shall send detachments to take any Americans who may land at the ports, and, coöperating with you, I feel assured, also, that we shall capture every member of the rebel government. In another month there will not be a single Texan in arms against us."

Ned read the letter aloud, translating into English as he went, and when he finished the Panther burst into a scornful laugh.

"So, the rebels are all killed, or about to be killed!" he said. "An' there won't be one Texan in arms a month from now! I'm willin' to give my word that here are six of us who will be in arms then, roarin' an' rippin' an' t'arin'! They'll sweep the country clean, will they? They'll need a bigger broom for that job than any that was ever made in Mexico!"

The others made comment in like fashion, but young Fulton was silent. His resolution was immutable, and it required no words to assert it.

"I guess we'd better take this letter with us an' give it to Sam Houston," said "Deaf" Smith. "Houston has been criticized a lot for not gatherin' his forces together an' attackin' the Mexicans, but he ain't had any forces to gather, an' talk has never been much good against cannon balls an' bullets. Still, he's the only man we've got to fall back on."

"You keep the letter, 'Deaf'," said the Panther, "an' now that we've got a horse for Ned I guess we can go a little faster. How you feelin' now, Ned?"

"Fine," replied Ned. "Don't you bother about me any more. I started on the upgrade the moment you fellows found me."

"A good horse and a good rifle ought to be enough to bring back the strength to any Texan," said Obed White.

They resumed their journey at a faster pace, but before nightfall they met another Texan who informed them that large forces of Mexicans were now between them and Harrisburg. Hence they concluded that it was wiser to turn toward the coast, and make a great circuit around the forces of Santa Anna.

But they told the Texan scout of what had been done at Goliad, and bade him wave the torch of fire wherever he went. He rode away with a face aghast at the news, and they knew that he would soon spread it through the north. As for themselves they rode rapidly toward the east.

They spent the night in a cluster of timber, and the Panther was fortunate enough to shoot a wild turkey. They made Ned eat the tenderest parts, and then seek sleep between blankets. His fever was now gone, but he was relaxed and weak. It was a pleasant weakness, however, and, secure in the comradeship of his friends, he soon fell into a deep slumber which lasted all the night. The others had planned an early start, but, as Ned was sleeping with such calm and peace, they decided not to disturb him, knowing how much he needed the rest. It was three hours after sunrise when he awoke, and he made many apologies, but the rest only laughed.

"What's the use of our hurryin'?" said "Deaf" Smith. "It'll take some time for Sam Houston to get any army together, an' we might keep in good shape until he gets it. Here's more beef soup for you, Ned. You'll find it mighty fine for buildin' up."

Two or three hours after they started that day they came to a large trail, and, when they followed it a little while, they found that it was made by Mexicans marching south, but whether they belonged to the main force under Santa Anna or that under Urrea they could not tell.

It was evident that the northern road was full of dangers and they rode for the coast. Several small Texan vessels were flitting around the gulf, now and then entering obscure bays and landing arms, ammunition and recruits for he cause. Both Smith and Karnes were of the opinion that they might find a schooner or sloop, and they resolved to try for it.

They reached, the next day, country that had not been ravaged by the troops of Santa Anna, and passed one or two tiny settlements, where they told the news of Goliad. The Panther, Smith and Karnes were well known to all the Texans, and they learned in the last of these villages that a schooner was expected in a cove about forty miles up the coast. It would undoubtedly put in at night, and it would certainly arrive in two or three days. They thought it was coming from New Orleans.

The little party decided to ride for the cove, and meet the schooner if possible. They could reach it in another day and night, and they would await the landing.

"We've got good friends in New Orleans," said Smith, as they rode over the prairie. "You'll remember the merchant, John Roylston. He's for us heart and soul, an' I've no doubt that he's sendin' us help."

"All the Texans owe him a debt," said Ned, "and I owe him most of all. His name saved my life, when I was taken at San Antonio. It had weight with Santa Anna, and it might have had weight with him, too, at Goliad, had he been there."

They rode steadily all the next day. Their horses were tough mustangs of the best quality, and showed no signs of weariness. They passed through a beautiful country of light rolling prairie, interspersed with fine forest. The soil was deep and rich, and the foliage was already in its tenderest spring green. Soft, warm airs swept up from the gulf. Five of the riders felt elation, and talked cheerfully. But Ned maintained a somber silence. The scenes of Goliad were still too vivid for him to rejoice over anything. The others understood, and respected his silence.

They camped that night as usual in the thickest forest they could find, and, feeling that they were now too far east to be in any serious danger from the Mexicans, they lighted a fire, warmed their food, and made coffee, having replenished their supplies at the last settlement. Obed White was the coffee maker, heating it in a tin pot with a metal bottom. They had only one cup, which they used in turn, but the warm food and drink were very grateful to them after their hard riding.

"Keeping in good condition is about three-fourths of war," said Obed in an oracular tone. "He who eats and runs away will live to eat another day. Besides, Napoleon said that an army marched better on a full stomach, or something like it."

"That applied to infantry," said Will Allen. "We march on our horses."

"Some day," said Ned, "when we've beaten Santa Anna and driven all the Mexicans out of Texas, I'm going back and hunt for Old Jack. He and I are too good friends to part forever. I found him, after abandoning him the first time, and I believe I can do it again, after leaving him the second time."

"Of course you can," said the Panther cheerily. "Old Jack is a horse that will never stay lost. Now, I think we'd better put out our fire and go to sleep. The horses will let us know if any enemy comes."

All were soon slumbering peacefully in their blankets, but Ned, who had slept so much the night before, awakened in two or three hours. He believed, at first, that a distant sound had broken his sleep, but when he sat up he heard nothing. Five dusky figures lay in a row near him. They were those of his comrades, and he heard their steady breathing. Certainly they slept well. He lay down again, but he remained wide awake, and, when his ear touched the ground, he seemed to hear the faint and distant sound again.

He rose and looked at the horses. They had not moved, and it was quite evident that they had detected no hostile presence. But Ned was not satisfied. Putting his rifle on his shoulder he slipped through the forest to the edge of the prairie. Long before he was there he knew that he had not been deceived by fancy.

He saw, two or three hundred yards in front of him, a long file of cavalry marching over the prairie, going swiftly and straight ahead, as if bent upon some purpose well defined. A good moon and abundant stars furnished plenty of light, and Ned saw that the force was Mexican. There were no lancers, all the men carrying rifles or muskets, and Ned believed that he recognized the younger Urrea in the figure at their head. He had seen the young Mexican so often and in such vivid moments that there was no phase of pose or gesture that he could forget.

Ned watched the column until it was hidden by the swells. It had never veered to either right or left, and its course was the same as that of his comrades and himself. He wondered a little while, and then he felt a suspicion which quickly grew into a certainty. Urrea, a daring partisan leader, who rode over great distances, had heard of the schooner and its arms, and was on his way to the cove to seize them. It was for Ned and his friends to prevent it.

He returned, and, awakening the others, stated what he had seen. Then he added his surmise.

"It's likely that you're guessin' right," said "Deaf" Smith. "The Mexicans have spies, of course, an' they get word, too, from Europeans in these parts, who are not friendly to us. What do you say, boys, all of you?"

"That Urrea is bound for the same place we are," said Obed White.

"That we've got to ride hard, an' fast," said the Panther.

"It's our business to get there first," said Karnes.

"Let's take to the saddle now," said Will Allen.

Ned said nothing. He had given his opinion already. They saddled their horses, and were on the plain in five minutes, riding directly in the trail of the Mexican cavalry. They meant to follow until nearly dawn, and then, passing around, hurry to the cove, where the schooner, without their warning, might be unloading supplies before nightfall into the very arms of the Mexicans.

Before dawn they faintly saw the troop ahead, and then, turning to the left, they put their mustangs into the long easy lope of the frontier, not slowing down, until they were sure that they were at least three or four miles beyond the Mexicans. But they continued at a fast walk, and ate their breakfasts in the saddle. They rode through the same beautiful country, but without people, and they knew that if nothing unusual occurred they would see the sea by noon.

Ned went over their directions once more. The cove ran back from the sea about a mile, and its entrance was a strait not more than thirty yards wide, but deep. In fact, the entire cove was deep, being surrounded by high forested banks except at the west, into which a narrow but deep creek emptied. The only convenient landing was the creek's mouth, and they believed that they would find the schooner there.

Ned, in common with the others, felt the great importance of the mission on which they rode. Most of the Texan cannon and a great part of their rifles had been taken at the Alamo and Goliad. But greater even than the need of arms was that of ammunition. If Urrea were able to seize the schooner, or to take the supplies, the moment after they landed, he would strike the Texans a heavy blow. Hence the six now pushed their horses.

At ten o'clock, they caught a glimpse of the sea upon their right. Five minutes later they saw a cloud of dust on their left, less than a mile away. It was moving rapidly, and it was evident at once that it was made by a large body of horse. When the dust lifted a little, they saw that it was Urrea and his men.

"It's likely that they have more information than we have," said the Panther, "an' they are ridin' hard to make a surprise. Boys, we've got to beat 'em, an', to do it, we've got to keep ahead of our dust all the time!"

"The greater the haste, the greater the speed just now," said Obed White.

They urged their horses into a gallop. They kept close to the sea, while Urrea was more than half a mile inland. Luckily, a thin skirt of timber soon intervened between Mexicans and Texans, and the six believed that Urrea and his men were unaware of their presence. Their own cloud of dust was much smaller than that of the Mexicans, and also it might readily be mistaken for sea sand whipped up by the wind.

Ned and the Panther rode in front, side by side, Smith and Karnes followed, side by side, too, and behind came Obed White and Will Allen, riding knee to knee. They ascended a rise and Ned, whose eyes were the keenest of them all, uttered a little cry.

"The schooner is there!" he exclaimed. "See, isn't that the top of a mast sticking up above those scrub trees?"

"It's nothing else," said Obed White, who was familiar with the sea and ships. "And it's bound, too, to be the schooner for which we are looking. Forward, boys! The swift will win the race, and the battle will go to the strong!"

They pressed their horses now to their greatest speed. The cove and the ship were not more than a half mile away. A quarter of a mile, and the skirt of timber failed. The Mexicans on their left saw them, and increased their speed.

"The schooner's anchored!" exclaimed Obed, "and they are unloading! Look, part of the cargo is on the bank already!"

With foot and rein they took the last ounce of speed from their horses, and galloped up to a group of astonished men, who were transferring arms and ammunition by small boats from a schooner to the land Already more than a hundred rifles, and a dozen barrels of powder lay upon the shore.

"Back to the ship! Back to the ship!" cried Ned, who involuntarily took the lead. "We are Texans, and a powerful force of Mexicans will be here inside of fifteen minutes!"

The men looked at him astonished and unbelieving. Ned saw among them a figure, clad in sober brown, a man with a large head and a broad, intellectual face, with deep lines of thought. He knew him at once, and cried:

"Mr. Roylston, it is I! Edward Fulton! You know me! And here are Captain Palmer, 'Deaf' Smith, Henry Karnes, Obed White and Will Allen! I tell you that you have no time to lose! Put the supplies back on the schooner, and be as quick as you can! Captain Urrea and two hundred men are galloping fast to capture them!"

Roylston started in astonishment at the appearance of Ned, whom he, too, had believed to be dead, but he wasted no time in questions. He gave quick orders to have the arms and ammunition reloaded, and directed the task himself. The Panther sprang from his horse and walked back to the edge of the wood.

"Here they come at a gallop," he said, "and we need time. Boys, hand me your rifles, as I call for them, an' I'll show you how to shoot."

The Panther did not mean to boast, nor did the others take it as such. He merely knew his own skill, and he meant to use it.

"Do as he says," said "Deaf" Smith to the others. "I reckon that, as Davy Crockett is dead, the Panther is the best shot in all Texas."

The Mexican cavalry were coming at a gallop, several hundred yards away. The Panther raised his long, slender-barreled rifle, pulled the trigger, and the first horseman fell from the saddle. Without turning, he held out his hands and Smith thrust the second rifle into them. Up went the weapon, and a second Mexican saddle was empty. A third rifle and a third Mexican went down, a fourth, and the result was the same. The whole Mexican troop, appalled at such deadly shooting, stopped suddenly.

"Keep it up, Panther! Keep it up!" cried Smith. "We need every minute of time that we can get."

While the Mexicans hesitated the Panther sent another fatal bullet among them. Then they spread out swiftly in a thin half circle, and advanced again. All the six Texans now opened fire, and they were also helped by some of the men from the boat. But a part of the attacking force had gained cover and the fire was not now so effective.

Nevertheless the rush of the Mexicans was checked, and under the directions of Roylston the reloading of the schooner was proceeding rapidly. They hoisted the last of the powder and rifles over the side, and two of the boats were putting back for the defenders. The schooner, meanwhile, had taken in her anchor and was unfurling her sails. Roylston was in one of the boats and, springing upon the bank, he shouted to the defenders:

"Come, lads! The supplies are all back on board! It's for your lives now!"

All the men instantly abandoned the defence and rushed for the bank, the Panther uttering a groan of anger.

"I hate to leave six good horses to Urrea, an' that gang," he said, "but I s'pose it has to be done."

"Don't grieve, Panther," cried Smith. "We'll take three for one later on!"

"Hurry up! Hurry up!" said Roylston. "There is no time to waste. Into the boats, all of you!"

They scrambled into the boats, reached the schooner, and pulled the boats to the deck after them. There was not a minute to lose. The schooner, her sails full of wind, was beginning to move, and the Mexicans were already firing at her, although their bullets missed.

Ned and Will Allen threw themselves flat on the deck, and heard the Mexican bullets humming over their heads. Ned knew that they were still in great danger, as it was a mile to the open sea, and the Mexicans galloping along by the side of the cove had begun a heavy fire upon the schooner. But the Panther uttered a tremendous and joyous shout of defiance.

"They can't hurt the ship as long as they ain't got cannon," he said, "an' since it's rifles, only, we'll give it back to 'em!"

He and the other sharpshooters, sheltering themselves, began to rake the woods with rifle fire. The Mexicans replied, and the bullets peppered the wooden sides of the schooner or cut holes through her sails. But the Texans now had the superiority. They could shelter themselves on the ship, and they were also so much better marksmen that they did much damage, while suffering but little themselves.

The schooner presently passed between the headlands, and then into the open sea. She did not change her course until she was eight or ten miles from land, when she turned northward.

only in the foreign banks of Mexico, but also large amounts of it in two of the great banks of London. The English deposits stand as security for the heavy sums that he owes me. His arm is long, but it does not reach to London.

"He cannot pay at present without putting himself in great difficulties, and, for the time being, I wish the debt to stand. It gives me a certain power over him, although we are on opposite sides in a fierce war. When you gave him my name in San Antonio, he did not put you to death because he feared that I would seize his English money when I heard of it.

"The younger Urrea has heard something of these debts. He is devoted to Santa Anna, and he knew that he would have rendered his chief an immense service if he could have secured his release from them. That was what he tried to force from me when I was in his hands, but you and your friends saved me. You little thought, Edward Fulton, that you were then saving your own life also. Otherwise, Santa Anna would have had you slain instantly when you were brought before him at San Antonio. Ah, how thoroughly I know that man! That he can be a terrible and cruel enemy he has already proved to Texas!"

The others listened with deep interest to every word spoken by Roylston. When he was through, the Panther rose, stretched his arms, and expanded his mighty chest. All the natural brown had returned to his cheeks, and his eyes sparkled with the fire of confidence.

"Mr. Roylston," he said, "the hosts of our foe have come an' they have devoured our people as the locusts ate up Egypt in the Bible, but I think our worst days have passed. We'll come back, an' we'll win."

"Yes," said Ned. "I know as truly as if a prophet had told me that we'll square accounts with Santa Anna."

He spoke with such sudden emphasis that the others were startled. His face seemed cut in stone. At that moment he saw only the Alamo and Goliad.

The "Star of the South" sped northward, and Edward Fulton sat long on her deck, dreaming of the day when the Texans, himself in the first rank, face to face with Antonio Lopez de Santa Anna.